SEVEN SURRENDERS

Also by Ada Palmer

Too Like the Lightning

SEVEN SURRENDERS

TERRA IGNOTA,

BOOK II.

by Ada Palmer

A TOM DOHERTY ASSOCIATES Book
NEW YORK

SEVEN SURRENDERS

Edited by Patrick Nielsen Hayden

A Tor Book
Published by Tom Doherty Associates
175 Fifth Avenue
New York, NY 10010

www.tor-forge.com

Tor® is a registered trademark of Macmillan Publishing Group, LLC.

Library of Congress Cataloging-in-Publication Data

Names: Palmer, Ada, author.
Title: Seven surrenders / Ada Palmer.
Description: First edition. | New York : Tom Doherty Associates, 2017. |
   Series: Terra Ignota ; book 2 | "A Tor book."
Identifiers: LCCN 2016043354 (print) | LCCN 2016051783 (e-book) |
   ISBN 978-0-7653-7802-6 (hardcover) | ISBN 978-1-4668-5875-6 (e-book)
Subjects: LCSH: Utopias—Fiction. | BISAC: FICTION / Science Fiction /
   General. | GSAFD: Science fiction.
Classification: LCC PS3616.A33879 S48 2017 (print) | LCC PS3616.A33879
   (ebook) | DDC 813/.6—dc23
LC record available at https://lccn.loc.gov/2016043354

Our books may be purchased in bulk for promotional, educational, or business use.
Please contact your local bookseller or the Macmillan Corporate and Premium Sales
Department at 1-800-221-7945, extension 5442, or by e-mail at
MacmillanSpecialMarkets@macmillan.com.

First Edition: February 2017

Printed in the United States of America

0 9 8 7 6 5 4 3 2 1

SEVEN SURRENDERS

BEING A CONTINUATION OF *Too Like the Lightning*,
A NARRATIVE OF EVENTS of the year 2454

Written by MYCROFT CANNER, at the
REQUEST OF CERTAIN PARTIES.

Published with the permissions of:

The Romanova Seven-Hive Council Stability Committee
The Five-Hive Committee on Dangerous Literature
Ordo Quiritum Imperatorisque Masonicorum
The Cousins' Commission for the Humane Treatment of Servicers
The Mitsubishi Executive Directorate
His Majesty Isabel Carlos II of Spain

And with the consent of all FREE AND UNFREE
LIVING PERSONS HEREIN PORTRAYED.

Qui veritatem desiderit, ipse hoc legat. Nihil obstat; nihil obstet.

Recommended.—Anonymous.

I won't be certain who the killer is until I meet them, but if it is
Mycroft, be merciful. Keep them alive, and safe, and working. You
need them. If you have lost me, you need them. There are things I
leave undone that only Mycroft Canner can complete.

—APOLLO MOJAVE.

CERTIFIED NONPROSELYTORY BY THE FOUR-HIVE
COMMISSION ON RELIGION IN LITERATURE.

RATÉ D PAR LA COMMISSION EUROPÉENNE
DES MEDIAS DANGEREUX.

Gordian Exposure Commission Content Ratings:

S4—Explicit but not protracted *sexual scenes*; *rape*; references to *sex* with *violence*; *sexual acts* of real and living persons.

V5—Explicit and protracted scenes of *intentional violence*; explicit but not protracted scenes of *extreme violence*; *violence* praised; recent incidents of global *trauma*; *crimes of violence* committed by real and living persons.

R5—Explicit and protracted treatment of *religious themes* without intent to convert; theological abuse; theological assault; recent incidents of global *religious controversy*; *religious beliefs* of real and living persons.

O3—Opinions likely to cause *offense* to selected groups and to the sensibilities of many; subject matter likely to cause *distress or offense* to the same.

Persons APPEARING IN THIS HISTORY

Bridger . . . . *a child*
The Major . . . . *a veteran*
   Aimer . . . . *his lieutenant*
   Looker, Crawler, Medic, Stander-Y, Stander-G,
      Nogun, Nostand . . . . *his men*
   Croucher . . . . *a malcontent*
Mommadoll . . . . *a homemaker*
Mycroft Canner . . . . *their guardian*
   Saladin . . . . *his lover*

Thisbe Ottila Saneer (Humanist) . . . . *a smelltrack artist*
Ockham Prospero Saneer (Humanist) . . . . *Officer of Security*
Lesley Juniper Sniper Saneer (Humanist) . . . . *a security officer*
Ojiro Cardigan Sniper (Humanist) . . . . *a pentathlete and living doll*
Eureka Weeksbooth and Sidney Koons (Humanists) . . . . *data analysts*
Kat and Robin Typer (Humanists) . . . . *twins*
Cato Weeksbooth (Humanist) . . . . *a mad science teacher*
Carlyle Foster (Cousin) . . . . *their sensayer*

J.E.D.D. Mason (minor) . . . . *a Tribune*
   Madame D'Arouet (Blacklaw Hiveless) . . . . *His mother*
   Gibraltar Chagatai (Blacklaw Hiveless) . . . . *His housekeeper*
   Martin Guildbreaker (Mason) . . . . *His investigator*
   Dominic Seneschal (Blacklaw Hiveless) . . . . *His sensayer*
   Heloïse (minor) . . . . *His nun*

Cornel MASON (Mason) . . . . *an emperor*
The Seventh Anonymous . . . . *a political voice*
   Brody de Lupa (Humanist) . . . . *his proxy*

Bryar Kosala (Cousin)................................. *a chairperson*
   Vivien Ancelet (Graylaw Hiveless).............. *her spouse, the Censor*
   Jung Su-Hyeon Ancelet Kosala
      (Graylaw Hiveless)............... *their bash'child, the Deputy Censor*
Ganymede Jean-Louis de la Trémoïlle (Humanist)........... *a president*
Hotaka Andō Mitsubishi (Mitsubishi)................. *a chief director*
   Jyothi Bandyopadhyay, Chen Zhongren, Huang Enlai,
      Kim Yeong-Uk, Kimura Kunie, Lu Yong, Wang Baobao,
      Wang Laojing (Mitsubishi)...................... *his colleagues*
   Danaë Marie-Anne de la Trémoïlle Mitsubishi.............. *his wife*
   Jun, Sora, Michi, Ran, Harue, Naō, Setsuna
      (minors)............................ *their bash'children*
   Masami Mitsubishi (Mitsubishi)........... *their bash'child, a reporter*
   Toshi Mitsubishi
      (Graylaw Hiveless)........... *their bash'child, an analyst for the Censor*
   Hiroaki Mitsubishi
      (Cousin)....... *their bash'child, an analyst for the Cousins' Feedback Bureau*
Casimir Perry (European)........................... *a prime minister*
Isabel Carlos II of Spain (European)...................... *a king*
Felix Faust (Gordian)................................ *a headmaster*

Julia Doria-Pamphili (European)........... *Head of the Sensayers' Conclave*
Jin Im-Jin (Gordian).................... *Speaker of the Romanovan Senate*
Darcy Sok (Cousin)............... *Head of the Cousins' Feedback Bureau*
Lorelei Cook (Cousin)............. *Romanovan Minister of Education*
Ektor Carlyle Papadelias (European)...................... *a detective*
Tully Mardi (Graylaw Hiveless)...................... *a warmonger*
Aldrin Bester and Voltaire Seldon (Utopians).............. *ambassadors*
Mushi Mojave (Utopian)...................... *a Martian entomologist*
Apollo Mojave (Utopian)........................... *in memoriam*

Too like the lightning, which doth cease to be
Ere one can say, 'It lightens.'

—William Shakespeare, *Romeo and Juliet,* act II, scene ii

Nihil Obstet

Nihil Obstat—'Nothing prevents it'—was the old license-by-fiat which kings and inquisitors pronounced in stifled ages when no printing press could give its inky kiss to paper until Tyrant Church and Tyrant State had loosed censorship's universal gag. But 'nihil obstet' is something else when He appends it to our permissions page, Good Jehovah Mason. 'Obstet' is a prayer, one He made over and over to the many authorities who guard humanity: His Imperial father, the Cousin Chair, the King of Spain, the Sensayers' Conclave, the far-seeing Censor, Brill's wise Institute: 'Let nothing prevent it.' They feared as much for Him as for themselves, tried to sow doubt in Him, asked Him by His many names: Are You sure You want to do this, J.E.D.D. Mason? Tribune? *Porphyrogene?* Prince? Tenth Director? Tai-Kun? Xiao Hei Wang? Jed? Jagmohan? Micromegas? Jehovah Epicurus Donatien D'Arouet Mason? Are You sure You want this snarling, wounded Earth to learn so much of You? But Madame D'Arouet, who raised Ἄναξ Jehovah in that strange bash'-out-of-time she cultured in the gold-drenched heart of Paris, also taught Him numbers: one and many, less and more. So, the same grim calculus that compelled Cicero and Seneca to give their lives for bleeding Rome compels Jehovah now to end the desperation-pain of the ten billion who cry for answers, even at the cost of worse pain to those dearest to Him, and Himself. For your sake, reader, He prayed, to one, to many. And for His sake I pray too, to That One Power—absent from our permissions page—Which could still stop us, as It stopped firebrand Apollo. The many mouths of Providence have swallowed up a thousand histories, and could swallow one more. So I pray: Let nothing obstruct this book and the Good it aims at. If there is benevolence in You, strange Creator, *nihil obstet.*

Sniper's Chapter

RESTRICTION: THIS SECTION MUST BE EXCISED BEFORE THIS DOCUMENT MAY BE PUBLISHED OR DISTRIBUTED. PRIVATE ACCESS MAY BE GRANTED BY JUDICIAL ORDER.

RESTRICTION ORDERED BY: The Conclave of Sensayers of the Universal Free Alliance.
REASON: Libelous attribution of criminal acts to a licensed sensayer.

RESTRICTION ORDERED BY: Cousins' Legal Commission.
REASON: Potential harm to the public peace, potential harm to minors herein discussed.

RESTRICTION ORDERED BY: Ordo Quiritum Imperatorisque Masonicorum.
REASON: Instigation of violence against a *Familiaris Regni*.

RESTRICTION ORDERED BY: Universal Free Alliance Commissioner General Ektor Carlyle Papadelias.
REASON: Strong evidence that substantial parts of this document are an alteration or forgery with destructive intent.

DURATION OF RESTRICTION: Five years, renewable pending review.

* * *

Howdy, fans and foes! This is your very own Sniper. First, let me assure you that I'm alive and well. The fugitive lifestyle suits me fine, my wounds are healed, I have plenty of allies, and I will kill Jehovah Mason for you, that I swear, today, tomorrow, a year from now, however long it takes. They can't guard the little prince forever. Tyrants and assassins have a great symbiosis. Assassins are always evil and despised (even when our effects are good, we're still a bad means to a good end) until tyrants crop up. Then suddenly assassins are heroes, lifelines; suddenly we alone have the power to save the world without a revolution and the destruction revolutions bring. You admit you need us. But, between tyrants, you forget that assassins will only be here, ready, when you want us if we've been here, ready, the whole time. You feel dirty keeping such a weapon in the house, but somebody has to keep one or it won't be there when the bad wolf comes to huff and puff. My office is no less a pillar of this age than Censor or Anonymous. I serve with no less pride.

Second, I should say I'm only writing this one chapter, and Mycroft will take over again when I've had my say. Mycroft went to great lengths to contact me so I could describe this event, which did come next in sequence. I agreed to relate it only on condition that they promise not to touch a word of what I wrote. It's a privilege I intend to abuse to the utmost, and I'll have my say about Jehovah Mason before I'm done. But I'll start first with the part that will make your usual narrator squirm the most: correcting their willful omission and giving you a proper physical description of Mycroft Canner.

Mycroft is average height, shorter because they stoop, and swimming in their oversized uniform, like a statue wrapped in sacking, waiting to be restored. Their hair is curly in that classical Greek way, off-black, closer to a grayish tint than brown, and overgrown around the sides and forehead, as if they imagine so marvelous a creature could hide itself beneath a few stray locks. Modern science has kept their face as fresh at thirty-one as it was at seventeen, when all it took was a glance from Mycroft Canner to make the strongest shudder, but now those devil eyes lock tamely on the floor. They're brown eyes if you get a look at them, bright brown and antique feeling, like the brown tint which makes old wine richer than new. There's a scarring on their upper lip where violence has split it once too often, which gives a sense of hidden fangs. But the real prize comes when you strip away their uniform and bare the skin beneath, a tapestry of scars, all shapes, all vintages: the crumpled edges of old cuts and bites, the roughness of burns, strap-sores around the wrists and ankles, the ley lines of surgery, bullet holes round like little kisses, all layered on top of one another like a graffiti wall which tempts you to add your own mark. There's a story behind every scar, and I've spent many lucky hours tracing that skin and asking about each; Mycroft answers about one-third of the time.

The Mycroft you remember from the news was lean, all muscle like a starving scavenger. That hasn't changed. The wildest stray goes soft after a year of warm laps and petting, but not Mycroft. I don't believe Mycroft starves themself only as self-punishment. It could be that they don't want to taint such a body with whatever unhealthy slop Servicers' patrons tend to offer, but I suspect it's just that our predator finds common food hard to choke down after what they've tasted. Their famous hat (and even I was surprised to learn it came from Dominic Seneschal) is round, brown, something like a newsboy cap, though more patches than cloth at this point, with only the remnants of what might have been a brim. Mycroft lied to you, you know. They said there was no Beggar King to command the Servicers, but the sight of that hat makes the others snap to attention as surely as a crown. It's not for the crimes that the other Servicers idolize Mycroft, it's what Mycroft's done since. Even in Hell they're stunned to find an angel among them, willing to be as much a guardian as a fallen angel can.

Today's Mycroft genuinely is as obsequious in person as they are in print, a self-styled slave in this world which has none. But if you sit with them awhile, and talk, and coax, the formality fades, the hunch which hides the still-strong shoulders loosens, the hands begin to splay like claws, and eventually the beast I call True Mycroft pokes its nose above the surface. It's not a prisoner in there, not fighting to break free, just resting inside Slave Mycroft like a ship in harbor, saving itself for something. Slave Mycroft has only one expression: apology. As for True Mycroft, their expressions are unreadable, or rather you're wrong if you try to read them, like when the shape of a dog's face makes it seem to smile or frown where really you're just projecting human expressions onto an inhuman thing.

Like most of us, I first laid eyes on Mycroft Canner on the news just after the capture, as the police wheeled them past row on row of emergency forces. Mycroft was so serene then, basking in the procession as if that transparent coffin-cage was a triumphal chariot. We'd already heard Mycroft's reasons for the Mardi killings from the recorded speeches they left beside the later bodies. This was the supreme act of violence of this century, done not by a government, not a Church, not a tribe, not an army, but by an individual. Ever since villagers first wielded sharpened sticks in their chief's name, the State had held a monopoly on supreme violence, but the Hive system ended that. Mycroft called their killings a demonstration of a liberty our era had not realized we possessed, proof of history's progress if seventeen deaths were enough to shock the world; historically, seventeen deaths is a good day. Philosophers had long speculated about Savage Man, whether the conscience is innate or implanted by society, and whether the human mind is actually capable of willing evil for the sake of evil—even the most heinous killers still tend to imagine some goal (revenge, profit, personal pleasure, some mad command). It's an important question, fundamental really—can we choose actions that purely make the world worse without any perverse perceived benefit?—but we couldn't discover whether the true Human Beast could exist back when the Beast was like a craftsman in an age of mass production, negligible beside the infinitely greater evils: Democide and War. There before the cameras Mycroft preached that, in these days of peace when we choose our Hive and values for ourselves, human individuals finally have the chance to be the worst thing in the world, and the right to be proud of our choice if we are not. That was the first time I fell in love with anyone outside my bash'.

It was a month after the arrest that Eureka told me Mycroft Canner wasn't executed after all. We had to make them ours, that was clear. My crush aside, I always say a killer can smell a killer, and with yours truly on the news every five minutes, Mycroft had surely scented me by now. Eureka tracked Mycroft down among the Servicers, and Ockham paid the visit. It took moments for each to recognize what other was. Laconic Ockham delivered simply, "Come," which Mycroft matched with an instant, "Yes, Məəəer Saneer," in Mycroft's signature vague diction which lets you think they're saying 'Member' but underneath it's really 'Master' leaking out. Lesley and I had spent weeks concocting blackmail enough to collar the beast (and keep them silent, which was Ockham's concern), and were a little pissed to find our schemes superfluous. We'd sent the trapper after a wolf and caught a fawning puppy; there was no choice but to adopt it. It was supposed to be my puppy, but Thisbe set their sights on it, and when Thisbe stirs even O.S. trembles. I still got Mycroft as a playmate, storyteller, sparring partner, but only Thisbe got them at night, and (as I've learned now) never touched them. Just as well; as one learns from the obituaries of the wealthy perverts Mycroft used to prostitute themself to, raising money to help other Servicers, if you sleep with Mycroft Canner you don't live long (and thanks to reading the first half of this history, I now know to call that phenomenon Saladin).

Enough authorial abuse for now. My kidnapping on March twenty-seventh, that's what I'm supposed to talk about. It happened at six A.M. by my schedule. I'd just endured a nasty (but deserved) chewing out from my fencing coach (obnoxious but worth putting up with, since it's so hard to find a coach who won't fall in love with me). I'd removed my tracker for a shower when an odorless and fast-acting drug knocked me cold.

It's hard to say when I awoke, since the world I woke to was so like a dream. I couldn't see; I couldn't move; I couldn't speak. I wasn't bound or gagged. It was my hands, my arms, my legs, they all lay limp, and when I tried to call for help, not only would the sound not rise but even my lips refused to form the words. I could feel, and recognized at once that I was lying in the molded contours of a Lifedoll box; I know the shape, since fans often ask me to have myself delivered in the packaging so they can have the pleasure of unwrapping me. My first thought was that I might be one of my dolls come to life (no, at the time I did not know about Bridger's power to bring toys to life, it's just that my profession made me think hard about these things), but my tongue could move, enough to keep me from choking, and I found the notch on the inside of my top left molar which no doll has, which I had etched there for just such eventualities (I told you, I thought hard about these things). Clearly, then, I was no doll. I was breathing. I could swallow (with difficulty), could blink and move my eyes (though the packaging strap across my eyes was as solid as a blindfold), and I could control my bladder and anus enough to keep from soiling the box. A few other muscles did tense slightly as I strained—my jaw, some spots on my belly, one spot in my neck—so I set to exercising them, to see if I could get my blood pumping a bit and so flush chemicals from my system faster, if chemicals were the cause. With concentration I detected spots of soreness scattered around my body which I guessed were remnants of however this paralysis had been achieved. Fear? I didn't feel much fear. I thought about trying to induce panic to get my heart rate up, but better to keep myself sharp, and ready.

The first words I heard were muffled, both by the box and by a voice distorter, which left the syllables gritty and robotic. « Now, let's see this surprise that was worth dragging me out here. » I do not speak French, but I hear it often, and Spanish gives me enough of a start to piece the simple stuff together.

« It might have been dangerous bringing it to Your Holiness's office. I tried to decorate this place to make you feel at home. »

« It's perfect. All my favorite posters, and the rug's so cushy. »

« I am a professional. »

« Mmm. That you are. »

The two paused and, from the sound of it, made out. There were two voices, both veiled by distorters. I'm not going to use names. The police promised (in writing) not to use this testimony as evidence against anyone, but the police aren't so good with that sort of promise. You know which sensayer was promised Sniper in return for handing over the Cousin Carlyle Foster to a certain Blacklaw. If I omit the names then I maintain reasonable doubt.

« Is this the surprise I hope it is? » Hands made the packaging flex.

« If you've guessed, it isn't a surprise. »

I felt clean air on my chest as the box opened. « Oh! Gorgeous . . . » Hands explored my chest. « It's real? The real Sniper? »

« I pay my debts, Your Holiness. » Another hand guided the first to test my pulse.

« The real Sniper. That's really the real Sniper? »

« I'll give my oath on it, if you doubt. »

« Did you get them to consent? »

« Of course not. I knew you'd want to do that part yourself. »

« Mmm. How did you snatch them? Did you take the Canner Device for a spin? »

« And draw a swarm of Moonmen down upon my head? No, no. Stealth and patience, Your Holiness, stealth and patience. »

Hands lifted my arm, the touch delicate but not gentle. « They're limp. Are they unconscious? »

« That would be no fun. It's conscious, just frozen like a doll. It can hear us, and when you unwrap the eyes it'll be able to see, so make sure your mask stays in place. »

Hands played with my fingers, bending them to test resistance. « How did you do this? »

« The paralysis? A very delicate application of this and that. It's not my invention; Madame's had this sort of special request before. It's not permanent, it needs to be refreshed every few hours, but I can arrange another round if need be. »

« Oh, you've outdone yourself! You can have Carlyle! You can have any pawn you want! »

The other laughed. « You deserved a prize today. That imaginary friend you identified from the boy's drawings was just what I needed, trick worked like a charm. »

« That child you asked advice about, you broke them successfully? »

« Am breaking. No need to rush. I've three of his little friends hostage, and you wouldn't believe what treasures are already flocking to the bait. »

« Little friends? I hope you're not breaking any Black Laws, harming minors? »

« Nothing of the sort. Besides, I'll hardly need such bait once I have little Carlyle to finish things for me. »

« And God? The common God, I mean, are you making progress? You dropped such taunting hints. »

Another hush for kisses.

« God's almost mine. »

« How long? »

A chuckle. « Patience is a virtue, Your Holiness. Think of it as a balance for today's delicious vice. Your doll awaits. »

"Mmm." Practiced hands gripped me under the arms and eased my torso forward until I flopped into an embrace. Some long hair caught in my lips as my face fell against bare skin, and I felt breasts against my chest. "Oops! Careful!" They switched to English to address me, laughing as they adjusted my head so my cheek could rest on their shoulder. "What a fragile thing you are, Sniper, and so light! I always imagined the real thing would be heavier than the dolls."

« Careful you don't strain its neck. Actually, better put this neck brace on it. I didn't want the brace to spoil the effect when you opened the box, but there's real danger of straining something, like with babies. »

"Well, we can't have that, can we, Sniper? Can't have you getting hurt. Come here." My New Owner (what else can a doll call the one to whom it's given?) held my head still for the Gift-giver to strap the brace in place. That helped, kept my head centered as my Owner tipped me forward into a cuddle. It was an intense embrace, no awkwardness, no holding back, the kind of hug two people can only achieve after long intimacy, but anyone can give in an instant to a stuffed bear. Amazing. "There, is that better? Now let's get you out of your box and settled somewhere comfortable."

« Let me help. » I felt the second person's hands now, midsized enough to belong to either sex, but fierce as clamps. « On three, ready? One, two, three! »

The two of them carried me a short way, then laid me on soft carpet with my head and shoulders propped against a cushion.

"There." My Owner laid my hands neatly at my sides. "Much better. Now, let's get this packaging off so we can see your pretty eyes."

They picked at the packing strip which protects the doll eyes during shipping, splitting the seal with fingernails which (almost) succeeded in not scratching my skin. Even common lamplight seared after such darkness, and I closed my eyes at once, flinching as much as I had power to flinch.

"Oh!" my Owner cried. "Did the bright light hurt you? Here." They leaned close enough to veil me with shadow, and restored complete darkness to my left eye with a soft kiss on the eyelid. "Let me make it better." The kiss moved, one eye, then the other, then down my cheek. "There, that's better. Now open your eyes. It's okay."

Squinting at first, I saw a clean white half mask covering the upper half of a light face, with a wash of black hair behind it, leaking over a bare body which was probably not as beautiful as I remember, but I'm about as objective here as Mycroft is about Thisbe. The room behind my Owner was a collage of me: posters, portraits, some quite rare, all different costumes, naughty, nice, formal, skimpy, all five sports, all seven Hives, and dominated by the 2442 limited-edition of me slumped shirtless in a chair with puppet joints drawn on my skin and the strings of a marionette holding me half-upright. I've always liked people who like that one.

"There. Welcome home, Sniper."

As they kissed my lips which could not kiss back, I felt, at last, my long-sought, threat-free love. In my years as a professional living doll I can't count how many times I've been brought home by a fan who'd dreamed of a night with the original, but the consummation often fails to meet their expectations. Those who want a doll as a lover tend to be timid, shy of being touched, more comfortable with plastic and make-believe. I've made myself as benign as possible: hairless, childlike, not strongly gendered either way, and I always let myself be dressed, be fed, be led, but I still touch back, kiss back by reflex, have the potential to be active. That potential spoils the illusion, like when you know a ba'sib is in earshot in the next room, and the fact distracts you even if they do nothing. As long as I could act, Owners weren't as safe with me as with my dolls. Bondage doesn't solve this, makes it worse, actually, since the bonds are just reminders of the power they're restraining. Here, though, with my power not constrained but gone, my Owner was as comfortable as when you sit naked in an empty house, or sing in the bathroom, so I tasted at last that easy affection which only dolls and dildos had enjoyed before. I could feel how much it was changing me even as it happened, the granting of such a visceral wish rewiring things inside my mind, not just the conscious iceburg tip but down into those black depths that even Brillists barely understand. At the time, Thisbe and Eureka hadn't told the rest of the bash' about their "black hole" in Paris or what lurks in it, so I had no way to recognize that this was trickle-down of the same threat. My Owner didn't study with Madame D'Arouet, but absorbed through the growling Gift-giver the same techniques, as through some dark umbilical: sniff out the forbidden appetites that people don't admit they have, and make them so real that afterward the normal world feels dull as black and white. Mycroft showed you how Chair Kosala and the Anonymous can't kindle the fire anymore without their 'he's and 'she's and lace and waistcoats. Mycroft was right to use the word 'addiction.'

"And now for the real mystery." My Owner's hands traced a slow path down my sides toward the second packing strip which protected my most private parts. They glanced over their shoulder at the Gift-giver. « You've been waiting for this, haven't you? »

« Actually, I already saw. » The Gift-giver stood behind my Owner, also masked, and with a black cloak which hid everything but a spot of shadowed throat. « Apologies for not waiting for Your Holiness, but I had to towel it off and get it boxed up. It was quite suspenseful, the rumors being so contradictory. »

« I know. » My Owner eased my thighs apart. "You're a naughty thing, Sniper, spreading confusing rumors to keep us guessing." I couldn't look down, but saw a subtle smile as their fingers cracked the seal. (I thought hard about whether to reveal this here, but it's time. I remain infinitely grateful to everyone who helped me keep the secret this long: the Celebrity Youth Act, my coaches, doctors, teammates, journalists, my many fans who knew, and many more who burned to know but respected my request so much you even rioted outside *The Scoop* that time they threatened an exposé. But it's time to free you all from that silence, that mystery, to let you see completely what I was, now that my doll days are over.) "A boy," my Owner announced. "Not surprising. No, wait." They leaned closer, their long hair tickling my thighs, which could not twitch. "Both! Oh, excellent." They lifted my penis gingerly and reached past to feel the vaginal folds behind. "You sweet thing, you didn't want to disappoint fans who got used to either model. How thoughtful!" They spread me further, the room's air cold against the wetness of my labia. "It's a beautiful job, seamless!" They turned again to the Gift-giver. « Which sex were they originally, do you know? »

The Gift-giver leaned forward. « I couldn't tell. Everything down there looks genuine. I could take some hair to the lab. »

« No need. This is how Sniper should be, now that I think about it. » My Owner withdrew their hands from my penis carefully, as if handling a baby bird. « Oh! It twitched. » They chuckled their delight. « Can they perform? »

« Of course. The paralysis is very selective. It'll take some massage, but you can get it up if you want. »

« Mmm. Not much massage from the look of it. Somebody's enjoying themself. » My Owner ran a finger up my cheek. "Aren't you?"

Knowing no answer would come, my Owner tasted my lips again and eased me forward, their affection washing over me like a good movie, which takes you to all the peaks of passion without you having to lift a finger.

They were used to my body, knew just how my shoulders swing, and at what height to hook my chin over their shoulder.

« How long can I keep them? »

It was a burning question for me, too.

The Gift-giver shrugged. « That's up to Your Holiness. If you want to keep it permanently I can bring what you'll need, but it'll be difficult keeping its Olympic physique from deteriorating in captivity, and there'll be quite the manhunt. I recommend catch-and-release: you enjoy yourself, then have me return Sniper to the wild and take it again when next you're in the mood. »

« Would that work? »

« Certainly. I estimate another two hours until the rest of the bash' realizes Sniper's missing, but they'll hunt in secret for at least a day before letting the news get beyond His Grace the Duke. So long as we get Sniper back this evening there won't be any larger fuss. We can erase its memory as extra security if you like, but I'm sure it won't breathe a word of this to anyone. » They switched to growling English. "If I can do this much to it when I'm calm, it can imagine what I'd do if I were angry."

My Owner hugged me closer. "There's no need for threats. My Sniper won't want to spoil this, not when I'm done. I know what Sniper wants. I've known for ages what my Sniper really wants."

You probably imagine I thought something defiant and heroic here. Some addictions only need one dose.

« Of course, Your Holiness. I apologize for insulting your abilities. »

« Mmm. I'll have you do some penance for that later. »

« As you wish, Your Holiness. »

My Owner stroked my hair, flicking stray black strands out of my eyes. "Sniper's turn first, though."

The computer distortion made the Gift-giver's chuckle sound like a computer's dying scream. « Maybe you should keep it permanently. There's enough nastiness around its bash', it might be safer here with you. »

« I'll think about it. »

I thought about it too, realizing that all I could do was lie and wait for my Owner to make this decision which would literally determine my entire world, and have a big impact on everybody else's. Duty was enough to make me wish for freedom, but that was the only moment I can remember that I've ever wished the duty wasn't mine.

The Gift-giver turned to go. « I have work. I'll be back before the paralysis wears off. I brought some doll clothes for dress-up, they're in the chest back there. »

« Thanks. »

« Give me a call if you see any twitching. Athletes often have a fast metabolism, so there's a chance things will wear off faster than normal. »

« Right. »

The Gift-giver came within my line of sight as my Owner shifted me onto their lap. I searched for hints of identity (skin color, weight) beneath the cloak and beaked plaster-white mask, but this foe was too practiced. « Enjoy. »

Enjoy my Owner did, every inch of me, but I'll skip the details. It was not all sex. A lot of it was being held, that warm, trusting embrace. A lot of it was talk. My Owner talked about what it's like being able to see people's hidden obsessions, like having X-ray vision and spotting all the ailments doctors haven't discovered yet. They talked about the nature of secrets, speculating about why one feels the need to share secrets with someone, whether one imagines something might happen if one says them aloud, like knocking on wood, or whether it just feels more real when there's a witness. They talked about the state of the world, about ideas of God which I won't repeat, and a lot about gender. Gender they called a universal language which we're all supposed to pretend we can't read. Most just play blind or try (as we know we ought) to eliminate the traces of it, and the ancient inequalities those traces threaten to revive. But, they said, cunning folk can use that language to attack targets with body rhetoric we can't acknowledge, let alone resist. My Owner used a strongly gendered persona intentionally to make people uncomfortable, just as I used my neuter one to set people at ease. We were two house cats who had both learned again the true purpose of claws and fangs; my Owner had taken to hunting, while I had tried to have myself declawed. Now, having read the first half of Mycroft's history, I know to blame Madame D'Arouet for these ideas. Mostly, though, my Owner talked about power.

"I need a break from power, Sniper. It sometimes feels like I've been playing the manipulation game forever, and once you're in you can't stop. I enjoy it, I wouldn't give it up for anything, but my rival is also very good, and I have to turn everyone around me into a pawn on my side to keep them from becoming a pawn on theirs. I need a break, just once in a while, like this. It's different with you. You can't try to use me, and I don't want to use you even though I could. You're off-limits to my rival, so I can safely make you off-limits to me, too. I can relax. There's no power with the two of us like this, just fun. I'm sure you need a break too. It's a very hard game you play keeping Ganymede in power. It must be exhausting, all the train-

ing, and competitions, and stunts to keep voters from thinking about anyone but you and Ganymede. But there's no spotlight here. With me you
can stop performing, and you don't need to worry about your obligations
when there's absolutely nothing you can do about them. You can relax. Isn't
that what you really want, Sniper? A life where you can finally relax?"

I could have tried to answer somehow, give a long blink, a distinct breath,
but that would have spoiled it, undone these hours which truly were the
pinnacle of my avocation. There's a word to chew on, 'avocation': a second
great occupation that takes you away from your vocation, like a musician
sidetracked by acting, a teacher by politics, Thisbe by making movies, or
my ba'pa designing dolls, all important tasks but secondary still. I don't
blame the parents who made me and Ockham rivals for O.S. (it made us
stronger), but when Lesley entered the picture it was clear there would be a
winner and a loser when we grew up, no ties. When the fuss over being a
Lifedoll model made me a child star, I saw a second path before me, a surer
shot than the fight for bash' leadership, which was always fifty-fifty. The
rest agreed a celebrity in the house would be a good addition to our ar-
senal, so I worked like a maniac to secure my fame: studying for the press,
keeping informed, full of jokes, always the most fun to interview, then finding a sport at which my small body (neither exceptionally strong nor fast)
could excel, and working to remain competition-worthy through three
Olympiads and counting. I loved my avocation, suffered for it, and I took
very seriously the duty of belonging to everyone who loved me. But that
still came second, and my bash' vocation first. I do apologize to all who
were in love with what I was. I miss you too, and if you contact my underground and host me for a night I'll do my best to be your Sniper again, but
that comes second. My Hive, all Hives, come first. I am a Humanist because
I believe in heroes, that history is driven by those individuals with fire enough
to change the world. If you aren't a Humanist it's because you think something different. That difference matters. I will not let Jehovah Mason undo
the system which (as Mycroft sacrificed so much to prove) gives us the right
at last to be proud of what we choose to be. The Hives must be defended.
Never before has one tyrant been in a position to truly threaten the whole
world, so never in history has my true vocation been so necessary. I will
kill Jehovah Mason for you; please accept that as my apology.

I'm over my five-thousand-word limit already. What else should I cram
in before I go? The Bridger parts are true. There's proof. Unlike Mycroft, I
won't let you get away with pretending it's madness. Don't trust the gendered
pronouns Mycroft gives people, they all come from Madame. The coup is

happening, don't let anybody tell you different. As for the resistance, I'm not expecting most of you to volunteer to fight and die, but if you support my side, all it means is that you love your Hive, and that you'll cheer for us when the deed is done. The First World War was the moment humanity learned to count its casualties in millions, but as a Humanist I must ask, as my bash' founders asked: which changed the world more? The loss of millions or of that handful who would have been the next generation's heroes? Wilfred Owen left behind a tiny collection of poems, not enough to even make a book, but still the most upsetting things I've ever read; if Owen had lived they might have revolutionized literature, spurred presses and politics away from the guilt-laden bravado which would light war's fire again, or driven countless readers to suicide. Karl Schwarzschild corresponded with Einstein from the trenches and deduced the existence of black holes while rotting knee-deep in muck; if Schwarzschild had lived they might have accelerated physics by fifty years, enabled *Mukta* two generations earlier, or given the Nazis nukes. Owen and Schwarzschild; calculate carefully which firebrands to snuff and one death can redirect history better than any battle. That was the foundation of O.S.

—*Ojiro Cardigan Sniper, Thirteenth O.S., May 23rd, 2454*

* * *

END OF RESTRICTED SECTION. PUBLIC ACCOUNT RESUMES.

Chapter the THIRD

O.S.

"Your Grace President Ganymede, O.S. is here."

"Send them in."

This fifth day of my history plunges us into a sea of scenes I did not witness. I was a prisoner, trapped at Madame's by Dominic's orders, and by the certainty I would be lynched if I ventured on the streets, where murmurs of the Seven-Ten list theft, corruption at *Black Sakura*, the dread Canner Device, all had been swept away by the shockwave revelation unleashed by warmonger Tully Mardi: Mycroft Canner hides among the Servicers. Dominic Seneschal now carried my tracker in his pocket like a trophy, deactivated 'for my mandatory rest' by order of my court-appointed sensayer Julia Doria-Pamphili. I was blinded, mute, trapped without even the lifeline of a newsfeed. But I am not cut out for objectivity. I fill in: an expression I did not see, words I heard only in paraphrase, a gesture I know was there, though no witness can prove it. Why do I do this? Because, imaginative reader, you are human. You will fill in for me, invent faces and personality as you invent your own Alexander, your own Jack the Ripper, and your own Thomas Carlyle. You have never met the people I describe, so your imaginings will be less accurate than those of someone who has toiled beside them in these rooms, and seen them sweat. Caught between two lies I give you mine, which has more truth immixed.

Ockham Saneer owns only one suit which their spouse Lesley may not doodle on, and it is used only for trips to La Trimouille. They met in the most secure room of the Humanist Presidential Mansion, the Treasure Cabinet: hexagonal, walled with a honeycomb of glass-faced cases containing carved stones, signet rings, miniature portraits, and curiosities both animal and mineral. Duke President Ganymede Jean-Louis de la Trémoïlle outdid the treasures, his mane as glaring as gold in sunlight, his eyes as biting as blue diamond. The ice-pale Duke expressed his displeasure by today's choice of silks, a deep pearl color almost dark enough to be called silver, which is as grim on him as black on any other man. Ockham, beside him, with his warm Indian skin and black hair like the fertile ash after a forest fire, seemed a real, organic human being beside some icy idol.

"Member President," Ockham greeted his Hive leader with a stiff but awkward nod, which wanted to be something more formal, but the customs of our peaceful era will not permit the honesty of a salute.

The Duke President gestured Ockham to the bench opposite his. "Why is Sniper not with you?"

"Cardigan is AWOL, Member President."

In the crisis, the Duke did not even pause to smirk at Sniper's middle name. "AWOL?"

"They disappeared from their gym this morning sometime between 11:14 and 11:40 UT. We believe it was a kidnapping."

"What?"

Ockham would not have showed his fear. "Lesley has our Humanist Special Guard investigating, but I thought it best not to report the incident to Romanova yet. It may turn out to be one of Cardigan's fans, unrelated to the *Black Sakura* affair."

"How could you let this happen now?" The accusation came from Chief Director Hotaka Andō Mitsubishi. He paced the tiny room, agitated steps making his spring-patterned Mitsubishi suit rustle, as if a fox were stalking through its pattern of night-darkened bamboo.

"My apologies, Chief Director," Ockham answered crisply. "There were holes in my security."

"That's clear." These cold words came from a fourth man, who sat tensely on a seat's edge at the far side of the little room. "Holes named Cato Weeksbooth and Ojiro Cardigan Sniper."

Ganymede's blue eyes flashed murder. "You will not denigrate what Sniper does for us, Perry. They are our bulwark in this, as is Ockham."

Perry held his tongue. This the first time you have seen him take the stage, "the Outsider" as you have heard the others call him at Madame's, Europe's Second-Choice Prime Minister, Casimir Perry. He has spent these past days busy in Europe's capital at Brussels, securing friends, flattering neutrals, and bargaining with the opposition that gnaws forever at the roots of his tender coalition. When the King of Spain was the European Hive's Prime Minister, His Majesty kept the peace among the member nation-strats with grace, relying on the general goodwill that others give the man who has been so good to them, his father so good to their fathers, his grandfather so good to their grandfathers. Casimir Perry they work like a workhorse. Physically he is a fine man, as tall as the Emperor, European in complexion but tanned and healthy, with a square face creased by a hundred kinds of stress, and a nub of brownish ponytail. He wears the full arm-band of his Polish nation-strat and finely tailored European suits, which sit well on him. Today's is a deep mustard shade with a double-breasted coal black vest and black lapels, but his tailor's efforts always look pathetic in the Parliamentary photos which show Perry where one's eye expects the King. There is a strain in Perry's voice when he speaks, making every phrase seem slightly urgent, and his hands strain too, latching on to armrests like barnacles, which conquer seas and tides only by clinging to the leviathans.

Ockham did not acknowledge the dirty glances traded by the three Hive Leaders who faced him like a triad of Romanovan judges. "The primary hole in my security at the moment is that we're without our Mitsubishi Special Guard. They had the privilege of handling Cardigan's personal security."

The dirty glances were for Andō now, but the leader of the Japanese nation-strat had the most reason of all to scowl at this reminder of his Chinese rivals' interference in the 'security drill' at the Saneer-Weeksbooth bash'house two days before. "Every link in the command chain responsi-ble for that debacle has been disciplined. Severely."

"Including the top?" Ganymede pressed, fixing his eyes on Andō. "Prob-lems in the Mitsubishi Directorate pecking order are only your private business so long as they don't endanger the rest of what we've built. I haven't seen any heads roll high in China's ranks. Which was it this time, Shang-hai or Beijing?"

Andō's almost-black eyes felt blacker as they narrowed. "Heads have rolled. Privately. With dignity. And permanence."

The Humanist President ran his alabaster fingers through his mane, holding the onlookers transfixed, like knights before a vision of their grail. "All right. For the time being, Ockham, I shall send you some of my own personal guard, to aid your search and substitute for the missing Mitsubi-shi. Perhaps Director Andō will do the same?"

It took Andō some seconds to master himself. "My personal guard? Yes, I can spare some."

"Thank you, Chief Director," Ockham acknowledged, glancing to Perry next.

"Right. I . . ." The Second-Choice Prime Minister trailed off.

Indulgence and gloating commixed in Ganymede's smile. "It's all right, Perry. We know you don't have private forces. Andō and I shall see to things. As always."

"Thank you as always, then." Casimir Perry scratched his forehead, hiding behind the gesture.

In lighter days, the smile on Ganymede might have matured into a laugh. The Duke is in the French nation-strat, so can vote in Europe if he wishes, even as a Member of another Hive, and I asked him once whether he himself had voted for Perry in the absurd election after Ziven Racer's attempt to fix the polls made the too-honorable King of Spain drop out. The Sphinx has no more smug a smile. "Ockham, I want reports on your search for Sniper at least every two hours. When you have leads, communicate with my own guard, and you have leave to request as many of my forces as you need. If the time comes that you think you need to contact Romanova, come to me first, and we shall go directly to Commissioner General Papadelias, no middletypes."

"Yes, Member President. Though, Papadelias is a problem already."

"Oh?"

Even Ockham sometimes needs a breath to steel himself. "Martin Guildbreaker is with Papadelias as we speak."

Pacing Andō stumbled in his alarm. "Martin with Papadelias!"

"Yes, Chief Director. Our set-sets have been tracking them. Martin Guildbreaker entered the Alliance Police Headquarters in Romanova nearly three hours ago, and Papadelias has not left in that time. If they are together, I believe that means Guildbreaker has strong suspicions of our activities, but no proof."

"How could they have suspicions?" Andō cried. "You said Martin hadn't gotten near your equipment, or Cato's lab, and you don't keep records anyway."

The Duke President sighed beneath his silks as he saw Ockham frown. "Martin got to Cato?"

"For sixteen minutes, yes," Ockham confirmed. "At the museum. Cato reports that Guildbreaker mainly asked about their teaching, science club, their books, nothing touching directly on the rest of the bash'. Cato ended the interview in a state of some agitation, but believes they discussed nothing which might betray our work. More alarming, in my assessment, is the fact that Guildbreaker also approached Cato's psychiatrist Ember Balin, and later accessed the records of Cato's suicide attempts."

All frowned, familiar with O.S.'s weakest link.

"Do Balin's records contain indications of what caused the attempts?" Perry asked. "Did Cato drop hints?"

"No, never. Cato is fragile, but no traitor. Lesley and I have both personally screened every record. But Cato's suicide attempts precede our hits quite regularly. Regularly enough that an intelligent person could see the pattern in the conjunction of crashes and suicidal episodes. I am approaching this presuming Martin Guildbreaker is as skilled at their work as I am at mine."

Ganymede nodded agreement.

"Guildbreaker has no way of detecting the hits which did not involve our cars," Ockham continued, "but, for the crash deaths, they can't fail to find it striking that Cato made these attempts before, not after, people died riding our cars."

Again Ganymede nodded. "Where is Cato now?"

"Sequestered at home. Martin has made no further attempt to contact Cato, but early this morning they sent for details about Esmerald Revere."

Outsider Casimir Perry rubbed his chin, in need of shaving. "I know that name."

"Our late sensayer, Prime Minister," Ockham prompted. "The one who realized what we were doing, and couldn't handle it."

"Ah, yes. Unfortunate. Then Revere was a hit?"

"Yes. Our second-most recent, before the Mertice O'Beirne hit to silence Sugiyama's Seven-Ten list."

The three Hive leaders' faces—severe Andō, exhausted Perry, dazzling Ganymede—all took on that signature determined darkness of mourning someone whose death you chose, and would choose again.

"Did you use a crash for Revere?" Andō asked. "Or one of Cato's inventions?"

"Neither, Chief Director. Thisbe handled Revere."

"Good, that should be difficult to link to the O'Beirne crash, or anything Martin can find."

Ockham took an unhappy breath. "Unfortunately, Chief Director, Thisbe assisted with the O'Beirne hit as well."

The Chief Director's frown grew even graver. "I thought you alternated techniques."

"We try to. Practical details are not always so accommodating."

I am glad to say that all three Hive leaders nodded here, respecting Ockham and his judgment. Less worthy commanders might have snapped at him with the corrections of hindsight, but an officer as steadfast and excellent as Ockham Saneer deserves respect, and here receives it.

Ganymede drew all eyes to him with a tossing of his mane. "How much do you think Martin Guildbreaker has pieced together?"

"Much, but certainly not everything, Member President. Not yet. If

Guildbreaker had proof they'd go to MASON. If they've turned to a sleuth-hound like Papadelias, it means they have the scent, not substance."

Andō had no patience. "What action do you propose?"

"I don't have enough data to propose action yet."

"What data do you need? You know the direction of the investigation."

Ockham paused to think. "I need to understand the degree to which we can or cannot trust Tribune J.E.D.D. Mason."

For three dead seconds no one even breathed.

"I have to ask, Excellencies," Ockham pressed. "I know Martin Guildbreaker works for Tribune Mason. You yourselves arranged to put this investigation in the Tribune's hands, I thought because they are personally close to you and can be trusted. But then you yourself, Member President, gave Cardigan a very intense if incomplete warning to keep the Tribune away from our 'weaker' bash'members. I've heeded the warning, but I remain deeply confused, and that confusion is compromising my ability to make decisions, especially about how to handle Guildbreaker. What is Tribune J.E.D.D. Mason to us? Friend or foe? I need to understand."

What are these glances that they trade, Andō, Ganymede, and pursed-lipped Perry? So many labels—fear, doubt, optimism, affection, shame—both fit and fail.

"I . . . am . . . aware that I know Tribune Mason less well than my colleagues . . ." It was Perry who began, looking from Andō to Ganymede and gaining momentum as he found both willing to let him answer first. "But, as I understand, personal duty, family duty, is more important to them than any Hive. Or at least, personal duty is the Tribune's tiebreaker, when they have multiple Hives tugging at them. And they have strong personal ties to both of you, yes?" His eyes flicked between Andō and pensive Ganymede.

"Tai-kun honors me as a father," Andō answered, darkness clearing from his face as he put it into words. "And Ganymede is one of Tai-kun's bash'parents."

The Duke President frowned. "Bash'sibling is closer, despite our age difference, but yes, we rise from the same bash'. Great pains have been taken to give us some privacy, much as with you and Sniper."

Ockham nodded his semiunderstanding. "If personal relationships are Tribune Mason's tiebreakers, might it not be best to break the truth to them directly? The moral calculus is on our side. We have reams of evidence that our strikes have been beneficial to everyone, tipping the world back from crisis time after time, helping not only our three allied Hives but everyone. And we can easily show how disastrous it would be in the present climate if our system and its history was revealed."

Andō frowned for some reflective moments before shaking his head. "I don't believe Tai-kun is capable of that kind of ethical compromise."

Ockham frowned. "I thought Tribune Mason often helped you and others conceal secrets. I keep being told that's what their investigating team is for, sensitive cases that are threats to Hive stability."

Andō, who has known Him so well, so long, could only sigh. "Normally, yes, Tai-kun does precisely that for us, and is brilliant at working with all seven Hives while hiding from each what would hurt the whole if it came out. But deaths are different, for Tai-kun, absolutely and infinitely different."

"Even though revealing our activities would certainly result in far more harm? The economic and political disaster aside, in the current climate riot deaths would dwarf the lives we take, hundreds to one or more."

The Chief Director shook his head. "I don't think Tai-kun's capable of that kind of choice. We aren't discussing a normal . . . person here." What word almost slipped out in that gap, I wonder? "Tai-kun is psychologically unique, without precedent even in the annals of Brill's Institute. You cannot predict their actions or reactions, not if you don't know them. Words, ethics, the decisions where we every day see gray and compromise are to Tai-kun as rigid and precise as mathematics."

"Math is on our side. Fewer deaths against more."

"No. If we made it an equation, death is infinity by Tai-kun's moral mathematics, so both ends of the balance are negative infinity, and equally unacceptable. The question itself would be crippling."

Concentration tightened Ockham's black brows, as he attempted to imagine such a mind. "Crippling in a useful way for us?"

Andō shook his head. "Tai-kun is not capable of concealing the outward signs of wrestling with such a question. It would be instantly obvious to Martin, to Dominic, to many others, including MASON themself."

Frowning Ockham still turned hopeful eyes on Ganymede. "What about your persuasive influence as a ba'sib, Member President?"

After a moment's hesitation, the Duke switched to Spanish, leaning forward as he spoke now Humanist to Humanist. "Understand this, Ockham: your own bash' has a strict hierarchy, for a vital reason. So does mine. Sniper, for all their fame and worldwide power base, does not for an instant supersede your judgment or command." He waited for a nod from Ockham to confirm that his points were clear so far. "I do not supersede Their Highness Prince Mason."

The sound of Spanish had relaxed Ockham, like breeze in summer, but these last words stiffened him again. "¿Then to say you have influence over Tribune Mason would be better reversed?"

"The influence is bidirectional, and strong, but not equal." Ganymede made his syllables fast and deeply accented, to make extra certain Andō and Perry could not catch many words. "Yourself and Sniper are not poor comparisons. The titles 'duke' and 'prince' are real to us."

"I see." Ockham pursed his lips in thought. "You know my office does not recognize such titles. 'Prince' Mason is not a Humanist, and has no authority over O.S."

"Nor have they authority over myself in matters of state. My oath of office as Humanist President trumps any ties of birth or aristocracy, just as when the King of Spain serves as Europe's Prime Minister. I recognize that, as does Prince Mason, and rest of our bash'."

"¿Then you believe your ability to act as President is not compromised?"

"Absolutely not, when I am acting in my office as President. But if I step outside my office and approach Their Highness ba'sib to ba'sib to persuade them to keep silent, there I would be a petitioner rather than an equal, and there lies hazard. I would avoid that if I can."

"Understood." Ockham smiled, to show his restored confidence. "Thank you for making that clear, Member President."

The Duke inclined his head.

"¿What do you think Tribune Mason will do if they learn? ¿Tell the Emperor?"

"They must not learn." Ganymede switched back to English here. "Our hope in all this is that Martin has not yet informed Prince Mason of their . . . it is still just theory."

Casimir Perry frowned as he scratched his fraying ponytail. "You think young Guildbreaker would go to an outsider like Papadelias before they'd go to their own boss?"

Andō breathed deep. "Martin knows how devastatingly painful Tai-kun would find all this. I believe they would want to be absolutely certain first."

Ockham nodded. "Then we have time. It will not be easy for Guild-breaker to assemble real proof, even with the help of Papadelias."

"And we can slow them down," Andō confirmed. "I will tell Tai-kun I am displeased with this slow progress, and have them order Martin to focus on hunting down the Canner Device and Seven-Ten list thief. Tai-kun is very willing to be told to pursue one question but avert their attention from another. That's why we all agreed to put this in their hands in the first place."

"Yes, that's consistent with what I've seen," Ockham agreed. "Tribune Mason only came in person to the bash'house once, and after some . . . very strange interactions exposing the Mitsubishi traitors within my security, they left saying they were afraid that, if they stayed, they'd learn too much. They intentionally avoided investigating more."

The ghost of a smile on Ganymede's somber face tempted the others to curse inside that there were no cameras to make it immortal. "Their Highness tried their best, then. Martin is the problem."

"And Papadelias now," Andō added. "Tai-kun can control Martin."

Ockham turned to Perry, who was fidgeting with the wrinkled fabric of his trousers. "Papadelias is European. Do you have any influence with them, Prime Minister?"

"Me?" Perry looked from face to face. "I . . . It's true Europe will suffer if O.S. comes out, but, from what I know of Ektor Papadelias, they're a detective first, a Greek fifth, and a European Member somewhere around priority twenty, after many other things like truth, and the Alliance, and reliving the glory days of Mycroft Canner. I don't think even the King of Spain could have persuaded Papadelias to hush anything up, not for Europe and politics."

Quiet faces mulled on that.

"As far as Papadelias goes, Excellencies," Ockham braved, "my instinct is that we do nothing."

"Nothing?"

"The biggest danger is giving ourselves away. If some intervention hinders the investigation, that will only make us look more guilty. Martin has a pattern, nothing more, and there is no true proof against us that I know of, not outside the bash'house itself, which neither Martin nor Papadelias can access."

The Duke President nodded agreement. "There are no tracks for us to cover. If we leave it alone, and continue to demand that Martin concentrate on uncovering who planted the Seven-Ten list, they won't be able to waste more time chasing shadows. Do you agree, Perry?"

Europe's Second-Choice Prime Minister sat forward on his little bench, where he preferred to sit silent, absorbing the conversation like a patient sponge. It was half deference that made him the quietest of the three Hive leaders here, but half exhaustion. History does not give with both hands. If the European Union enjoyed an easier birth than the other Hives, its apparatus a century old before the Great Renunciation, it pays the price whenever its nation-strats rehash their ancient grudges: you seized my borderlands, you executed my hero, you conquered me a thousand years ago and I remember. All Europeans are equally guilty, English, Flemish, Kurdish, myself no less, for I catch myself from time to time rejecting good sense just because it came from a Turk's lips. The strat delegates who make up Europe's Parliament, and the strat leaders—Presidents and Premiers, French, Belgian, Laotian, Canadian—who sit on her Executive Council, they all answer, not just to Now, but to the pride of Then, and every problem must consider the silent wishes of countless ancestors. For Casimir Perry, a man who is no king, to herd these vindictive cats toward compromise takes every card in statecraft's deck, and more hours than any man should spend awake. "I'm calling a hit," he said.

Ockham's eyes grew round as planets. "A hit now, Prime Minister?"

"It can't wait. We have a Hive to save." Perry's gesture brought the files up in all their lenses. "The Cousins are toppling, not just weakening, toppling, the whole Hive. Masami Mitsubishi is your ba'kid, Andō, how could you let them put Cousins' Feedback Bureau Chief Darcy Sok on their Seven-Ten list? Have you even seen the footage from Casablanca? With the furor after the theft of the list, there are more journalists at the CFB now than employees. The Feedback Bureau is the heart of the Hive. If word gets out what's really been going on in there, that's it for the Cousins, they're dead, and I don't just mean Bryar Kosala. It doesn't matter they're the second-largest Hive, after a blow like this they'll shrink to smallest in no time, if they manage to stay together as a Hive at all."

With feather-smooth motions and an embroidered handkerchief, the Duke made art even of blowing his nose. "Is that bad?"

"The dissolution of a Hive? Of course it's bad! We're not talking about the Masons here. The Cousins may not be in our alliance, but all our members benefit from them, depend on them, every day."

Andō frowned, impassive. "The Masons and the Cousins agree too often. Between them they have 48 percent of the population."

The claim made Perry stiffen. "Masons and Cousins never agree, they're polar opposites."

"Exactly, they propose opposite plans, then compromise, and reduce any debate to reconciling their two proposals and ignoring everybody else's."

"If you were ever there for the debates," the Duke added, "you'd understand."

Andō took charge before the Outsider could return the slight. "You know my bash'child Toshi works in the Censor's office in Romanova. Before all this began, their prediction was that, within two years, the Masons plus Cousins will go over 50 percent, and the 36 percent we have between the three of us will shrink to 33 percent or less. The Seven-Ten list mess has only accelerated that; it could happen this year. We can't let the Masons and Cousins create a real majority."

Perry clutched the rim of his bench, as if clinging to a more stable past. "You planned this. You're trying to tear the Cousins down!"

Is that a smile on Andō's face? "Whatever the cause, the Cousins failing would mean one point seven billion Members seeking a new Hive. You said yourself Cousins and Masons are opposites. Ex-Cousins are unlikely to become Masons, and they're certainly not going to turn Utopian. A lot may linger as Whitelaws for a while at least, but Hivelessness is only so appealing. That leaves Gordian or us, and one point seven billion people are not about to convert to Brillism overnight."

Perry sprang to his feet; a kiss from sparkling Danaë could not turn a man so red. "You expect ex-Cousins to join us after O.S. is exposed? Or had that by-product not crossed your minds when you dispatched your little thief?"

"Thief?" Andō repeated. "You misunderstand. We had nothing to do with the theft of the list, we would never jeopardize O.S. like that."

Ganymede nodded confirmation. "Never."

"The three of us," Andō continued, "you included, Perry, agreed at our last meeting that we had to silence Sugiyama's Seven-Ten list article about François Quesnay, or there would be a disastrous anti-Mitsubishi backlash. So long as my Toshi was writing the substitute list, it seemed a good opportunity to bring the world's attention to the corruption in the CFB. I suggested that Toshi consider putting CFB Chief Darcy Sok on their list, just to weaken the Hive a bit, no more. This theft, which has turned a slight nudge into an earthquake, that was someone else."

Perry made fists. "This violates the spirit of O.S., Andō. You took advantage of a hit we all agreed on to advance an agenda we never talked about."

Andō scowled. "I don't recall the terms of O.S. requiring me to give you equal access to my adopted children, as well as to my assassins."

"They're not *your* assassins," Perry spat, "they're *our* assassins."

Ganymede's gilt brows narrowed. "In fact they are *my* assassins."

"Regardless," Perry plunged on, "the terms of O.S. clearly require the three of us to share with the others any agenda which might affect Hive balance. Dissolving the Cousins more than qualifies!" The Prime Minister's breath grew fast, the ferocious enthusiasm of a speaker accustomed to being heeded only when he made it seem the sky was falling. "You set a bomb without telling us, and it's gone off at the worst possible moment. Thanks to this theft, the whole world's read Sugiyama's article about François Quesnay and the so-called failure of the Mitsubishi land-focused philosophy. Mitsubishi stocks are already showing the impact, and worse, Sugiyama's list put the spotlight back on Ziven Racer too, which has shredded what little confidence Europe was starting to have in me, not to mention Sniper being on their list instead of Ganymede. Polar opposites or not, if the Cousins go down right now the Masons are going to seem a lot more appealing than Mitsubishi whose philosophy is doomed, Europeans with a leader no one wanted, and Humanists whose President only stays in office at the whim of a living doll with no attention span." His hot fist slammed the inlaid cabinet behind him. "I'm calling a hit. I called the O.S. set-sets earlier to have them look for a way to deflect the press from Darcy Sok and the CFB."

"You went directly to our set-sets?" Throughout the leaders' conference Ockham had sat as stiff as a foot soldier before the wrathful Major, but now his stiffness grew cold. "That isn't how this system works, Prime Minister."

A weak master is quick to slap what dogs he can. "With Sniper missing, and you too incompetent to keep the chaos out, it works however it has to work, Saneer. Understood?"

Ockham did not answer, but his eyes flashed to his President, full of silent warning.

"Now," Perry ploughed on, "the set-sets have found a hit that will trigger the retirement of Darcy Sok and several other CFB staff. With new people taking charge, the press won't find it strange if they can't answer many questions, and the consequent chain of promotions will put your Hiroaki Mitsubishi in a position to alter the most damning files." He nodded to Andō. "If we do this, the Cousins are safe for now. If you really do want to tear them down, we can always expose them later when the public doesn't think we're all dirt."

The Duke President and Chief Director debated with their eyes.

"We can't hand the Cousins to the Masons on a platter!" Perry pressed, his words racing as if some demon chased him, tossing Members into

MASON's maw with every heartbeat's tick. "The three of us together, even with O.S. behind us, we're still constantly losing ground, Gordian too, and Utopia, you've watched them both shrinking, Census by Census, while bloated MASON swells!" He gasped a breath. "I love this Alliance, love it, and my Hive, with every fiber of my being, the best and greatest work of politics the human race has ever seen! And we, poor as we are, are its custodians. Do you really think the system can endure if the Masons slurp up the Cousins and make the Emperor dictator of a true global majority? I don't believe this hit will expose O.S., I trust Ockham and their bash' better than that, but even if it did, we could endure that, a blow, yes, but we few who knew about O.S. would fall upon our swords, while our Hives would live. The system would live. But there's no recovery from the stranglehold of true majority, more and more youths will choose what seems the default path, while what other Hives remain will diminish until we're as rare and impotent as Hiveless. We must act, now, or this—the only golden age the human race has ever seen that is no myth, no propaganda spun by its or later ages' flatteries, this real golden age—will die in our keeping!"

On this impassioned climax Perry waited, at the edge of panting, like an actor at the finish of some famous speech. I want to say more of Casimir Perry, of the inner man, what dreams and appetites course through this heaving soul who built from nothing his stairway to power, baking each brick in the blister-fire of his determination. But he may not have been like that at all. I do not know the Outsider, as I know these others. I have not poured his wine, paced his hallways, memorized the tics of his lip and eyebrow so I could anticipate when to attend and when to cringe. I know his words, but not the man beneath, who watches now as Ganymede and Andō trade in glances their fears, agreements, counterarguments, all the subtle signals of debate which intimates need no words to share with one another. Will they heed him? Will they, in their security and condescension, think this Second-Choice Prime Minister is crying wolf?

Ockham could only hold his tongue so long. "I must advise against the use of O.S. at this time, Prime Minister. It isn't safe."

Perry scowled. "Using the cars now would be stupid, I agree, but Cato's one-time-only concoctions should be as untraceable now as ever. Am I wrong?"

Ockham's voice did not lighten. "Since I don't know what methods Guildbreaker and Papadelias might employ, I don't know what would be traceable or not. One does not gamble with the flagship. I don't know what it is in the CFB that the three of you are trying to conceal, nor should I know, but it is difficult to believe it could be as devastating as the exposure of O.S. If the President gives this order, I will execute it, but under protest. Member President?"

I believe Ockham is the only person in the world who can address the Duke as 'Member President' and win a smile. From others it is a reminder of discomfort, of disconnect, too contemporary for this living fossil dredged back from the aristocratic days of yore by DNA retrieval and Madame's strange education. His Grace is an exile in time, and it is madness to him that his subjects are his by vote, and not by birth or conquest. But strict, soldierly Ockham, and the absoluteness with which he almost-salutes his leader, that, at least, to this living anachronism named Ganymede, feels right.

"I agree it is a risk," the Duke President answered, "but Perry is correct, we must consider it. There is no return if MASON takes a true majority. We must prepare means to prevent that, even if it might increase the risk of exposure. Do you agree, Andō?"

The Mitsubishi Chief Director paused, brows locked.

Casimir Perry is not a man to let a silence last. "All Martin Guildbreaker has is the alignment of some of Cato's suicide attempts with some crashes. Cato's own techniques are unique each time, no pattern, untraceable. The risk of O.S. being exposed because of this one hit is tiny compared to the disaster which is certain. A Masonic majority, not just in our lifetimes but this year! What was O.S. created for if not for this?"

Gazing down at the pleading European as grimly as storm-willed Poseidon, Andō gave his single, rigid nod.

Sun-bright Ganymede holds a different kind of grimness, just as chillingly divine. "Prepare for this hit, Ockham, but take no action yet. Have Cato choose a means, then look it over yourself and see what flaws you can detect. I don't want to give this order, but I want you ready if I have to. Meanwhile we shall, all of us, try every other means we can to calm the Cousin situation, and to deflect Martin and Papadelias."

Ockham nodded, his shoulders easing at the promise of delay. "I'll prepare the hit right away, Member President, but I hope we will not need it."

"You will divide your efforts between preparing this hit, and finding Sniper. All my personal forces are at your disposal, and if you want official Hive forces, request anything you like, no need to check with me."

"Thank you, Member President."

"Now, leave us. We have other business to discuss."

"Yes, Member President." It must be from old war movies that Ockham learned to click his heels like that, so the clean metal frames which vein his deerskin boots sing like chimes.

Andō breathed a long sigh, shifting from a formal to a friendly posture as Ockham latched the door behind him. In fact they all shifted, shoulders stretching, hips relaxing, legs sprawled at ease, postures of comfort, now that the subordinate was no longer there to make them wear their masks.

Speech did not change so fast. "I must clear this possible hit with the other seven Directors," Andō began, "but they're in no position to argue at the moment."

Perry frowned. "Seven? You still haven't told Director Bandyopadhyay about O.S.?"

"Nor do I intend to," the Chief Director answered stonily. "Greenpeace was not part of this arrangement before the merger, and is not now."

Prime Minister Perry leaned back with a hissing sigh. "I still think it's risky trying to conceal O.S. from one of your Nine Directors, while all the others know. Any one of them could tip off Bandyopadhyay, and earn a lot of favors in return. If you tell them yourself, you get the favors."

Andō's eyes narrowed. "Your lack of confidence in my fellow Directors verges on insult, Perry. The Greenpeace-Mitsubishi merger was a source of strength, not weakness, and we have kept Greenpeace Directors successfully at arm's length for more than sixty years. Do not presume our strat balance is as deceitful and self-defeating as your own."

The European sighed contrition. "I'm sorry if it seemed like a criticism. I just meant it as advice, really. Things are much more peaceful and manageable on my end now that I've told the rest of my coalition leadership about O.S. It's united us, both with the feeling that we have an extra tool in our belts, and with the knowledge that, if one of us sells out, we all go down."

Ganymede's gold brows knit. "You told your entire coalition about O.S.?"

Perry adjusted the Polish strat band around his upper arm. "Why not? I've been head of the Special Means Committee for almost twenty years; most of my close allies either knew or suspected what that really meant. It was an administrative nightmare operating O.S. when it had to be secret from the Prime Minister, the Commission, the European Council, and my own personal coalition. Now that His Inconveniently Catholic Majesty isn't in charge anymore, there's no reason to keep things so compartmentalized."

The Duke's light fingers trembled. "You're talking about how many allies here? Five? Ten?" He waited. "Twenty?" Still no nod. "More?"

"Most of my coalition already knew. It was no end of difficulty trying to run Europe's end of O.S. alone while Spain was Prime Minister, trying to guess what the Hive needed when most of our leadership didn't know I was important enough to bother informing of pending trouble. I had to have allies who knew, just to have enough ears to the ground to know when to act. Andō does the same."

Ganymede frowned. "Andō asks permission every time they discuss *my* assassins with any breathing soul."

Perry gave a tired smile. "Then I envy Andō, having time to visit you so often."

The Duke President glared, and glared more when he caught a smirk on Andō's face. "Levity has no place in this. Every person who knows is that much more danger."

"Andō has told their allies, I told mine."

"Seven Board Directors is not fifty-plus unstable coalition allies."

"It was the right call," Perry insisted. "It's smoothed everything. I finally have Parliament in hand, really in hand. Now that they know I can call on a power like that, they snap to like a *Familiaris* in front of MASON!"

"You will not reveal O.S. to anyone else without my express permission. Ever."

Perry sighed his consent. "I'll check with you whenever I can, but sometimes I need the extra leverage at a moment's notice."

"Ever," Ganymede repeated.

"I'll do my best. I'll always tell you afterward."

"You will find your own means to keep your house in order, or I shall send a housekeeper."

Perry's eyes glittered coldly between their nests of care-lines. "I'll thank you to leave Europe to the European."

At that the Duc de la Trémoïlle rose to his feet like wrathful dawn. "Your presence in my house is a privilege, Perry. You advise me on the use of my assassins as a privilege. You access my ba'sibs at Madame's as a privilege. You keep your precious coalition and your seat because I refrain from calling a few friends to say I am tired of you. I do not need to threaten to expose how you used Ziven Racer to oust Spain from office; I can unseat you by hinting that I wish it so. You will not insult me ever again. And you will not speak of my O.S. to any breathing being."

The Prime Minister drew slow breaths, staring up at backlit Ganymede, whose blazing mane turned his pale face to silhouette, like the moon at the eclipsing of the sun. What is that that Perry swallows down now? Words?

Or pride? "Yes, Your Grace." He bowed his head. "I'm sorry. I'll never do anything like it again."

The eclipse passed. "You will supply me with a list of everyone who knows, and you will not question how I choose to deal with them."

"Of course, Your Grace." Not quite all pride was swallowed. "Doesn't Andō get a chiding too?"

Blue diamond eyes flashed murder. "What for?"

"Me telling my allies caused nothing, just stability. Shanghai and Beijing brought traitors into the Saneer-Weeksbooth bash' itself! It was Andō's job to vet the Mitsubishi Special Guard, make sure they were the loyal among the loyal. And there's the Canner Device."

Andō paused in pacing the room, his stony frown darkening to something worse, a stony smile. "What about the Canner Device?"

Perry looked nervous. "You . . . you made it, didn't you? Japan keeps coming up in all of the reports. It's a big, sophisticated tool, hijacking the entire tracker system, millions of tracker signals at once. You've had it for more than a decade and never shared it with us? This alliance is supposed to be complete, coequal, sharing all we have to guard our stability against MASON's. The only reason to hide something like that from allies is if you plan to use it against us."

Ganymede turned on Andō, anger on his golden brows. "Is this true?"

Andō shrugged, still smiling. "I have no plans to use the Canner Device against you or anyone."

"But it's true? You made it?"

Still the Chief Director smiled. "A predecessor made it."

Hurt mixed with anger on the Duke's face. "You knew who made the Canner Device? You didn't tell me?"

Andō stepped close enough to smile down at the delicate Duke. "You didn't need to worry yourself about it."

Gold brows tightened. "That isn't your decisi—"

"Yes it is."

Ganymede stared up at him. "You cannot hide a thing as serious as—"

A kiss rendered the Duke mute as Andō seized him, a fast, practiced embrace which pinned the Duke's slim arms to his sides. Ganymede's eyes answered the kiss with wet anger, then some moments of serene enjoyment, then anger again as he craned his neck away. "Not . . ." He stopped—how could he finish? Not here? Not now? Not in front of this worm Perry? Any of those would have proved to Perry that elsewhere, elsewhen, the Duke would have submitted.

"What?" Andō answered with a sibling's nonchalance. "Perry's been invited upstairs, it's nothing they're not going to see a thousand times." He
pressed the Duke President against a wall and took his lips a second time.

"Upstairs!" Perry cried in full-bodied delight. "You asked Madame?
I'm in?"

Andō has practiced this, one arm to pin the fragile Duke in place, the
other down his trousers to tickle Ganymede's seat of pleasure, and drive all
words from his lips with gasps of joy. "Not me." Ando's words took turns
with kisses. "I convinced Spain . . . to ask Madame . . . It had to come . . .
from them . . . from me it . . . might've seemed an insult . . . You'll be
inducted . . . tomorrow."

"Tomorrow?" Different kinds of delight chased each other across
Perry's rapt face. "Does this mean Madame approves of me staying
Prime Minister? The others approve? MASON approves?"

"They're reconciled to you . . . Eventually they might want . . . to shunt
you off . . . some high office in Romanova . . . Senate Speaker maybe . . .
reinstate Spain . . . but you're inside now . . . we'll keep you at the top . . .
somewhere."

"I did it?" Perry voiced a little laugh, slow, like a timid chick, uncertain
whether it is truly time to leave the shell. "I made it? Madame's inner circle.
It's done. I'm done."

"I've paid your dues for this year. I know you've nowhere near the means
to pay yourself, but we'll discuss the balance of your debts in time."

"Thank you!" Perry's voice cracked. "Andō, thank you! I can never th—"

"No, you never can, and never will."

The Prime Minister froze, then bowed his head. "You won't regret this,
Andō, both of you, I swear. I'll make you glad to be my sponsors, every
hour, every day!" Sponsor was an interesting word choice, avoiding the dread
word 'patron' as the Servicer Program avoids the dread word 'slave.' Sponsor feels so legitimate.

"I have high expectations," Andō warned.

Perry filled himself with a deep breath. "I'll exceed them."

Ganymede wriggled in Andō's grip. "Stop. This is serious. The Cann—"

Again Andō stole the Duke's words with a long kiss. "The Canner Device?" he finished. "That's old business. Don't worry your head about it.
The guilty have been well punished. It's done."

Ganymede wriggled. "No, you—uuuh." A fresh gasp broke his words.
"It's done."

I do not know, reader, whether Andō mounted Ganymede here in front

of Perry or spared him; it is the sort of detail a gentleman omits in interview. Perhaps Andō backed off, but, after Ganymede's show of ducal fire at
Perry, Andō might have taken this chance to drive home to both the others
that he is and ever shall be first among (un)equals. Besides, I know Andō
enjoys how the Duke's unwilling buttocks clench like a virgin's on these
rare occasions when he is not 'in the mood.' You may choose for yourself,
reader, how thorough a congress to imagine.

"Is this a perk that comes with being invited upstairs?" Perry asked, a
freshness awakening in his face as he watched, as when a dozing dog pricks
up its ears at footsteps.

Andō enjoyed that question. "Watching is. The twins are one flesh, and
both of them are mine, as sure as man and wife and otherwife." Fresh
touches made sure Ganymede had no breath to contradict. "I paid for them,
more money than you'll see in your lifetime. The boy I leave free to share
himself when he fancies, but the last man who glanced too long at Danaë
is not here to remember it."

"Understood." The trial-weathered Prime Minister smiled as he
stretched back to watch politics play out before him. "I really can never
thank you enough, Andō. Tomorrow night. It hardly feels real; just one more
night."

Providence

SHARE NOW MY HORROR, READER, AS A LIVERIED FOOTMAN returns my confiscated tracker, and the first sight in my feed is Carlyle Foster stepping across the threshold of Madame's. Dominic plays our puppet strings with a musician's precision, like the grim matron who made him. He knew just how long he could keep me off the tracker network before Papadelias would go berserk, so he had my tracker delivered to my hands minutes before the Commissioner General would have called the Romanovan cavalry, and seconds after our sweet young sensayer had passed the door. That door, festive with its gilded ironwork of twining vines; I would have plastered it with warnings to match the gates of Hell, had I been free to reach it before Carlyle. Did Dominic know that I had tapped Carlyle's feed? That I watched, live, as a pair of blushing housemaids swept the Cousin up, happy to serve as teeth for Dominic's bear-trap. "Sister Heloïse is expecting you," they crooned. "She's just through here. She's so been looking forward to your visit." Their lies poured out like syrup as they coaxed their victim on, just a little further, through these suites, these doors, these bolts. I groaned inside. My warning had failed to save Carlyle, the instructions I had left with my fellow Servicers when I left them packing up Bridger's toys to ship to Sniper's doll museum: warn Carlyle to stay away, far away from Madame's, from Dominic, and danger. But Carlyle had come fluttering to the flame, lured by the false invitation Dominic had sent in Heloïse's name, and lured too by Carlyle's conclusion that J.E.D.D. Mason was something not unlike a miracle. How confident the Cousin was that, in this golden age of peace and ever-watching trackers, a virgin with a bag of gold could walk across the Earth without danger. Our modern moths have bounced so many times off lightbulbs, they aren't prepared for torches, and forget that wings can burn.

But thou canst save Carlyle, Mycroft. Thou art close at hand, yes? As I understand it, this whole house is thy large and roaming prison, strange haven from the wrathful world that calls anew for Mycroft Canner's blood.

You are right, good reader. I am but four stories above the young sensayer, a few halls past screaming distance.

Thou must save Carlyle then. The Cousin is a fool to come, but still does not deserve what lies in wait.

Would that obedience were easy, compassionate master. But, while I may rival greyhounds over open ground, I am as helpless as any man in Madame's labyrinth of doors and doorkeepers. I began at once to plead my way past the many checkpoints of the house, strong doors and their strong keepers, but even as I raced I feared that slow was too slow.

Call on thy tracker, then, and warn the victim of the trap.

Alas, the sweet sensayer knew my name now. The ears of Carlyle Foster were deaf to the words of Mycroft Canner. If I called, Carlyle would cut me off in seconds. I might get in a sentence or two first, and I would save those for the true crisis moment, when it came. Better to head down in person, since a switch's flick could not silence me if we stood face to face. So I raced, and watched, and dispatched a silent prayer too as I watched, on the off chance that This Universe's God was not as deaf to me as was His priest. You may, if you wish to aid us, pray as well, reader. The Hand that weaves Providence knows everything from creation to infinity, and takes account of the future when He plans the past; if prayer has any power to sway Fate, then even though, from your perspective, Carlyle was either saved or not saved long ago, it could still be your prayer, now, as you read, that swayed the Judge. Free and righteous as you probably are, you may pray for any intervention you imagine: a timely call from a bash'mate, Kosala wandering by, a house fire. For myself, low creature that I am, I dared not ask so much: only that Fate might be so kind as to let Carlyle find Dominic in a gentle mood, as I had found him thirteen years ago, the first time I begged my way back into that house.

Should I share that scene too with you, reader? The gentler version of what Carlyle may be about to face? It was long ago, my first day as a slave, the day I donned my Servicer uniform, still hostile in my heart to the changes that were remaking me, and unused to coming as a suppliant. But I had to see Jehovah Mason again. Some weeks had passed since my trial, my first encounter with He Who Changed Me, and my soul was still one great wound after my transformation. My old self had been so armored in conviction that it had never hesitated, even as I made all the world my enemy. My new, raw self did not yet know to name these icy stab-wounds 'doubt.' I had to see Him again. If the only way was to throw myself upon the mercy of the looming dragon who seemed to control access to this Prince, so be it. I slipped my tracker, and slinked my way to the alley behind Madame's. A young and fierce Chevalier dragged me inside, and hurled me at the feet of Brother Dominic, seventeen then and not yet ordained. How did kind Fate have me find him? Naked in his cell, his youth-firm breasts and hips just starting to swell with Venus's fertility, all callously bare, as when a bandit chief plays with his drawn sword, watching the wide white eyes of prisoners follow his naked blade. Dominic's posture was all power, his expression too as he dismissed the Chevalier only after a lazy, appraising stare which said that he could have enjoyed this servant during our meeting had it been worth his time. Brother Dominic chuckled at my stammering petition for an audience with He Who Had Shattered My Illusory World, and he consented at once to teach me of the real world, and what my place in it must be if I wished to have access to our Master. Dominic had pets in those days, gifts from Madame, a lion, a leopard, and a wolf bitch, almost tame, and as he lectured me on the Enlightenment, and secret politics, and the rules a slave must follow when addressing God, his pet beasts squabbled, competing to lick the meat-sweet monthly drippings from his cunt. Such a scene I prayed might wait for Carlyle Foster in Dominic's room, but Providence was not so merciful.

"Wait, that's not Sister Heloïse, I . . . Wait!"

Carlyle sought escape at once, but the two maidens who had been his traitor-guides flitted away fast as summer butterflies, and bolted the door too firmly for pounding fists to even rattle it. That room reminds one why prisons and monasteries are both composed of 'cells.' It is dim, no softness, no color, no throw pillows or smiling toys, just bare walls, raw wooden furniture, and books in piles, much fingered but not loved. Madame insists on printed books for her creatures' education despite the expense, for an electronic text ceases to be quite real the instant it leaves the reader's lenses, easy to forget. Paper, with its must and bookmarks, lingers in the corner of the eye, refusing to be unread. Dominic has all the theologians as his roommates: Calvin, Ramanuja, Augustine, lazing on every surface of the room like flies so persistent that one no longer bothers to shoo them away. Carlyle found Dominic there on his knees, his back to the door, hands clasped in prayer, with the shapeless folds of a monk's long habit pooling around him like sacking. It was a Dominican habit, a black mantle over white beneath, the rough layers rustling with the rhythms of his prayer, like the wings of a hooded hawk. Dominic's feet, half hidden in the folds, were bare, and his wig discarded, so it no longer hid the blush-red bare patch of his tonsure. Nothing remained of his daily gentleman's costume except the tracker at his ear and the long, hooded sensayer's scarf draped across his shoulders like a priest's stole. On the wall above, where Dominic focused his devotions, hung the room's sole decoration, framed in plain gold against the bare plaster: a portrait of Jehovah.

Carlyle collapsed at once and vomited into the trash can, which waited by the door for victims such as we. She convulsed over it, wriggling like a half-crushed maggot as her body usurped the mind's control in its desperate need to purge itself. Hot tears followed the waste, forced out by the violence her muscles did to themselves. She fought, not to rise, not even to stop retching, but just to breathe.

'She,' Mycroft? For Carlyle thou meanest 'he.'

No, reader, I refuse. It is wrong, this pronoun they commanded me to force on her, they who are so proud to number the prince and heir of la Trémoïlle among their playthings, but it is wrong. Look at this kind and tender Cousin, her giving smile, her flowing wrap, her courage strengthened daily by the knowledge that her existence helps so many others. Has Carlyle made one choice in all this history that does not declare the strong and beauteous 'she'? I will not erase Carlyle's choices anymore, not in deference to this mad law, revived in Madame's antique pageant world, that only penises inherit. Let censors change the pronoun later if they wish; I shall lie no more. And you, reader, you need Carlyle to be 'she' here too. Do you remember when you first smelled the rot? When alien Danaë, armored in the extinct pelt of 'woman,' drew forth my secrets? Perhaps your better age is finally past it, reader, but my society—despite our neuter efforts—still shoves gender down our throats, imbibed in toddlerhood when a child whom the adults label 'girl' gets chided just a little more for getting her nice clothes muddy than a child we see as 'boy' and associate with snails and muddy puppy tails. The residue of ancient archetypes embedded deep in Mycroft Canner knew that I was supposed to become the shining knight when Danaë presents the tearful princess. That learned, unconscious chivalry made me helpless before her, and you would not have understood why if I had not given Danaë her 'she.' Just so you need it here, Dominic's overwhelming 'he' as Carlyle's 'she' responds with that tender, honest, feminine goodness which makes this fell bloodhound smell prey. Carlyle is a thousand times stronger than I, fights back where I surrendered, but it is still millennia she battles, the learned detritus of millennia, deep inside her.

Are these thy true motives, Mycroft? Thou claimest that this sudden switch to 'she' is for my better understanding, but this feels more like thy prejudice, that, because Carlyle is the victim here, thou seest suddenly the 'weaker sex' and concoctest these excuses to justify thy change.

I wish I could prove you wrong, reader. When I ask myself why I reach for 'she' here it feels as if it is for you, your better understanding, and for Carlyle, respecting her choice to be a Cousin. Those motives feel so real. But I cannot be certain these are not veneer over some grosser instinct. The poison of millennia is in me too.

Methodical Dominic finished his prayer, the rote-swift syllables punctuated by the music of his victim's nausea, before he turned to gaze upon his prey. "Tell me, Cousin Foster," he began softly, "what's it like getting up in the morning every day knowing thou hast a coward's religion?"

Carlyle barely had the strength to raise her eyes as she retched over the can.

"The unexamined can get away with it," Dominic continued, not rising from his knees but gazing over his shoulder at his shaking visitor. "But as a sensayer thou knowest perfectly well that, of the hundreds of faiths thou'st studied, thou'st fixed on the most toothless. Deism, the comfortable fancy that all religions are coequal puzzle-piece interpretations of the same Clockmaker God, Who made this universe but does not interfere with blights or miracles, trusting Nature and mankind to run ourselves with the hands-off guidance of His beneficent, rational laws. Thy studies have taught thee well how cowardly that is."

"Ho-o-w?" Carlyle gasped, choking on her own hair which stuck to the spit and stomach juices mingling on her chin. "How did you know I was a Deist? Did Jehovah Mason tell you? Is that their power? Some kind of telepathy?"

Dominic shifted, kneeling more erectly now, the waves of his habit straightening like a stormy ocean gathering into tsunami. "Thou darest not face a universe without a God, but thou refusest to diminish human freedom, so thou honorest this Clockmaker, Who does not interfere with Fate or freewill, just steps in at the beginning with a happy plan, and the end with a happy afterlife."

"The invitation didn't come from Heloïse, did it?" Carlyle accused. "It came from you. You lured me here."

Dominic would not let his victim break the rhythm of his words. "No commandments to follow, no angels to fear, and all religions are equally valid in the eyes of thy vague God, so thou dost not even have to say that anybody else is wrong. They're all right, thy parishioners, thy fellow sensayers, the priests and martyrs of every faith in history, everybody's right except the atheists, and thou canst tell thyself the atheists too would be happy with a God who does not judge or interfere. Has there ever been a faith that required less of its adherents?"

"Stop this right now!" Carlyle tried to rise, but slumped back into the corner, barely strong enough to raise her head. "This isn't the Eighteenth Century, it's the Twenty-Fifth, and there are rules! You can't lure people into your house on false pretenses, you can't wear a costume that declares your religion publicly, and only my sensayer gets to talk to me about my religion!"

No predator has ever worn so cruel a victory smile. "I am thy sensayer."

"What?"

Dominic's gesture brought the document before Carlyle's lenses, a sensayer transfer, signed and validated, effective that day by order of Conclave Head Julia Doria-Pamphili. "Thou knowest well it is unhealthy to spend thy whole life seeing the same sensayer, and it is unfair to the world, too, one parishioner hogging so many of the great Julia's sessions. She's the most popular sensayer on Earth. There are leaders and philosophers on a two-year waiting list for one of her transformative sessions, while she wastes two hours a week on one spineless, unchanging little Deist."

Carlyle coughed. "What did you do to Julia?"

Without rising, Dominic settled onto a three-legged wooden stool that waited by his side. "I'm not permitted to disclose what goes on between me and my sensayer."

A sharp breath. "Julia's your sensayer?"

"She's been teaching for ten years, did it never occur to thee that she had other students?"

"You . . . 'A coward's religion,'" Carlyle quoted, her voice softening as understanding bloomed, "that's how Julia described Deism too, when we first met."

"It would be a shame if the world's most penetrating sensayer had no apprentice capable of using her techniques." Dominic gestured to a cup of water, waiting on his table for his victim's need. "Thou shouldst be happy, Carlyle. As thy sensayer I can't lay a finger on thy body or I could lose my license. There are only a handful of people in the world I'm not allowed to touch, and most of them are on the Seven-Ten lists."

Where art thou, Mycroft? Thou promised thou wouldst race to Carlyle's rescue.

I am coming, reader, coming, as quickly as I can.

Carlyle wolfed the water down, breathing easier as wetness rinsed the acid from her throat. "I'm never accepting this," she began with new strength, sweeping her matted hair out of her face. "Even if you've forced or bribed Julia—"

"Thou dost not think she's beyond bribery, then?" Dominic interrupted. "Thou'rt perceptive when thou allowest thyself."

Carlyle's fist tightened around the pewter cup, ready to hurl it like a sling stone. "Even if you have, I'll go to the committee—"

"And petition for a transfer? Feel free. They'll interview me if thou dost, and I'll so enjoy telling them about thy tawdry affair with Thisbe Saneer. It will be thee who loses thy license then."

"I haven't touched Thisbe Saneer."

"No judge in this world will believe that." Dominic drummed the side of his wooden stool. "Thou'st spent thirty hours in her bedroom in the last five days, and you went to a brothel together. What wilt thou say, that thou wert there chasing a miracle child? Or wilt thou ask Mycroft Canner to vouch for thee?"

Keep in mind, reader, that Dominic's 'thee's and 'thou's feel far stranger in print than they do in person. He does not exaggerate them as bad actors do, but mumbles the archaisms with the calm slurring of common speech, so the syllables fly past too quickly to feel unnatural. Read his lines aloud to a friend saying 'thou'st' and 'what'rt thou' as quickly as you would say 'you've' and 'what're ya,' and, more often than not, the friend won't even notice archaism rearing plain as day.

The Cousin still had fire to spit. "You sound stupid making empty threats. Thisbe will vouch for me, that's all I need."

"Thisbe?" Dominic repeated. "Thisbe's ambitious. She'll sacrifice thee in an instant if I offer to help her climb Madame's ladder. She's tasted what we have; she won't turn back until she's glutted herself. Thou must see that."

Carlyle sat up fully now, glaring defiance, the hints of blond in her hair catching the light like old gold. "You know, Bryar Kosala had almost talked me into being okay with what Madame does here, that Madame was just using gendered sex to vent people's urges and foster inter-Hive collaboration, but the real problem is encouraging others to imitate that. Even if there's still sexist residue that makes it harder for a woman to get ahead outside, sitting here using sex to pull strings isn't going to end that inequality, and encouraging normal people like Thisbe to do it too is just going to reduce the number of competent women that are out there trying to make things equal." She frowned, seeing a stifled snicker twist Dominic's lips. "Have I said something funny?"

"Thou hast it backwards. Madame isn't here pulling strings because it's hard for a woman to make it to the top out there, it's hard for a woman to make it to the top out there because Madame's here pulling strings. No one gets to the top now except the ones she chooses, and, however good she is with all genders, she finds the traditionally masculine the easiest to draw in and control. Fifty years ago half the Hives had female leaders, fifty years ago the Seven-Ten lists were always different, and fifty years ago this building was a music conservatory."

Carlyle wiped her chin and soiled hair with a handkerchief Dominic had left on hand for her. "You're saying Madame's artificially re-created sexism so they can manipulate the world with it? That's absurd. I can't believe one brothel could have that much influence."

"Reawakened, not re-created—the old dragon but slept. They did not finish it off, thy ancestors, after their surface victory, they did not chase the worm to see how deep it coiled." Dominic leaned back, the black over-cape of his habit falling back to let the white folds of the lower layer pool between the roundness of his breasts. "We spent ten thousand years perfecting gender, more: gendered clothing, gendered gestures, gendered language, gendered thought, a hundred thousand tools of seduction, so literally all a maiden had to do was let a glimpse of ankle show beneath her skirts to blind almost anyone with thoughts of sex. Since the worst of both sides in the Church War were also those that separated the sexes most, fear wedded gender to religion's poison in the survivors' minds. Suddenly neutered dress and speech were mandatory to proclaim one's allegiance to the 'good guys,' and anyone who used skirts and ties and 'he's and 'she's—even in nontraditional ways—invited the label 'zealot.' So the Great 'They' Silence fell, but our ancestors didn't purge the libraries and history books, didn't ban the costumes from the stage and screen, and those are enough to teach us gender's old language, the cues of dress and gait, which even today thou understandeth as clearly as 'thee' and 'thou.'"

"Understand and hate," Carlyle spat back.

Dominic shook his tonsured head. "Yes, it is easy to mistake other strong feelings for hate. But you know what you feel here isn't hate. The outside world has had barely three centuries to develop neuter seduction, while gender had millennia. Once thou bitest the peach thou canst not stomach bland gruel anymore. I knew thou wouldst come back. It's amazing what members will do to keep coming back. Selling out a friend or fixing a vote is nothing, I mean real work: founding a business, starting a career in politics and fighting to the top as Casimir Perry has, because they know that at the top the fruit is sweeter. Madame doesn't just make them ad-dicts, she uses the addiction to make them vocateurs."

"No. It's strong, it isn't that strong."

"Read any Eighteenth-Century novel, or, better yet, nonfiction. Thou thinkest Marie-Antoinette commanded the nobility of France with her good diction?"

"I don't think six hundred years of social progress can be undone that easily."

Dominic's eyes sparkled. "And since everyone agrees with thee, no one's resisting. As with smallpox, you are more vulnerable now than in the filthy past, since without exposure you build no resistance, yet we do not vacci-nate against a thing defeated. The more people insist that feminism has won, the more they blind themselves to its remaining foes." He paused to slurp an eager breath, as if braced by the wind of his own words. "But we are not here to talk of gender, but of theology. Thou hast not had a session in three weeks, and thou'st had a number of theological shocks in that time."

Carlyle crossed her arms. "You're not my sensayer."

"Dost thou really believe in thy Clockmaker? Is that genuinely belief thou feelest inside thee, or something weaker, a wish, wishing it were so, this easy answer, while in truth thou fearest something worse?"

"I refuse to do this."

The stool creaked as Dominic leaned forward. "Does that not prove me right? If thy belief were strong, thou wouldst have nothing to fear in letting me nip at it. Thou wishest desperately for thy Clockmaker to exist, but desperation is not faith. How canst thou tell if thou believest?"

"Because I love God!" Carlyle declared, with all the strength and fervor with which she had risen from bed that morning, every morning, marking on her calendar how each day was sacred to so many names for God.

Dominic's smile widened. "Thou lovest Him, dost thou?"

"I do. I love God and I love this universe They made: nature, humanity, all Creation. Sometimes I look out the window, or bite into an apple, and actually start crying at how wonderful it is that everything exists. God did all that. The world is our window onto God, and it is so infinitely beautiful that sometimes I think I'm just going to burst with how much I love it!"

The grim monk scratched the bare rim of his tonsure. "And thou think-est thou canst not love something that thou dost not believe in?"

"Exactly." Carlyle dug her fingers into the time-grayed fringes of her own long scarf. "I've heard your arguments before, from Julia, that there are so many reasons to want to believe in Deism that you can't be sure if you really do. I do sometimes feel rational doubt, for that reason or others, but then I see the infinite detail of an insect, or taste snow, and then I know I love, and I believe."

Dominic's eyes narrowed until only the black remained; I have seen him glare so at Heloïse passing in the halls with her tranquil smile, and sometimes at myself. "It is easy to love something one does not believe in," he began. "Think of an idealist, a dreamer, a Utopian, how often you see them burst into tears at the beauty of a future they imagine. Thou hast read books, seen movies, wept and rejoiced at the sorrows and triumphs of fiction. What is that if not love for something thou knowest does not exist?"

"That's not the same."

"Why not?"

"I won't deny that that's love, but there are lots of kinds of love, like the love one feels for bash'mates, or friends. This is different."

"Stronger?" Dominic tested.

"Y-yes." Carlyle's voice was weakening.

Where art thou, Mycroft? Stop this. Stop this soon!

"Thy love is special, then? Thou lovest thy God more truly than others love that which they love most?"

"No. No, of course not." Carlyle lost the strength to look at Dominic, her eyes ranging the room, the floor, the ranks of books stacked by the walls, Spinoza, Nietzsche, Averroes, ready with a thousand portraits of God, or of His absence.

Dominic leaned forward. "Why not call thy love special? Thou art not merely a sensayer but a vocateur. Thou hast devoted thy life to thy God, sacrificed thy leisure hours for Him, thy studies, thy passions. Few men weep daily for love of anything, as thou dost. Is that not the sort of special love that Saints are supposed to have, and Prophets?"

"No." Carlyle had seemed almost prepared to rise, but slumped again against the door, hiding behind her hair. "It's not special like that. I'm not special like that."

"Because if thou wert special thou wouldst not have fallen?"

Carlyle choked. "You stole my files. . . ."

Dominic adjusted the stole-scarf across his shoulders. "I didn't have to steal them, I'm thy sensayer. Four years ago a parishioner let slip in a session that she was plotting murder to avenge her lost ba'pas, and thou brokest thine oath and tippedest off the police."

"I couldn't—"

"Thy *sacred* oath," Dominic pressed, "for we all hold our oaths as sensayers sacred, secular as they may be. One who loved God as perfectly as thou claimest to should not hesitate to die, or let another die, to keep a sacred oath."

Wetness leaked in tracks down Carlyle's cheeks. "Please stop."

"Thou brokest thy sacred oath," the monk jabbed, "because thou didst not trust thy God enough to let Providence judge whether the victim should live or die. A Deistic God asks practically nothing of His priests, but still thou hast managed to betray Him. Very impressive."

"Stop!"

"Thou falteredest because thou dost not truly believe, thou only wishest to."

"I do believe!"

"Thou dost not, here's thy proof: thy love remains unchanged to this day, yes?"

"Of course."

"Yet today thou knowest thy Clockmaker does not exist. Thou hast seen Bridger, Bridger's power, miracles. This Universe's God does not sit back and let the world tick on its way. He intervened before thine eyes. Thou hast proof that thou wert wrong about the nature of thy God." Dominic leaned forward, eyes alight with victory. "If that did not affect thy belief, then thou didst not believe to begin with. Tell me I am wrong."

"I . . . I didn't want . . ." Sobs wracked Carlyle's frame, like storm waves lashing at a buoy tethered in harsh current. "It's true. The Clockmaker, if . . . They wouldn't . . ." Words failed. Sobs swelled. Carlyle dug her fingers hard enough into her scarf to cut the fibers with the dull remnants evolution has left of human claws, and, like an infant, screamed.

Thou art overtardy in thy rescue, Mycroft. Thy God, too.

I know, reader. I feel it worse than you, for you simply read, while I can hear the screams Dominic wrings from this shaking wretch. But what can I do? There are many doors between the study where I had been serving and Dominic's distant cell. As for the tardiness of God, Providence must answer to its own unknowable design before it answers prayers, reader, even your own.

Hungry Dominic was not yet sated. "I saw the child in the shower, thou knowst," he pressed. "I had been curious, after I watched him on the beach, why such a playful child swam fully clothed. Mycroft's orders, I imagine."

"Huh?"

"He has no navel."

Carlyle choked. "What?"

"The child Bridger has no navel, no belly button. He wasn't born, not from a human mother anyway. There is your final proof. The child was created, with no placenta or umbilical, miraculously by thy God, whom thou canst no longer call Clockmaker."

Hopefully, reader, you can remember some fond day when you laughed so hard it hurt. You emptied your lungs, sprained the smiling muscles of your cheeks, and still the laughter forced itself from you, though you had no breath left to give it wings. Here Carlyle cries that hard, and Dominic watches, patient as his victim's strength dims sob by sob, like failing fire.

"Divine intervention." Carlyle was the first to say the words. "Real, undeniable divine intervention. This changes everything, for the whole human race, forever."

"Still hiding behind thinking of the human race?" Dominic clucked, like a chiding mother. "What of thyself? For whose sake dost thou truly want This Universe's God to be a Clockmaker? For thine own? Thou art His priest. All thy life thou hast wanted desperately to see Him, to have Him set a miracle before thee and prove His presence. Why then didst thou imagine Him a Clockmaker who never shows His face? That wasn't what thou wantedst."

It took Carlyle some seconds to gulp enough air to speak. "The Clockmaker is most fair, most universal. It wouldn't be right for God to be just one God, to reveal Themself to just one people and let the rest be wrong. A Deist God, Who answers to every name people call Them by, is . . . would have been . . . the only just God."

"Exactly." Victory fire surged in Dominic's eyes. "It was for the others thou preferredest the Clockmaker, not for thyself. Thou dost not want the others to be wrong, dost not want their God not to exist, their universe to be unkind to them. They need the Clockmaker, not thee. Deep down thou hast always wanted to pray for a miracle, for proof, but thou couldst not ask for it. Thy God must be perfectly fair, and a fair Clockmaker would not violate His own rule to show Himself to an unworthy fallen priest. Am I right?"

"I don't—"

"Am I right?"

"Yes!" Carlyle shrieked out. "Yes, of course I always wanted God to make an exception for me, to show Themself. I wanted it more than anything else in the world. But I couldn't ask for God to be so unfair, to come to me when They didn't to so many others. I didn't deserve it, not after what I did. I still don't."

"Yes, thou dost."

Every inch of Carlyle trembled. "What?"

"Thou thinkest thy fall makes thee unworthy? Just the opposite." Dominic leaned close, his calm brows suddenly more grave than cruel. "Thou hast fallen from thy God and yet thou servest Him still, even though thou no longer considerest thyself 'special,' or 'chosen,' or worthy of His Love. Thou art willing to devote thyself to a God whom thou expectest to hate thee, and before His wrath thou declarest, 'Damn me if Thou wilt, Lord, I shall love Thee still!' That is a far stronger loyalty than the placid worship of the pure who expect Salvation or Enlightenment; they get a bribe, while thou, for all thou knowest, gettest Hellfire, and still thou lovest. It is not hubris to call such devotion special."

"I . . . hadn't thought about it like that."

"Few do."

Carlyle raised her eyes anew to her tormentor, who sat with his crossed arms buried in his habit sleeves, contemplative. It is strange to see Dominic's face without aggression, passive, but it happens from time to time, as when, after feeding, a serpent knots itself up to sleep, and squirrels and monkeys play freely in the branches around it, sensing by instinct when the hunter is benign. Snakes sleep most of their lives, you know—they stir only to feed.

"Dominic," Carlyle began with trembling lips, "have you also fallen?"

"We are talking of thy faith, not mine," the monk interrupted quickly, "but it does seem that thou and I are both among the rare creatures that have recognized the necessity of hypocrisy. Thy fall saved someone's life; surely thou believest thy God intended that. Thy God, like us, knows that oaths must sometimes be broken, but that doesn't mean the oaths meant nothing; in fact, to we who agonize again and again over the choice of when to break and when to follow, oaths mean more."

"I guess so."

"Nothing in thy life has made thee think more about thy God than the time thou brokest His rule. If thou hadst chosen a God with more commandments, or made more vows to Him which thou wouldst then suffer to keep or suffer more by breaking, thy faith would have grown even stronger for it."

The Cousin realized now that she was hugging herself, and felt strong enough to stop. "You really were a monk once, weren't you, Dominic? A real monk?"

"I am thy sensayer, and may not speak to thee of my religion."

Again Dominic's hands stirred deep in his sleeves, but I recognized the gesture from when he does the same in his public costume, for even lace cuffs cannot conceal the fidgeting as he fingers on the skin around his wrists. There are no scars now, but there were when I first faced Dominic in that same cell. It was sincere, that session when I let you hear Dominic 'confess' to Julia his weekly sins, breaking his vow of chastity. Sincere too was young Dominic's conviction when he took his monastic oath: obedience, poverty, chastity too, to seal away forever that appetite which Madame had raised him to wield as a master swordsman wields his blade. At fifteen Dominic could already break a man with ease, but he determined to sacrifice his plea-sures to honor his Lord with a life of pious deprivation. Madame would not permit such wastage. After he took his vows, she granted Dominic one month of his new life, just enough to feel the habits taking hold, then she had him dragged from his cell, and sodomized, and tormented until he un-leashed his wrath and now-forbidden appetites upon his tormenters. So, calculating mother, she taught Dominic how much more powerful he was now that his lust was charged with guilt, the fire of his flesh channeling the burn of his Master Jehovah's disapproving gaze. You cannot call Madame's order a 'crime'—they were all Blacklaws. You can call it abuse, but Dominic would not wish away his past, and the powers it gives him, any more than would Eureka, Toshi Mitsubishi, or Voltaire.

"There is no need now, Foster," Dominic continued, "to pretend that thou wishest thy God to be a Clockmaker. He has answered thy secret prayer, and proved that He is not. That was thy true prayer, was it not?" Dominic did wait, but Carlyle hid behind tears, and let her sensayer finish for her. "He gave thee Bridger. He has shown Himself to thee, to us, to we two fallen creatures out of all the priests and faithful of the Earth. A window to speak to our Maker is in our hands, not those of the untainted sensayers thou hast long envied. Ours." Dominic's eyes led Carlyle's to the corner of the room, where Bridger's No-No Box sat open on the table, with its crucifix, its Buddha statue, and its black rubber ball. "This Universe's God has recognized the special fervor of thy devotion since thy fall, and He has heard thy prayers above all others."

"This Universe's God?" Carlyle repeated.

"What of Him?"

"You always say 'This Universe's God,' as if there were some need to specify."

In that instant, two fast knocks rang out against the door. "I'm com-ing in."

At last, Mycroft! Thou and thy Providence are tardy rescuers indeed.

It is not I, reader. Providence chose a nobler instrument here to slide the bolts back and let freedom's air into that cell: Voltaire Seldon, his bright Utopian coat breaking the cell's dim blankness with its vista of ruins baked in sparkling sunset. "Where's the Traceshifter Artifact?"

Dominic's eyes twinkled. "French or English, please, I don't speak Moonman."

"Where's the Canner Device?"

Dominic pointed to a bookcase. "On top of Maimonides."

The Utopian lifted a cloth sack from its seat on top of the old volume, and checked the deadly tool humming away within. "How long have you had it?"

"Three days," Dominic answered. "I found it by one of the emergency exits from the understructure of the Saneer-Weeksbooth bash'house. Whoever used it to deliver the Seven-Ten list knew you'd catch them if they used it again, so they dropped it then and there. Our thief expected you Utopians to be called in, and they were willing to sacrifice such an expensive toy just to plant that little piece of paper in Ockham Saneer's trashcan. Whatever this enemy is that we're hunting, it is a rare bird that I look forward to tasting."

Carlyle rose now, as if the new figure looming over her made her suddenly realize she was still slumped on the floor. "That's the Canner Device? *The* Canner Device? From the Canner Murders? The one that tricks the trackers?"

Dominic chuckled. "You must've switched it on yourself, Carlyle, when you knocked against the bookcase, and our pet Utopian tracked it." He flashed a smile at a volume of Seneca on the desk beside him. "How Providentially improbable."

Carlyle gaped, and the digital eyes shown by the Griffincloth surface of Voltaire's Utopian vizor seemed to lock on her. "Who is this Cousin?" the Utopian asked. "They're not in the client registry."

"The Saneer-Weeksbooth bash's sensayer," Dominic answered. "Carlyle Foster. Carlyle, may I introduce one of the Emperor's *Familiares Candidi*, Voltaire Seldon."

Voltaire frowned. "You know this is a warded zone, Dominic, inside the defense orbit for the Alphas present. Variables are pandoras. Foster, you will let me shuttle you to the exit."

A playful smile on Dominic's face always seems monstrous, like those nightmare fish of the deep sea that lure prey with their false, sweet lights.

"Foster is not an outsider, she's my parishioner, which makes her a member of the household. Isn't that right, Foster?"

Carlyle had one second here to think, facing those strange digital eyes, before she had to choose: remain or go? "Yes. Yes, Dominic's my sensayer."

"This is a session?" Voltaire asked.

Dominic made Carlyle be the one to answer. "Yes."

"It's private," Dominic added, "so kindly take your toy and leave."

Voltaire spirited the device into the sunset depths of his long coat. "You should have given this to us as soon as you found it."

"I've been busy."

"You wasted human effort, slowed our progress, aided entropy."

"I've been very busy."

Digital eyes turned again on Carlyle, squinting, while Voltaire's fingers played at controls within the sleeves whose Griffincloth transformed the wall behind into a honeycomb buzzing with phosphorescent fox-wasps. "Foster, you will hold still, please."

Carlyle shied back as the Utopian reached for her throat. "What are you doing?"

Voltaire's hand locked on the Cousin's slender shoulder. "You will hold still. This will not hurt or harm."

I was impressed that Carlyle did not scream as snakes shot from the Utopian's sleeve. The first fast-striking serpent wrapped itself around Carlyle's neck to hold the target steady as three others slid into place across her cheek and shoulders, like roots crawling over stone. Only their front sections emerged, white scales glistening like old ice, while the rest of their long bodies stayed in the depths of Voltaire's sleeve, so one could not guess how deep the coils ran.

A dog learns fast to cry for help to its protector. "Dominic!"

"It's all right, Carlyle. Seldon here belongs to *Maître* Jehovah." Dominic refuses to call the Utopian by the name of the Patriarch. "He will not harm thee, though one could wish he were a bit better house-trained."

The central serpent opened its jaws to bare gold-bright connectors, which it plunged into Carlyle's tracker. "They're transmitting video." Voltaire's digital eyes narrowed as data flowed in from the serpent. "Someone's scrying."

Dominic's eyes hardened. "A spy? Didst thou know, Foster? Answer carefully."

Carlyle's throat twitched, but fear of the snakes gave her a good excuse for silence.

Dominic's fingers flexed as if hungry for the sword which did not hang at his rope belt. "Who's listening, Seldon? I can think of several possibilities."

"Six seconds and I'll know." Another snake, or perhaps a different part of one of the first few, let a coil peek out of Voltaire's neckline as it slid across its master's shoulders. Swissnakes they're called, an infinitely useful U-beast, and I've never been certain how large a colony lives inside that coat. I've never spotted more than six heads at once, but I have seen so many different-seeming heads, armed with everything from a radiometer to a corkscrew, that I would not be surprised to see Voltaire dispatch twenty at once, or for the entire coat to dissolve into a weft of serpents.

"It's Mycroft Canner," Voltaire concluded.

Dominic laughed openly. "Mycroft must like thee, Foster, to be spying. He must have worried for thy safety in my lair, or perhaps for the safety of our mutual young friend. We must ask him."

"Should I counterspell?" Voltaire offered, snakes purring in readiness.

"No point. Our Mycroft is a little hydra, they'll grow two eyes where you put one out." Dominic smiled darkly at Carlyle and, through him, at me. "Thou wouldst be wise, Mycroft, to concentrate on thine own work for the time being, and stay far away from mine. As dear to *Notre Maître* as thou art, my patience has its limits."

So did the Utopian's. He retracted the snakes, like inhaled smoke. "If you'll excuse me, I have progress to progress."

"Of course." Dominic dismissed Voltaire with a bored wave. "I might call you if I find anything else useful."

The Utopian paused in the doorway. "You should register Foster as a formal client. Security aside, you know Madame doesn't like you giving it away."

Carlyle clutched her wrap, as if to assure herself it was intact. "We haven't—"

"You could do the registration for us, couldn't you, Seldon?" Dominic asked, almost sweetly. "That would be much more convenient."

"I could . . ."

"What do you say, Foster?" Dominic invited. "Wouldst thou like to let the Utopian handle thy registration, while we finish our session? There was another question thou wert about to ask, was there not?"

Watching through Carlyle's tracker I could see Voltaire gazing at her, intense eyes trying to advise in silence, but the vizor's electric shimmer would not let them seem earnest.

Carlyle took a deep breath. "I'll stay."

I saw Dominic swallow down their surge of victory drool.

Voltaire turned away. "As you prefer."

This is no rescue! Giving the monster everything he wanted! Thou hast mocked me, Mycroft, inviting me to pray when thou knewest what outcome waited.

Ah, reader, I understand it is your kindness which fills you with this hubris, but it is hubris still. You presume, not only to advise your Maker, but to demand that He respond to your advice by revising the infinite and perfect Plan of His Creation precisely as you—with your flawed and finite wisdom—recommend?

Thou, hypocrite, art the one who invited me to pray in the first place.

True, reader, and I too succumbed at the time to that universal human hubris we call prayer. I prayed for a smaller thing, that Carlyle might find Dominic in some more kindly mood, a gentled doom; one tainted by par-ricide dares ask no more. But if I have encouraged you, reader—a nobler creature, worthier of our Maker's ear—to raise your thoughts in prayer, it was not to deceive you, not to mockingly declare that our Creator is a deaf, unyielding Clockmaker after all. No. He hears, our Maker, all of our ad-vice, I know He does, and Acts on it, as suits His Will. His Plan. Which is not our plan. I bade you pray because He answers sometimes, in His distant way, and when He doesn't, it always means something to be heard—the prisoner shouting his last words from the gallows understands that. I will not offer you philosophy's old comforts, what the theologians cramming Dominic's shelves repeat so many times. I will not say that Providence requires trust, and patience, that what seems cruel from our limited perspective will turn out to be for the best in the end. I will not tell you that He left Carlyle to Dominic because it was somehow better for Carlyle, or the wider world, or you. There is a Will behind this universe, reader, that I know. There are miracles, and a Divinity behind those mira-cles, Who has a Plan, but have you ever, reader, heard me claim that that Plan is benevolent?

"The Canner Device didn't get switched on by accident, did it?" Carlyle asked the instant Voltaire closed the door behind him. "You switched it on before I got here, so we'd be interrupted and you could make me say you were my sensayer."

Dominic chuckled. "You're a sharp one. I see why Julia likes you."

"Forcing me to say it won't make me actually accept it."

"Forcing thee?" A laugh rose in Dominic's throat, thick as honey. "And what force did I use? Did I threaten thee? Did I tie thee down and beat thee?"

"No, but—"

"What other sensayer, pray tell, is capable of handling thee now? Who else can talk to thee of Bridger, miracles, and of thy fall? Wouldst thou rather return to trading lies with Julia?"

Carlyle again evaded Dominic's eyes, gazing across the stacks of Theophrastus, St. Ignatius, and Chandrakirti. "No."

"I can grant thee access, to this house, to Madame, to Mycroft, even to *Maître* Jehovah."

Carlyle gulped. "What is Jehovah? They have a power too, like Bridger, don't they? A second Intervention?"

A long breath. "That privilege too, to know, to speak to Him, that may be thine in time, but only here. I can be thy patron, and together we can use all the resources gathered here to guide and protect Bridger until he fulfills his Maker's purpose."

It was easier for Carlyle to feel strong with her eyes closed. "You know, I never expected to say this, but you're right. I didn't understand at first why God would show Themself to me, but you're right, maybe we are stronger because we fell. God didn't just show Bridger to me, They showed them to you, too. They chose us, us two." Her cheeks relaxed, almost enough to smile. "I thought I was sent to keep Bridger away from you, but maybe not. Maybe the two of us are supposed to save Bridger from Mycroft Canner together."

Dominic paused and let his tongue play across the flavors of his mouth, his victory. "Then turn thy tracker off."

"What?" Carlyle clutched by instinct at the device at her ear.

"We can't plot to rescue Bridger with Mycroft Canner listening. Turn it off."

Carlyle hid behind her hair. "I don't . . ."

"Foster, I'm not going to rape thee. It's not even in my mind. Bridger likes thee and thinks I'm a monster. Thou art the only person in the world who could possibly persuade the boy to work with me. Thou thinkest I would jeopardize my only window to This Universe's God just for some quick sex? Turn it off."

"You said it again, 'This Universe's God.'" The Cousin wiped her cheeks at last, hoping, I imagine, that there would be no more tears.

Dominic fingered the ends of his own sensayer's scarf, coarse white cloth on one side and black on the other. "Thou shalt not ask thy sensayer about his religion. That is the law."

Carlyle sighed. "For a minute there you'd stopped being a hypocrite.

You can't just say it outright like that. You're supposed to dodge around the question, not admit point-blank that I struck home, that tells me what you believe anyway. You think Jehovah is a god."

The monk's eyes flickered. "Thou wishest me to use the formulaic dodges they teach us in sensayer training?" Dominic stretched, sleeves falling back to reveal red-speckled bandages fresh on his arms. "Thou knowest the same tricks, and can spot them if I use them. Isn't it better that I volunteer to be the hypocrite, rather than making us both pretend?"

Carlyle frowned at the bandages. "Are you all right?"

Dominic's glance barely acknowledged the injuries. "It's nothing. Minor bites. I had set a . . . rat trap on our back stoop, and found instead a rather fierce stray dog." He leaned toward her. "Thou canst not put it off forever, Carlyle Foster. Choose now: am I thy sensayer, patron, and ally in guiding Bridger's miracles as thy God intended? Or am I thine enemy?"

Carlyle raised a steady hand, and groped for her tracker's off-switch.

"Wait, Carlyle!" I cried through the tracker to her ears alone. "You're asking the wrong question! I used to think the same way, that Bridger was an answer to my prayers, but if the miracle was meant for us, we would've been given what we prayed for directly, without a child as intermediary. Providence pays infinite attention to detail. Whatever God is doing requires Bridger's specific power to make toys real, and it has to be wielded by the child Bridger, and the adult that Bridger will grow up to become. This Intervention isn't for you, or me, or any one person, it's for the whole world, the human race, the universe! The real question isn't 'Why me?' it's—"

Carlyle cut me off, chopped off the monster Mycroft Canner's words, half said. But I knew Carlyle Foster. She was a sensayer. She had read those volumes that lurk in Dominic's cell, and hundreds like them, the thoughts and prayers of the dead, pious and impious, so many of whom had prayed as fervently as she to see a miracle. To see Proof. However desperately she did not want to hear it, a true sensayer could not keep herself from following my logic, and arriving at the question, that same question great Achilles asked when gray-eyed Athene appeared before him by the tearstained ships, when war had already swallowed ten bloody years: "Why now? Divinity, child of the thunder-wielding heavens? Why come now?"

If Anybody in the World Can

BRIDGER CLOSED APOLLO'S *ILIAD* AND SLID THE TIME-GRAYED volume back into his pocket where it always lived. "Next I want to rescue Mycroft."

Should I not have given him the book? You say I have put a lighted torch in the hands of an infant, but what more do I know than a child of the infinity of the Universal Plan? I had no right to deny what was so obviously meant for him. The book was given to me and I to Bridger—what line of inheritance could be more clear? *Thou hast lied to me, Mycroft. Thou claimedest thou wert raising Bridger to be a normal child, then a normal man, so he might grow up to wield his powers on behalf of all of us, but it was a lie: thou art raising him to be Apollo Mojave.* No. *Thou darest deny it? Thou speakest of the two of them with the same worship, steepest the boy in history and philosophy no average child needs, and now thou hast made him keeper of this little book whose import I can guess if not its precise contents.* You are wrong, reader. If I had wanted Apollo back, there was a statue in Romanova waiting to be awakened by Bridger's touch.

"You want to rescue Mycroft?" the Major repeated in a flat, tired tone, neither approving nor criticizing, just listing one more fact in a world which has too many facts in it.

"Yes," the boy declared. "Mycroft's always rescuing everybody else, it's time somebody rescued them."

Some of these scenes are hard for me to re-create from interviews and stale research, but not this one. The safe house Saladin chose to hide the child from Dominic would be warm and snug, walls stacked high with the sorts of games and entertainments a thug would want when forced to lie low. Mommadoll would have set to work stripping the room of 'inappropriate' materials, while Boo nested in the cushions, and the army men pitched cautious camp on the bedside table, ready to leap to instant cover should my Saladin return. I'm happy to say the hostages were free once more; Privates Pointer and Nostand and Lieutenant Aimer, who were captured when Dominic had stolen Bridger's clothes and backpack from the cave, had been successfully snatched back from that circle of Hell which is Dominic's desk drawer. Operation Ariadne, as the Major called it, had been planned for three careful hours and executed in forty-seven seconds, a six-man extraction team guided by Looker scrying through the crystal ball, with Bridger at the teleport controls. Success. Medic was now treating the captives' wounds with Bridger's potions, their hands and feet where Dominic had pinned them to a slab of cork like butterflies. They bore it bravely, Lieutenant Aimer especially, determined not to cry out with the Major watching. The others ringed them, cheering on the rescued, hailing their endurance in the face of monster Dominic, a heroes' praise from all except paranoid Croucher, who glared up from a bunker he had built from loose puzzle pieces on the far side of the table, and muttered to the walls.

"You've searched it through and through?" the Major asked, nodding to the pocket of Bridger's recovered wrap, where the lump of the *Iliad* showed through fabric long since warped to fit its corners.

"Yup," the boy answered, "it's all there, no missing pages. The bad sensayer cracked the spine a bit, but nothing's gone. And they didn't bug it or anything, I used the crystal ball and everything. I know you're mad I let it get stolen, and I know it's really, really important, but it's safe now, so it's time to work on Mycroft. You can lecture me after we have them back, okay?" An unsettling resolution tensed the child's tender brows, as when sculptors give Hermes or Dionysus a child's face but a man's expression. When Providence and the Major first granted me the undeserved blessing of Bridger's friendship he was not yet six years old, that recipe of tiny hands and games and tantrums which awakens the instincts to protect and nurture, even in Mycroft Canner. At first the sheer wonder of helping a child grow was enough for me, but soon moments started cropping up, after a fight over clipping his nails, or when I stumbled reciting a favored bedtime story, when he would glare, and show me for an instant, not infancy, but personality, a flash of the person he would be when he grew up. With time, I began to see him less as a blossom swelling to its proper shape than as a buried statue, waiting for the sand around to fall away. I loved the child, but was waiting for the man to come and wield his power with this kind of confidence. We all were.

The veteran shook his head. "Spiriting Mycroft away is no simple matter. Only Dominic will notice we took Aimer and the others, but Mycroft is part of a larger world, connected, watched. Many will notice if they vanish to the far side of the Earth."

The boy's blond brows stayed locked. "But they do it all the time. If

Mycroft disappears everyone'll assume they did a clever Mycroft thing and got away. All we have to do is wait until no one's looking."

"No." The Major sighed, as ships sigh strained by tides too huge for eyes to spot beneath the petty waves. "If it were that simple, he would do a clever Mycroft thing and get away. You've seen it. Mycroft's not trapped there by a cell, or a chain, he's trapped by choice, his choice, something that's keeping him from trying to leave."

"I know," Bridger answered, though I suspect he did not like knowing. "Mycroft disappears a lot. That's where they go isn't it? That house in Paris where the bad sensayer took the others?"

"'Mycroft disappears a lot . . .'" the Major repeated. "They must say that in Paris, too, whenever he's here with us."

"Unless they know exactly where he goes." Croucher's voice rose cold and thin, like the glitter of his teeth, the only part of his face visible beneath his helmet's shadow as he peeked out from his puzzle-fort. "Mycroft Canner, he knows who all these enemies are, what they want, but will he tell us anything about them? No. He's scheming behind our backs, I've always said that, and now the trap is springing shut. You know it, you just don't want to admit you were wrong."

"Enough."

"The great hero duped for eight years by a clever slave!"

The Major stretched back across the dominos that served him as a bench. "Don't tempt me, Croucher! As for you, Bridger, Mycroft would take on every monster Hercules faced to get to you, but they won't leave that house. That means whatever's there is worse than monsters. It's not somewhere you should even think about going. Leave it to Mycroft's killer friend who dresses like Apollo."

Bridger leaned on his elbows, gazing down at the tiny soldiers like some Egyptian monolith. "Mycroft's scary friend has been gone a long time."

The Major frowned. "It's only been a few hours. Paris is an ocean away, and travel like that takes time, even today. Wait here and stay safe, that's what Mycroft would want."

"Sometimes what Mycroft wants isn't what's best for Mycroft."

"True. Mycroft wants what's best for the entire world, and most of all for you."

The boy breathed deep. "You and Mycroft always say you have to keep me away from people until I'm big enough to decide for myself how to use my power. Well, I've decided. I want to do this. I *should* do this. You always say someday I'll be able to use my power to save everybody in the world. Right now I want to use it to save Mycroft."

I can see clearly in my mind the expressions of the others, Nostand, Medic, Lieutenant Aimer putting on a brave face after his ordeal. They watch raptly, hanging on every syllable of this quarrel between their absolute commander and their young creator. It is enough to make these brave men shake. But you are braver still, reader. Yes, you, who trust your life to distant leaders whom you cannot watch firsthand, and whose Creator decides your fate invisibly, without warning, explanation, or apology—and yet you rise to face each morning, head held high. Brave reader, these happy army men are here to hear their maker's argument themselves, and will hear the verdict firsthand, instead of having to deduce it from a thousand years of experiment and guesswork. And, best of all, they know that both these beings, Bridger and the Major, love them. Benevolence, real, before their eyes. Do you not envy them? Does it not make you call This Universe's God a little cruel? These are the sorts of questions Ἄναξ Jehovah calls me to His rooms to ask, that He was asking me at that very moment as I sat beside His desk, forgetting Carlyle downstairs, forgetting the investigation, forgetting even Bridger as His questions made the present seem just a drop of history. I rarely manage to offer Him any answer, but it is a comfort to Him that at least I understand.

The Major shook his head. "Mycroft does not want to be saved. I know him, Bridger. If he lingers on as someone's captive, it is because of some relationship he has to that someone, awe, honor, fear, something."

The boy wrinkled his nose. "Then I want to know why. I want to go and ask. I'm not going to let anybody see me. I just want to talk to them. The crystal ball isn't good enough, I need to really see, and hear, and have Mycroft hear me. I want to try to talk them into leaving, that's all. Just one try."

"It's not like you can stop the kid, Major." Trust Croucher to pounce on the truth nobody wants to hear. "He can just unmake you if you try to stop him."

"I wouldn't do that!" Perhaps this kind maker blushes with guilt that the thought was in his mind. "I don't want to do that. Major, I want you to help me. I want your advice, your planning. There has to be a first time I try going out and really doing something, so walk me through it, talk me through it, guide me, make it a surefire victory. If anybody in the world can, you can."

"'If anybody in the world can, you can,'" Croucher repeated in a whine. "What'll it be this time, Major? Give in? Or sit and sulk while the kid goes off and dies?"

Quick as a striking carp, the Major hurled his pocket canteen at Croucher's face. It flew true as a javelin, striking the cheekbone below the helmet's rim hard enough to split the skin. Croucher vanished into his puzzle-fort like a seal beneath the waves, and closed the entrance with a last piece, which almost muffled his curses. These soldiers are made of fiction, reader—did you think they would coexist in boring harmony?

Even Lieutenant Aimer required urging from his comrades before he dared address the red and glaring Major. "We could think about it for half an hour and then decide?" He smiled, trying to make the balance of sweet and sturdy in his young face tip toward sweet.

A long breath and the Major's fingers stopped crawling toward his weapons. "Let it be. Tonight. The black of the morning Paris time." He raised his eyes to Bridger. "You'll have your chance. But you will not leave this room until we've planned out every breath, every step, until you can recite it backwards. You understand me?"

Bridger's grin displayed his bright teeth, like an open piano. "I won't make a single move without discussing it with you first, and I won't touch anything, or try anything hard, just words."

"Words? Words will be the hardest part. Persuading the persuader. He'll have a thousand reasons marshaled against every one of yours. You know who this is you're arguing against?"

The child swallowed. "I know."

The Major softened. "Well, perhaps words from you will mean more."

"I hope so." A brave smile.

"If things go wrong while you're out there—"

"If things go wrong," the boy took over, "just tell me what to do and I'll do it in an instant, no questions, I promise. I'll be like a new recruit on my first mission. I have to have one sometime, right?"

The veteran shook his head. "No, you don't. You know how hard we worked to make you not be like us? Not be like a soldier? We want you to enjoy these days of peace."

"It hasn't seemed very much like peace lately."

"I'm glad you think that."

Here's an expression a child's face should have, wide eyes, a curiosity still willing to ask any question, never fearing answers. "Why?"

"It means you have no idea what war is." The Major rose and hauled over a pack of gum to serve as table as he set to work. "We'll watch My-croft until he falls asleep. They're unlikely to leave him unguarded. Crawler, you'll head up a team to take out guards if necessary."

"I should do that," Lieutenant Aimer interrupted, smiling.

"What?"

"Head the team." The Lieutenant rose, testing his hands, tender but nimble after the healing potion. "That's usually my job."

The Major's fists slammed the pack of gum before him. "We just got you back! You're not going to think about going near that house again or, by Hades, this time I'll be the one who nails your feet to the gods-damned floor! Now sit down!"

The white-faced Lieutenant more fell than sat down as the Major's words flew like blows.

"As for the rest of you," the Major continued, "if any of you catches the Lieutenant anywhere near the teleporter, or the armory, you have stand-ing orders to knock him out and strap him to the nearest immovable ob-ject, is that clear?"

Most of the men frowned apology at the Lieutenant as they answered. "Yes, Major."

"Good. All three of you who just escaped the enemy's abuse, I want you to think of nothing but rest today. Crawler will head the team, with Stander-G, Looker, and Nogun. I shall head the standby team in case of misfor-tune, with Medic and Croucher. You hear me, Croucher?"

A mumble rose from the puzzle pieces, so vague that it might as easily have been poetry as profanity.

"So I can hear you!"

"Yes, Major! Understood!"

"Good, now, equipment check. Bridger, you first."

Bridger smiled as he held forth his sea-green backpack. "I've got every-thing, Major."

"I believe you, but if we're going to do this we're doing it in baby steps. I won't be satisfied until I watch you put on every item. You got the ta-laria?"

Hermes's winged sandals gave a little flutter as Bridger drew them from the sack. "Yup."

"Invisibility cloak?"

The old blanket shimmered as the child tied it across his shoulders. "Yup."

"Force field armor generator?"

"Yup."

"Thor's belt of strength?"

"Yup."

"Excalibur?"

The boy fondled the plastic hilt. "Yup."

"Phaser?"

"Yup."

"Teleporter?"

"Yup."

"X-ray specs?"

"Yup."

"Magic mirror?"

"Yup."

"Magic wand?"

"Yup."

"Spare magic wand?"

He tapped the pair of chopsticks in his pocket. "Yup."

Has any potentate ever traveled with such protection?

"Healing potion?"

"Four of them."

"Resurrection potion?"

"Two of them."

"Paper and markers to make more?"

"Twenty sheets."

"Scissors and tape?"

"Yup and yup."

"Apollo's *Iliad*?"

The boy's nod was grave enough for an adult. "I won't let anything happen to it ever again, I promise. I know it's the most important thing in the world."

The Major shook his head. "No, Bridger—you are."

Normally the boy would smile at that. "Major?"

"Yes."

"You don't want to say anything, but I know you're thinking it."

"What?"

"That it's getting too dangerous, that we might need to abandon Mycroft, not see them again. I want you to know, I don't think I could cope if I lost Mycroft."

The Major cracked his knuckles. "Listen, Bridger, Fate takes people sometimes. I have lost a lot of people, people I thought I couldn't live without, whole worlds, but I'm still here."

"I know, but you're . . ."

"I'm what?" the veteran invited. "It's all right, say what you're thinking, I won't snap at you."

"You're not somebody who should have my powers. The world needs me to be sane and stable, or I could wreck everything. I need to keep being me. And for that I need Mycroft back. If we can't get them then I don't . . . I just need Mycroft back."

Chapter the SIXTH

The Room Where Mycroft Canner Died

« Young Master Jehovah, Madame wants you to send Mycroft up to the *Salon de Versailles*. »

Before you see my next failure, reader, you must understand the power of the room we are about to enter. Here my trial took place. Here was the neutral ground the Powers chose to meet in secret and decide the monster's fate, while the world outside called in unprecedented unison for blood. Madame had suggested it, hanging on the Emperor's sleeve as she pleaded for a chance to see this rarest of human beasts before they put it down, and the excuse of satisfying her girlish whim had let all of them pretend the choice to hold my trial here was not political—in truth it could not have been more political, for where else than in her sanctum were the Seven free to help each other cheat their own laws?

When the police stormed my vivisection room and caught the murderer, still elbow-deep in Mercer Mardi, they dosed me with more drugs than even my preemptive antidotes could counter. I awoke in my coffin-cage, arms locked behind me in a gel, as gentle as water against my skin but inescapable as steel, which the Utopians, in their rage, had invented in those few days, just for me. Within the cage was silence, the walls clear from the outside but opaque to me, so I knew nothing of the crowds past which the police paraded me, though I could feel the gentle bumping of the box, and peace when I was set down in what I assumed must be my prison. I would guess I had two hours' peace before a switch turned the speakers on and made the walls transparent, leaving me squinting at the sudden light and bare as a lab rat before the red-faced and panting Anonymous.

"This letter, is it yours?" Rarely have I heard words so urgent. "Tell me!" He slammed the tired green sheets against the glass, youth-arrogant scribbles dating from the days when Saladin and I, fourteen and giddy with the power of our intellects, had begun many ingenious little projects to show the adult world our brilliance.

"Yes. Yes, it's mine," I answered.

"Who helped you?" he barked at once. "Was it Kohaku? Did Kohaku Mardi know I'm the Anonymous?"

"No one helped me," I answered, almost too quickly. "Not Kohaku, not anyone. I figured it out myself." If Saladin and I are one flesh then I spoke the truth, for we had deduced it together, and written this letter, addressed to the Anonymous's true identity, to boast that we had guessed, but we never sent it. We realized mid-draft that such a stunt might endanger our greater project, so we left the letter in the negligible clutter of my adopted bash'house, scraps which only Papadelias would think to go through.

"They knew you're the Anonymous?" It was the King of Spain who asked it, striding forward to frown beside the Anonymous like a teammate after a bad game, the blue and gold sash which marks Europe's Prime Minister set aside for mourning black.

The Anonymous nodded, grave. "It even gives the reasoning they used. It's brilliant."

My eyes adjusted to the dazzle slowly. I took in the room: silk-paneled walls, sofas of gold and velvet, and figures lounging over brandy like friends drawn close by troubled times. I did not recognize most of them at first, but seeing the Anonymous answer to his secret title with eight people watching was enough to make me doubt the structure of the world. How many knew? How many people here were privy to what was supposed to be, after the name of MASON's successor, Earth's second-strictest secret?

"Canner figured it out?" It was Ganymede who asked, still the Humanist Co-Consul, not yet President. I knew him only slightly then, and it was a strange aesthetic privilege seeing Ganymede in his mourning clothes, that shade of midnight blue that chases the sun toward sunset, so the dark cloth made the translucence of his skin glow bright as moonlight. *For mourning, should it not be black?* It should, reader, but remember that, however deeply the others mourned the Mardi bash', it is unlikely the Duke actually cared.

The Anonymous faced the others. "This is why the police have had me in protective custody the last four days. They found this letter in Mycroft's things and thought I might be targeted as well." He backed away from my cage, and, with a clearer view, I recognized Andō Mitsubishi on the couch beside Ganymede, his black hakama stark against the sumptuous hall.

"That's why they wouldn't let me see you?" The voice let me recognize Cousin Chair Bryar Kosala, hoarse with tears. She was huddled on a couch, resting against Gordian's Headmaster Felix Faust, as a niece rests against an uncle. "That's why you've been locked away?"

"I'm sorry, Bryar, they wouldn't let me tell you." The Anonymous went to her and lifted her into his embrace. "They didn't want anyone to know that they knew Mycroft knew."

The Anonymous still wore his outside clothes, tiger-striped with the wrinkles of his captivity, which Kosala ruined further as she pressed against him.

My mind raced as I counted: the Anonymous, the King of Spain for Europe, Chair Kosala for the Cousins, Headmaster Faust for Gordian, Duke Ganymede for the Humanists, Director Andō for the Mitsubishi . . . six of the seven pillars of the Earth stood before me here, in black together like a bash' in mourning. It was wrong. I had been in the Twenty-Fifth Century that morning, yet here I found myself in a world of petticoats and incest. I was not some amateur. I was trained by the Mardi bash', by Senator Aeneas Mardi, by Deputy Censor Kohaku Mardi, by Felix Faust's prize pupil Mercer Mardi, by Apollo. I knew more of the world than the world did, its trends, its fears, the currents churning beneath the ripples of property and population. Yet, of these secret relationships between the Powers—Ganymede and Andō, Kosala and the Anonymous—I had no idea. My teachers, my great teachers, had known nothing. In another life, I mused, I would want to study this, to see what other secrets lie behind these frills and petticoats. But I was a dead man, and nothing would make me miss my appointment with the executioner who would carry out the General Will and make the whole world murderers.

With Kosala warm against him, the Anonymous relaxed enough to let his own tears fall. "You can't kill Mycroft Canner. I know what they've done, I know the public wants it, but you can't. I'll take it to my Proxy if I have to."

"When did they realize?" Spain asked, grave as a portrait on a coin. "When did Canner figure out your true identity, what year?"

The Anonymous swallowed hard. "The letter's dated twenty-four thirty-five."

Felix Faust let out a long, delighted whistle. "Before even our Donatien? Spectacular."

Ganymede rolled his murder-blue eyes. "Please, Faust, in 'thirty-five Canner was what, fourteen years old? Much less impressive than the Prince's six."

The Anonymous shook his head. "First is first."

"The next Anonymous?" Kosala held her lover's eyes. "No! I know the rules of your succession, but you can't make Mycroft the next Anonymous, they're a monster!"

The Anonymous caught her hand, in those days not yet brightened by the sparkle of a wedding ring. I pitied him. No monarchy has ever had so suspenseful a succession. An impotent king may wait decades for an heir, but at least he can try aphrodisiacs, affairs, placebos. The Anonymous can only wait and hope for the day some bright young thing will reason him out and come to claim the apprenticeship, as he came to his predecessor, and she to hers, back through six generations. Such a helpless wait, and now the bright young thing had appeared before him, but I had already thrown my life away. Yes it's true. I could have been the next Anonymous, the second most powerful political voice on Earth. But I gave that up to teach you, gentle reader, what violence the human beast can sow when we are free. It was hardly the greatest sacrifice I made—I sacrificed my life as well, and worse, I would die in a hangman's arms, and not my Saladin's.

"I know Mycroft can't be the successor now," the Anonymous answered, "but however sick they are there's so much potential there! They're seventeen, for goodness sake! A child! We all heard the hopes the Mardis had for Mycroft." He turned from Power to Power, searching for one whose eyes would not shy away. "Andō, you were there when Kohaku and Chiasa first brought Mycroft to my office. Ten years as Deputy Censor and Kohaku was barely faster than Mycroft aged nine. We all know Aeneas was grooming them for the highest office, and Felix!" He turned to Headmaster Faust, on the couch behind. "You had Mycroft at the Institute. You know we can't throw a mind like that away." He choked. "Murderer or no, Mycroft's all we have left of the Mardi bash' now, and of Apollo. We—"

"Mycroft Canner will live."

No stone on stone, no hammer on anvil, no thunderbolt striking the heart could fall so heavily as the Emperor's words. I spotted him now too, the seventh of the Seven, sitting at the room's end, his uniform of imperial gray like ash against the festival of silk and gold that played across the walls. He would spare me? MASON, who had glowed in Apollo's presence like a dead coal brought to life, the one among the Powers I had trusted to crush my throat with his own hand if the others faltered—now he talks of sparing me? It was beyond my ability to even think it. That cage was my coffin. I had sacrificed my life eight days earlier when, hand in hand, my Saladin and I set the torch to the wicker prison which held the maimed but living remnants of Luther Mardigras. Luther was the fifth to die, but was the turning point, the moment that we knew I had left traces enough that the police would catch me, not right away, but someday, even if I stopped. For the week since I lit that torch, I had lived in the unique and absolute philosophic calm of one who has already drunk the hemlock, or already sees his heart's blood streaming from the wound. A dead man's philosophy. When Hope left she took Doubt with her, leaving only resolution, and a quiet curiosity about the larger nature of the universe. I mused, those seven nights, abstractly about what forces had conspired to put me in such a place, and make me such a person that I would choose this. I almost thought the dread word 'Providence.' But my path was set, and the possibility that I would be denied death was not hope to me now—it was betrayal. How dare the world make me do what I had done and then threaten to deny me my execution! I opened my mouth to object, to scream, to spit my curses at the Powers and demand death, but Caesar finished first:

"It is Apollo's will."

I had not imagined the Anonymous could tremble. I had not imagined I could anymore either. "Apollo's?"

I recognized the page as Caesar raised it in his black-sleeved hand, the title page of Apollo's *Iliad*, ripped out, with hasty lines scribed on the back in bloody red, so like Apollo. "I won't know for certain who the killer is until I meet them," Caesar read aloud, "but if it is Mycroft, be merciful. Keep them alive, and safe, and working. You need them. If you have lost me, you need them. There are things . . . there . . . there are . . . things . . ."

MASON's throat froze, a tremor in his bronze cheeks threatening to prove that even Caesar can cry. I think he would have, there in front of everyone, in front of me, had not the Lady beside him on the sofa laid soft hands on his shoulders and kissed his temple. She wore a formal mourning gown, as I remember, black lace pooling across the arms which reached around the Emperor, like the wings of a black swan. She seemed strange, less like a person than a shell waiting to enwrap something, a haven whose gentle gestures promised to lift Caesar from his grief, if only he surrendered. That was the first time I laid eyes on Madame.

"There are things I leave undone," a fresh voice finished where the Emperor failed, "that only Mycroft Canner can complete."

It was Mushi Mojave who stepped forward from a corner which, in my bonds, I could not turn enough to see. The constellations of Utopians have, to my knowledge, no rank nor hierarchy, but if, like stars, they may be said to have magnitudes of brightness, then surely Mushi Mojave is one of those

Crowns of Heaven that pierce even city smog. "Except ants" is Mushi's motto. Humanity is forever boasting of its 'unique' achievements: "Humans are the only creatures who build cities, use agriculture, domesticate animals, have nations and alliances, practice slavery, make war, make peace; these wonders make us stand alone above all other creatures, in glory and in crime." But then Mushi corrects, "Except ants." How proud the day when Mushi rushed in to tell the young Apollo and the other Mojave ba'kids that even man's greatest achievement, Space itself, was no longer a monopoly. The terraformers had found ants, stowaways in one of the nutrient shipments, which had escaped and built a colony in the new Mars soil, spiral tunnels woven like DNA around a leaking oxygen pipe. The first city on Mars was not built by humans, but under them. Science needed an expert, and Mushi Mojave leapt on the chance. First entomologist on Mars, now there's a title for a hero.

"Apollo knew?" The Anonymous looked to Mushi, then to Caesar. Then to me. "Apollo knew Mycroft was the killer?"

"They foreglimpsed, it seems," Mushi answered. "We don't know how early. We ask . . ." Mushi's voice quavered, hard words for one of the ba'pas who raised this light of lights from infancy, ". . . we ask that you honor their request."

The Anonymous peered hard at the Utopian, perhaps wondering whether grief's red around the digital eyes was real. "You want us to spare Mycroft?"

"I don't," Mushi corrected at once. "Apollo did. Collectively Utopia sides with Apollo."

The Utopian halted in the center of the room, a knife-stark silhouette wounding the salon's veil of antiquity. Mushi's Utopian coat fills the world with ants, billions upon billions, the incomparable colony that ants would erect if the whole world were given over to their intricate industry. A lesser imagination would leave it there, but Mushi reads deeper, for ants' paths, as they weave about their work, may by chance trace the shapes of letters, and with time such letters may by chance form words. While fools wait infinitely for the monkeys at their typewriters to reproduce Shakespeare, Mushi's coat collects and displays the new, alien poems ants write as they march. But the ants were dead now, the ant world switched off, leaving the coat a block of flickering static, flat and shapeless as if someone had sliced a hole in space. Those who lived through it cannot forget the days after Apollo's death, when across the globe the coats which should be windows to so many other worlds turned blank. When a Utopian dies before his

time, the Hive mourns together, all the coats in the world turning to static
for as many seconds as their kinsman lost years—thirty seconds for a centenarian, ninety for someone full of midlife's promise, a full two minutes
for a child. Apollo's murder was different. For him their mourning would
not stop. They left the static for hours, days, four hundred million walk-
ing holes in space, their vow that they would catch the killer and end this
nightmare where all other Hives had failed. It was terrifying, wounds of
static around every corner, everywhere and organized, reawakening a fear
Earth had not tasted since the Set-Set Riots. I saved Apollo for near the
end of the seventeen because I knew I could not last long once I woke that
sleeping dragon, but even I underestimated their speed. Four days is all it
took. They caught me with my work unfinished, Mercer still breathing, Tully
still free. Poor Papadelias will never stop cursing the fact that they, not
he, took down his long-awaited Moriarty. The static stayed, though, for
eleven hours after I was caught. The popular assumption has always been
that they were waiting for Caesar to carry out my execution. It is half true:
they were waiting.

"I side with Apollo too," MASON pronounced, forcing the words out
stiffly. His eyes fixed on me, my first taste of the rage which has not dimmed
in thirteen years. "You will live, Mycroft." I already knew him well, Cornel MASON. I knew his smiling eyes on soft afternoons when he came to
see Aeneas, Geneva, or Apollo. I knew his rich bronze face aglow with pride
as he showed his capital to me and the Mardi children, as if we and we
alone were the posterity who would inherit this greatest of empires. This
was a different man. "You will live. You will finish the Mardis' work:
Geneva's, Aeneas's, Mercer's for Faust, Kohaku's for the Censor, Jie's for
Andō, Leigh's for Kosala, Apollo's most of all. All of it."

"No!" Bryar cried. "You're talking like they can all be replaced!"

"Of course they can't!" Caesar bellowed, his full power, which before
that time no man had ever heard. Even the World's Mom fell silent.

"Caesar, please," cooed the dark Lady whom I did not yet know to call
Madame. "My salon is not the place for harshness." She stroked his black
hair, her touch dispelling the electric anger in the Emperor's stance.

"Apologies, Madame."

She kissed him again upon the cheek, as if the tender courtesy were her
apology for having to be strict.

"And you, Déguisé," she continued, holding out a slim black mask to
the Anonymous, "one must observe the forms."

"Sorry, Madame." He donned the mask, and seemed at once more confident and comfortable, more like himself than his fake outside persona. Madame's quick eye caught mine, saw that I was watching, and she had a smile for me, sweet as a mouse, before she locked the crosshairs of her attentions back on the Emperor. My mind, honed by so many leaders, caught more and more the scent of something rotten.

"Of course they can't be replaced," Caesar began again, more calmly, "but the pieces that remain must be picked up. They were all Mycroft's teachers. Apollo especially spent hours with Mycroft every week, telling them everything from research ideas to what's supposed to happen in the unfinished chapters of their ridiculous science fiction *Iliad*." His eyes locked again on me. "You'll finish writing that book for Apollo, Mycroft. You'll finish everything. You'll work until you die."

"I refuse." In those days I was headstrong enough to match Caesar glare for glare. "You think I killed Apollo and the others just to become them? I'm not some psycho lashing out for revenge or lust or fame. I loved the Mardis more than any of you! I know perfectly well what great things they would have accomplished if they'd lived. If there had been better people in this world I would have killed them instead. I've destroyed something wonderful just for destruction's sake, proving once and for all that the human animal can do evil for the sake of evil. I'm not about to undermine that by replacing what I've destroyed."

"You have no choice," the Emperor countered, Madame's hands reminding his fist not to slam her gilded chair. Who was this Lady who could chide and temper MASON and Anonymous?

"You're the ones with no choice," my young self shot back. "The world won't rest until it sees me dead. That's how it ends. They'll keep chanting my name until I've had my day in court, and there the world will see that it's possible to choose evil over good, over happiness, over family, over love, over the future potential of the human race, and over life itself. When the axe falls, or the electricity turns on, or whatever you decide to use on me, the world will taste again the base satisfaction of getting its hands dirty, as the human animal was meant to do. You can't avoid it. The world won't let you, and neither shall I!"

Does it sound rehearsed, reader? It was. I felt giddy in my cage, drunk on the idea of that supreme moment when all men would become killers again, and my Saladin watching, proud. Saladin would live, and hide, and watch what humanity became after we taught it that, with the death of

Nations, the supreme predator on Earth was once again Man. That I would be the one to die and Saladin to live had been determined by Providence—which in those days I still called Chance—nine years earlier, when the rescue workers found me after the explosion, but left Saladin for dead. He was out there at this very moment, waiting to see his Mycroft hold his head high in the court, and recite to the world these speeches we had practiced a thousand times. I would not betray him by surviving.

The Emperor did not lighten. "I do what I will."

"To Masons maybe." I was tempted to spit, but did not want to smear the precious window of my cage. "I'm no Mason."

"Silence that monster, would you, [Name]?" Caesar spoke the true name of the Anonymous, which, though you know it, I refuse to use before the desperate day.

"Happily," the Anonymous answered, though it was Mushi Mojave's hand which worked the controls, which means it was Mushi's choice to set the cage so I could still see and hear, though not bark back.

"But I'm afraid Mycroft's right, Cornel," the Anonymous continued. "The world wants them dead. I suspect most of the people in this room do too, am I right?"

Mute in my cage I trembled—first names, reader. MASON and Anonymous were supposed to be strangers, two lords in distant citadels who keep a cold and distant eye on one another like Light and Dark Manichean gods, and here they call each other by first names? Curiosity matured to a fearlike itch as it became clearer and clearer that this was not the same political landscape I had studied with Aeneas and Apollo.

"Well, I'm against killing Mycroft Canner," Headmaster Felix Faust volunteered first. "I'd never have so rare a specimen put down. Spain? Thumbs up or down?"

The King stroked his temples, already graying at forty-six despite science's efforts; he had been on the throne eleven years now and a widower ten, long enough to begin to gain those character lines which give portraits of older men more interiority than those of youths. "I think, as world leaders, we should not set a precedent by reviving the death penalty when our personal friends are killed. Andō?"

The Chief Director took a long breath. "Mycroft would be useful if rehabilitated. Ganymede?"

The Duke Consul shrugged. "What I'm worried about is how to justify it to the public. We can't exactly say we spared Canner because they were going to be the next Anonymous, and saying we're doing it because a Utopian wrote a note on a scrap of paper isn't going to fly, not with a victim from every Hive involved."

Headmaster Faust sniffed. "Why bother justifying it? We just have to refuse to suspend our own laws, no justification needed."

Ganymede sniffed back. "It may not matter to you, Felix, but some of us have to get reelected. Right, Spain?" The Duke-Consul seemed happy that the King–Prime Minister had no good answer. "We have to give the mob a trial, and we have to let Mycroft speak at the trial or we'll have lawhounds on our backs. Mycroft was tutored in oratory by two Senators; if they want the crowd screaming for blood, it will."

Andō shook his head. "No trial. We can't allow a trial. The more the world thinks about this business the more harm it does. There hasn't been an incident of global trauma like this since the Set-Set Riots. No trial or the world will go mad."

Ganymede frowned. "What if we get an actor to impersonate Mycroft in court and play penitent? That'll calm the mob, then we can accept whatever the judges decide, fake an execution if need be, and Caesar can do what they like with the genuine article."

Prime Minister Spain shook his head. "I will not so abuse the law."

"Besides," Andō continued, "even a false trial will have devastating effects on the world."

Upon your Hive you mean, Mitsubishi, as the police probe your Canner Device.

"It must be stopped," the Director pressed, "at all costs."

The Duke scowled. "Does anyone have a better solution?"

"No, but we all agree we—"

Kosala's voice, though soft among men, was still strong enough to interrupt the King. "I haven't agreed."

"Bryar?"

"I haven't agreed to letting Mycroft live." She shuddered, tempting the Anonymous to tighten his embrace. "Oh, I'll go along with it, I'll even supply a justification for you, but I don't agree."

Ganymede arched an eyebrow. "You'll put a humanitarian veto on the trial?"

"I'll get one of my charities to. Everyone expects Cousins to do that sort of thing, it'll seem natural. I'll tell the public how Mycroft Canner is a poor, sad trauma victim, and all this is the tragic lashing out of a bash'orphan who needed help. From me they'll accept it. I can even make them feel good about themselves for being so forgiving, but I want all of you to re-member that I'm against this. When a dear, beloved, wonderful pet dog starts killing people, you put it down. If you don't, more people die."

The husk of Felix Faust's body was, even back then, barely strong enough to sigh. "I appreciate the thought, my dear, but it won't work."

She scowled. "You think I can't control my own Hive?"

He smiled, but one can always feel the scientist behind the man read-ing numbers instead of faces, and judging by Brill's criteria, as arcane as craniometry or horoscope. "It's not that, Bryar, it's just that you're a bad liar, and you need at least another two weeks to recover from Leigh's death enough to talk about this in public."

"You think I can't—"

"Make a speech," he challenged. "Make a speech for us right now about how Mycroft Canner is a poor puppy who got kicked once too often. If you can orate on the subject for two minutes without crying, then I'll believe that you can get us out of this."

Rage swelled in Kosala's face, but turned at once to tears.

The Anonymous pressed her to him. "I think Felix is right. You're pro-posing that you lie to your own Hive about your opinions. It's a brave offer, but do you really want to live with that? I don't think any of us could do it, and I don't want to ask it of you."

"Quite right." The unknown Lady spoke up now—'Madame' they had called her? She seemed all smiles and good sense beneath the mask of makeup which made her seem as otherworldly as a china doll. Are you surprised, reader, that she stayed quiet so long? What cares she what hap-pens to this little murderer when the fact that only her salon can solve the crisis is a victory itself? "We'll find another way to persuade the populace, one that doesn't put all the strain on one person, or endanger reelection, or precedent, or the law." She glanced from Power to Power as she listed each one's concern. "I have all the resources we could want here, and no one expects this decision to be quick. We'll take our time and sort it out as friends. That is what my salon is for."

She looked straight at me during the last sentence, exposition for the outsider's benefit, to make sure I understood her, what she was, her place among the Powers. Doubt burned through me. What I had done I did in the confidence that I knew how the world worked, how it would react, how the Hives and strats and laws and numbers ebb and flow, as Geneva, Aeneas, and Deputy Censor Kohaku taught me to predict. Now, just as Eureka Weeksbooth would thirteen years later, I found a snarl in my web. I felt like an old astronomer, who had spent a lifetime plotting the courses of a flock of distant stars, only to discover on my deathbed that there was a great black something out there pulling all astray—what doom did this spell for the rocket I had launched, loaded with hopes and false calculations? Curiosity is a dangerous thing for a dead man; it tempts one to want to live.

That moment was when I saw the Child. I do not know how long He had been there, standing close beside my cage, a volume of Cicero forgotten in His hands as His studies found a new object. He wore a tiny mourning suit, fresh from the tailors, period and perfect, trimmed with a *Porphyrogene's* imperial purple, since at eight years old He had not yet discovered that the adults would accomodate if He voiced His preference for pure black. His eyes reminded me of the late King Isabel Carlos the First, whom Makenna Mardi had brought me to meet upon his royal deathbed at the venerable age of one hundred and forty-nine. There had been something unfair in the old king's eyes, a hunger to snatch this world back from the foolish children who had inherited it. I remember shuddering, thinking my generation would have stood helpless against his political guile, honed over a century and a half, that only death relieved us of the necessity of parricide. And now those terrifying eyes seemed to stare at me once more, from a Child's face.

Seeing me spot Him, Bryar Kosala called to the Child. "Jed, honey, come away from there. It's not good for you."

I shuddered in my bonds of Cannergel (Utopia later named it for me). You had a birth bash', reader. You know the special way your ba'pas gazed on you, grave and loving, parents even if it was not their blood coursing through your veins. The Powers all looked at Him that way now, the King, Director, Headmaster, Anonymous, even Bryar who is everybody's Mom was His Mom more. There is no glue like a child to keep a quarreling couple from cutting the knot, so what of quarreling empires?

Madame called now, since the Child did not move. "Jehovah, mon Petit, viens ici." She made room for Him on the couch between the Emperor and herself.

Still the Child lingered, staring, thinking, crafting His words. For me. "You disappoint me, Master Canner. I thought to see the Liberated Man, but you still hid behind a cause."

This was the death of what was Mycroft Canner. It was impossible. The Child saw in an instant the hypocrisy that I had not quite admitted even to myself. He was right. I was never strong enough to do evil for the sake of evil. Saladin was the true, free beast. I had merely followed, leaning half on him, half on the crutch of a hidden good that lay beyond the Mardis' deaths. The Child saw, as if my inmost self were an open book before Him. He was monstrous, with powers humans should not have, and here the Seven leaders of the Earth were doting on Him as on a Son. Panic is too weak a word. Metamorphosis, perhaps? An ant which strays onto someone's clothes, and is spirited in a car to an alien land incomprehensibly far from home and colony, could not feel more lost. All my strength had stemmed from the conviction that I could read the shape of the future as it unrolled interminably from the present. That present had been a lie, the rivalries, the enmity between Mason and Mitsubishi, the competition among Hives, all lies. Was I wrong, then? Had they not had to die, Luther, Geneva, Kohaku, Laurel, Seine? Apollo? I suffered many injuries during my capture, but only this wound bled.

Spain took the Child by the hand, His small fingers locking around the royal thumb with the speed of habit.

It does not matter what I screamed at that moment, for, through the cage, no one could hear me. I realized who the Boy must be. Everyone knew the Emperor had an adopted Son, but the young *Porphyrogene* glimpsed in heartwarming shots in newspapers had no more factored in my calculations than the child of any Senator.

"*Fili*," Caesar addressed the Boy as He settled on the couch beside him, "what do you think we should do with Mycroft Canner?"

The Child Jehovah looked again at me, and through the glass my eyes begged Him to read me again, to tell the others how deeply He had struck me, how desperately I wished to see more of this new world which proved the old a lie.

"He is benign, *Pater*. Make him a Servicer."

"Benign?" Bryar Kosala knelt before the Child, her skirts and Madame's cocooning Him with silk. "No, sweetheart, that's a very dangerous criminal who's done terrible things."

Even in those days His shell did not move to look at things, only His eyes. "Benign means something which can do no harm."

"That's right, and—"

"This man is benign." He even raised His hand to point, a child-stubby finger which seemed to touch my soul, which in that moment I started to believe in. He was right. If I had been wrong about everything, the world, Apollo, I could be sure of nothing. If my teachers were wrong about politics, were they wrong about science, too? Metaphysics? Philosophy? Was man incapable of willing evil? Did Evil exist? Did Good? Did God? Was there a divine Maker scripting this universe? A Maker of souls? Did some Divine Force plan Apollo's death? From that moment I could not be sure enough of my world to tread on an ant which might—who knows—be Apollo's reincarnation, let alone to kill a man.

"You're sure Mycroft is harmless, Tai-kun?" Andō asked.

A lesser creature would have answered "Certain," or "Absolutely," but nothing is more absolute than Jehovah Mason's "Yes."

Ganymede stretched. "If Caesar wants to work Canner to death, the Servicer Program is a fine way. It'll give us all equal access, so the Censor can use them when they want to, Faust too, and I trust the Utopians would consent, yes?"

Mushi Mojave breathed hard. "It doesn't matter whether we consent or not if Mycroft won't. You heard them, they want the trial and they want to die."

Jehovah answered, "No. That desire was. It is not."

With my hands bound in the Cannergel I could not wipe the tears which itched down my cheeks like burning wax. It was the truth. Conviction's end had left me a newborn, vulnerable again to fear, hope, curiosity, hunger for knowledge, and, above all, to life's fierce desire to see tomorrow. I sobbed. Saladin was out there, still in our old illusory world, waiting to see his proud Mycroft mount the gallows. I'm sorry, Saladin. I'm sorry.

The Anonymous breathed deep. "How do we do it?"

That quickly, reader, they accepted Jehovah's judgment, a child's claim that Earth's most savage killer was benign. Oh, perhaps there were other arguments, doubts, details of how to smuggle me through the bureaucratic shadows, but why repeat what came to nothing?

"It would be different if they were a *Familiaris*," the Anonymous growled, "then we could do what we want, but—"

The mountain that is Caesar trembled. *"Familiaris."*

"Cornel?"

"Madame, is there a printer in this room?" MASON asked with sudden urgency.

"Behind the third sconce on the left," she answered. "What did you remember?"

He rose. "To make Mycroft Canner a *Familiaris*."

Bryar looked to the others. "You can't make them a *Familiaris* after they've already committed the crime you want to punish, even your law doesn't work like that."

"Not after." He slid the crystal half-chandelier aside to bare technology beneath. "It's finished, set and sealed, all it needs is Mycroft Canner's signature accepting the appointment." His quaking left hand fumbled as he accessed the panel. "Apollo requested it, nine days ago. They came to me, frantic, insisting I start the process to make Mycroft Canner a *Familiaris* immediately. I thought it was because Apollo thought Aeneas had wanted it, and was trying to carry out a dead friend's wishes, but that wasn't it. Apollo suspected Mycroft even then, and wanted to put Mycroft's fate in my hands."

"To make sure the Mardis were avenged," Bryar Kosala suggested at once. "Apollo knew if Mycroft was a *Familiaris* we wouldn't have to change any laws to execute them, you could order it yourself. Perhaps Apollo meant—"

MASON turned on her, all thunder. "What would you know about what Apollo meant!" He caught himself, bottling his rage as a sailor seals the cabin door against a storm. "I'm sorry."

"It's all right." She smiled it away; Mom can smile anything away.

The Emperor tore the page from the printer's jaws. "We'll tell the public Mycroft was already a *Familiaris,* and that I have dealt with them as I saw fit. Everyone will assume that means an execution, and that will be the end, no trial, no questions, done. Can you free Mycroft's hand enough for them to sign the page?"

Mushi Mojave worked the controls, liquefying the Cannergel enough for my right arm to stretch semifree in its rubberband grip. "I've spoken with Apollo's bash'," the Utopian recited, sullen. "In this case we will suspend *modo mundo.*" Had it not occurred to you, reader, that—as a Utopian's killer—I, much more than Chagatai, deserved to be banished from the kingdoms of fiction? Utopia had its own plans for me. "At least until the book is done." From the depths of the coat's static, Mushi's unwilling hand produced Apollo's *Iliad,* treasure of treasures, scatterbrained and far from finished, which I had cursed not finding on Apollo's corpse. It was at that moment, as the book slid through a slot into my waiting hand, that Mushi's static gave way to ants, and across the world the millions of Utopian coats showed again their nowheres. In every corner of the teeming globe people relaxed, believing I was dead. You were not wrong.

Cornel MASON slid the *Familiaris* contract in after the book, and a crayon with it, squished from a long stint in his pocket, Laurel Mardi's perhaps, which the little prince had used to scribble fancies as he played beneath the Emperor's desk. "You will become my *Familiaris,* and a Servicer," MASON pronounced. "You will work without rest to cover every service your victims would have done for us, and when no task is given to you, you will think what Apollo or the others would have done with those spare minutes and still work. If I ever judge that you are slacking in your duties I shall deal with you as I choose, and my Capital Power knows no limits. On these terms and these terms alone you live. Sign it."

"Will I get to see that child again?" I asked. I knew my words could not escape the cage, but I hoped He did not need to hear to understand.

Jehovah Himself answered, "Yes."

On those terms then, reader, I live, my long penance, thirteen years and counting. It is my privilege among my many tasks to hear Jehovah's words and follow His commands, even His order on the twenty-seventh that I obey His mother's summons return to the *Salon de Versailles*, whose scent still weakens me like fever. I was half in the past as I mounted the steps, thieves and Seven-Ten lists fading as I saw the Powers still staring at me through my coffin-cage. I hope now you will understand my failure as I stumble across the threshold and there let fly the name which a decade's interrogations had not forced from me: "Saladin!"

He should not have been there. I would have given anything in the world to have him never see this place. But there he was, curled on the floor of a cage which stood just where mine had, though larger, metal bars this time instead of Utopian genius. He cried out, "Mycroft!" in the same breath that I called, "Saladin!" and we rushed to each other, the world around melting away as we embraced, the bars between us no more impediment than the core of the Earth is to its two hemispheres. He was trembling, naked except for bandages around fresh wounds, and rank with sweat.

"A pair?" Madame fluttered toward us, her skirts a garden of hand-painted Chinese silk. "Dominic, thou didst not tell me Mycroft and thy stray pup were a pair."

"I did not know, Madame." Dominic hobbled forward, facing Madame with as proper posture as he could manage on crutches, with his right foot dragging stiff. Remember, reader, all that time down in the cell with Carlyle, Dominic knelt, or sat, but never stood. "The beast attacked me out of the blue, I knew nothing."

"Wast it thou, then, Mycroft, who trickedest the tracker system into registering this lovely creature as a dog?" Madame swatted at me gently with her fan, azure painted with a hunting hawk. "Thou shouldst have told me of that trick, I could have used it many times."

I stroked Saladin through the bars, counting his injuries, and recognized around his throat the pinprick stab wounds of Madame's mancatcher. The mancatcher may be the most medieval of inventions, a metal collar, spiked on the inside and mounted on a pole which, when thrust just right, locks around the enemy's neck, as savage as a bear trap. Madame's of course is not medieval but Enlightenment, gilt silver filigree with mother-of-pearl inlay, a birthday present from the King of Spain. I did not then know that Dominic had set a trap for Bridger, how he had murdered the imaginary friend 'Redder,' stolen Bridger's backpack and captured three of the little soldiers, or how that bait had brought to Paris not the boy, but my beautiful monster. Still, I could envision the battle clearly, Dominic pacing in the shadows of the back stairs when Saladin lunges, all claws and teeth, tackling this rival predator who would dare target his prey. The two would match one another bite for bite, cracked rib for snapped ankle, snarling like lions until, in some opening, Madame snares the stranger with her mancatcher, as delicate as a violin bow in her hands. « Dominic, » she chides, reeling her captive high with a twist of the inlaid handle, « thou art frightening the ladies with thy ruckus. Is this delightful monster thine? »

« No, Madame. This is not the prey I was waiting for. You caught him, you may keep him. »

So it would have gone, the many creatures of the house jeering through cracks and windows as the beast was dragged inside. Saladin does not whimper. Even here, blinded by gold and crystal, he had stayed as silent as a captured stag, but I could feel exhaustion in the arms which gripped me, like a drowning man clinging to life. «What is this, Mycroft?» he asked in rasping Greek. «It's like another world.»

«I know.» I stroked him. Thirteen years my silence had bought him, thirteen more years free in our old illusion. How I had prayed this day might never come. «Bridger?» I whispered close to his ear.

«Alive. Safe.»

My heart beat easier. «And Tully Mardi? Please tell me you've killed Tully Mardi.»

Apology's shudder half stifled his answer. «No.»

Madame sighed down at us, white wig curls playing across her shoulders. "And here I thought I'd keep the new pup, but if they're a pair I suppose I must give both to Jehovah."

"No need, Madame," Dominic counseled. "Keep the new one if you wish. I'm sure *Maître* Jehovah would say Mycroft is enough for His needs."

Her fan concealed her thoughts. "Perhaps."

Even Dominic looks like a suppliant when he has to petition her for favors. « Madame, may I speak with the pair privately for a moment? »

« Certainly. » She floated back, hovering like a summer butterfly just out of whisper range.

Dominic crouched over me, producing from a pocket a small tablet, on which he summoned a scanned handwritten page in hasty ink, one I knew as well as my own face in the mirror. "Thou shouldst be more careful with thy holy relics," he warned. "Apollo's *Iliad* in the hands of a child?"

My breath caught. "Where's the original?"

"The boy stole it back, along with my hostages, leaving behind only the pitter-patter of extremely tiny feet. I'm curious, didst thou pick the name Bridger, or did the little soldiers?"

Fear mixed with prayers of thanks within me that the boy and men were safe. "Bridger chose it himself."

"Thou knowest, Mycroft, when I heard the great Apollo Mojave had left behind an unfinished novel I didn't expect it to be . . . how can one put this delicately?"

"Terrible?" I volunteered. "Apollo was one of the busiest vocateurs on the planet, they didn't have time to master writing, too."

"Apparently not. Tactics, military history, weapons technology, combat, not writing—that's strange for a Utopian. Or is it?" He leaned almost close enough to lick my ear. "Thy mate here wore a fascinating pelt when he was taken."

Saladin's eyes caught mine, offering silently to strike out at this enemy who stood within claw's reach, but I shook my head. "What are you going to do with it, Dominic? It's not to your advantage to break Caesar's heart right now."

I hate Dominic's smile. "Done is done."

In the pause, I heard voices at the far end of the room, tense and familiar; we weren't alone:

MASON: "This technology, there's no denying it was designed for killing?"
Voltaire: "Among other things, Caesar."
MASON: "Killing people."
Voltaire: "It has lethal and nonlethal applications, Caesar."
MASON: "And it's not just one person's work, there was industry behind this, science, many planners."
Voltaire: "Yes, Caesar."
MASON: "Many people were involved. A large conspiracy."
Voltaire: "It is a prototype, Caesar. Most likely never intended for field use."

MASON: "The theft was thirteen years ago—it's held up well for a prototype."

Voltaire: "It was made well."

MASON: "Were others made?"

Voltaire: "If so, they have not been used."

MASON: "You're sure?"

Voltaire: "Yes, Caesar."

MASON: "You know that, if it came out that a Hive had developed technology like this, the public backlash would be incalculable."

Voltaire: "Likely so, Caesar."

MASON: "Deadly technology."

Voltaire: "Yes, Caesar."

MASON: "Just like the Canner Device."

Voltaire: ". . . The public might react similarly to the two, yes."

MASON: "The two have the same purpose."

Voltaire: "Likely not, Caesar. I only recovered the Traceshifter Artifact an
hour ago, but it is already clear its powers are not intended for combat.
It may be an assassin's tool, or forged for some larger cursecraft: espionage, mass-scrying, surveillance."

MASON: "This is worse than the Canner Device, then. This is for killing."

Voltaire: "For war, Caesar. Offense and defense. If the Canner Device is an
assassin's tool, a saboteur's, this is a soldier's."

"Give it back!" I screamed across the chamber. "Give it back! You don't
need it! The Utopians have already surrendered! They've given you two of
their best as hostages! They won't resist you, they can't! Whatever you've
asked of them they've given. You don't need blackmail!"

Madame's smile was enough to make Saladin shudder, but MASON
was worse, storming toward us from the far side of the room with the coat
in his arms, so the program in its Griffincloth transformed the Emperor's
gray Eighteenth-Century uniform to a different uniform, sleek modern
panels of black and gray, with the Masonic sigil on the breast in porphyry
purple, like old blood. "This was Apollo's coat!" He thrust it forward, the
computers making his hard hands bloodstained. "I'd know it anywhere."

"Yes, Caesar, it's Apollo's."

"You said you didn't have it!" His limp was back, that limp that stays
only in Caesar's mind, and worse than I had ever seen.

"I didn't have it, Caesar. Saladin di—"

His fist slammed my cheek against the bars hard enough to splash blood on Saladin's cheek. "What was Apollo doing? There are more than twenty weapons inside this, a third of them lethal!" He let the coat fall open, so all could see the pockets and slots within, the glint of handles. "Do you have any idea how devastating this could be if it fell into the wrong hands? Did Apollo?"

I licked my blood from Saladin's cheek without thinking. "Of course we did."

Caesar was shaking. "I couldn't protect the Utopians if this came out. No one could! Why? Why did Apollo make it?"

"I'm sure Apollo's reasons were the best."

MASON's black-sleeved left hand locked around my throat, and Saladin's hands about his wrist, a stalemate which left me pinned against the bars.

"You think I'm deaf?" Caesar spat. "That you're the only one watching dark corners?" He tapped his tracker with his free hand, and the speakers played back Tully Mardi's voice: "How would you defend yourself if it did come to war? Do you know? Armed Masons and Mitsubishi flying through every street, exchanging bombs? Can your waste converter be turned into a weapon? Can your child's toy? You can't just flee the combat zones like they did in the Church War, there will be no centers, no neutral ground, not with all Hives spread across every city in the world. If you want to defend your bash' you need to become a soldier, but how can you learn when there aren't any left to teach you? Weapons change as——" MASON silenced the recording there, his own words worse. "What were the Mardis doing?"

"They were . . . economists," I choked out, "historians."

He squeezed me harder, ignoring Saladin's claws as they tore at his wrist. "What were Apollo and the Mardis doing?"

Death, reader, Death was in Caesar's grip around my throat, the only terror that could have ripped from me the word: "War!" The force of my cry left me wheezing. "They were war historians. They were all war historians, whatever else they pretended to be, it was always war. Why else would they shorten Mardigras to Mardi, Mars-day, War-day? You dined with us dozens of times, did we ever once not talk about war?"

His hand stopped tightening. "Kohaku Mardi's numbers, 33–67; 67–33; 29–71. You told the Censor they were when Kohaku predicted a recession, but that wasn't it, was it? They predicted war."

I wondered for a moment whether MASON had had a spy in the Censor's office, or whether the Censor had leaked the facts himself. "War between the Masons and Mitsubishi," I confirmed. "Apollo went so far as to start experimenting with weapons, preparations to defend Utopia if war broke out. They were all preparing, Aeneas running for the Senate, Kohaku working for the Censor, they were all trying to influence you and the other leaders, get ready for the war."

"To stop it," he tried to finish for me.

"No, Caesar," I corrected, "to start it. 33–67; 67–33; 29–71, those numbers don't make war inevitable. They make it possible. The landgrab, Nurturism, those were potential fuel. They needed a spark. They were pushing to make that happen."

Madame came to the Emperor's side, and her touch on his elbow made his grip ease on my neck. "You're saying the Mardi bash' wanted to start a war?" A fold of Apollo's coat fell across her too, replacing antique silks with the bleached white of a nurse's uniform.

"They thought war was inevitable," I answered, "locked in by human nature, that there will always be another war, now or two hundred years from now, sometime. How long ago was it, Caesar, that Geneva Mardi first asked you their favorite question? 'What was the nastiest war in history?'"

He swallowed hard. "We were still students."

"And what answer was Geneva fishing for?"

"The First World War."

"A war . . ." I choked a moment as his fingers flexed. "A war that came after a long period of relative peace and smaller conflicts, combined with accelerating advancement. Earth had never seen anything like that before. Antiquity, the Middle Ages, the first four centuries of the Exponential Age, they had all seen frequent war, large-scale war compared to the population, but Nineteenth-Century Europe confined the conflicts to its colonies and border zones, while at home they engineered their long and rosy peace. Technology kept changing, made new, worse ways to kill, but military experts had no opportunity to realize how the new tools would change the face of war when the big powers finally fought each other directly. When the Twentieth Century saw total war again, soldiers didn't have the dignity of dying at the enemy's hands; they rotted in trenches, froze in winters, wandered in jungles, blew themselves up on kamikazi missions, drove themselves mad attempting genocides, as deluded commanders kept urging them onward to their noble deaths. The Church War may have killed more people, but at least then it was the zealot enemy that killed you, not your own side and stupid ignorance. The Mardis thought that three things make wars more or less terrible: the length of the peace before them, the amount of technological change, and how little the commanders know about war's up-to-date realities. We've had three hundred years of peace now, Caesar. Can you imagine what the next war would be like? With the trackers? With the transit system? With every spot on Earth a two-hour hop from every other? With the Hives all scattered equally across the Earth? No homelands, no borders, and without a single tactician who's ever taken the field in any kind of war? It will be Hell on Earth. Even the wonders Utopia has made will turn to war."

MASON's hand was trembling. "I can't believe Geneva would want to start a war."

"They thought it would be a mercy having the war now, that putting it off longer would only make it worse. If war is inevitable, and if every invention makes it that much more probable that mankind will wipe itself out when the next war comes, the best thing was to get the next war over sooner, while technology has changed less and while the Mardis were there, experts ready to predict and guide it. Better a smaller war now, when it might be contained, than an unplanned war in a hundred years, when Earth might destroy itself. Doesn't that sound like something Geneva would say?"

"No."

"Lies don't suit you, Caesar. Think about it. The Mardis were brilliant scholars; why did they publish almost nothing? Why were all their files so carefully encrypted that even the police couldn't unlock them after the murders? Why did they network so carefully into every Hive, getting close to all the leaders? Why did a bash' of eleven adults have only three children among them? Most of them didn't want kids to grow up in the world they planned to create. Tully's still here trying to start the war all by themself, what kind of life is that?"

"Dear, modest Mycroft!" Madame cried, hiding her expression with her fan. "All these years thou hast pretended to be evil, when really thou didst it to prevent another World War! Our secret hero."

It burned hearing so much of the truth at once. Jehovah had sensed a hidden good behind my actions, but He was merciful enough not to voice it. "Don't praise me, Madame," I pleaded. "I did it to keep violence in the hands of individuals. My solution was for us all to turn back into beasts and kill each other one-on-one instead of en masse. I wanted..." Even in His absence I could feel Jehovah's eyes forbidding me to lie within His house. "I also wanted to prevent the war. But it doesn't matter, I was wrong, and the Mardis were wrong too. This place, Madame, Ἄναξ Jehovah, He's a tie between Caesar and Andō, between all the leaders, too strong for war to break out between any of the Hives. Kohaku's numbers mean nothing. As long as this place exists, and He exists, the war the Mardis were afraid of can't begin."

Madame dared chuckle. "Flatterer—now I'm the one preventing the next World War?"

"And Apollo?" The Emperor had to release me now, for fear he really would forget himself and strangle me. "What about Apollo?"

I looked at the coat in Caesar's arms, Dominic showing through it, his monk's habit replaced by another modern uniform of black and blue. "Apollo's only concern was that Utopia survive. War now, war later, the important thing was to prepare. That special Utopian coat and those weapons were developed for defense."

"They work, too, the weapons. The rest of the Mardis were sitting ducks, but Seine and Apollo very nearly killed us instead." I thought for a moment that my dead past self had risen to speak this boast, but it was Saladin's voice from behind me, dark and proud.

MASON turned cold eyes on the caged beast. "You were Mycroft's partner in this?"

"In everything."

I spread myself as a wall between Caesar and Saladin. "Please don't listen to them, Caesar. They're mad, developmentally disturbed, they don't know what they're—"

One blow knocked me from my knees to the floor; a second kept me there.

"Who are you?" MASON demanded.

A serpent smile spread across Saladin's hairless face. "Mycroft Canner."

"It's practically true, Caesar," Madame cooed, lace fluttering about her elbows as she restrained MASON's poised fists. "We ran a skin sample, it's a genetic match, and the tracker system refuses to admit this is a human being at all, it thinks he's a dog. Isn't that delightful?"

"I won't ask again." The Emperor loomed. "Who are you?"

Saladin still smiled. "Nobody. A wild dog. A ghost."

I saw a computer search flicker in MASON's lenses. "Mycroft had a ba'sib named Saladin who died in the explosion twenty-two years ago. There was a fire; you did a skin graft and used Mycroft's skin as the source." It was fast guesswork, but Caesar is no fool. "So, which of you two killed which of the Mardis? Or did you do them all together?"

"Caesar," Madame interrupted, her voice honey in his ear, "now is not the time. The Seven-Ten list mess is what needs you now. Save yourself for that, and leave this to me. In a few days I'll have the beast's answers flowing on command."

MASON turned to her, letting fatigue show for a moment as he limped a step away. "Madame, if the law offers no protections to this creature you have caught, do to it what you will."

She let a smile peek over her fan.

I raised my head. "Caesar . . ."

I had to dodge to keep his heel from falling on my hand. "I'm dealing with the present now, Mycroft. The past can wait. Voltaire!"

"Yes, Caesar?"

Apollo's coat creaked in Caesar's grip. "Take it away." He bundled it into Voltaire's open arms. "We'll never speak of it again."

"Give it back!" I shrieked. I did not stand but sat straight, startled at the unaccustomed force in my own tone. "The coat is ours, Caesar!"

He turned. "It is Apollo's."

"When you slay the enemy hero you rip the splendid armor from his back and haul it back to Troy! You know this, Caesar! It's ours! Our spoils! Our right! Apollo would agree."

Mason stood frozen, unable to face the ghost of Apollo which welled, I'm sure, before his mind's eye as it did before mine. I was right. He knew I was right.

What is Woman's office if not to step in where Man's pride makes him helpless? "Let's compromise." Madame lifted the coat from Voltaire's arms, carefully, like a bundled infant. "You know Mycroft can't walk the streets anymore, Caesar. You've asked me to keep them safe here, and I shall keep the coat safe here too, in reach of our Utopians and out of reach of any prying public. That's fair, and safe, and fully in your power without separating trophy from victor. Now come, Caesar, you have affairs of state."

MASON's chest was heaving, quaking breaths which he forced down with the iron of his will. His hands hungered to rip the coat from her, as he would have ripped life from me, if Apollo let him. The call of state let him retreat in silence. Well done, Madame.

"Art thou injured, Mycroft?" She approached and bent low over me, or squatted, the architecture of her gown made it impossible to distinguish.

I licked blood from my lip. "I'm fine, Madame. Thank you."

She laid the precious bundle in my arms, the Griffincloth turning my

Franciscan habit to a uniform, not quite a Servicer's, dappled with dirty camouflage. "Thou'lt want this, too." She drew Apollo's vizor from the depths of her frills. "Caesar never saw it."

I shuddered with true gratitude. "Thank you, Madame."

"Thou'st had a hard few days." She rose again and moved toward a sideboard, where I saw my bowl waiting. "What time zone dost thou sleep by these days, Mycroft?"

"Any I can, Madame."

"Wouldst thou like to spend the night inside the cage with thy stray?"

"Yes, Madame, I'd like that very much!"

Her chuckle told me I had answered too eagerly. "Just don't tire thyself out too much to work."

"I—" I caught myself on the verge of promising too much. "I'll try my best, Madame."

"Do." With a face as much smirking as critical, she handed me my bowl, loaded with lopsided petits fours and mangled omelet, twice my usual portion.

"Thank you, Madame."

"Not at all, Mycroft. Rather I should thank thee and thy stray." She leaned low as she unlocked the cage to let me in, whispering so only Saladin and I could hear. "Mycroft knows this already, but Apollo Mojave was my only rival for the complete affections of the Seven." She winked at wide-eyed Saladin. "Thanks to you two, I won."

I felt a sense of safety as the bars locked fast behind me, Fate's promise that Saladin and I would not be ripped apart again until that lock clicked open once more. For thirteen years we had enjoyed only those rare hours when I could slip my tracker, or stolen seconds between its bleeping my excitement and Papadelias's cavalry charging in. Now a whole night stretched before us, infinite as the sea. It was an undeserved mercy, snowfall to cool my burning patch of Hell.

«Mycroft,» Saladin whispered as we wrapped ourselves around each other. «Where are we?» His Greek felt hollow, like a child's song lost in a cavern.

«The secret capital of the world,» I answered.

«Who was that woman?»

«The secret Empress. I'm sorry, Saladin. I wanted to die for you, but after what happened to me here I was too weak, and now they're going to do it to you, too.»

His eyes seemed old, too old, life without medical treatments letting the years show in his face as in portraits of ancients. «Who is Jehovah? You mentioned the name Jehovah.»

I stroked his hairless cheek. «Tomorrow. The world can end tomorrow. For tonight, let's let the world cease to exist.»

He tasted my ear. «Why are you crying? I'm all right. These wounds are nothing.»

«We killed Apollo.» My voice cracked as I said it. «Apollo's dead and we killed them, I killed them, and the reasons were all lies . . .» I drew Apollo's coat tighter around us, as if we could hide in its reality. «What kind of God would plan this?»

His eyes grew wide. «Mycroft, since when have you believed——»

«Even if Apollo had to die, They could have used disease, or an accident, or lightning. Why us? Why murder, and why make us, both of us, live to see that we were wrong?» I pulled him around me like a shell. «We killed Apollo, and tomorrow, and the next day, forever, we'll still have killed Apollo. Tell me it's a nightmare, Saladin. Just for tonight, tell me it isn't true.»

He held me as I wished, but his breath against my cheek was slow with thought. «Mycroft, where did Bridger come from? Apollo didn't have a child. Seine wasn't pregnant, we know that, but the resemblance is too strong, so where——»

«Shhh. Not here.»

Chapter the SEVENTH

Treason

"Yes, I'll sign for it. Wheel it in."

Lesley signaled the bash'house security to let the postman wheel the box across the threshold. In the stress of the crisis, her doodles had strayed off the margins of her clothes to streak her skin with veins and spirals.

"Member Lesley Juniper Saneer," he read off after she signed. "I thought I recognized you. I still remember that speech you made to the cameras after your bash'parents died. I showed that video to my little ones. 'If you ever lose your ba'pas,' I told them, 'I hope you do something as brave and good for the world as that Lesley Juniper.'"

Lesley smiled at the postman, and at the signature tracks his Humanist boots stamped on the hallway carpet, quotes from Milton woven into branching spirals something between fire and a tree. "Thanks, that means a lot."

Compliments aside, Lesley could not get rid of the outsider fast enough, and practically shoved him out across the threshold in her haste to be alone with the doll box, which now lay in the hallway like a festive coffin. "¿Cardie? ¿Are you in there?"

"Yeah." Sniper's voice was muffled by the packaging. "¿Could you give me a hand out? I've been drugged, not moving very well."

She attacked the box at once. "¿Are you hurt?"

"Just groggy. ¿What day is it?"

"Still the twenty-seventh. You disappeared this morning, fourteen hours ago." Something caught in Lesley's throat as she found her celebrity bash'mate within, naked and wincing at the light. "¡Ockham!" she cried. "¡Cato! ¡Come here now! ¡And bring the first-aid kit! ¡And the crime kit! ¡Sniper's back!"

Lesley eased Sniper forward gently, until it flopped against her, like a fawn learning to walk. "It's not your fault if they got you to talk; with enough drugs and pain anyone will."

"It wasn't like that." Sniper let its arms flop over Lesley's shoulders as she eased it forward. "Just a crazy fan, nothing to do with the break-in."

(I realize, reader, I should apologize for deceiving you in my first book, with Sniper's pronoun. Before I received its chapter, I had not imagined it would consent to have its sex revealed, so, in the first half of my history, forced to choose between the standard genders, it seemed best to give Ockham's rival and successor the same pronoun as Ockham.)

The cavalry arrived now, Ockham swift and grim with Cato in his wake, lab coat flying, armored with gizmos. Ockham brought only questions. "¿You're certain it's unrelated to the break-in?"

"I'll be certain once we runbwa ba wff thhff . . ." Sniper sputtered as its head flopped forward into the massed twists of Lesley's soft African hair. "Once we run a blood test," it tried again. "If there's nothing in my bloodstream that would mess with my memory, or make me blab in my sleep, then we're safe."

Ockham's dark face grew darker. "Connected or not, anyone who targets one of us is a threat to the global peace and will be dealt with." He wore his favorite shirt, sleeveless and so intricately layered with doodles that hardly a thread of silver gray still showed between the black.

"Hey, it's not all bad." Sniper's smile sagged like a stroke victim's. "Proves what a good job I'm doing seducing the fans. Better than polling data."

Ockham had no smiles. "You have forty-seven minutes, Cato. Check everything: the box, skin, blood . . ."

"I know my job." From a braver man the words might have sounded sharp.

"Forty-seven minutes," Ockham repeated.

Sniper's eyes narrowed. "¿What's the rush?"

"I've called a house vote. We need to finish before Japan hits rush hour."

"¿A vote on what?"

"The possibility of disobeying orders."

I shall spare you the details of Cato's findings, or lack thereof; you know the skills of Sniper's captors. Instead we follow Ockham, who spends those forty-seven minutes pacing the bash'house's Spartan trophy hall as the rest of the bash' assembles. I call it Spartan, not just because their true vocation is too secret to add awards and trophies to their walls, but because they find no shame in its bare simplicity: what would a true Spartan care for trophies? As the fallen of Thermopylae care only that Sparta knows they died obedient, so, if Ockham had his way, his hall would stand bare but for one inscription: "We are O.S."

"A quorum of bash'members having been reached," Ockham began, "at 23:14 UT, 18:14 local time, I hereby commence this meeting of O.S."

Picture them convened around *Mukta,* her fresh-waxed hull reflecting the evening ocean, which is in turn reflected by the glass-ringed mountainside of Cielo de Pájaros. Five bash'mates sit on the ring of sofas: Lesley first, sketching invisible doodles across Sniper with her fingertips as it shelters in her lap. The hermaphrodite has rubber exercise balls in its hands, exertion freeing its muscles fiber by fiber, while its face tries to show nothing. Thisbe Saneer sits next to Sniper, her black hair loose, her landscape boots clicking as she hides her thoughts behind her tea. One set-set has crawled onto the couch for the occasion, Sidney or Eureka, though the two set-sets are hard to tell apart, faces and hair erased by so much apparatus; the other stays on duty in another room, watching the cars prepare for dinnertime to dawn on the Pacific rim. Last, fidgety by the window, sits one of the Typer twins, just one, for so fierce is the enmity between the pair that when one speaks up the second is not only obliged to contradict but to condemn all who do not follow suit, so, tired of war within the house, Ockham decreed that only one twin may attend such meetings. *And Cato? Where is our poor Mad Science Teacher?* He attends too, reader, by the lab door, huddled in the whiteness of his coat like a rabbit in its winter fluff. But, from where you sit, you cannot see him, for, gazing out through *Mukta'*s mirrored windshield, you can see the couches and ocean window, but not the side doors, nor Ockham, who stalks around the car, impatient as a wolf. Yes, reader, you are here too, inside *Mukta,* or rather you watch through the eyes of someone hidden within, our witness for this secret conference, spying from inside the ancient car.

"At 14:01 UT," Ockham began, "nine hours thirteen minutes ago, I met with our three Commanders. Prime Minister Perry said that the press investigations incited by the *Black Sakura* theft are now targeting the Cousins' Feedback Bureau, and they think this will expose an important secret, whose nature they did not specify, but which is likely to result in the dissolution of the Cousins. The Prime Minister called for a hit—"

"¿Now?" Sniper interrupted. "You must be joking."

"No joke. They want us to trigger the retirement of Bureau Chief Darcy Sok, to deflect the investigation away from whatever the CFB is hiding."

"¿And what's supposed to deflect the investigators that are after us? ¡A hit right now is insanity!"

Ockham's sigh agreed. "Perry stated that they had violated protocol and already made direct contact with Sidney and Eureka, to have them pick a target."

<that's true,> the set-set confirmed, <the p.m. called direct. we thought it was weird, but the world is weird lately, so weird things coming are normal.> Will you be more comfortable, reader, if we decide this is Eureka Weeksbooth, not Sidney who attends? Eureka you know, and the two are as interchangeable as two ants, whom only Mushi Mojave could differentiate as they trundle by. They are not the same, though, in the eyes of a tribunal. Eureka Weeksbooth was born to this bash', sent to set-set training for this purpose, and their parents baptized them in the transit computers as soon as their young set-set eyes had opened enough to gaze in proper wonder at their digital universe. Sidney Koons, on the other hand, was sent for set-set training by an enterprising bash' in expectation of a fat check when someone hired their living little nest egg, much as the bash'es that sold Madame the source genes which made Ganymede and Danaë are doubtless still living off the proceeds. Sidney had several fatter offers when hiring day came; they chose O.S.

"¿Weird how?" Lesley pressed, bending to help Sniper retrieve a dropped ball. "¿How is the world weird lately?"

<you wouldn't understand.>

"Try me. Perry's saying the Cousins are in danger. ¿Can you tell from what?"

<¿you see the sea?>

Lesley gazed out the window at the bird-speckled waves afire with sunset. "Yes."

<in my sea, the currents are getting violent enough to grind against each other. human earthquake.>

"¿How bad?" Lesley asked. "¿How bad compared to . . . what's the worst we've had, when that Anti-Mitsubishi Land Bill went up in 2449?"

<this is five times as salty.>

Fear rose on faces that rarely show it.

Not Ockham's. "Then O.S. will steer it back again. The question is precisely how. The President and Chief Director indicated that they had intended this leak to occur so the Cousins would be dissolved, but both agreed with the Prime Minister that if this occurs now, while Mitsubishi and Humanist popularity is low, it could cause a disastrous swing toward the Masons. They talked about a real population majority. The President asked my advice, and I advised against O.S. taking any action while Martin Guildbreaker's investigation is ongoing. The President—reluctantly—ordered that we prepare this hit, but said we are only to prepare, and to do nothing further without orders."

So sweet is Lesley's face that even her frown feels rosy. "¿Is that it?"

"Yes."

"¿So, the order may not come?" she suggested.

"It may not, but it may. Before it does, I want votes from all five of you on whether or not we should obey it if it does."

Five? Correct me if I err, Mycroft, but by my reckoning there are nine members of this bash', not five. There are, reader, but nine members is not nine votes. Cato gets no vote—his abject terror has led to so many consecutive abstentions that no one bothers to ask him anymore. Only the attending Typer votes, and the set-sets share one vote between them, since they think so identically, as two rats in a lab respond to the same shocks and treats, that a council convened to poll diverse thinking does not give two votes to one opinion. Lesley votes, Thisbe, Sniper, one twin and one set-set, a good odd number to prevent a draw. Ockham does not vote; Ockham decides.

"¿You think we shouldn't obey?" Lesley asked first.

Ockham steps forward into your view now, his back to *Mukta's* windshield, as if he dares not speak such words while facing the Saneer birthright. "I think we must weigh this carefully. Making a hit now would greatly increase the danger of exposure. I am the twelfth O.S. I do not intend to be the last."

"Before we weigh the sides, Ockham," Kat or Robin Typer interrupted, "one of us should say what we're all thinking. ¿Isn't this sort of thing exactly why we killed our ba'pas?"

Thisbe nodded emphatically.

"I mean," the twin continued, "it's us on the couches this time and no kids yet to eavesdrop, but this is the same scene as five years ago. We all agreed back then that our ba'pas deciding to choose for themselves when to use O.S. instead of taking Presidential orders was reason enough to . . . ensure they wouldn't be around to follow through on that decision."

"What they intended was treason," Ockham supplied at once, the word as heavy from him as from any Masonic Judge.

"Yeah," Kat or Robin nodded, "and this is too." One must say Kat *or* Robin since those present had no more way than you do, reader, to tell the twins apart.

You have not yet met the Typers, have you? Not surprising—if one is home on duty then the other has inevitably stormed out after their daily row. Their sameness goes beyond matching clothes and hair to matching body language, matching scars, and they switch trackers frequently, despite police complaints, for what can the police do when the twins have singed off those offending fingerprints that dared make them differentiable? Each twin watches through the other's tracker at all times, so one cannot test them by mentioning some earlier encounter; both know all. Once at their birthday party I saw one get drenched with punch, and in a wordless second both ripped off their differentiating shirts. What are the differences between these intentionally identical archenemies who refuse to move to separate bedrooms after thirty years of constant war? Kat Typer I know is fascinated by the pseudoscientific spiritualism of the Nineteenth Century: meters to quantify ghostly presences, meticulously catalogued séances, ESP research, but it is not in the supernatural where Kat finds wonder. It is the late Nineteenth-Century mind that fascinates, these scientists who were simultaneously so rigorous and so poetic, so critical and so credulous, so expert and so wrong. It was a unique mind-state, Kat thinks, fleeting, a psychological mayfly possible only in the moment when science was rising quickly in respect and use, but lagging behind in power. Medicine was not yet competent, workweeks not yet humane, so these minds, trying to be modern, still faced premodern trauma levels, and channeled that into the most sophisticated double-think we have ever achieved. That is Kat's current theory anyway. Robin Typer likes bikes. Each of these interests may extend to the other twin as well, but I have only once had a conversation with each twin when I was certain which it was, so that is all I know: Kat, spiritualist double-think; Robin, bikes.

<it's not the same,> Eureka objected.

Kat or Robin snorted. "¿No?"

<our ba'pas wanted the set-sets to start choosing targets for o.s. themselves instead of following the commanders-in-chief. this isn't choosing a target, it's refusing a hit for the defense of o.s. and the whole hive.>

"Yeah," the twin agreed, "but the thinking is the same. They wanted to take O.S. into their own hands. ¿Why? Because five years ago the three Commanders-in-Chief were all crappy leaders. Perry's Special Means Committee was so paranoid about P.M. Spain catching on that Perry hardly dared to come to meetings, Andō was having so much trouble with the Chinese blocs it took a month to get the Directorate to agree on anything, and Ganymede was flipping insane."

"*President* Ganymede," Ockham corrected firmly.

Kat or Robin frowned. "Regardless, O.S. wasn't getting any orders worth following; that's what our parents said. Here we are five years later. Andō is on the verge of losing control again, Casimir Perry's turned out to be a dickhead, and *President* Ganymede is still flipping insane. Fess up, Ockham. ¿Do you want to disobey this order because it's stupid or do you want to disobey it because *they're* stupid?"

"¡That's too much!" Lesley scolded. "Ockham wants to disobey the order because it puts the entire Hive in danger, nothing else. ¿Can we check this off as the point in the meeting when you gripe again about Sniper not being President and move on?"

"Hear, hear," the celebrity agreed.

"Wait."

Lesley and Sniper looked up, startled to have Ockham rein them in. "¿What?"

"I don't approve of Typer's tone, nor do I agree with their opinions of the three Commanders-in-Chief, particularly the President, whom I might add Typer has never met in person, while I have, and I deem them competent. Nevertheless, Typer's question is valid if rephrased. ¿Do the current leaders, competent or no, have the right to jeopardize, not just the generation that elected them, but all the past and future generations of Humanists?"

<and europe and sanling,> the set-set added, using the Chinese name for the Mitsubishi; perhaps this is Eureka after all.

Ockham took a slow breath. "O.S. was created to serve the Humanists. If subsequent Humanist leaders judged that the Hive was best served by lending this power to two allied Hives, that does not add those Hives to our mandate. I want you to think only of our main Hive as you vote on this. ¿Do our leaders have the right to order O.S. to put itself in danger of exposure? ¿Lesley?"

"No." She swallowed as she said it, bright eyes apologizing for voicing what her spouse would not want to hear. "In chess you're not allowed to move the king into check, even if it'll check the opponent, too. In a few days, maybe, if something makes Guildbreaker and Seneschal back off then sure, but not now, *and*"—she raised her voice as she saw Kat or Robin preparing to jump in—"I don't think it's a matter of disobeying the President. It doesn't sound to me like the President wants us to do this. It was Perry's idea. You said the President told us to prepare the hit but do nothing, probably because they didn't want to refuse outright with Perry there. We can send Cardie to meet with the President tomorrow and verify, but my money says the President doesn't want to give this order, not until the heat's off."

Ockham breathed deep, weighing all before he nodded. "¿Cardigan?"

"We serve the Humanist Membership," Sniper stated simply. "They elected Ganymede."

"Thank you. ¿[Sydney/Eureka]?"

The set-set stretched within their electrode mesh. <¿you're asking if we should take a small risk to prevent the cousins crashing down? yes, we should. of course we should. you haven't seen these numbers. the sky is falling. yes, we should catch it before it buries everyone alive.>

Again Ockham breathed deep. "That's two for following the order, one against. ¿Thisbe?"

The witch Thisbe gazed down into her teacup. (*Mycroft, must we have this fight again? No talk of witches.*) "We should make the hit. We're in no danger. Even if the investigation is looking at the cars, they can't track my personal technique, and I'm sure Cato has a dozen fresh methods lined up. Martin Guildbreaker and Dominic Seneschal have no better chance now than ever of catching a one-time Cato concoction. If switching methods every time let an amateur like Mycroft Canner kill seventeen people in a week with the whole world chasing them, I think the nine best-trained killers on Earth can manage one hit without being caught by an uptight Mason and a perverted Blacklaw."

"And Ἄναξ Jehovah," I would have added had I been there, "He Who sees what cannot be seen, and judges all by His unknowable Law. He too is watching." So I would have warned, but I was not there, reader, nor am I even listening with you in *Mukta*. I am at Madame's still, nestled in the unmerited heaven of Saladin's arms. It was irresponsible of me, I know, to let the world spin on without watching. I who owe you seventeen lifetimes of service have no excuse.

Eighteen lifetimes, Mycroft, don't forget; thy victims' and thine own.

"I'm right. ¿Aren't I? ¿Cato?" Thisbe prompted, scraping one boot across the other so the squeal of the surfaces penetrated even *Mukta*'s vents. "There's no way they'll catch you, you're too good at this."

His demonstrations of static electricity, famous at the science museum, do not make Cato's wiry hair stand more on end than Thisbe Saneer. "¿What? Um . . . yes. I mean, I've already picked out a method. It's normal. As untraceable as normal, I mean, which means it could be traced only if you know what I don't know . . . I mean, I don't know how it could be traced, but nothing's impossible. If somebody knows more than me maybe . . . except nobody . . . ¿is it hot in here?"

Thisbe tossed her head. "It was a yes or no question, Cato."

"Yes," he answered, quick as a kicked pup. "I mean, no. ¿What was the question again?"

"¿Do you think you can make the hit without danger of exposure?"

His answer came slowly, like a pulled tooth. "Gggggggyyyyyyes. Yes. It'll be ready to go in a few hours, as safe as it ever has been, assuming they don't have any resources we don't know—"

"Et cetera, et cetera . . ."

His black brows furrowed. "Don't 'et cetera' it away, Thisbe. This universe contains infinite possibilities, therefore it's possible that we'll be caught. It always is." Cato had more conviction in his voice here than you have ever heard from him, strength, one might almost call it, hope, for it was hope to Cato, that tiny thousandth of a percent of a chance, each time they made him do this, that it might be the last time.

"Yes, yes," Thisbe granted, "but no more probable now than ever, that's what I'm saying. Frankly, I'm not worried about this little puppet investigation."

"¿Puppet investigation?"

"If an independent party like Papadelias got involved," she continued, "it might be a threat, but Seneschal and Guildbreaker both work for J.E.D.D. Mason. We're in no danger there."

<¿no danger? ¿have you forgotten what j.e.d.d. mason did here two days ago? ¡they're a psycho cult leader!>

"I agree, Thiz," Sniper added. "President Ganymede warned me emphatically to have the bash' avoid contact with J.E.D.D. Mason at all costs. I've never heard the President sound genuinely scared before."

She sniffed. "That's as may be, but we have Andō Mitsubishi on our side, and if Andō asks J.E.D.D. Mason to call off the hounds they will."

<¿why should they?>

Thisbe looked ready to laugh. "You know why."

"It really is hot in here," Cato interrupted.

Ockham frowned. "I asked the Chief Director and the President directly about J.E.D.D. Mason."

Thisbe rolled her eyes. "You hardly have to ask. Andō's J.E.D.D. Mason's real father. Everybody knows." She looked to Sniper. "Your whole nation-strat knows."

Sniper always frowns, being lumped in with its Japanese mother's nation-strat, whose insignia it never chose to wear. "¿You believe that stupid rumor? ¡It's gibberish! A fantasy Mitsubishi made up to make themselves feel powerful, that J.E.D.D. Mason is really Andō's son, and they spy on the Emperor and then sit in on Directorate meetings as the unofficial 'Tenth Director,' giving secret advice to help battle the Masons. ¿We're supposed to believe the Emperor's being duped by something billions of people know?"

Thisbe's eyes have a special glitter when she knows something you don't. "I heard it from Andō's own mouth, that J.E.D.D. Mason is their child."

Sniper's child-wide eyes grew wider. "¿From Andō?"

"President Ganymede was there too."

"¿Where?" Ockham asked quickly.

"At a place."

"What place."

"A place I was, that's all."

"Thisbe . . ."

<¿that's the black hole right? ¿location 133-2720-0732?>

"¿Where?" Ockham does not like to repeat himself.

<the invisible nexus where every hive has ties. thiz went there checking up on . . . i forget why.>

"¿Thisbe?"

Thisbe snuggled deeper among the cushions, enjoying the shock that spread across her bash'mates' faces as one enjoys a winter fire spreading through dry logs. "I'm not allowed to repeat the details, I'm afraid."

The twelfth O.S. loomed toward his sister. "You will repeat them to me."

"No, I won't," she answered calmly. "The *President* told me not to. All I can say for now is that little Tribune Mason is like a living contract between the Masons and Mitsubishi not to screw each other over. With that in place—"

"Stop," Cato whimpered. "It's too hot in here." He is out of your sight behind *Mukta*'s steel ribs, but perhaps you can still imagine the mad science teacher sweating beneath the lab coat he never removes.

"¿Why did you meet with the President without informing me?"

"We just ran into each other, it was a complete surprise."

"¿What were you doing at this secret place?"

"Checking out what kind of threat J.E.D.D. Mason was. It is my job, Ockham, I do my job."

"Not without reporting it to me."

She took a deep breath. "Look, the name aside, the President made it very clear that—"

"Stop!" Cato half shouted.

All turned, as startled as you are to hear the coward Cato raise his voice.

"¿What's wrong?"

"It's hot in here."

What you cannot see from sitting inside *Mukta* is that, for some minutes, Cato's hands have been playing with the controls of some mad devices he wears strapped to his forearm under his sleeve. "It's hotter in here than the system thinks it should be," Cato repeated, "I'd say two point six degrees hotter than seven people should make it."

Perhaps about now, reader, you realize, as our witness does, that Ockham has backed out of sight behind you, stalking around the back of *Mukta*, maybe drawing some weapon from his belt while you cannot see. Panicked, you wonder: does he realize? Does he too see what a perfect hiding place this old museum piece provides? Perhaps in childhood he played hide-and-seek inside the ancient car with Lesley, or made a play-fort of it as he and one twin weathered a pillow-bombardment from Sniper and the other. If you had my pacemaker, eavesdropper, it would bleep alarm.

"¡A spy!" Ockham rips the hatch open faster than you can turn, and presses a weapon to your back, just at the neck's base where even a non-lethal dart could cripple. Before he even speaks, a prick injects you below the ear, and your vision wobbles as the muscles of your limbs lose two-thirds of their strength. "Hands where I can see them!" he orders in cold English. "No fast moves. Back down out of the car, now."

And who is the intruder whose eyes and ears you have shared while spying on this deadly conference?

"What? Carlyle!" Thisbe recognized her first, rising with a despairing condescension on her face. "Oh, you idiot!"

It was Carlyle indeed, shivering like a fevered child as the drug magnified the after-stress of Dominic's 'session,' a cocktail worse than vertigo. It has been four hours since we left Carlyle, switching off her tracker in Dominic's cell, and the flight from Paris to Cielo de Pájaros takes barely one.

Lesley sighed like a melting snowdrift. "Again? I really liked this one, too."

"Quiet, all of you!" Ockham ordered, digging his fingers into Carlyle's scarf as he walked her down *Mukta*'s extending stair. "You used your clearance as our sensayer to get inside?" he asked.

"Yes." Carlyle's voice cracked as she answered. "I had an appointment with Sniper but I showed up early. The computer let me in but no one was here and . . . I just wanted to look at *Mukta*, and then I was so tired, I fell asl—"

"How much did you hear?"

"Wait!" Lesley cried, suddenly shrill with hope. "It was all in Spanish! Cousins don't speak Spanish. They won't have understood a thing, right, Carlyle?"

"Exactly!" Carlyle agreed at once. "I have no idea what you were discussing, I was just—"

A kick from Ockham brought the prisoner to her knees. "That's one warning. You don't get two. Your bash' is half Humanist, you think I haven't looked you up? I run security here, I check every molecule that passes through my door, and you'd do well to remember that I have the right to exercise lethal force on intruders I judge to be resisting."

"But not to assassinate innocent people at the President's command," Carlyle shot back, braver, perhaps, than you imagined. "Or to drive your old sensayer to suicide when they found out."

Ockham's sigh did not weaken his grip on the prisoner. "You did understand."

"Crap," Kat or Robin groaned. "Now what do we do? We can't bump off two sensayers in a month, even an idiot would notice."

<¿thiz, you have those memory drugs, right?>

"¡Have you been snooping in my bedroom!"

<sorry.>

"Wait!" Carlyle cried. "It's better that I know! I'm not going to tell anyone. I can't tell anyone, I'm your sensayer! I've taken a vow to hold all parishioners' secrets secret, no matter what they are." The captive twisted in Ockham's grip. "I can help you. I've helped murderers before. You think they sent a novice in here after your last sensayer killed themself? You murdered your ba'pas, don't you want to talk about your guilt?"

Pride made Sniper draw its pistol too, though Lesley had to support its arm with hers. "We can do it now," Sniper suggested, "say we shot them before we realized who it was. It'll seem natural enough after the break-in two days ago."

Cold sweat broke out across the sensayer. "You don't need to kill me. I'm here to help. Look at Cato! How many times has Cato attempted suicide this year, a dozen? They need me! You all need me! Having a sensayer who knows the truth may be the best thing that could happen to this bash'."

Ockham held his prisoner fast. "Not if it leaks."

"You don't believe I can keep your secret?"

"I believe that you think you can, but—"

"Leave Carlyle to me." Thisbe rose, slowly, letting the softness of her house self fall away.

"That may not be the best way, Thiz—"

"Ockham!" She spoke it urgently, her black eyes blacker with warning. "I'm not going to kill them. We all want a sensayer we can trust, who knows our real work, so we can have proper sessions, and don't have to go through all this again. That's better for all of us, right?"

A quick debate of glances flashed among the bash'mates, Lesley wary, Sniper suspicious, Cato petrified, but a contaminant tainted their cautious instincts—a contaminant called hope.

Faces alone told Thisbe she had won. "Then leave Carlyle to me."

The others backed off as Thisbe stomped toward the prisoner, her Humanist boots pressing contours of grass and roads into the carpet, a continuation of the landscape whose labyrinth wound its way across her boots' false leather. She snatched Carlyle's scarf from her brother's hands as one snatches the collar of a wayward pup, and dragged the staggering sensayer down the stairway to the depths of her secluded room.

No Rest for the Virtuous

I WONDER SOMETIMES WHETHER THE FURIES WERE VENTING their wrath on Carlyle that night, since Providence had ordered them to leave me be. In my experience the Furies are a fairer portrait of Fate than any smiling angel. They are not good, not merciful. The sufferings they sow are not steps toward some incomprehensible Good; rather, in this kingdom where the virtuous must suffer, at least the Furies make the wicked suffer more. This I can believe in, Fates who spin and mark and cut our threads of life and hide no benevolence behind their shears; some other goal, perhaps, but not benevolence. I know enough of what we mortals mean by "Good" to know that I have never seen it. I do not deny the Plan—a world without a Plan would not have spared Apollo's killer only to grant me Apollo's legacy—I simply refuse to be party to the optimistic hubris which labels the Goal behind that Plan as "Good."

"Carlyle, Carlyle, Carlyle. What are we to do with you?"

Not even Thisbe's bedroom was private enough for her purposes tonight. She chose the flower trench, the grass at once alive with evening's chorus and dead in the absence of the child whose golden smile transformed night to day. Carlyle followed her close, not by choice, for Thisbe still held Carlyle's scarf like a mother lion carrying her cub.

"I'm sorry," Carlyle began. "I was here searching for clues about Bridger, I didn't mean . . ."

"Carlyle," Thisbe interrupted, softly, "it's time to stop lying."

Carlyle gulped air, even raised a pointing finger ready to justify herself, but her conviction melted into the tremors of a sob. "I'm sorry. You're right, I shouldn't lie, not to you. You've shared Bridger with me, the most important secret in the world, and I couldn't even tell you . . ."

"Couldn't tell me what?" Thisbe released the sensayer, facing her with arms crossed but eyebrows pleading. "What couldn't you tell me?"

"I was sent!" Carlyle broke down, her whole frame deflating as she confessed. "To protect you, mostly to protect you. After your last sensayer killed themself, the Conclave guessed there might be a secret reason, some kind of secret pressure on your bash'. I was sent to find out what."

"The Conclave guessed?" Thisbe repeated. "Collectively?"

"Yes. Well, no, not the whole Conclave."

"Julia Doria-Pamphili," Thisbe supplied.

"Julia sent me, I . . . that's what I do, I take on tricky cases where other sensayers have . . . fallen . . . before."

Thisbe sniffed. "A professional spy?"

"No! No, I didn't come to spy, I came to protect you!"

"By eavesdropping from inside *Mukta*?"

The Cousin winced. "I needed to know the truth. And you needed to tell me, all of you, Cato especially. Could I have gotten you to share the secret any other way?"

Thisbe's sigh could be no heavier. "I never expected to hear 'the ends justify the means' from a sensayer."

"Sometimes they do! Not often, but when the gain is so much bigger than the harm done, yes, they do. The harshest sensayer sessions are often the most productive, it's amazing, you should try it too." Carlyle tried a deep breath to steel herself, but it collapsed into a sob. "I learned that again today."

Thisbe leaned back against a patch of rain-smoothed trash wall. "From Julia Doria-Pamphili?"

"Yes! Well, no, not today, today for me was . . . but anyway, the first time was with Julia. It was incredible, painful, but back then I was on the verge of suicide and Julia saved me, transformed me. We can do that for Cato, too, for all of you, but you have to let us in first, and you weren't going to do that on your own."

"And you and Julia arranged this for us out of the kindness of your hearts?"

"It's our job. The Sensayers' Conclave cares for the well-being of the world. You're one of the most vital bash'es to protect. Imagine if Cato flipped out one day and decided to end it by making all the cars crash at once! The world can't take a disaster like that. The world needs your bash' to have a sensayer you can talk to!"

"Who? You or Julia?"

"Me, me, of course, at least . . ." Tears' beginnings awoke the diamond sparkle in Carlyle's blue eyes. "No, that's not true. It would have been me at first, but then I'd have referred you to Julia." She crouched down in the grass, picking seed heads as she avoided Thisbe's eyes. "I knew it when

Julia assigned me here, whenever they assigned me anywhere, they always said it was so I could help people, and I pretended I believed it, but we both knew. Julia sends me in to get people's trust, so I can refer you to have a session with Julia, and then . . ."

"Then what?" Thisbe's tone grew coaxing.

Carlyle's chest heaved, her still-weak stomach threatening again to purge itself as the truth flowed forth. "Julia will make you keep coming back to them. If Julia wants, they can make anyone keep coming back, but you have to consent to that first session first." She sank into the softness of the grass. "I knew what Julia was really doing. I pretended I believed them, but I knew. I have such an innocent demeanor, people who don't trust anyone are willing to trust me. That's why Julia took an interest in me, trained me to lure people in." She wiped her nose on the sleeve of her Cousin's wrap. "I know about the incident, a few years back, Julia tricked Cato into coming in for a session, but Cato ran. That was smart. Julia tried for years to get your old sensayer Esmerald Revere to refer one of you to them, but they wouldn't, so Julia leapt on the chance when they died. When you killed them."

Thisbe offered Carlyle a tissue from her pocket. "Ockham has pledged to execute any bash'member who talks to Julia Doria-Pamphili."

"What?"

She sat on the ground beside Carlyle, not quite close enough to share warmth. "Eureka and Sidney can smell what's rotten in the CFB; you think they couldn't smell what's rotten in the Conclave? Julia Doria-Pamphili, sensayer to the great and influential, commanding a network of parishioners with links to every center of power." She smiled. "Sounds a lot like Madame D'Arouet."

Carlyle had a good nose blow. "Yes, that's what it is, just like Madame, a secret empire, but worse, taking advantage of people's religion directly. Julia pitched it as defensive, that we're fighting back against corruption, building an empire to oppose an empire."

"To fight Madame?"

"Madame? No. No, we didn't know about Madame. Julia still doesn't. At least, I think they don't."

"Who are you fighting, then?"

"Danaë Mitsubishi."

"Danaë Mitsubishi?"

Carlyle sniffled. "Mm-hmm. Danaë and Andō Mitsubishi, you know they've adopted all these ba'kids? Ten of them."

"I heard something like that."

"What you didn't hear is that they're all set-sets."

"Set-sets?"

"Yeah. Some weird new kind, and now they're systematically infiltrating everywhere, even inside the CFB. I'm sure they're part of whatever Perry and your President are so worried about."

Thisbe stroked her lips. "Set-sets . . . Are you a Nurturist after all, then?"

"No. Well, maybe a little, uncomfortable with set-set training, not opposed. But that doesn't really matter. The Mitsubishi set-sets were an excuse, the excuse Julia used to justify it all, the excuse I used to justify it to myself. I pretended I was doing good. Protecting the world. Just being part of that, it made me feel . . ."

"Powerful?"

"Less powerless, I guess?" Carlyle wiped her eyes. "The world is full of so many bad things, sometimes it seems like good can't even make a dent unless we do something a little underhanded. Julia's network was supposed to let us keep the peace, fight back against Danaë and the set-set corruption, but it was all a lie, wasn't it? Dominic was right, from the beginning, not just every word Julia's said to me but every word I said to Julia, both ways it was all a lie."

Thisbe cocked an eyebrow. "Dominic?"

"I talked to Dominic today. Dominic's a perverted sadist living in a psycho whorehouse, but at least there we could talk about the truth. With Julia it was all lies, even this!" Carlyle tore the long scarf from her shoulders and hurled it away, the worn knit flopping in the grass. "Julia told me it used to belong to Fisher G. Gurai. Maybe I did believe it at first, but I've studied Gurai, all sensayers have. I've seen the photos, that scarf wasn't in them. It just made me feel important pretending it was true."

Thisbe stretched her shoulders. "So you've been luring in important people for Julia's network, but for how long? Years?"

Carlyle nodded, wiping tears from the salty tracks still fresh on her cheeks. "Years and years. I've been Julia's pimp." Carlyle's tense hands took her rage out on the grass. "Julia told me once about this special order of monks in the Middle Ages. They took in priests that had fallen, broken their vows, and been expelled from other orders. They helped them reform, retrained them, then sent them out on dangerous missions, not just dangerous to life and limb but full of temptations, to brothel centers, corrupt courts, bandit camps, places likely to make anybody fall. Because these priests had fallen once before, they knew how painful it was afterwards, so they would be less likely to do it again, that was the logic. And even if they did fall again, at least . . . at least they kept somebody pure from falling." She swallowed hard. "That story kept me going. After my fall, if I could do that, I thought, if I could be like that, stronger than the pure are, going to spiritually dangerous places to help people where no one else can, it would be worth it. But it was all a lie. There was no order of fallen monks. Julia made it up. I knew. Whenever I asked about dates or documents they changed the subject. I knew it was a lie, I just wanted to believe." Her breaths grew short. "Maybe Dominic's right, maybe that's all I ever did before Bridger, just want to believe in things, in doing good, in God, but I never believed deep down, and now that I have proof I can't handle it."

Thisbe drew a pocketknife from inside her jacket and started picking at the dirt beneath her nails. "You were so upset two days ago at how Madame is pulling strings, when all this time you were helping Julia do exactly the same thing."

"I know!" Carlyle cried. "I'm a hypocrite! Pimping for Julia just like that Chevalier for Madame. No, not like the Chevalier, like Heloïse, playing innocent, half believing it myself, while I let Julia twist my beliefs to make me into the puppet they wanted me to be. The puppet I wanted to be!" She hiccupped, too weak to speak and cry at once. "Julia, Danaë . . . I've been a pawn in their stupid power game because that's what I wanted to be. To feel like a savior, and avoid having to think about my choices."

Thisbe didn't meet Carlyle's eyes, didn't try to, just watched Carlyle's hands as they shook faster and faster. "All these years you've been pretending to help people find their religions, when really you've been helping to turn them into what Julia wanted."

"It's true!" Carlyle cried. "It's all true! I shouldn't be trusted with your bash's religious guidance, or your secrets, or with Bridger. I shouldn't be trusted with anything!"

"How many people?" Thisbe asked.

"What?"

"How many parishioners have you led to Julia? How many people have you tricked into becoming pawns? Dozens?" she prompted. "Hundreds?"

"Around . . . a hundred." Carlyle was shaking too hard now to fumble with the grass.

Thisbe frowned sympathy. "And Julia's been twisting your beliefs to fit their scheme for so long, are you sure you even had any beliefs of your own to begin with?"

"No." Carlyle hugged herself. "No, I had nothing, and Julia made me into this! Oh, God! What am I? What have I been doing all these years, in Your Name?"

Reflections of the streetlights on the bridge above played across Thisbe's knife blade. "You were going to bring Bridger to Julia, weren't you?"

"Oh, God! You're right! I would have! I hadn't decided on it but it had already crossed my mind. It was instinct! I would have handed Bridger to Julia, handed God to Julia! And what have I done instead? Now I've agreed to hand Bridger to Dominic!"

Thisbe scowled. "To Dominic?"

"Julia's given me to Dominic! I didn't see it before. Julia's done using me as a pawn so I got traded to Dominic. They know I have the perfect belief system to make me jump when anyone who knows how to push my buttons says jump. Julia must have briefed Dominic, told them what to say to make me do what they wanted. I was too blind to see it! Mycroft was right, I shouldn't have access to Bridger. Bridger should be spirited as far as possible from me. I should never see them again!"

Thisbe fingered the knife's black handle. "That's not enough."

The Cousin's eyes grew wide. "What do you mean?"

"It doesn't matter whether you separate yourself from Bridger or not. You'll still be serving Julia's plans elsewhere. You can't just undo years of being trained to be a pawn. They're going to keep using you, even if you try to break off on your own. So long as you continue being a sensayer you're going be making people into what Julia's taught you to make them, like you tried to do with us. And if you stop being a sensayer—"

"Stop being a sensayer!"

Thisbe's nose wrinkled at the discourtesy of interruption. "Even if you stop, you won't be able to keep yourself from talking to people about religion. You won't be able to stop doing what Julia's made you so good at doing." She smirked. "Cato would say it's like a retrovirus. The virus pumps its RNA into a cell and the cell keeps pumping out more virus every chance it has, until it dies. It doesn't even know it's doing it."

Sobs came too fast for Carlyle to speak.

"There really is no escape for you, is there?" Thisbe pressed. "The network you helped Julia create is everywhere now, and Madame, and Danaë, and Dominic are everywhere. Anywhere you go they can find you, send an agent, and teach them what to say to get you back. You're just going to keep luring in more and more victims. You can't stop it."

"I can stop it."

"You can't. It's not like you can run when the poison is inside you."

"I can stop it."

"How?"

"Like this!" Carlyle snatched the knife from Thisbe's hands, and leapt to her feet.

"Carlyle—"

"Don't try to stop me! It's the only way to protect you. To protect Bridger. To protect everyone!" Carlyle lifted the knife toward her own throat. "You're right! As long as I live I'll draw everyone around me toward Julia. It has to end! God won't forgive me. God shouldn't forgive me, but at least this way it'll be over. At least this way God knows I'm doing what's best for everyone." Tears swelled to a river on her cheeks, but a smile broke through them. "I'm sorry, Thisbe. I liked getting to know you, and really did intend to help you, all of you. It's best this way. Bridger will be safe, your bash', your secret will be safe, everyone. Even me."

Carlyle closed her eyes and thrust at her throat with the full force of both trembling hands. Smooth as a diving fish, the edgeless trick blade collapsed into the hollow handle with a pathetic squeak.

Slowly, softly, a laugh rose from the depths of Thisbe, swelling like a downpour as a vicious smile bloomed across her cheeks.

"Thisbe, what?" Carlyle stared uncomprehending, testing the knife again and watching the fake blade slide in and out of the trick hilt.

Thisbe raised her hands, applauding clumsily as the fervor of her laughter made her arms weak. "Beautiful performance! I should have let you squirm longer, shouldn't I? Pleaded with you not to do it. I could have gotten at least two more farewell declarations out of you."

Carlyle's jaw quivered. "I don't understand."

"Drop it."

Thisbe snapped her fingers, and the knife tumbled from Carlyle's hands, her whole frame weakening as despair's soft trembling turned to crippling terror.

"Thisbe, what . . . what's happening?"

Thisbe rose to her feet, her laughter subsiding into a darker smile. "You're starting to realize, aren't you?"

Trembling took the sensayer's legs. She staggered, collapsed into the grass. "What have you done to me?"

Thisbe chuckled. "I'm a witch."

"What?"

What?

"Did you imagine Bridger was the only one with powers? The child plays with toys. I'm a grown-up, I play with grown-ups."

"A witch?"

"You needed punishment. You can't just waltz into my house, or meet with enemies like Dominic, without permission." Thisbe prowled around Carlyle, the cat circling a sparrow too wounded to flee. "Let's get things clear here, Carlyle: this house is my domain. I may bring in strays like you, and Esmerald Revere, and Mycroft Canner, but that doesn't make you any more important than those plastic toy soldiers. You jump when I say jump, you dance when I want you to dance, and you'll bite your own tongue out and choke to death any instant I choose."

Carlyle tried to rise, but tremors pinned her, helpless. "A witch?"

Mycroft, is this really happening?

"I've been watching you." Thisbe raised two fingers to her forehead as if to point out a third eye hidden beneath the skin. "Ever since you stumbled through my door I've been watching. You fool, you're not Julia's pawn or Dominic's, you're my pawn, and you're going to stay my pawn, and stay alive, precisely as long as I want to keep you that way."

Thisbe's black eyes were too harsh for Carlyle to meet. The sensayer looked at the ground, at the toy knife lying in the grass before her. "You made me do that just now? You made me try to kill myself!"

The witch shrugged, basking in the web of hair around her shoulders, blacker than night's black. "I was bored. You think I want to listen to your whiny theolo-gibberish? Besides, you needed to learn the lesson. Forget Julia and Dominic: you're my puppet, mine alone. My hexes are worked into your flesh too deep for anyone to break."

Mycroft, what is happening?

I'm sorry, reader. I failed to prepare you for this, just as I failed shivering Carlyle. I tried my useless best, but with the sensayer my warnings were too subtle, and with you, I think, too blunt to be believed. She is a witch. I told you from the start. I still can't make it sound sane. It's fear that makes me fail, fear of Thisbe, her spells that can cripple me as fast as Tully's Canner Beat, while my eclectic skills provide no armor against her craft. I fear her, rare for me. It isn't that I'm otherwise fearless—I fear a thousand things: Tully's scheming, MASON's left hand, Bridger—but the witch is altogether different. She should not be part of this, that's what it is. She is an unexpected threat, outside the palette of the possible, as when a fortress city, whose death-stained towers have stopped a hundred battle lines, is brought low by a pestilence within. Why would this stage of Gods and Emperors suddenly contain, of all backwards absurdities, a witch? I fear, abjectly, and will fear still, even if you tell me limping science can explain away her spellcraft. When Utopians forge Earth's rare metals into dragon fleets that feed on sunlight as they bear their masters across the sky-white surface of the Moon, they are wizards, even if they use science to deny it. Just so, when a black-hearted spinster lures a stray priest to her bedchamber to rape her soul and laugh, she is a witch.

"I'll let you continue as our sensayer," Thisbe began, running her fingers through the length of her black hair. "You're right, it'll be a convenience being able to talk about our work. Maybe you can even help fix poor Cato. You'll help us, help them, guide them all the way I think they should be guided, and if you start taking any of them in a direction I don't like I'll take over your body and talk through you like a meat puppet."

Carlyle started to speak, but Thisbe waved two fingers, and the words froze dead.

"This is what you need, Carlyle," the witch continued. "Don't you see? You want to be free of Julia, but you never can be, you'll never undo years of Julia's worming into you, making you think what they want. If you know the truth about us, or about Bridger, Julia and Dominic will make you tell them someday. Except not now. Now you know I'm watching. You know I can snap my fingers, speak the magic words, and . . . what would be the best threat? Instant death is boring, a stroke maybe? Pain and paralysis? Insanity can be fun, leaving you a nice lunatic babbling about the end of the world? Is that scary enough? Yes, that's the right level of twitching. You see? And that terror will keep you from blabbing. You have a check now, a backup plan. The moment you get close to letting something slip you'll remember this . . ." She loomed. "You'll remember this to your dying day. And that memory will keep you quiet." She took a satisfied breath. "I'll be your gag. That's what you really need, a gag, to make you free of Julia, to keep us all safe. And if you ever do transgress." She clapped her hands, and the body at her feet convulsed with shock. "I'll end it. And fear of that will keep you from doing what you don't want to do. That way we can all have everything we need: my bash' can have a good sensayer, Bridger too, and you can finally be free of Julia. How does that sound?" A flick of her fingers freed Carlyle's voice.

"D-d-d-does Mycroft know?"

"Know I'm a witch?" Thisbe savored another chuckle. "Mycroft's a clever one. They figure it out about once a week on average, but I don't let them remember. It's much more fun to let them guess, to see what gives me away each time. Good practice for not getting caught by others. You, though, I think it's best for everyone if I let you remember this time."

"Th-is time?"

The witch's eyes sparkled with secrets. "Sensayers are used to fearing God, so you know the right way to fear me, don't you?"

Carlyle tried to swallow. "B-uh . . . bash'ma-ates know?"

"They know not to mess with me." She played with her own footprints as she circled, her boots stamping patterns into the grass. "I haven't let most of them taste my full powers, though, it would cause unnecessary anxiety." She grinned. "You see now why this little investigation is no threat to me doing a hit. But the others still worry, so considerate of them."

Thisbe let Carlyle's flesh relax at last, and the Cousin inchwormed side-ways, trying to watch as Thisbe circled him. "Whaa—now?" she gasped out.

"What now?" Thisbe cocked her head. "Now you're going to say, 'Thank you, Thisbe.' And I'm going to go back and tell my anxious bash'mates that we have a trustworthy new sensayer, and no one has to worry about you blabbing."

Carlyle's body rocked, her lips attempting words. "Th . . . th-th—th."

Thisbe sighed. "Was I too rough? You're a frail thing, aren't you? Oh, well." She leaned down, close enough to kiss. "Run away, little sensayer. Run home and talk to no one. I'll be watching, my creatures too, my imps and sprites—I conjure darker things than plastic soldiers. I'll be watching you, in the cars, in your bash'house, in your bedroom with all the pretty birds painted on the ceiling. It's a good design—maybe I should make you paint my bedroom too?" She slapped Carlyle gently on the back. "Rest up tonight, but I expect you here promptly tomorrow morning. Ockham will want to debrief you when you've recovered, plus Sniper needs their session, and I'll see if I can corner Cato for you."

Frozen Carlyle could only twitch and watch as the witch retreated slowly, the grass with its army of hidden crawling things caressing her gleaming boots. Thisbe paused at the door to let herself taste Carlyle's fear-sweat a moment longer, sweet as gingerbread.

"Thiz!" Sniper cried from within the instant she opened the door. "Tell me everything you know about J.E.D.D. Mason!"

Her voice was ice. "Don't come into my room without permission, Cardigan."

"Sorry. Did it go well?"

"Swimmingly." Thisbe moved to block Sniper's view of the collapsed Cousin, but Carlyle could still hear their words across the stillness of the grass. "Carlyle's comfortable with everything, and I'm sure we can trust them now."

The living doll held the door for her. "Great. Should I get Ockham?"

"No, Carlyle's tired tonight. I've told them to come in the morning. Why are you here, Cardie?"

"Tell me everything you know about J.E.D.D. Mason. Ockham was telling me more, things the President said, but it doesn't add up. Thiz, doesn't it bother you that Andō's supposed child doesn't look half-Japanese? A bit of something East Asian in the mix maybe, but not what you'd expect of Andō's child."

The door closed behind the ba'sibs, leaving Carlyle slumped like a carcass abandoned when the hunt has too much prey to carry home. The shock was too absolute, too saturated to be confined by names like terror or despair. She did not try to rise, but flopped onto her back as trembling gave way again to tears. Just tears. It doesn't matter how long she lay there, ten minutes, an hour, two; feelings that deep dissolve the illusion that time can be measured.

"Ruff! Wuff wuff! Auuuuuw Auuuu!" Hearty as home's lights through a storm, Boo's bark rang through the flower trench. The blue dog trundled over to the sensayer, sniffing and wagging, its curious nose trailing wet warmth across Carlyle's trembling hands.

Carlyle stirred. "Boo? What are you doing here?"

"Rrrruf! Ruf!" Boo licked Carlyle's face, and the sensayer could not help but stroke its tender ears.

"Here, drink this milk, you'll feel better."

It was Mommadoll, riding on Boo's back, her dress of checked red gingham studded with seeds and burrs. She held a thermos, giant as a barrel between her four-inch arms, while a sack strapped across her back leaked the scent of fresh-baked cookies.

"How did you—" Carlyle began.

"Teleportation. Drink your milk, dear."

"Where—"

"Milk first!" Mommadoll ordered, shoving the thermos into Carlyle's hands. "No arguments. And as for you, Stander-Y, I have a hot pot pie for you, and you're eating all the vegetables this time or else you're not getting any cobbler afterward. Well? Come out!"

After a few breaths' pause, a tiny figure in sand brown crawled out from the shadow of the stairs up to the walkway above. "Mommadoll, a secret spy mission means no one is supposed to know I'm here spying."

"Oh, fiddlesticks," she countered, gold curls bouncing. "The Major left me in charge while they're on the rescue mission, and I say you get a hot dinner." She produced a tiny pie. "It's not right you getting stuck by yourself all night. The least the Major could do is see you get a decent meal."

Carlyle stared at the thermos in his hands, despair's tears turning to relief's. "You were spying on me?"

"No, we're spying on Thisbe." The tiny soldier's eyes glowed as Mommadoll lowered the pie into his arms. "And the bash'house. We've moved Bridger to safety, but best to keep an eye out here. There could still be evidence, and Dominic could get to Thisbe."

Carlyle gulped the milk, and gasped as Mommadoll opened her sack to display the chocolate chip treasures within. "I can't believe you brought me milk and cookies."

"You need it after facing one of Thisbe's bullying moods." Mommadoll offered a napkin from the stash in her apron pocket.

Carlyle sprayed crumbs. "Did you know?"

Stander-Y snorted. "Know what? That Thisbe's a scary-ass psychopath? Of course."

"Language!" Mommadoll chided.

"Sorry, ma'am. It's true, though. Thisbe's scarier than Mycroft. Reliable in her way, but scary."

Carlyle paused, facing the ageless question of whether to dip her cookies or keep her milk crumb-free. "You knew Thisbe's a witch?"

"That's nonsense!" Mommadoll smiled the thought away with rosy cheeks. "Thisbe just says that to play with people. Thisbe's upset. I'm sure that's the only reason for this bullying tantrum just now. It's been a trying time for poor Thisbe, police stomping around the house. I'll bring more cookies later."

Carlyle frowned. "You saw what Thisbe almost made me do."

Stander-Y took a long breath. "I don't know if Thisbe's really a witch, but I do know she can do . . . something. Witchcraft would explain a lot, actually. Just now, where I was standing, it felt like I could feel all the same things you did, sad, then really sad and ashamed, then suddenly terrified when Thisbe snapped her fingers the first time, then weakness in my legs, and when she shushed you I choked too, like in a dream when you can't speak. Maybe Thisbe and Bridger have powers from the same source, something about this place."

Carlyle gazed into her milk. "The place wouldn't explain J.E.D.D. Mason. . . ."

Stander-Y shook his head. "I think you should stay away from J.E.D.D. Mason. Mycroft said they'd die before they let you close to them, and Mycroft Canner is a man who's thought a lot about their death and how best to use it."

Carlyle's frown deepened as she took a long breath, two. "I've been wondering, does Bridger . . ."

"Does Bridger what?"

The sensayer closed her eyes, as if afraid to face the question and the world at once. "Does Bridger have a belly button?"

"Good question, if a little out of nowhere." The soldier smiled. "No, he doesn't. First real belly button Bridger ever saw was Mycroft's, and the kid thought it was another bullet scar."

A cleansing tremor shook Carlyle's frame: laughter. "That's proof then."

"That Bridger had no parents?"

"Yes," Carlyle answered, though her eyes dodged the others'. "No parents."

"Yep, the kid sprang from nowhere," the soldier confirmed, "the belly button and the thumbs prove it."

"Thumbs?"

"You didn't notice?" Stander-Y fished through his pie for chicken bits among the vegetables. "Bridger has little red welts on his thumb tips, like scarred-over acne. Mycroft scanned them. When an infant sucks its thumb, wouldn't you call it a substitute for a nipple? A toy nipple, in other words?"

"Then . . . Bridger nursed themself?"

The soldier nodded. "Take that, conservation of matter and energy." He smiled again. "You must be feeling better, thinking about metaphysics again?"

"Yes. Yes, I'm feeling much better. Thank you." Carlyle gave panting Boo another scritch. "You rescued me."

"You needed it."

"Agreed," Mommadoll announced. "And now, Carlyle, you are going home to get some rest. Everything will be better after a good night's sleep."

Carlyle breathed deep. "Thisbe's not really watching constantly, are they? They were surprised when I said I'd talked to Dominic. They didn't realize I was hiding in *Mukta* until Cato Weeksbooth noticed. Even the details . . . there are photos in my profile where I'm in a bedroom painted with birds, but that's a bash'mate's bedroom, not mine. It was a lie. Thisbe's not watching. They want me to think they're watching."

The soldier nodded approval. "You're quick."

Carlyle sniffed. "Julia trained me well." She closed her eyes for a pensive second. "You need to go. Both of you, Boo too. Now."

"Why?"

"I'm finally strong enough to make an important call."

Foster: "Hello? This is Special Informant Carlyle Foster, calling for the Commissioner General. It's an emergency."

Desk: "Patching you through."

Papadelias: "Foster! You finally worked up the courage to testify against good old Julia Doria-Pompous-Head? Now's a great time!"

Foster: "It's not about Julia. It's about the Saneer-Weeksbooth bash'."

Papadelias: "Ooh . . . you have my full attention now. What's up?"

Foster: "I think Thisbe Saneer just tried to kill me."

Papadelias: "Great! How? When? Where? Why?"

Foster: "I don't know, in the trench in their backyard, about . . . a little while ago. We were just talking, and Thisbe did something, and suddenly I tried to kill myself. It was so fast, I don't know how it happened but I'm sure Thisbe did something, they said they did."

Papadelias: "Suicide on cue, that's perfect! Stay there! Stay exactly where you are. Don't move! Don't touch anything! Don't move anything! Don't alter the chemical composition of anything! I'll have forensics there in ten minutes, just hold still!"

Foster: "I will. I'm ready."

The Visitation

IT NEVER SEEMS TO STOP, THIS LONG NIGHT OF THE TWENTY-seventh. Here in Paris it has already been March twenty-eighth for some hours, but no mathematician's prescription will ever force the mind to call those stifling hours of black before the dawn 'tomorrow.' I did not want that night to end. With Saladin around me, the universe outside our cage might have melted away with me uncaring. Only the coat around us reminded me of the present, Griffincloth heavy like womb-water, but on every second or third tossing or turning my elbow would nudge a weapon nested in the coat and remind me that, at least once upon a time, there were members of the human race beside we two.

"Mycroft? Mycroft?" This part was not a dream, I think, though as I dozed in the ambrosia of Saladin's arms, it seemed one. "I've come to get you."

"Leave me."

"Your friend looks hurt."

I stroked the bandages; Saladin has always been the deeper sleeper. "I don't know what I was hoping for. It was inevitable Saladin would get caught up in this someday, I just thought maybe they'd get killed first, fighting a monster somewhere. That would've been a good end. There are monsters in the world these days, more than just the two of us." I raised my eyes now, seeking the visitor's shadow in the shimmering dim that darkness makes of Madame's gilded halls. "You shouldn't be here."

"And you should?"

"Yes, I should."

"Why?"

"Because there are important people here who need the things that I can do, and it's my fault that I'm the only one left who can do them."

The voice drifted closer, confident, and a gust of dry air moved with him, like birds' wings or old breath. "Then why shouldn't I be here too?"

"I wish you could be." Our whispers could not wake Saladin, but I feared my breath might, silent sobs against his side. "I wish you could have been here all this time, but you're too dangerous. The things you would have made us do. You were going to destroy the world."

A pause. "I don't want to destroy the world, I want to help it."

"No, you don't. You've never been looking at this world, only at the future you see stretching on and on." I pulled the coat tight over me, afraid to see his blue eyes peering down. "I remember when we were in the garden with Geneva. You asked if we would destroy a better world to save this one. I would. I did, I destroyed the world that had you in it. But I always knew, for you it was the opposite. You would destroy this world to save a better one. You tried to."

"Mycroft, I don't . . ."

"Caesar's sworn an oath to protect the three billion Masons who are living now, not in the future, now. If I hadn't killed you, Caesar would have had to do it. Wouldn't that be worse? Being the one that killed you hurts more than just losing you, a thousand times more. It's better for the world that I'm the one who has to live with that, not Cornel MASON."

"Killed me?"

"You would have died anyway." Tears trickled far enough to touch my lips. "You knew that. You would have been a front line soldier. The odds of you living even through the first few weeks of the war were next to zero. At least this way we had our battle, you and Seine against the two of us, no innocents, no civilians, the best kind of battle, both sides knowing exactly what we were fighting for. The only battle of your war. You lost."

The stranger reached through the bars and lifted aside the edge of the coat to bare my eyes. "Mycroft, I'm not Apollo Mojave. It's me." He let the cloak of invisibility around him fall back, just enough to show his blue striped child's wrap, and Excalibur's plastic scabbard hanging at his side. "The Major said you wouldn't really be locked in a cage."

"Bridger." New tears followed the old tracks down my cheeks. "I asked to be locked in here."

"Why?"

I scanned the room for spies, shadows within the shimmer of dim gold where hounds might lurk. "Is the Major with you?" I asked.

He shook his head. "The Major's watching, but I came alone. I'm here to rescue you. Will you come with me?"

I shuddered as I answered. "Do you need me?"

His smile shed more warmth than fire could. "I always need you, Mycroft."

"But do you need me right now? Are you hurt? Is there trouble? Something urgent?"

"No." His frown, though sweet, felt like a criticism. "The only problem is that you're gone. Come home."

The child's smile went from warm to wriggling as the winged sandals tickled his ankles, flapping at each other in their boredom. I gulped a fast sigh. I really had believed it was Apollo, that he had come in Hermes's place to offer me death's rest. No other has the right to absolve me of my labors, yet he never would, not he who wept with rage whenever illness threatened to steal an hour from him, and preached that one should never snuff a candle which can still burn. Even after the battle, given the choice between cyanide's painless end and one last hour facing the tortures Saladin and I had prepared, he chose life. Sane men may call him a fool, but in that hour we three—Apollo dying, I expecting soon to follow, and Saladin long dead—explored realms of philosophy which, if they were not virgin, at least no traveler had ever yet returned to share their riches with the living. Apollo will leave me here to eke out every last second this living carcass can endure, just as he did himself.

"Come on," the child coaxed, "it's easy." He grasped the iron bars, pliant as straw in hands where Thor's magic strength surged. "We can teleport away, your friend too, home safe."

"No." I grabbed his wrists to stop him. "I have work to do here, important work. I'll come soon, soon as I can, I promise. Now please, go, now! Someone might find you."

Bridger frowned. "I know it'd be selfishness if any other kid said this, but it's true for me: I'm the most important thing in the world. No matter what you're doing here, it can't possibly be as important as making sure I do whatever it is I'm here to do." The softness of his face grew softer. "I know you believe in Providence, Mycroft. You think there's a reason we met, and you think there's a reason for my powers, they didn't just appear by random chance. I'm supposed to do something and you're supposed to help me find out what."

My throat grew tight. "You're not going to leave until we hash this out, are you?"

"No," he answered flatly, "I'm not, and I know how dangerous it is here and I don't care. I'm leaving with you, or with a good reason you can't come, or not at all."

I reached out through the bars and patted the carpet, motioning him to sit close so he could almost lean against me through the cage wall. "You're right. You're right you're that important, Bridger. It's good that you know that. I think the Major's right, I think you can save everyone, everyone who's alive now in the world and maybe even everyone who's ever died, that's why you're here."

"I want to." His fists clenched with the force of his conviction; I remember days when my fists clenched like that. "I want to help everyone," he said, "save everyone, but I have to be careful, you and the Major taught me that. Everything I do I have to think and plan. If Mommadoll had my powers they'd fix all the world's booboos and have no plan for how to save the economy from chaos when suddenly nobody dies anymore. It would wreck the world. This!" He pulled a vial from his pocket, a glowing, mottled orange like cold lava or living gold. "I made this resurrection potion for Pointer, but I can make more, a hundred more, a hundred billion more, but what will happen if I do?" Small fingers trembled as he held the tube between us, close enough for me to snatch—such trust. He managed half a smile. "Thanks to that sensayer Carlyle I'm not worried anymore about dragging people back from heaven or whatever. I agree with Carlyle, if there's a God out there running an afterlife They wouldn't let me do it if They didn't want me to. I'm worried about what happens here." He hiccupped. "If I start resurrecting dead people, how will we adjust? What will happen to the Hives? To society? Where will the extra people live? Ten billion people is as much as Earth can handle and Mars isn't ready yet. Should I make another Earth for the extra people to live on? Is one enough? Should I make six more Earths? Who will own them? Who will run them? Should I make teleporters to take us from Earth to Earth? Who will run those?" His face grew red as he recited his questions, an old list but longer this time than when last I had heard it, a few more details worked out, transit and property, the kind of things we grown-ups learn to think about. "And what if I don't just bring back people who died recently, what if I bring back people from ages ago, from the Middle Ages, all ages, how will they adjust? How will we adjust to them? How will we even talk to them? Should I make them all speak modern English? Will they even be the same people they were if I change them like that? I don't know!"

"Neither do I." I tried to sound soothing.

"I—hic—I know you don't, but—hic—at least you can help me think about it." This was a new phase, I thought, the child learning to suppress sobs into hiccups, almost more mature. "A President—hic—can cause famine and chaos just by making the wrong economic policy, so how—hic—can we possibly protect the world from the changes I want to make?"

He leaned his brow against the bars, eyes closed, as if the pressure against his temples let him feel like he was hiding. "I need you, Mycroft. You know more about the way the world runs than any ten people. You know about politics, and history, and economics, and people, everything."

"I don't know everything."

"I know you don't—hic—but you know as much of everything as anybody can, especially about power." He glanced sidelong into the gilded dark of the salon. "You say there are important people in this house who you're working with, who need you, well, I need them. I need you to get them on my side. I need the Emperor's power, the Utopians' skills. I need Chair Kosala to organize hospitals and aid workers to distribute the stuff that I create. I need Felix Faust to pick the right people to put in charge of things. I need the Censor to track the impact I'm having, and predict disasters. I need the Anonymous to convince everyone to cooperate. I need the Humanists to get excited about it as a big achievement and work for it, and the Europeans and the Mitsubishi to warn me when what I'm doing sounds like something that went hideously wrong when their nations tried it in the past. I need all that, but I wouldn't know I need all that if I hadn't had you to teach me about it." His gaze seized mine. "I need you, Mycroft. No one could possibly need you as much as I do, and I think you need me too, more than anyone." He stroked the thick hem of Apollo's coat, his fingertips disappearing as they slipped beneath the Griffincloth. "Providence gave us to each other."

I tried to keep my sobs as quiet as I could. "Yes. Yes, it did. There is a reason it was me of all people who stumbled on you all those years ago, and there's a reason you grew up outside Thisbe's bash's house and no other. But there's a bigger question besides 'Why me?' and 'Why there?' There's 'Why now?' Why did this miracle come now?" I caught his hand, making my lecture gentler with a squeeze. "There must be a reason you were born in the year twenty-four forty, not thousands of years ago when people first started praying for immortality, and not a thousand years from now when we might have the technology and resources to support all the dead people you can resurrect. I've been working on that question, why now, ever since I met you. I think the answer is a person called Jehovah Epicurus Donatien D'Arouet Mason."

"Your Tocqueville," Bridger supplied, remembering my code phrase.

"Yes, my Tocqueville." I caught myself looking at his hands, but a child needs eye contact, reassurance. I tried my best to give it. "There's a crisis happening, Bridger. I don't fully understand it yet myself, but it is happening.

Apollo and the Mardi bash' saw fragments of it years ago, and I silenced them because back then I still thought it could be averted. I was wrong. It's happening. The Censor and Anonymous have realized, and Felix Faust and Papadelias aren't far behind. I'm sure Madame is at the heart of it, and Caesar . . ." I paused. "Caesar is finally running out of ways to pretend they don't see."

"You mean war, don't you?" Bridger's stubby fingers clutched the lump of the book under his wrap. "I've read Apollo's notes. It's been three hundred years since anyone fought anyone and we don't know what technology can do now. For all we know the first strike might accidentally wipe out the world. I can stop that." He tried to smile for me. "I thought hard about it, but I think it's obvious God put me here to stop that."

I shook my head. "That wouldn't take a miracle. If you're God you can make the detonator accidentally fail, or make a mutation make us all immune to whatever toxin we concoct, or just make us not have this war." I poked at Bridger's tummy through the bars, making him smile. "Your Creator could have given you a belly button, Bridger, but They didn't. They wanted you to be proof of Their existence. I think Jehovah Mason is a big part of the reason why."

He shook his head, brows tight. "I can't believe that."

"You don't know Him."

"I don't need to!" he hissed, almost too confident to whisper. "I don't believe God would make a miracle for just one person. It's too unfair. Everybody in the world for thousands and thousands of years has wanted to know the truth about God and the afterlife. The more books you give me the more it seems like nobody in history ever really wanted anything else. If there is a God, I don't think They'd be so unfair as to show Themself for one person after ignoring everybody else."

Pride surged in me. The child wasn't just parroting his teachers' conclusions, he was making his own. "I didn't say I thought you were here to give Him proof. I think you're here because He's here."

His young brows narrowed almost enough to wrinkle. "Why? What makes Jehovah Mason so important? No half answers," he warned. "They have influence over every Hive Leader, I know that, the Major looked up their bio, but that just tells me what everybody knows. I want to know what you know."

"I can't tell you."

He batted at the bars, forgetting for a moment his god-strength, which dented them like butter. "Can't or won't?"

I met frankness with frankness. "Won't. You need to form your own conclusions. I met Jehovah Mason too young. I was seventeen and vulnerable, and He destroyed me and made me into something else. I'm not objective enough to talk about Him, to you or anyone."

Even a child's blue eyes can grow cold. "You're not objective about Apollo Mojave, but you still talk about them."

"Not freely," I answered. "Not even to you."

His brows accused. "You've answered every question I've ever asked about Apollo. Have you been lying? Lying to me?"

"No, never, Bridger, never." I stroked his fingers through the bars. "I've told you everything about Apollo, every fact, but I haven't told you my opinions, what I think those facts mean. Even when you read Apollo's *Iliad*, I never talked to you about what I think Apollo meant by it. I want you to put the pieces together for yourself, because I know if you do you'll make a different picture than I would, a better one."

"But you know more than me! If we have different conclusions I'm bound to be the one who's wrong." He grabbed my sleeve. "I trust you, Mycroft, or I would if only you'd tell me things. I want to know." His free hand crept toward the plastic scabbard at his side. "Don't make me make you."

I felt glad that he had grown strong enough to threaten me. "Listen, Bridger," I began again, "I realized a few years ago that I believe Jehovah is a God, and—let me finish," I warned as I saw him part his lips to speak. "I don't believe it because I've seen proof, or because I was actively convinced, it's just that He acts so consistently like a God, and I've spent so long around people who believe He's a God, Himself and others, that I absorbed it, the way if you spend too long with Mommadoll you start thinking of everyone as children. Jehovah will say something and I'll think to myself, 'Oh, He thinks that because He's a God.' It's the truth to me now, the way I think, and I can't stop thinking that way. It's like how you can't stop thinking that up is up, even though you know there's no real up in Space, or how the army men can't stop thinking that Stander-Y is the enemy even though there never was an enemy, and how I can't stop being sure that what you're going to do with your powers is the most important thing that's ever happened to the human race, even though I don't know what that thing will be."

Bridger hid behind his eyelids. "Do you think I'm a god too?"

Now I hid behind mine. "You could be. I've been considering that possibility. Just because the twelve Olympians are hiding on their mountain it doesn't mean that newborn gods can't walk the Earth. Assuming there really are Olympians, that is. I don't know, Bridger." I squeezed his hands again, both of them, the best embrace that I could offer through the cage. "The one thing I'm sure of in this world is that I don't know anything for certain, not what you are, not why, not any of this. All I can do is trust the Plan, and while I can't understand its ends, I have to trust that they make sense to Someone."

I could feel him shivering. "But what if the ends are bad?"

"There's nothing I can do about it if they are, so I have to trust they're . . . if they're not good or kind, at least they're for something. Something real. Better some end than none." Leaning close, I could almost pretend we were in the soft dark of Bridger's cave. "The Greek Stoics said a human being is like a dog tied behind a moving cart. The dog can struggle, tug at the rope, dig its heels in, choke and suffer as it's dragged, or it can trot along content and trust the Driver, though it still can't understand the purpose of the journey, or its end." I paused, watching distaste wrinkle his nose. "You don't like the simile?"

"No."

I nodded slowly. "Jehovah hates it too. He said any just Driver would let the dog sit with Him in the cart, and a just God would not create a creature incapable of understanding the journey." My fingertip traced Bridger's thumbnail, just starting to lose childhood's softness. "You will learn about Jehovah, Bridger. You'll meet Jehovah, it's inevitable. I just wanted to wait until you'd grown up more, until you were mature and had a bash', and solid grounding, and a plan. Until you were formed enough as a person that meeting him wouldn't destroy and remake you the way it did me. But the crisis won't wait. You need to learn about Jehovah now. Just not through me. Do it yourself. Spy. Scry. You have your crystal ball, your magic mirror, and your little army. You can watch Him from a distance, invade His house invisibly, read His notebooks, hack His tracker, see more than anyone can, without letting Him speak to you. Watch Him, judge Him, if you have questions for Him tell me and I'll ask Him for you. When you understand enough about Him to be sure you can approach Him without being changed, then come to Him, and the two of you can figure out what must be done."

The child's fingers locked around mine. "I will if you come help me."

"No."

"You don't have to tell me opinions, just tell me facts, like with Apollo."

"No. I'm needed here."

"Why?"

"Because Jehovah doesn't have Mommadoll, or the army men, or Boo. Because everybody needs someone they can talk to freely about beliefs and doubts, and I'm the only one Jehovah has. Because Jehovah's still young too, barely twenty-one, which may seem old to you but—"

"It doesn't," he interrupted. "I know twenty-one's still young. With responsibilities like these fifty's still young."

"It is." I smiled. "Most of all, I have to stay with Jehovah now because, if this crisis tears the world apart, Jehovah will be the One expected to make things right again." I brushed back a spray of stray hair trapped by the sweat on Bridger's forehead. "You're right that you'll need me, Bridger. When you're ready to reshape the world you'll need me to hook you up with the powerful people who can help you, but that's the future, ten years or ten days from now, not tomorrow. Jehovah needs me tomorrow. It's His time. He needs me to help Him keep the world on track, and to ensure that those powerful people I can call on are still here to help you when your time comes. That's why I have to stay." I squeezed his shoulders. "That's why you have to go."

The child swallowed hard. "How long will you stay?"

"Not long, I promise. Jehovah never keeps me for long stretches at a time. He knows a lot of people need me."

"I won't promise not to come back." Bridger crossed his arms. "I'll watch Jehovah, but I'm also watching you, and I'll snatch you away if I decide I should. You know I can."

I nodded acceptance. "I know you can, and I can't stop you. But I trust you, Bridger. You've grown up a lot, and you're ready to make hard choices like this. I trust you not to come back for me unless you're sure you should."

He smiled. "Do you want me to set your scary friend free?"

I stroked the underside of Saladin's bruised arm. "You can't, not anymore. The need to know will just bring them back. It's all right," I comforted quickly. "It's not your fault this happened to them. It was inevitable."

His frown did not believe me. "This is why kids grow up, isn't it?"

"What is?"

His words grew timid, sensing goodbye's approach. "It's probably special for me, since I'm pretty sure if I don't want to grow up I just won't, I can decide that. But things like this, where you see what's happening in the grown-up world and realize that you have to do something, you can't keep out of it, this is what makes kids want to grow up, so we can become able to make a difference."

I gave his fingers one last squeeze. "I don't know, Bridger. I never really grew up, I was made into what I am now all at once. Don't let that happen to you. I don't have the right to pray for anything, but if I did pray it would be for that to never happen to you."

He gathered the cloak's invisible folds around him. "You don't have to pray, Mycroft. I'm prepared. I've been prepared for years. I've had you as an example. I realized a long time ago it would be a disaster if something like that happened to me, transformed me into something bad, or unstable. I won't let it happen." Bridger curled against the bars, holding my arm around him. "Mycroft, can I lie here like this?" he asked softly. "Just for a little bit? I know I have to go, but—"

"Of course you can." I drew my hat from my habit and offered it as a pillow as he snuggled against me. "Nap for now. I'll wake you when it's time."

I tucked the cloak tighter around him, and tucked Apollo's coat around Saladin and myself, so between the Griffincloth and the invisibility magic the two of them vanished, and I seemed to lie alone on the cage floor in the soldier's uniform, sandy tan and gray, which Apollo's coat made of my habit. Am I still alive then, Apollo, in your prediction? As we fall one by one in your computer's simulated battles, so we vanish from your nowhere, and your coat, passing across a street, reduces crowds, half to soldiers, half to emptiness. Saladin has been dead to you these thirteen years, and profited well from a ghost's invisibility, but how can I be still alive? You knew I would have been like you, a frontline soldier, doomed to fall in the first months of your young war. Has chance spared me in every calculated battle? Or, when you programmed the coat, had you somehow already recognized the conspiracy of Fate which dooms me to survive?

"Want me to kill the kid now?" Saladin whispered inches from my ear.

I laughed inside at myself. I had half known he must be awake, and half not cared. "No," I answered. "I know Bridger could destroy everything, just like Apollo, but there's too much to gain if it goes right. We have to gamble on this one, Saladin. We have to trust the Driver."

CHAPTER THE TENTH

Stalin in One Weekend

IMAGINE, READER, THE VIEW THAT LUCKY STARS ENJOY AS YOUNG worlds orbit, rich with life. The star catches brief glimpses as its children spin, of living oceans, lichen jungles spreading new dirt across still-cooling rock, and the first sentiences raising curious eyes to their bright parent. Such a view Martin Guildbreaker shared, seated in the main hall of the Utopian Transit Network as its technicians circled from computer to computer, their coats showing birdman cities, giant mushroom forests, seas of dark ghosts, anthropomorphized animals striding in armor through medieval castles, and a dozen other teeming worlds. Their creatures circled too: a fat, snoozing Techupine bristling with detachable tools, a Gilded Owl, a rambunctious two-headed dragon, Crystal Bats transparent as glassfish, and a rainbow cloud of Hummerlights, glowing hummingbirds as colorful as orchids, which schooled around the room like minnows in fast-forward. Did Martin ask himself, I wonder, as suns must: How long until these wonders launch to the heavens on their self-made wings, and do not need me anymore?

"Guildbreaker, the set-set you hired just attempted murder!"

"What?" Martin rose at once, too slow to intervene as the Utopians seized the set-set who sprawled on the floor at Martin's feet and ripped the wires from their mesh of sensors. The set-set screamed. The Major once described to me a time he saw a man struck blind and deaf by a blow from a flying rock. He told me he had never heard so pitiful a scream, the soldier, still a boy, shaking more from terror than from pain, floundering helpless in a silent, death-black world with two of five senses lost; imagine then the set-set's scream losing forty of forty-five.

"What are you doing?" Martin reached out a strong hand to the set-set, who latched on like a drowning man.

"They tried to make a car crash." It was Aldrin who answered, seated on her unicorn whose panther-black skin merged with her coat of deep space to stream night and stars around the rider.

<what? i did no such thing!> the set-set protested, wiping tears of
shock. For legal reasons the name of this set-set must remain confidential,
not that many would care which of this race of bonsai brains had answered
Martin's call.

"That was live data!" Aldrin shouted. "Can't you tell the difference?"

<live data?> The blinded set-set's fingers trembled as they dug into
Martin's arm.

"You just tried to delete a data point from the set you were viewing."

<i wanted to see what impact it would have. i was going to put it back
later.>

"Put it back? That data point was a fifty-nine-year-old Cousin named
Harper Morrero. If we hadn't parried, they'd be dead now."

The set-set's breath raced, enough to make their tracker bleep concern.
<dead? a person? wait, what is this data?>

Aldrin's fists clenched her unicorn's ink-black mane. "You didn't tell the
set-set what data they're sifting?"

Martin gave the set-set's shoulders a comforting squeeze. "They didn't
need to know. They said they'd work better if they didn't."

<ten billion points,> the set-set typed faster than speech, <ten billon
people, that's the whole world. is this the tracker system? have I been hooked
to the tracker computers without knowing it?>

Martin sighed at Aldrin. "Why did you give them access to live data?
I told you to show them old records, not—"

"They asked for it," Aldrin interrupted.

<wait, you said a car crash. the transit network! this is the transit
network, isn't it? not the trackers. cars! am i in cielo de pajaros? where are
sidney and eureka?>

"Why did you try to kill that person?" Aldrin pressed. "What fallout
did you prophesy?"

The set-set's breath raced. <i didn't mean to hurt anyone! attempted
murder? am i going to prison now? i didn't know those data points were
people! i'm not a murderer!>

"It's all right," Martin consoled. "We know you didn't know. I called
you in here, you won't be held responsible. You had no way to know."

<then all the points i found that were deleted, those were people too?
murders!>

The Masonic iron of Martin's face softened for a moment. "Just remember, it's not your fault. I didn't tell you what we were investigating. You

aren't responsible for what's going to happen when we release this information, I am. I could have hired anyone. None of this was you."

\<release? you can't release this! it'll cause worldwide panic!\>

"They'll just keep killing if we don't."

\<you don't understand.\>

"How many did you find?"

\<what?\>

"I had you look for deaths—deletions—that had a large global impact,
and which only a Cartesian set-set would know how to predict. How many
did you find?"

\<maybe it's not true. this is new data to me. where are sidney and eureka? sidney koons and eureka weeksbooth, they work on the transit network, they're the ones you want! ask them!\>

"You knew Sidney and Eureka well, didn't you?" Martin asked softly.
"You were sort of ba'sibs?"

\<of course. with the cousins and lorelei cook sabotaging set-set training, there's only one place left that trains cartesians. you must've read the
black sakura seven-ten list article about it.\>

How could Martin not wince? The whole world had read by now, not
only Masami Mitsubishi's original editorial about Romanovan Senator and
Minister of Education Lorelei "Cookie" Cook, but the follow-up articles,
penned by quick-striking journalists ever poised like mantises in search of
prey: the nighttime raids which, increasingly of late, had been ripping infant set-sets from their pod-beds, smashing their computers, burning their
bash'houses down, was this more than the sleeping dragon Nurturism releasing a scorching snore? Was this Nurturist surge deliberate? Traceable
to Lorelei Cook, and through the Cousins' most prominent Senator to
the Cousins themselves? Perhaps this sigh from Martin wishes for a world
where that had been the largest crisis.

\<where are sidney and eureka? they must be here.\>

"This isn't the Six-Hive Transit Network," Aldrin answered, cold. "It's
ours."

Fresh fear spurred the set-set to finally lift the blinded interface hood
from their eyes and look. The walls were the computer, a forest of rod-
thin processors glittering within columns of sparkling coolant.

\<the utopian network. then you watched? you saw everything i found.
you utopians, you're the ones trying to expose this, aren't you? the world
goes down and you suck up the profits like parasites and shoot them into

space!> They dug their fingers into Martin's sleeve. <don't let them use you like this, mason! the utopians know the truth already, but they want the announcement to come from you instead of them, so no one will realize it was their plan. when the saneer-weeksbooth bash' is arrested, they'll control all global transit, just in time to exploit the chaos!>

"It isn't the Utopians."

<of course it is! who else wouldn't care about the consequences of exposing this?>

"I don't care," answered a new voice, tired and cracking as it rose from the depths of a thick grove of computers. "I'm not allowed to. Law and only law, that's my job."

<who's that? who's there?>

"Police Commissioner General Ektor Carlyle Papadelias." Papa strolled forward, flexing their work-stiffened shoulders, slim and ancient like a cliff-face tree that keeps its trunk pole-thin as it puts the growing strength of centuries into its roots. "The Mason and the Utopians are both working for me on this one, me and Romanova, and so are you. Now, start from the beginning and tell me what you found. Everything."

The set-set paused to catch its breath. <i was reviewing old records like the mason asked me to. this database doesn't just track the cars, it tracks the people, patterns and relationships, everyone on earth, utopian and not, so it can predict when people will call cars. but it can predict a lot more than that. i was looking for times when a single point got deleted and had a conspicuously good impact on the rest.>

"Good impact?"

<the system gets tense sometimes, clusters of internal pulls that make masses of points twist or clash. remove just the right point and millions of ugly tensions vanish at once. what's a comparison you'd understand? it's like you're listening to a symphony, and it's all tense and agitated, then suddenly one discordant note stops, and all the harmonies fall into place. someone's been detecting these points, and deleting them.>

"Guildbreaker showed me your initial report from earlier this morning." Papa shooed a Salamanderfly out of his face. "You'd found eighty-one murders by then."

<points,> the set-set corrected, <please call them points.>

"Hiding from the label won't help. I've looked into those eighty-one. Half were killed in car crashes, some were suicides, the rest were the kinds of random incidents that look like accidents until you dig too deep, but they were murdered, every one of them. At my age, the nose knows."

The set-set clung tighter to Martin's arm. <this morning's list was partial. these points are hard to spot, even for me. i mostly work investment trends, sanling clients. i didn't realize the points were people. i had no idea deleting a live datapoint would kill someone.>

"Don't worry, you're not in trouble. But you've found more murders since, yes? More deleted points than the initial eighty-one?"

<yes.>

"How many more?"

<some.>

"I'm not a dentist and I don't like pulling teeth. How many?"

<9.4 per year, like i said before. actually, it starts out at 9.1, then goes up to 9.4 later.>

Papa's nose twitched. "After how long?"

<the first thirty years or so are 9.1, the rest are 9.4.>

"Thirty years?" Papa looked to Martin, who met him with equal pallor. "That's a lot more than seven years."

<you know what, i refuse to do this. i don't care what you do to me. i won't be complicit in wrecking everything for everyone forever.>

In seventy years of service, how many attempts at self-sacrifice to save a friend has Papa watched, and watched fail? "You can't save Sidney and Eureka."

<you think it's sidney and eureka i care about? you're a european, you must see the consequences for you, too!>

"European?" It was Aldrin who repeated it, but that steely tone might as easily have risen from any of the digital faces that ringed the set-set. "You can't masquerade here. You recognized this data. Ten billion points in seven groups with two percent floating, you know the proportions as the Hives. You know which Hive is which by size, so you know which are the masterminds, which benefited."

The skin of sensors shifted over the set-set's trembling limbs.

"Tell me," Aldrin pressed, "when you tried to delete a point yourself just now, were you trying to save the whole, or the Mitsubishi?"

<lies! i didn't know!> The set-set groped for Papa, unused to judging distance with their eyes. <you must believe me, commissioner general, i didn't know anything!>

"I don't give a goat's crap if you knew or not. Somebody tell me how many murders are on that list before I confiscate every hard drive in the building, furry or otherwise!" Papa swatted at the Techupine, which lumbered to safety behind its master's knees.

\<you won't get it from me. ask them, the spying utopians. they know everything already. they're the ones that want this. let it come from them, not me.>

Rarely in my history, reader, have I been tempted so to lie. It was Utopia who supplied this last inch of fuse which let the spark reach the powder keg. They were innocent, as innocent as the Emperor who had sent Martin on this quest with no motive but justice, but you will not believe that. You distrust Utopia already. You distrusted them the instant the name 'Apollo' made you shout inside: *A cult! A cult!* You have hungered these many chapters for some evidence to let distrust mature into suspicion. Even when I prove another guilty, when I put a name to that gloved hand which dropped the Seven-Ten list in Ockham's back room, you will still believe Utopia consented, knew, as shamans know what sky will turn to storm, or what village boy will grow into a monster. They didn't know. I don't care if you don't believe me. Utopia knew nothing of O.S., Apollo knew nothing, and if the Mardis knew enough of human nature to sense a predatory darkness pent up by these years of peace, they did not know to call that sin O.S.

"We have been tagging the points the set-sets focused on." At Aldrin's nod one of the other Utopians, shrouded in a nowhere future where Earth and her sister planets had been disassembled rock by rock and spread into a shell to catch every last drip of daylight leaking from our dying sun, brought up the list. Martin made it through the first hundred names, then fell back into his seat, the data thundering on him like a waterfall. Papa took it standing up, though not in silence, the blood of a Greek and of a grandparent making him too much a storyteller to resist reading the juiciest parts aloud.

"Death of Akker Anaba in a car crash in 2392 enabled the Greenpeace-Mitsubishi merger? That's more than sixty years ago!"

\<keep scrolling.>

"Death of Gillian Joiner Dao in a car crash in 2262 enabled the Olympian-Hollyworld merger which created the Humanists. That's . . . how far back does this go?"

The set-set sighed surrender. \<all the way.>

"What do you mean, 'all the way'? To the Paleolithic period?"

\<to 2210. that's when the sanling developed cartesian set-sets. that's when the olympian-run saneer-weeksbooth bash' started using us on the transit network. that's when the system's natural crash rate dropped from 96 per year to 9. actually it dropped from 96 to 4, but they told the public it was 9, so they could use the extra 5 for this.>

"2210." Papa repeated with a long whistle. "That's two hundred and forty-four years. Five crashes a year, plus four or five extra deaths carried out by other means than crashes, we'll say nine victims per year, so . . . over a thousand victims?"

<two thousand, two hundred and four.>

We reach a breach here, reader: which are you, my near contemporary who breathed these troubled days alongside me, or remote posterity? If you lived through it, you must remember vividly when you first heard that number, where you were—out shopping, sharing dinner—who first told you, what the wind smelled like. Tens of thousands of days fade into memory's melting pot, but not the day Death first took someone you loved, nor that day. If, on the other hand, you join me from remote posterity, then the picture must be altogether different. Two thousand, two hundred and four: in the coldness of a history book it must seem like nothing—Stalin killed as many in one weekend—and it must fade too beside the millions of the World Wars. Not so for us. For three centuries we had lived out our rose-tinted daydream, convinced that we were peaceful creatures, good at heart, like Locke or Jean-Jacques's Noble Savages; now we woke to find ourselves still brutish humans in the thrall of Hobbes.

Papa took a breath and held it, one last pause. "Mycroft was right, then."

"What?" Martin asked, already pale.

"To smear blood all over the Altar of Peace in Romanova. Three hundred years of world peace. Don't you see it, Martin? This is why."

"No. No, it can't—"

<it's true. i ran sims where those points weren't deleted. it's exquisite what sidney and eureka have been doing. if all those discords had been left in place, it would have fallen into chaos, all of it, a dozen times at least. they saved the world.>

"Made the world, more like," Papa corrected. "They made this world. Two thousand, two hundred and four deaths buy one golden age."

"Sede te, domine! Tua culpa non est! Domine!" (Calm yourself, sir! It's not your fault! Sir!—9A)

It was not to the room that Martin cried, but to Jehovah. Had you forgotten that the *Porphyrogene* can watch at any moment through His Martin's tracker? This investigation was assigned to Jehovah Mason, and Martin's silence—here's the cruelty of it—Martin's silence made the kind Prince check in on him. He was Witness at this dark unmasking, and His Mind's great Eye saw at once past petty politics to the greater horror, that our Creator, the Mind That Wills This Universe, creating Man (perhaps in His own image?) made Man this. I should have been with Him. I count it a mercy that I was not awake to hear Jehovah's words of pain, but I should have been. That is my duty in the house, to sit with Him in troubled hours and listen to the inner questions of a God. It was Dominic who kept them from fetching me, Dominic who bade the other servants leave me be, so he could claim this moment for himself. Can you see him, reader? The blood-hound limping as quickly as injury allows toward the Young Master's bed-room, his lips twitching at the sound of his God's cries as if tasting some rare liqueur? Already in Dominic's hot imagination he tastes Jehovah's tears, sees his God pressing Himself into his arms, shuddering like a pet bird. This is the consummation he has drooled for, that day of weakness he has wanted ever since Madame first held the Infant in her arms and cooed, "Look, little Dominic, here is thy Master." He might have had it too, his victory day, seen tears—true tears at last!—leak down his Master's blank and distant cheeks, had Mercy in the form of Heloïse not beat him to Him. Her cell stood close by Jehovah's study, and her legs, though tiny, were un-injured, so she flew to Him prompt as a mother. Dominic, arriving second, heard her voice along the corridor. She did not comfort Jehovah—in her world it is not woman's part to console man—rather she had Him tell her of His grief, and, hearing of the deaths of innocents, she wept, she sobbed, she shivered fragile in her habit's rough embrace, so her God had no choice but to comfort her, and make Himself again the strong One. Dominic has always hated happy Heloïse, but until that day there had been others he hated more. Still, with Bridger almost in his pocket, he could wait.

"That's Epicurus Mason on the line, isn't it?" Papa asked, the Greek choosing the Greek name from Jehovah's many. "They're watching? They heard?"

"Yes. Yes, *Dominus* heard it all."

Papadelias frowned sadly. "Are they all right?"

Martin's voice quavered. "No-o. But neither is the world."

<cover it up!> the set-set interrupted. <tell them it's not too late to cover this up! right now no one knows except us in this room. you don't even have any proof except my testimony, and i won't testify in court, you can't make me, not against a ba'sib. you need a cartesian to see it, and not a one of us would go to court against eureka and sidney, i can tell you that. without us you have no evidence and no way to get it, you can legitimately drop the case. stop now and save the world. three hundred years of world peace, we can let there be three hundred more! two thousand deaths, in olden days they'd lose that in a week!>

Ektor Carlyle Papadelias drew a long, wheezing breath, and slowly let it out. "I bet the Utopians would cover it up if you asked them. And you certainly could, Martin. The only one you'd have trouble hushing up is me, but you could give that the old college try. I'm far from invincible, and probably far from expendible . . ." The Commissioner General trailed off, playing out the strategy game in his mind, how he would try to kill or blackmail himself, in Martin's shoes.

Martin was shivering. "Your orders, *Domine?*"

From far across the Earth, His own kind words. "Protect Harper Morrero."

<who?>

Aldrin's digital eyes glared. "The Cousin you just tried to kill, had you forgotten?"

<i didn't mean to kill them! i just had to delete that data point, i couldn't help myself! there were so many tensions it would fix! i reached by instinct, i couldn't even think!>

"Nobody cares if you meant to or not." Papa turned to Aldrin. "Who is this Harper Morrero?"

"Harper Mertice Morrero . . ." another Utopian scanned the bio. "They're a Cousin, skier, tree doctor, not a vocateur . . . ah, they're the spouse of a ba'sib of Cousins' Feedback Bureau Chief Darcy Sok's grandba'pas' live-in nurse. We're not set-sets but we have charted the set-sets' work enough to retroparse. It may sound like an unreasonable number of links in the chain, but if Harper Morrero dies, Darcy Sok will resign from the CFB, and the press around the Cousins will locust nap. Go dormant," they translated.

Papa frowned. "Press nosing around the CFB qualifies as a world-destroying tension?"

<you haven't seen the data. if we don't stop it, it'll rip the hive apart, everything. i can't explain it in your terms, it's just obvious, painful even to experience. that's why i had to do something, had to delete that point. it wasn't even a choice, i had to, like a compulsion. it's like coming home finding a friend with a knife sticking out of their guts, you can't just leave it there, you have to pull it out and help.>

Papa gave a shallow sigh. "If you pull the knife out it'll hemorrhage and get worse." He looked to Martin, hoping for a laugh, but found the Mason rigid.

"From their own mouth," Martin muttered.

"What?"

"A compulsion. Don't you see, Papa? This is where we get the final proof." Martin's voice swelled quickly, like an eager avalanche. "*Dominus* has given us the answer. We don't need a set-set's testimony. If our set-set can't resist this hit, the enemies' set-sets can't either. Harper Morrero, they're going to try to kill them. We can catch them red-handed!" Martin's own hands shook at the prospect. "Aldrin, put a team together. I want you to surround this Harper Morrero with a wall of surveillance and invisible defense no one could penetrate."

Aldrin frowned. "You think they'll strike now? They must know we're scrying."

"If the set-set's right about its impact, this is bait they can't resist. Stay untraceable. Don't let the subject know you're there, but watch them, listen to them, test their food, their air, everyone that goes near them, have agents ready to intervene at any instant. Our assassins seem to have a lot more than cars at their disposal, so check anything they could use: medical conditions, habits, allergies, emotional instabilities, dangerous pets, old ceiling beams, ex-lovers, anything. Cost is no object; the Emperor will pay if Romanova can't. I don't just want to protect the target's life, I want you ready to detect the attempt when it happens, and to trace it step by step back to the perpetrator. We don't know when it'll happen, tomorrow, the next day, in two months or two minutes, but I want us ready. I want enough proof to convict."

The others looked to Aldrin, who took a long breath, making the coat of stars about her swell. "I want this order to come from Papadelias. We don't want Utopia to be accused of siding with one Hive against the others. If we do this, we do it for the Alliance Police, not for the Emperor, or you, Martin. Or even for you, Micromegas." She raised her voice on the last phrase, to make sure her words would carry to His distant, most important ear.

<you see!> the set-set leapt in, as quick as you are, reader, to accuse. <they're trying to cover their tracks! it's them. the utopians wanted this exposed. they planned it all! they knew!>

"Enough."

<think about it, why should they care if the humanists, europeans, and sanling are conspiring against the masons, cousins, and brillists? they aren't the target, there aren't even any utopian victims, there can't be, they use a separate network, and no one would dare target them anyway, because . . . >

"Because they'd catch them," Papadelias supplied.

Martin and Papa stared at Aldrin and her peers, waiting for some answer, some comment, but they faced only blank, digital eyes. What do you think they feel as they uncover our sins? These 'clean' Utopians? Three Hives targeting three Hives leaves them aloof, like Noah safe in his ark while a sick world drowns. Is that what you think, reader? Noah had assurances from God that he and his would live: infallible, omnipotent protection. Utopia does not. Imagine what fear Noah would have felt without that promise, seeing the waters rising, countless neighbors turning greedy eyes on his small ship.

"Do it." Papa ordered. "As Alliance Police Commissioner General, I am commissioning you to protect Harper Morrero, and trace anyone who attempts to kill them. Report to me directly."

"Acknowledged." Aldrin, the others with her, their attendant beasts, and who knows how many other individuals, teams, and cities which formed a constellation lacing the human empire from Paris to Luna City, nodded.

"That's it, then." Martin's shoulders slumped within his square-breasted Mason's suit. "If they make this hit that's it, we have them."

Papa shook his head. "No."

"No?"

"If they make this hit, we can prove someone in the Saneer-Weeksbooth bash' has attempted one murder, but that's all. We need one more thing to land the big fish."

"More? We're lucky to have even this. What more can we get?"

"A confession."

"What? Whose?"

"Time to make a call."

Call logged 03:42 UT 03/28/2454

Papadelias: "Foster, how are you hanging in there? I hope my forensic team wasn't too rough."

Foster: "I feel like I've been dry-cleaned."

Papadelias: "I know the feeling. It'll pass."

Foster: "Do we know what Thisbe did to me? Do we have a plan? If it really was witchcraft we're all in danger!"

Papadelias: "Give the lab time, Foster. I've called in some Utopians. Whether it's fake witchcraft or real witchcraft, they'll know better than anybody what to do."

Foster: "I guess."

Papadelias: "Look, Foster, I don't have time for friendly. Give me the recording."

Foster: "What recording?"

Papadelias: "I haven't been stalking Julia Doria-Pamphili eleven years for nothing. I know how they work, and how they train their pawns to work. They
taught you to eavesdrop, and if Thisbe Saneer tried to kill you it's
because you stumbled on something major. Julia's also taught you to
record everything on your tracker so you can review it afterwards.
I need that recording."

Foster: "There is no recording."

Papadelias: "It's not a violation of your vows, I'm not asking you to tattletale
on something from a session, this is an unrelated scene that you
happen to have witnessed."

Foster: "There is no recording."

Papadelias: "I know what you're thinking, you're thinking you wouldn't have
been there if you weren't their sensayer, that you have to protect your
parishioners, whether it was a session or not, but that's bull."

Foster: "There is no recording."

Papadelias: "You know what they are, don't you? The Saneer-Weeksbooth
bash'. They're just going to keep killing."

Foster: "A sensayer can't be forced to testify about planned crimes."

Papadelias: "Do you know who they're working for?"

Foster: "I don't know anything."

Papadelias: "Did they say who they're working for?"

Foster: "I don't know anything."

Papadelias: "You think you're protecting your parishioners, but you're not.
You're protecting their bosses. We're going to catch the bash'members,
that's a certainty at this point, and you know what'll happen when we
do? They'll take full responsibility themselves, tell the world the assassinations were their idea from the start, and destroy any evidence to the
contrary. Your parishioners will go to trial, Cato Weeksbooth will kill
themself, and their bosses, the ones who've been forcing them to do
this, they'll sit back content and find a new way to get their killing done."

Foster: "You're sure they're working for someone?"

Papadelias: "I know who, I know how, I know since when, but what I have
won't convince a judge. If you give me that recording I can land the bosses,
and probably get Cato and a couple of the others to testify against
them and get lighter sentences as a consequence. That way the parties
truly responsible get what they deserve, the killing stops, and those who
were forced unwillingly into doing the dirty work get the more lenient
justice they deserve. It's your call, Foster. Justice is a lot less blind in

our day but a sword is still a very clumsy instrument. It's up to us to guide the blade."

Foster: "Tell me what you know."

Papadelias: "What?"

Foster: "You said you know who, how, and since when, so prove it. Tell me. You haven't even directly said what crime it is we're talking about."

Papadelias: "I can't tell you, it'll prejudice you as a witness."

Foster: "I'm not going to testify. If there were a recording and I did give it to you, I'd agree to give a written deposition explaining how I got it, but that's it. I won't take the stand against a parishioner, the precedent would rip the Sensayers' Program apart, and no law, certainly not Cousins' Law, can make me do it."

Papadelias: "No chance your conscience will make you, is there?"

Foster: "Not likely when you won't even tell me what cause I'd be supporting."

Papadelias: "Fine, you want it spelled out, you got it, but if you breathe a word of this to Julia or anyone but me, you'll be under arrest faster than you can say Greenpeace-Mitsubishi Merger, clear?"

Foster: "Clear."

Papadelias: "Two hundred and forty-four years ago, the Six-Hive Global Transit Network, developed by the two Olympian doctors Orion Saneer and Tungsten Weeksbooth, started using Mitsubishi-trained Cartesian set-sets. They rapidly discovered that set-sets hooked to the transit computers could identify people whose deaths would solve big tensions in world history, or help their Hive. The Mitsubishi and Olympians, later Humanists, made a deal to use this system for their mutual benefit against the other Hives. The Europeans got on board in the twenty-three thirties, forming what I'm calling the Saneer-Weeksbooth Set-Set Transit System Three-Hive Secret Alliance—O.S. for short—which has thus far claimed two thousand, two hundred and four victims, and will claim more if you don't help me end it."

Foster: "O.S.?"

Papadelias: "That's what I've nicknamed our assassins."

Foster: "Why O.S.?"

Papadelias: "It's easier to pronounce than S.W.S.S.T.S.T.H.S.A. The head of the bash' always has the initials O.S. Before Ockham Saneer the last leader was Ockham's mother Osten Saneer, before that Oyuki Sniper, Oleisia Sniper, Napoleon Weeksbooth Saneer who went by Ollie, before that Rong Oakhart Shen, Kiran Omi Saneer, Omid Saito, always O.S., back twelve generations to Orion Saneer, who put the system together. Even Sniper's full name is Ojiro Cardigan Sniper, and Thisbe is Thisbe Ottila Saneer. So, O.S."

Foster: "I am the twelfth O.S."

Papadelias: "What?"

Foster: "Ockham said it. 'I am the twelfth O.S., I don't intend to be the last.'"

Papadelias: "Heh. I didn't expect to actually guess the name right. O.S. it is, then. Twelve generations of murder, Foster. You can end it."

Foster: "You're sure you'll get their bosses this way?"

Papadelias: "Nothing's certain in this world, Foster, but this is as close as we're going to come."

Foster: "Fine. You're right, if it has to end, it should end with the right people going down. It should end with the truth."

File transfer initiated 03:56 UT 03/28/2454

Papadelias: "Thanks."

Foster: "Don't thank me."

Papadelias: "As you like. I'll make sure no one finds out it was you."

Foster: "No, let them know. Let everybody know."

Papadelias: "What?"

Foster: "If there are to be limits to what secrets a sensayer will keep, then everyone should know them. We've decided this is acceptable, that the recording isn't covered by sensayer confidentiality, so let everyone know who made the recording, and how, and why. Let them judge for themselves whether or not to trust us after this."

Papadelias: "You really want your name mixed up in this? We're not talking about twenty minutes of fame here, we're talking about your whole life. Even being a sensayer can't be the same after everyone in the world knows you as *that* sensayer."

Foster: "So be it."

Papadelias: "Even though you're a Gag-gene? Even twenty minutes of fame is long enough to bring out all kinds of old bad."

Foster: "I don't care about myself in this."

Papadelias: "And what about Julia Doria-Pamphili? It won't be easy keeping that name out of things if you do full disclosure on the recording and why you made it."

Foster: "Then let Julia's name be out there too. Julia and I have both been making too many judgment calls for other people. I think I've done right, and to some extent I think Julia has too. Time to see if the world agrees."

Papadelias: "It's four in the morning, Foster. Go to bed. After a night's sleep and a solid breakfast, if you still feel like destroying yourself and your mentor, then we'll talk."

Foster: "I'm not going to change my mind."

Papadelias: "Good night, Foster."

Foster: "I'm not! Believe me, I know when I'm sure about something."

Papadelias: "Listen, Foster, conviction is a virtue, but sometimes doubt is too. You've known Mycroft Canner almost a week, you should have picked that up by now. Go to bed, and make sure you sleep, okay? Come to me rested, calm and sensible and maybe, just maybe, I'll let you throw yourself to the media wolves tomorrow."

Foster: "All right. Tomorrow."

Call ended 04:02 UT 03/28/2454

HERE AT LAST THEN, WITH CARLYLE DOZING,
UTOPIA BUSTLING, JEHOVAH COMFORTING HELOÏSE,
BRIDGER SNEAKING OFF SOFTLY WHILE I SLEEP, AND DAWN'S
ROSE FINGERS ALREADY TICKLING THE EDGE OF NIGHT,
ENDS THE LONG FIFTH DAY OF MY HISTORY.

CHAPTER THE ELEVENTH

Providence Chooses Left

"SNIPER!"

The cry rose from one throat first, then many. It is a researcher's duty to stand objective before birth and death and all between, but the sight of Sniper, still sparkling damp from morning swim practice, swinging on a Tarzan rope through the spiraling, hypnotic architectural experiments which lined the Spectacle City heart of Ingolstadt would dumbfound even Felix Faust. In fact, it did. The Headmaster had been strolling with a patriarch's dawdling dignity along the grass beside a footpath whose electric keyboard stepping stones turned his students' hijinks into harmonies, but he stopped now, slumping against a crystal Spinosaurus sculpture, as if his frame had not the strength to simultaneously stand and study such a specimen.

"Sniper, my dear," Faust greeted. "Nice pants."

What else could one say? The living doll wore nothing else: gray riding britches which made the Olympic striping on its boots seem like the rank marks of an army, but from the waist up it wore nothing. If Sniper is, as many speculate, an Amazon, female by birth, then the surgeon who nipped in the bud the breasts which might have slowed the athlete down in sports, left no blemish on this matchless human canvas. The mist of nearby fountains served as polish for its skin, hairless and pale across the muscles which so many vitamins, exercises, and coaches have trained into the most perfect in the world. Or second-most perfect. I have seen the Major strip to tend a wound, his musculature sculpted by experiences so much more raw, more real, than Sniper's in the gym. Perhaps the Major shouldn't count.

Sniper's smile glittered. "I let my fans vote on how I should repay them for playing hooky most of yesterday. They voted for 'no shirt.'" The living doll turned, displaying every angle to the cameras which hovered about like flying saucers. "I was hoping for a chat, Headmaster, but you look like you're on your way somewhere. Am I interrupting?"

Faust laughed, not at Sniper's words but at its gesture, posture, the angle of its stance, which, to the old voyeur, betrayed more than a diary. "Not at all, my dear, your company is one of life's more fascinating pleasures. I was just strolling up to the Old City to discipline some absentees." He nodded toward the river, where sharp Bavarian towers still pined for knights and dukes and Charlemagne. "There is much hooky being played of late, not just by you."

Sniper was obliged to laugh.

"What did happen to you yesterday?" Faust asked. "I hear no one could find you for fifteen hours."

"Bash' business." Sniper winked. "We all have bash' business sometimes, even me." Its smile apologized for the half answer.

"Naturally. Well, walk with me. I'm eager to hear what's brought you to Ingolstadt, and to hear your comments on the question of the day."

The old gentleman offered Sniper his arm, and the hermaphrodite took it gingerly, like a falcon which settles on a high branch, only deigning to land where it is easiest to leap free. "What 'question of the day'?" it asked.

"Now I'm actually worried," Felix fussed. "Sniper a day behind on the news! The Earth will shake." The Headmaster is not one to exaggerate, and Sniper knew it.

The watching Fellows knew it too, students and instructors, researchers and researchees who leaked like fugitives from the bright pastoral ant farm of the Adolf Riktor Brill Institute of Psychotaxonomic Science. The Institute complex covered a series of artificial slopes above the festive city center, its dorms and classrooms, tiled in blue and white porcelain, nested among precisely measured hills and banks of flowers, still waiting for April to awaken them. Have you visited it, reader? The Cognitivist's city? I remember well when Mercer Mardi first brought me, eight years old and still on crutches from the accident, to limp my way through these too-calculated gardens: paths precisely wide enough to fight off claustrophobia, banks of carefully chaotic flowers, so test subjects can say what shapes they see in the living Rorschach. As Headmaster Faust's Heir Presumptive, Mercer Mardi had enjoyed the finest office with the finest view: three-quarters mathematical perfection, while in the corner of the window one could just see the Old City below, historic Ingolstadt, lurking like an archenemy with its one-horse-wide organic streets, its fort and cathedral towers alive with pigeons. Matter and antimatter must not meet, so, to separate the Institute from the Old Town, Brill conceived this Spectacle Strip between, where Faust and Sniper stand. Here the great sculptors and architects of each generation are invited to build 'abstract self-portraits,' anything they can dream, a rainbow tree, a singing obelisk, a warren of mirrored tunnels, a sausage stand in the shape of a chambered nautilus, anything so long as it is a reflection of themselves. Old Town, Spectacle Strip, and Institute; if only the most successful revolutionaries cease to fear their teachers, how better could Brill boast his conquest of Master Freud than to let his capital flaunt its Id, Ego, and Superego so conspicuously?

"So, what's the question of the day?" Sniper asked.

"The Cousins' Feedback Bureau."

The hermaphrodite did not flinch, but in the videos you can see Faust smile, spotting something. "You mean Masami Mitsubishi's *Black Sakura* Seven-Ten list article about CFB Chief Darcy Sok?" Sniper supplied. "Never let it be said that I'm completely out of touch."

"I'm sure it never will be. So, do you find it credible that the bureaucrats who sort the letters before sending them on have a major political impact on the Cousins? Traditionally you're the one at the bottom of everyone's Seven-Ten lists; this mess has quite stolen your spotlight."

Sniper scratched its black hair with childish modesty. "If the experts involved say they don't know yet, then certainly I don't. So far as I understand it, the letters sent to the CFB are actually sorted by computer. All the CFB people do is tell the computers what criteria to use. It must be true that those criteria influence things, but I've no reason to think they're any less objective than the criteria the World Food Production Index uses to count foods, or the Romanovan Censor uses for population and economy. No one doubts that the data that comes out of the Censor's office has more global impact than just about anything, but that doesn't mean that Ancelet dictates it. If I were a sinister conspiracy, Vivien Ancelet isn't the someone I'd try to bribe. Neither is Darcy Sok."

"You're speaking purely hypothetically, of course?" Faust tested.

"Of course." There is a tendency to hide normal expressions around the Master Brillist, fearing they give away too much, but Sniper had long since outgrown such paranoia, and gave the Headmaster the dark wink he was fishing for. "The Censor can't change the numbers, they just read them. I imagine the CFB is about the same."

"So you're not concerned at all?" Faust tested, winking at the knot of researchers (for all spectators in Ingolstadt are researchers) which had gathered, taking notes on the encounter, and whispering in the clinical German their great founder had judged to be the best language for a researcher to think in.

"Of course I'm concerned," Sniper answered, "I'm concerned what damage these rumors will do to the Cousins."

"Oh?" Faust glanced to his watching students, an arched brow promising to quiz them on their notes and readings after the encounter.

Sniper never minds an audience. "The CFB is the heart of the Cousins. All the other major Hives are run by political types, power brokers, from Mitsubishi directors to President Ganymede. They're vokers, too. They like power, it's their play as well as their work, and what they do in office is at least partly dictated by what will make the people keep them there. But the Cousins don't have elections, don't compete, they just get suggestions filtered by the CFB, and they put into office whatever generous soul is willing to take on something so onerous. That's what makes the Cousins a family, instead of a corporation or an empire. If people start doubting the CFB, they're doubting what makes the Cousins cousins."

As Chagatai, on those rare evenings when Ἄναξ Jehovah dines at home, savors afterward the leftovers and remnant dinner wine whose brilliant pairing the chef best appreciates, so Faust savored the thousand subtleties of Sniper's answer.

"Do you agree, Headmaster?" Sniper pressed.

"No," Faust answered thoughtfully, "if I were an evil conspirator I would definitely bribe the Censor, especially the current one, since you get the Cousin Chair's spouse in your pocket at no extra cost."

Sniper frowned. "That's not an answer. You're the one who quizzed me about the CFB, so you may as well return the courtesy. Do you agree the CFB is the core of what separates the Cousins from other major Hives?" Did you catch it, reader? Faust did: 'major Hives'—how elegantly we exclude Utopia and Gordian.

The Headmaster's eyes sparkled. "There, dear Sniper, you have hit one nail on the head. There are other traits most Cousins share, of course, I'm doing a seminar on that if you're interested, but you're right, if I wanted to weaken the Cousins—still speaking hypothetically—undermining the CFB would be a fine course. The Cousins don't have many weak spots, but the CFB is very like a jugular."

Sniper's black eyes flashed as it homed in on its prey. "I hear Chair Kosala's so worried they called an emergency meeting of admins and experts."

"That would not surprise me." The Headmaster turned off the main path, down an alley of rainbow-dyed waterfalls and toward the cobblestone border of the Old Town.

"Do you think they'll call in J.E.D.D. Mason?"

Faust's brows flexed. "Why do you ask that?"

"Young as they are, J.E.D.D. Mason was elected the Graylaw Hiveless Tribune again this year, and they're also a polylaw, and aren't they an executive of the Cousins' Chief Counsel's Office?"

"Yes. Quite the combination."

Sniper could not help but follow Faust's glance across to the observers. These now included several elite Fellows, their heads ostentatiously shaved to display the blotches of pressure spots, proof of their participation in the Institute's eternal mind-machine interface experiments, which crawl toward digital immortality as slowly as Utopia toward worlds past Mars. Even to hold the gaze of such a specimen is a compliment. Sniper took the lead as the pair squeezed single-file along the whitewashed alley, where the Gordian flag, with its brain-like gold knot against a scarlet field, competed with the brightness of spring laundry. "It must be hard to keep straight, J.E.D.D. Mason having so many different offices. Last I checked they held an office of sorts in every Hive except Utopia, despite still being a minor, and popular enough among the Hiveless to get elected Graylaw Tribune twice. Which way now, Headmaster?" Sniper asked at alley's end.

Faust pointed right with his cane, up a shopping street where fruit and candy tempted like jewels. "The Hiveless do have the most discerning taste."

"Did you know J.E.D.D. Mason met with the Mitsubishi Directors three days ago?"

"Did they? Well, they are a Directorate Advisor."

Sniper's eyes sparred with Faust's. "Don't you think that's odd? Cornel MASON's adopted kid being so close to the leaders of the Mitsubishi? Not to mention all the other Hives?"

"Not really. J.E.D.D. Mason's a very bright child, Sniper, much admired. Much like you."

Sniper's smile accepted the compliment. "The Directorate meets with J.E.D.D. Mason far more often than any other advisor. Some even call them the 'Tenth Director.' Some even say they're really Hotaka Andō Mitsubishi's son."

"I have heard such a thing said."

"Do you believe it? Do you believe J.E.D.D. Mason is Andō's son?"

Faust sighed, swatting at the cameras which buzzed close in the Old Town's unaccustomed cramp. "Is this why you came to see me? To bait me into embarrassing one of my colleagues in front of millions of viewers? Not a very elegant game, my dear."

Sniper shed its smile at once. "No game. I want the truth. That's what the public eye is for, to hold us accountable if we tell lies. I brought my witnesses, don't pretend you don't have yours."

It nodded at the crowd of Institute Fellows watching from behind a bread cart, like naturalists stalking a pair of wild tigers. The observers tried to hide at once, and old Faust snickered at their failure as they ducked behind a bread sign which concealed them from their chins up, but left bare their Brillist sweaters, spelling out their numbers like biographies. The Clothing as Communication Movement began in the 2170s, that same stretch of post-war regeneration when Chairman Carlyle proclaimed the Death of Majority, when Utopia launched the first terraforming ships to Mars, and yes, when Cartesian set-sets took Earth's bloody helm. As we left the Exponential Age behind us, the Clothes-as-Com leaders called for our new modern age to be an 'honest' one, where our clothing would proclaim Hive, work, hobbies, allegiance, a glance proclaiming what makes each stranger special. We tend to assume the Brillist sweaters sprang up in that same decade, along with Mason suits and season-changing Mitsubishi cloth, but it was actually earlier, 2162, when a freshly converted Thomas Carlyle was channeling half of Gordian's budget to the Institute, that Fellows began to home-knit sweaters which spelled out their numbers, the first digit coded by the texture of the knit, the second by the waistline, the third by cuffs, etc. I myself have found the code impossible to master, too unintuitive, like Brillism itself, but I have picked up four things: shorter sleeves go with better skills at math, the patterns on the fabrics get less complicated as a kid grows up, quiet types wear turtlenecks, and a hood on any Brillist makes me feel fear. Whatever Faust could see in his hiding students' sweaters, it won a belly laugh.

"My students aren't robots, Sniper," he answered, "I can't switch my audience on and off at will like you can. Isn't that a little unfair?"

"True enough," Sniper conceded. "If you won't be baited, answer me this: usually executive Mitsubishi pass their shares and influence down in the family, or at least within the bash', but Hotaka Andō Mitsubishi doesn't have any children, apart from possibly J.E.D.D. Mason."

"Andō has lots of children."

"Lots of adopted ba'kids," Sniper clarified. "Lots of half-trained set-set adopted ba'kids. Do you think Andō could really make one of them their political heir, the next Japanese strat-leader, with how much Cousins and Brillists hate set-sets?"

No man enjoys surprise so much as Felix Faust. "How did you know they're set-sets?"

"And here you accused me of being behind in the news." Sniper smirked. "There's a bio of Masami Mitsubishi, released by the *Rosetta Forum* this morning. *Black Sakura*'s not the only paper with top-notch snoops. There were details on Toshi and Ran Mitsubishi as well, and it's not hard to guess that, if these three are from one batch, the other seven adopted Mitsubishi ba'kids are the other seven children that Minister Cook's Nurturist saboteurs carried out of the ruins of the training lab. You know who I couldn't find a good bio on, though? J.E.D.D. Mason."

"J.E.D.D. Mason's still a minor, protected by the Celebrity Youth Act. Poor Masami, Ran, and Toshi didn't think it through when they took the Adulthood Competency Exam so early."

"You know J.E.D.D. Mason personally, though, don't you?" Sniper pressed.

"Yes, I do."

"They're a Fellow at your Institute, aren't they?"

"Of course."

"To study or be studied?"

Faust smiled at a flower seller who glowed at the sight of Sniper, as at a passing angel. "You ask as if the two were separate."

"I've heard a rumor—"

"You're ripe with rumors today."

"—that you have a whole room in your offices just for files on J.E.D.D. Mason: old toys and drawings, recordings, tests, that they're your favorite specimen."

The Headmaster smiled. "And I hear Ganymede offered to prostitute you to Andō in return for rent concessions. What imaginative things rumors are."

Even Sniper's cheeks sometimes grow grave. "Have you picked the next Gordian leadership yet?"

Faust snorted. "I can't make crowds swoon like you and Ganymede, child, but it's a little early to put me in my grave now, don't you think?"

"I don't mean the next Headmaster, I mean the Brain-bash'. You're supposed to pick the most innovative and original bash' you can find, with the rarest number combinations, and put them in charge of picking new political and intellectual directions for Gordian. 'The guiding light must be one that has never burned before, the spirit of the age personified in its rarest newborn,' isn't that what Chairman Carlyle wrote in their memoirs?"

Faust laughed. "Have you added constitutional scholarship to your list of hobby strats?"

"The last 'Brain-bash' was assigned almost seventy years ago, and the position's not hereditary. You must have your eyes on a replacement. Is it J.E.D.D. Mason's bash'?"

The German murmur of the watching fellows peaked.

Faust took his time enjoying Sniper's face. "It is fascinating to see you of all people trying to drag a minor into the spotlight, flouting the Celebrity Youth Act which you yourself have benefitted from more than anybody I can name. You must tell me what's set you so abruptly on this scent." Faust frowned as the street forked, both options lined with identical antique shops. "This corner isn't on my directions. Left or right, do you think?"

"Directions? We're not just meandering?"

Faust winked.

Sniper shrugged. "Left, then. What are J.E.D.D. Mason's numbers? Rare, I expect? Unique? Their bash'mates', too?"

"You know I don't release numbers without permission."

"Do you know what 'J.E.D.D.' stands for? I can't find it anywhere."

"I know your first name too, Sniper, but I don't use it in public, since you don't like it."

Sniper had to laugh. "Touché."

Take a moment, reader, to reflect that one of the most critical decisions of this century has just been made by Sniper without thinking. Left or right? In one direction lies the course history chose, and in the other, what? A longer conversation with the Headmaster? Different questions? Different world. Is this an act of Providence or of Freewill? Or both? Did God craft His creation Sniper so it would choose left? Or did our Maker know from time immemorial that Sniper would choose left, and so sculpted the slopes of Ingolstadt so the square best suited to the Enemy would be built in Sniper's inevitable path?

"What are they like?" Sniper pressed as it led the Headmaster across rain-scented cobbles toward an open square. "J.E.D.D. Mason?"

Faust frowned. "Surely you two have met."

"Actually, they're a Humanist Balloting Officer just like me, but, funny thing is, I don't think I've ever seen them at a Balloting Officers' meeting. Whenever I arrive they've had to leave or vice versa, ships in the night."

"Is that so? How improbable. Perhaps it's a conspiracy by the bash' that runs the transit computers to keep you two apart—you should look into that." Faust's chuckle invited Sniper to feign laughter with him. "No, couldn't be. You ride standard cars but I hear young J.E.D.D. Mason only rides Utopian cars." Faust met Sniper's eyes at last, and held them. "Why is that, do you suppose?"

I wonder how Sniper trained itself to cover fear so well. It laughed, naturally, delightedly, no hint in its warm dark eyes that Faust's teasing had touched so close to home. It took a deep breath, ready to answer, but Faust hushed it, the Headmaster's brows arching at new words, which floated toward them from the square ahead.

"We speak so smugly of economic determinism. We say the French Revolution was inevitable because an expanding population made it untenable for a miniscule nobility to keep monopolizing ninety-five percent of the wealth. We say fascism and Nazism were inevitable because the economic idiocies of 1919 made it impossible for peace to last. We say all this as if past peoples were not only locked into their choices, but were stupid not to realize that they were." The voice was thin, tired but used to being tired, just audible over the breathy shifting of the gathered crowd that filled the square. "But what did it actually feel like? Did a French peasant wake up every morning thinking about the inequitable distribution of wealth? Or that the Old Regime was on its last legs? Or did they wake up thinking that they were hungry while their noble masters weren't? They felt uneasy, unhappy, tense, they wanted things to improve, wanted them back the way they were, perhaps, in the imaginary idyllic past. But war? War wasn't in their minds."

Sniper craned its neck, even hopped with its Olympic grace, just high enough to see over the sea of heads. There he stood, Tully Mardi, perched on the steps of an old church. He was thin in his Hiveless gray, leaning on crutches as his legs—unused to Earth—threatened to fail despite their braces. The Enemy—as I shall always call him—had guards around his soapbox, Apollo's bar friends, sledgehammers and metal pipes more frightening in sober hands than drunk as they waited for me. "Who is it?" Sniper whispered.

Faust held a finger to his lips. "It's what has so many of my students playing hooky."

"And what do you feel when you wake up in the morning?" Tully pressed, quick eyes flicking from face to face across the crowd. "When you make out fat rent checks to your Mitsubishi landlords? When you see more and more Mason suits on the streets? When you pay huge royalties to Utopian inventors, and watch them squander the profits lobbing expensive rocks at Mars? Do you feel uneasy? Unhappy? Tense? Do you want things to go back to the way you think they used to be? The Romanovan Censor publishes new numbers every month, and you worry about your savings shrinking, a rent hike, a recession, as if a salary cut is the limit of what horror humans can inflict. Why not war?"

The back fringe of the crowd was starting to recognize the new arrivals now, whispering Sniper's name, and shying back from their Headmaster like guilty pups, but Faust just smiled, sliding his dry hands into the pockets of his sweater as he took his place as spectator.

"The restless French didn't see war coming," the Enemy continued, "but they had the excuse that back then economists didn't yet know how to see which tensions lead to war. The survivors of 1918 even called the second half of their World War by a separate name, as if unable to see the connection as the tanks rolled out a second time. We're being just as self-blinding. We have the evidence, but we refuse to believe, because it's a matter of faith to us that war's impossible. It isn't. War is the human norm. We've had three hundred years of peace after thousands of years of war. How can you think that we'll never do it again?" His pleading eyes hopped from face to face. "We say war ended with the Exponential Age, that humanity matured after the Church War, developed peaceful means to settle conflicts: sports, debates, elections; that we've shed nations, armies, all the apparatus of warfare, but the French peasants didn't have those either! They just had torches, and pitchforks, and very hungry children. It doesn't take a declaration, or an invasion, to start a war, all it takes is an 'us' and a 'them.' And a spark. You think there aren't plenty of sparks today? What if this Seven-Ten list theft turns out to be a plot by one Hive to sabotage another? What if this mystery at the CFB turns out to be Mitsubishi set-sets taking revenge on the Cousins for sabotaging set-set training bash'es? Remember the Set-Set Riots? Riots turn to war in a heartbeat when the situation is ripe, and then what? Don't think it would stop with fists and bricks and torches. What city in this world doesn't have a factory that could switch production from stoves to guns in an instant? What kid can't cobble together a rocket in chemistry class?"

"Magnificent specimen," Faust whispered, unable to stifle the delight in his eyes. "Preaching on a street-corner soapbox, when they could post it to the web and reach millions."

Sniper nodded softly, eyeing the sea of captivated Brillists. "It's a performance. One more nutcase on the web, no one would care."

"You don't believe me, do you?" Tully pressed, his voice edging to frantic. "Let me put it even more simply, then. I'm Tully Mardi, Mercer Mardi's child, the only survivor of the Mycroft Canner massacre. Some of you must remember when Mercer used to bring me here as a child. You know what I lived through. I've just learned, as you have, that Cornel MASON and Bryar Kosala conspired to protect Mycroft Canner after the capture. Would you be surprised if I tried to assassinate MASON and Kosala? And if I did, and afterwards if people said the Utopians helped me do it, how long do you think it would take for that to turn violent? Days? Hours?" Tully's gesture led the crowd's eyes to his fifth guard, a Utopian who slouched against the church wall behind the soapbox, shadowed in a nowhere sea where derelict ships of every age from Babylon to Space drifted through ghost-mist like frozen leviathans. "The Utopians were protecting me all this time, out of charity. Apollo Mojave gave their life to save me, gave me their seat on the Moon shuttle so I could get safely out of Mycroft Canner's reach, but, if I assassinated someone like Cornel MASON, how long would it take you to start wondering if it was a Utopian conspiracy? If they planned it? Did they cultivate me all these years on the Moon as part of a scheme to kill the Emperor? You'd think that, anybody would!"

I suspect Tully had never before faced a crowd so silent. Cousins will cheer politely, Europeans debate, Humanists cheer or heckle, but the expressionless Brillists just took notes in a dozen silent formats, or whispered technical terms in breath-soft German, as if safely separated from this fascinating subject by a mirrored wall.

"Obviously I'm not going to assassinate anyone," Tully continued, "and I don't really think set-sets are sabotaging the CFB, but is something similar possible? Could a spark like that really set the world at war?" He scanned the crowd, restless. "You tell me, you're the experts. You from the Institute know the human psyche inside out, what we are, what we can become. Is the human animal still like it was hundreds of years ago: aggressive, territorial, competitive, ambitious? Do we still think in terms of 'us' and 'them'? When drunks lash out at someone from another Hive, isn't that really the iceberg tip of something bigger? Or have we changed? Is the human psyche really better, wiser, more peaceful now? Are we really, as we are required to believe, incapable of war?"

"No."

All eyes sought the interrupter, glaring, a flock of scientists wondering what fool had shattered the walls of objectivity with that most dangerous of missiles: an opinion. All breathed relief to find it was not one of them.

"I'm capable of making war." Sniper stepped forward, the crowd parting before it like mist before breath. "I'm not a Brillist, and I can't speak for anybody else's psyche, but I love my Hive. I love my bash'. I love scanning the news each morning to see what great deeds my fellow Humanists have added to the sum total of human excellence. If something threatened to destroy that, I'd fight to stop it, kill to stop it, I know I could. And I can't be the only one who feels this way." The master crowd-pleaser slid slowly toward the podium. "If there's one thing I've learned from helping the President these past years, it's that the balance between the Hives is a lot more fragile than people imagine. They say the geographic nations were the cause of past wars: borders, nationalism, that Hives are better. But I think Hives could be worse. Our fellow Members are our comrades, not by chance, but because we think alike. We choose them. If in the past people would kill or die for the field they happened to be born in, then I think most of us would fight ten times more fiercely for the Hive we chose. That doesn't mean I hate the other Hives; of course I don't." Sniper spread its arms, its androgynous torso offering the world a broad embrace. "I love the other Hives too, all of them. They're part of this. There have to be multiple Hives to make the choice meaningful. But if another Hive threatened my own, I'm sure I'd fight back, I'd fight anyone: a Mitsubishi, a Hiveless, a traitor Humanist, even my own President if they somehow threatened what makes us us." Sniper's clear, almost-black eyes disarmed even Tully's guards, who stood frozen like caryatids as the celebrity, and hundreds of millions of viewers with it, stepped up onto the steps beside Tully's soapbox. "Would I fight for my Hive?" Sniper continued. "Yes. And I'd kill for it, I know that. I think I'd die for it too, though there's no way to know if I'd really be brave enough until the day comes."

Sniper smiled on Tully, who stood ice-stiff, as if he feared the slightest breath would dispel this apparition at his side. I like to imagine dark ambitions wriggling through Tully's mind here, scenarios tumbling mechanically like a Jacob's Ladder, his next five moves, ten, how best to exploit the weapon of celebrity that Chance had thrown him. But Tully is not such a creature. I have so many reasons to hate him, it would be a disservice to the true ones to pretend he is worse than he is. Tully was stunned by Sniper's presence, dazzled, and if any thought of personal gain pierced the veil of disbelief, it was doubtless no more than a prayer of thanks to whatever Power he believes in.

Marking Tully's stunned silence, Sniper shifted its smile to reassuring-mode, developed for that fragile genus of love-mad fans who burst into hysterics upon meeting their idol in the flesh. "You're a very brave person, Tully Mardi. You're trying to save the world by preventing, or at least preparing us for, what would probably be the worst war in human history if it came. You don't mind being called a crackpot, you don't mind sacrificing time and hobbies to be gaped at by ungrateful crowds, and you don't mind publicly implicating yourself in a plot to kill the most powerful person in the world, if that's what it takes to drive the warning home." It offered Tully its hand, clean calluses still soft from swimming. "You're right, there could be a war, and if there was one I'd like to hope that you and I would wind up on the same side."

Imagine, reader, a castaway, so long on his island prison that even the hunger for human company has waned, who spots white sails at sea. He cannot at first recognize the answer to the prayer he has long stopped chanting, but watches uncomprehending until, like a fever, hope, pain, loneliness, all the old passions make him charge shrieking into the surf. Just so, Tully accepted Sniper's hand slowly, gingerly, then clung for dear life. "Mojave, not Mardi," he corrected. "I prefer Tully Mojave."

In a kinder world, Saladin and I would have awakened trembling, breathless at this moment, sensing in our bones as the doom that we had sacrificed so much to fight became a certainty. But in a kinder world Sniper would have turned right.

"Nice to meet you, Tully Mojave," Sniper answered. "I'd like to introduce you to some friends of mine."

Snakes and Ladders

"MEMBER HIROAKI MITSUBISHI, PLEASE. TELL THEM IT'S THE Pontifex Maxima."

Julia Doria-Pamphili stretched back across her favorite sofa, copied thread by thread from Freud's. After a moment her office wall flickered to digital life, showing a suite in the distant Mitsubishi capital of Tōgenkyō, elegant Japanese architecture decorated with Ganymedist paintings, where Danaë's half-set-set brood lounged around their gaming boards and news feeds. The freshly promoted Cousins' Feedback Bureau Executive Assistant Hiroaki Mitsubishi is the frailest of the ten adopted Mitsubishi ba'sibs, ancestrally Korean if I guess right from her face. She was thin as a wisp within her spring silk Cousin's wrap as she crouched on the floor with the delicacy of a folded spider, sitting beside a game board, where Toshi Mitsubishi—whom you last saw with myself and Jung Su-Hyeon in the Censor's office—faced low-crouching Jun Mitsubishi, who took out her frustration at having failed to infiltrate Faust's Institute by playing an excessively aggressive game of Go.

Hiroaki waved. "Hello, Julia. Thank you for calling back."

"Of course," she smiled. "What's up?"

Frail Hiroaki hesitated, but Masami Mitsubishi spoke up for her, sprawled on the far side of the game board with the calligraphy-covered jacket of a *Black Sakura* reporter wadded beneath him as a pillow. "We need your help handling Darcy Sok."

"You're asking help from an opponent?" The Conclave Head waggled her finger at them, like a chiding aunt. "Are things getting out of hand?"

This is the first time you have seen Masami Mitsubishi in the flesh, the young journalist whose Seven-Ten list sparked so much. The boldness of his smile here is surely false, a mask for the exhaustion of four days dodging the grim slur 'plagiarist,' but it is a good mask, the strength of his jaw and the darkness of his face making all his expressions warm and confident.

Masami is the darkest of the ten ba'sibs, darker even than Africa-tinted Toshi, and he wears an Ainu strat bracelet, a rare Japanese ethnic sub-strat which stirs much comment when he stands at his adopted father's side. "Darcy Sok attacked Hiroaki at the CFB last night. Physically attacked." His frowning glance led Julia to the bulk of a bandage under the cloth that veiled Hiroaki's fragile shoulder.

"I'm not surprised. Exposing the corruption in the the CFB isn't some small revenge; you've destroyed everything Darcy Sok lived for, the whole Cousins Hive, and you've made it seem like Sok's fault."

"Sok has no evidence it was us."

Julia chuckled. "Masami, honey, a flailing, desperate person doesn't need real evidence, conjecture is enough. You put Darcy Sok on your Seven-Ten list, and Hiroaki was inside the CFB; that's coincidence enough for an angry imagination to blame it on you, even if you were innocent as babes."

"Not that a Nurturist bigot like Darcy Sok would've called us innocent, even as babies."

More than a few of the ba'sibs scowled, while others traded glances. Dark glances would have made sense, angry glances, chill, even hurt, but these were nothing so familiar, strange glances with something off about them, timed wrong, shifting wrong, something in the muscles of the cheeks, heads semiturning but not fully following the motion of the eyes. Perhaps you can see it best in tiny Hiroaki, how her arms—as thin as sticks within one of the sleeveless sweaters Danaë hand-knit to let her children boast their 'unnatural' Brillist numbers—don't quite move like arms which have climbed and roughhoused under Nature's summer sun.

Julia gave a sympathetic smile. "I know it means a lot to you, getting back at the Cousins for ruining your training, but I warned you, revenge is dangerous. Revenge has motive dripping off of it, and when your motive is obvious, people will link things to you even without evidence, and more when there is evidence."

"There is no evidence!" Masami protested. "Hiroaki didn't actually leak anything, or break any law! They were just an observer!"

Julia did not feel like feigning patience. "You're not a Gag-gene, Masami, and anyone with half an eye for body language can spot from how you move that your senses are half remapped. I'm sure the Brillists have guessed for ages, plenty of others too, but everyone held off while Minor's Law protected you; now that three of you are legal adults, any snoop worth their salt can find the records of your training bash', and who was behind the attack that broke it up. I wouldn't be surprised if someone warned Kosala and Lorelei Cook the very day you passed your Adulthood Competency Exam."

What leaked from Masami's throat was almost a growl. "It's Felix Faust, isn't it? They told Darcy Sok we're set-sets, told the Big Seven too, and now they're leaking it to the public."

Julia shook her head. "Felix Faust is a voyeur, not a player. They don't have to destroy you, they can sit back on their sofa and watch you bring this down upon yourselves. You should have been subtler. I understand going after Lorelei Cook; as Minister of Education Cook is practically keeping Nurturism alive by themself."

"And Kosala!" Masami interrupted. "Kosala's been covering Cook's part in the raids for years! Kosala's just as guilty!"

Julia nodded indulgently. "But Darcy Sok wasn't one of your enemies before this, and by destroying the Hive on their watch you've made an unnecessary enemy, one you can't unmake so easily. If Sok doesn't kill themself, they'll devote themself to revenge on the lot of you, with an undying, single-minded fervor, just as you have against Cook and Kosala. That's not the kind of enemy you want to make at a young age. Never create a personal enemy. Always keep layers of minions between yourself and someone you destroy, it's safer that way."

Frail Hiroaki frowned at the Cousins' wrap around her knees, as at an old cast overdue to be removed. "I never lied to Darcy Sok. I told them I wanted to join the CFB to fight corruption. They were the one stupid enough to assume I meant only other people's corruption, not their own. Or yours. Frankly, Julia, if Darcy really thinks you're the lesser of two evils they need to reread *Faust*."

Julia smiled at the compliment. "I've been too gentle on you kids. We've been playing games with no real risk, but bringing down a Hive is deadly dangerous, and I'm not just talking to Hiroaki. The lot of you have been very reckless in this, Toshi especially."

"Me?" The Censor's analyst sat forward. "I haven't done anything. Really I haven't."

"That doesn't matter. You have access to the secrets of the Censor's office. You could have leaked them to your ba'sibs, and people hunting for conspiracy will assume you have, whether it's true or not." Julia played with the long black coil of her hair. "Just because you're innocent doesn't mean you don't need to prepare an alibi. Innocence needs to be proved."

Self-conscious Toshi tugged at the fluffy twists of her own hair. "Do you really think that's necessary?"

"Revenge heeds instinct, not evidence. Besides, you did know what your sibs were doing, and you could have stopped it. That's complicity enough for blame to fix on you."

Hiroaki gave frowning Toshi a sisterly shoulder-squeeze. "Anyway, Julia, Darcy Sok is your parishioner. Can't you deflect them? Calm them? Redirect their anger someplace else? You could call them for a session right now. It would mean a lot to us. Please?"

Julia frowned. "Why doesn't your mother take care of Darcy Sok? Or your father? They have means enough."

Glances not-quite-right passed among the ba'sibs once again.

"You're ashamed to tell them, aren't you?" Julia's chuckle grew smug. "Afraid of a chewing out? This won't do, children. If you start keeping secrets within your own bash', things will fall apart faster than you can say Seven-Ten list." Her eyes narrowed. "Or are you afraid of something more serious than a chewing out? You told me and your mother that you didn't plan the Seven-Ten list theft. Was that the truth?"

"Yes!" the ba'sibs answered all together in a chorus.

"Do you know who stole it?"

"No."

"Really?"

"Cross my heart." Masami made the gesture with dark fingers stained darker by the archaic inks used at *Black Sakura*. "I wrote the list but didn't think to pull a stunt like the theft. I wish I did know who it was. I'd congratulate them on a plot well laid, then deck them."

Julia smiled sympathy. "I hear Papadelias is on the edge of learning to trace the Canner Device. I'm sure there will be sufficient decking when the time comes."

"Do you know who has it?"

"What?"

"Canner's prototype." Again they all said it together: Masami, Hiroaki, Toshi, Jun, Ran, Sora, Michi, Harue, Naō, Setsuna, all one crisp, inhuman chorus. "We have to find it."

A narrow smile. "Perhaps I do know who has it, but that's the kind of information you buy from an opponent, you don't get it out of the kindness of my adversarial heart. As for Darcy Sok, go to your parents. You made this bed, you get chewed out in it."

"Please, Julia." Hiroaki huddled adorably within her Cousin's wrap. "You could do it so easily, and so quickly!"

"We aren't asking this for nothing," Masami added. "We'll owe you, help for help."

"Mmm? Anything concrete to offer? Or do I get an open-ended boon?"

"We can help with a certain enemy you've made in the last days."

Julia half rose from her sofa, her oil-black hair unwinding down her back like a waking serpent. "An enemy? Intriguing. Who?"

"Carlyle Foster."

Julia stared for a frozen moment. "Have you been spying on my little Carlyle?" Her voice grew sweet and ominous at once, a teasing disapproval.

"Not more than normal," Toshi answered. "But nobody can fly that far out of pattern and not be conspicuous."

Julia stretched her shoulders. "Good spotting, bad interpreting. I've given Carlyle to Dominic as a present."

The ba'sibs exchanged looks, which a stranger might have read as nervous or questioning, but Julia knows that one who reads too much into the curve of a dog's inhuman brows gets bit.

"How long ago was it visible?" she asked. "Carlyle going out of pattern."

"I didn't spot it first," Toshi answered. "Jun, you did, right?"

Jun Mitsubishi only now looked up from the Go board. The would-be Brillist member of the brood is always quiet, with little smiles and little shrugs, as if constantly apologizing to the others for being the only one who looks classically Japanese, and drawing an unfair portion of great Andō's affection. "Who are we talking about?"

"Cousin Carlyle Foster."

"Who?"

"C-CF-003035."

"Oh, yes!" Jun cried. "Spectacular acceleration. There was some erratic behavior Monday, but it didn't get acute until two days ago, full swan dive yesterday."

Julia's fingers twitched as she mapped out the calendar in her mind. "Yes, that's about right."

Jun looked up. "Is 3035 not there yet?" she leaned back, eyelids sagging as she lost herself in the flicker of her lenses.

Julia perked. "Oh, is Carlyle coming to see me? Good. Perhaps I can ease the swan dive."

"They want to destroy you."

"Carlyle?" Julia laughed.

"I know what kind of dive I'm seeing."

Julia gave . . . patronizing isn't the right word, a matronizing smile. "Jun, I know what's happening to Carlyle, it's a case quite without precedent in your experience. There's no shame in an imperfect prediction."

"I know what I'm looking at. I can pull them up again, they're . . ." Jun clutched suddenly at the nearest warm arm, which happened to be Toshi's. "They're there now."

"What?"

"3035, C-CF-003035, Carlyle Foster. They're there now. Their location signal, there, in your office."

"Arriving?" Julia turned toward the door.

"No. There. Now. They've been there for almost an hour."

Julia frowned, gazed about her room, her seats, her desk. Her closet. "Carlyle?"

Carlyle: <C-CF-003035 is my tracker tag, isn't it, Julia? They've infiltrated the tracker system on top of all the rest, and you never told me.>

Julia Doria-Pamphili savored a long, smiling breath. "Time to end the call, kids. I'll handle this myself."

"They're there?" Hiroaki voiced it with the most fear. "3035! They heard! We talked about the Cousins!"

"Do not worry," Julia pronounced with a clear, commanding calm. "I'll handle it, then call you back. Give my best to your mother."

"Juli—"

Earth's Chief Sensayer killed the call, then watched, still smiling, as the screen cycled around to a slide show of her favorite Sniper posters. "They have a thrillingly original reincarnation theory, those kids; I'll send you the notes."

"Set-sets." With those black syllables, Carlyle Foster stepped forth from the closet. "Pythagorean set-sets."

"Yes, their notion of reincarnation is more Pythagorean than Buddhist, well done. How did you know?"

Carlyle is priest enough to tread with reverence in the Chief Sensayer's office, even now. "Jehovah Mason. When they first met Eureka Weeksbooth, their first question was 'Are both your set-sets Pythagorean?'"

"Ah," Julia smiled, "the infallible Jehovah Epicurus Mason."

Every inch of Carlyle was tense: pale hands clenched in fists, golden brows knit, a parody of threat from a creature too delicate to make it feel real. "Would those kids have been Cartesian set-sets too, like Eureka and Sidney, if their training hadn't been interrupted?"

"No, no." Julia flexed her shoulders. "A new kind. I've heard them say Oniwaban set-set, but I think they're just being dramatic. They claim they would have made Cartesians obsolete."

"Set-sets, Julia, on both sides of this: attacking the Cousins, and in the Saneer-Weeksbooth bash'. They are the poison after all, and you've been treating it like a game."

Her smile did not change. "Why are you here, Carlyle? Is there a problem in the Saneer-Weeksbooth bash'?"

"You taught me to be a spy, Julia. Don't think I haven't used it on you, too."

"Did you record the call just now?" she asked. "Should I say, 'Oops'?"

"I recorded that one, and dozens of others, today and many days." Carlyle's steps were slow, the fatigue of a grueling night weakening her limbs like flu.

Still Julia smiled. "You mustn't read too much into how I talk to them like it's a game. You and I really have been guarding the world from them, Carlyle, keeping the set-set poison out as best we can. I let them think I think it's just a game because it makes them give away so much to me, you heard how much."

"I don't believe you, Julia. But, right now, I actually don't care. I'm not here to confront you about our noble battle against the Mitsubishi brood being a sham. I'm here to make you save the Cousins."

"Make me?" Her smile brightened. "You are feeling stronger after your first session with Dominic. Did you enjoy it? I see you're not wearing your old scarf anymore."

Carlyle's throat was indeed naked for once. "I'm not going to let you bait me, Julia. This is serious. The CFB scandal is going to drag the Cousins down, and all that we've created with it, all the hospitals and orphanages, the greatest charitable network in history. You can stop it."

"I can?"

"Yes, only you." Carlyle sank into one of the pudgy armchairs. "You don't see how, do you?"

Julia leaned back. "I hadn't thought about it."

"I didn't think you would have. You have the CFB, Julia. You have Darcy Sok and the others. I encouraged you to make them your parishioners because I thought you were the best one to help them."

"Mmm. A wise decision."

There it flashed in Carlyle's blue eyes, the chill of diamond, almost keen enough for murder. "I know you've been exploiting Darcy Sok. Not a lot, not enough to threaten the world order, just having them push the Cousins in directions you suggest from time to time, plus . . ."

"Plus?"

"Plus the other sorts of things you like to make parishioners do. You've broken your vows, Julia, over and over. I've recorded that, too."

"Have you?" She picked at her nails. "How enterprising."

"Yes. And now that I know Dominic, I see where you learned your style from."

"Mmm. We cross-pollinated, Dominic and I. Did you like it? Dominic's technique."

Carlyle did not avoid her eyes. "We're not talking about me for once."

Julia laughed. "If you don't like what I do to my parishioners, why didn't you do something years ago? You kept feeding me more people, that makes you guilty too."

"True. I'm guilty. I wasn't even deluded, or, if I was, I was willingly deluded. I let things continue, spying, manipulating, because it made me feel good, and because I believed you were doing more good than harm."

"I still am."

Carlyle breathed a short sigh. "Only if you do this. There's one more chance, Julia. You can save the Cousins. It's not hard to prove you've been manipulating the CFB. All their key staff are your parishioners, and I'm sure, if an expert analyzed the way they've been editing how letters are sorted, they could see that it supported your goals."

"That's not proof."

"True, it's not, it's circumstantial, enough to cause doubt but not enough to bring to trial. On the other hand, if you confess—"

"Confess?"

"Confess that you have been calling the shots in the CFB."

"Why, in the name of sanity, would I confess?"

"Because, if everyone thinks you controlled the CFB, they won't look for anything deeper. The press smells blood, Julia. They're not going to let up until they've sunk their teeth into someone. It could be you instead of the heart of the Cousins."

Julia stretched back. "Mmm. Doesn't sound very appealing."

"No? The whole point of you sending me into the CFB was to help them fight more sinister outside control. You achieved that, twice in fact."

"Twice?"

"You helped the CFB fight back against the original outside manipulation, and you also slowed Danaë's brood down. If you tell everyone you only hijacked the CFB in order to keep Danaë out, we can expose what the Mitsubishi set-sets were doing, make it look like there was nothing rotten in the CFB before Madame started moving in on it, and no one ever needs to learn the truth. The Cousins stay safe, Madame is exposed, and you wind up a hero."

Julia's eyes went wide. "Madame? You think I was fighting Madame directly? That's very flattering, Carlyle, but honestly I thought I trained you better than this."

"Doesn't Danaë Mitsubishi work for Madame? If President Ganymede was born at Madame's, their twin sister was too."

Julia shook her head. "You're useless when it comes to period thinking, aren't you, Carlyle? When a lady weds she throws away all allegiance to her parents and transfers it to her husband. Danaë isn't working for Madame. It's Director Andō who wants the Cousins torn down, not Madame."

"Andō?" Carlyle trembled. "That . . . That's even worse! The Mitsubishi Director themself trying to tear the Cousins down. That's what you have to tell the police!"

"Why?" Julia shot back. "Why should I? I like Danaë, we have endless fun."

Carlyle's brows knit. "They're destroying a Hive! Is that not registering in your mind? Almost two billion people. There's never been a social disaster on this scale!"

"That may be true," Julia answered, "but it's for the world's good."

"What?"

"I know it is hard for you to see, Carlyle, but the Cousins have to go. The Masons are on their way to a monopoly which will destroy the Hive system. The Cousins are enabling that. You want to know what Darcy Sok was really doing in the CFB? Altering the sorting programs, distorting the data? They were trying to counter the control that's already there."

"Danaë's? No, Madame's?" Carlyle guessed.

"Neither. There's one voice dictating the CFB reports, controlling so many of the letters that the trends the computers find are really only ever one person's voice. Day by day, month by month, the trends the CFB extracts are dictated like clockwork. Darcy Sok was altering the postanalysis reports to try to counter it, fighting control with countercontrol, the closest we could get to freeing the Cousins, but that was just treading water."

Carlyle's throat was not yet too hardened to sob. "Who? Who's dictating the letters?"

"You haven't guessed?"

"MASON?"

"You really haven't guessed. Well, I'll tell you if you earn it." Julia stretched back. "Meanwhile, better to dissolve the Hive and let its resources spread among the others that at least have some integrity inside."

Carlyle made fists. "So you won't do it?"

"What?"

"You won't save the Cousins? You still can, all you have to do is go public about your battle with Danaë, claim that you two are responsible for all the corruption in the CFB. Do that and no one will look for anything underneath."

Julia stroked her hair. "No. No, I think it's time the Cousins went."

Carlyle took a long breath, wincing as if in pain, so reluctant was she to resort to sin. "How about saving yourself?"

"What?"

"I told you I have recordings, lots of recordings. I can prove a lot of things about you, what you do here that you shouldn't. If you tell the world you abused your position to manipulate the CFB and fight off Danaë, you lose your license for a year or so, but you save the Hive and become a hero. If you refuse to help, I'll see to it you lose your license for a much more ignominious reason, and a much longer time."

Julia's eyes glittered. "Are you blackmailing me?"

"Yes, I suppose I am. I've been gathering evidence for a long time, recordings, tracker logs, videos."

Julia shook her head. "Carlyle, Carlyle, Carlyle. The kinds of recordings you make by sneaking into places aren't admissible in court—"

"Unless I take them in specific circumstances and document them in certain ways, I know that. The Commissioner General taught me."

Julia blinked. "Papadelias?"

"I went to Papadelias a year ago, when I started to doubt what you had me doing. Papadelias was already on to you, but had no proof. I wouldn't testify then, but I had them teach me how to gather evidence, to build a case so we could take you down if you ever used your resources for something other than good. This is too much, Julia. Even if I weren't a Cousin I wouldn't sit back and let you destroy a whole Hive."

"You're bluffing, and you're not good at it."

"You just can't see me as a threat, can you?" Carlyle's inner tumult forced out tears. "I'm not bluffing. This is your last chance, Julia. Save the Cousins."

"No. I refuse to help a Hive that crows about being morally superior but can't support itself without lies and blackmail. You're proof enough in yourself. What's the point of all the Cousins' work keeping the other Hives civil if you're the first to turn into brutish backstabbers when crisis comes?"

Carlyle rose. "I'm serious, this is your last chance."

"No."

"Then it's over, Julia. I'm sorry." In this world one rarely sees apology unmixed with regret. Carlyle walked to the office door and opened it. "Come in, Papa."

Commissioner General Ektor Carlyle Papadelias entered with a soft voice, a grave face, and a full squad of backup. "Julia Doria-Pamphili, under the authority of the Universal Free Alliance, I arrest you as an officer of the Alliance Conclave of Sensayers for abuse of the official capacity of your office, and for misuse of official information; I arrest you as a Member of the European Union for willful communication of classified information, for bribery, for receipt of stolen information property, and for sexual exploitation; and I arrest you as a Member of a Hive pledged to respect the legal protections of fellow Members of the Universal Free Alliance for conspiracy to steal information property belonging to Cousins, Humanists, Masons, and Mitsubishi, and for conspiracy to commit espionage against Cousins, Masons, and Mitsubishi."

Julia smiled at the recitation. "Carlyle, you really did it?"

Centenarian Papadelias no longer bothers to hide his curses under his breath. "You told Julia you helped me, didn't you, Foster? I told you to say nothing. Should have cuffed you to my car."

Carlyle stepped forward, bold as a traitor before a tribunal whose verdict is already known. "I'm the one who did this to Julia, Papa. I should have the decency to face them."

Papa's raisin-wrinkled brows drew taut.

"Carlyle!" Even Julia's face can show astonishment. "You really did it? You really are a double agent? You betrayed me? That's wonderful! I'm so proud of you!"

"What?"

"You've become so strong! When I first took you in you were a spineless wreck, just waiting for somebody to tell you how to live and what to think. Now you've become your own person. You're taking initiative, doubting what you're told, making contacts of your own, and following through on what you believe. It takes a lot of strength to betray your teacher. I'm so proud of you."

"I did have a pretty good teacher to betray." The syrup in Julia's tone had Carlyle smiling. "That didn't come out right, did it?" Carlyle chuckled. "I mean that you were a good teacher, Julia, you showed me how to do something with my life, and how much the world needs help. And separately you really do deserve to be betrayed."

She nodded. "That's fair. And you were a wonderful pupil." She cupped Carlyle's cheek gently in her hand, like a proud parent. "Danaë Mitsubishi is your real mother. Twenty-eight years ago Andō promised Ganymede enough resources to make them the Humanist President if Ganymede would get Danaë to marry Andō. Ganymede took the bargain, and ten months later, at a certain house in Paris, you were born. The wedding was right after."

Carlyle blinked. "What?"

"You betrayed me. You didn't think there would be consequences, Gaggene?" Julia's smile deepened. "It's thanks to you that a certain person in Paris controls the Humanists and Mitsubishi now, and by giving Danaë to Andō your birth also gave the Mitsubishi everything they needed to destroy the Cousins. So you aren't personally responsible for the entire world being slaves to you-know-who, just three Hives."

Carlyle froze, too shaken even to tremble. "Why did you just tell me that?"

"When you start playing grown-up games, there are grown-up consequences."

"Danaë Mitsubishi?" Carlyle repeated. "Then I was . . ."

"Carlyle, don't . . ." Papa tried to intervene, but knows when done is done.

Still Julia smiled. "I've enjoyed sparring with Danaë all these years, but really, the two of us are just scrabbling over leftovers. Thanks to you, someone else already finished conquering the world."

The Gag-gene teetered as if to fall. "Thanks to me? Then, my mother . . . and my father? Who is my father?"

"Mmm. Well, now that you know your real birth-bash', you can go home and ask. I doubt your step-ba'sibs in Tōgenkyō know much, but you can try Paris. Dominic's an upstanding ba'sib, I'm sure they'll help."

Speech abandoned Carlyle, strength too, as she fumbled like one crippled by laughter or fever.

"Foster, don't!" Papa made a halfhearted grab as the sensayer crashed past him toward the exit, like a hound mad with the hunt's scent.

"Should we stop them, Papa?" The Commissioner General's men prepared to follow.

"No." Papa frowned at still-smiling Julia. "Too late."

CHAPTER THE THIRTEENTH

Rose-Tinted Daydream

SOMETIMES MADAME COMPARES HER REVOLUTION TO THE Renaissance. As she has made the Enlightenment her weapon today, so, starting in the Fourteenth Century, Italy, tired of the yoke of northern chivalry, dredged the legacies of Greece and Rome from the dust, and redefined art, learning, and nobility on their 'classical' model, half ancient, half invention, in which Italy was the automatic leader. Petrarch was their spearhead, whom you may know as the subject of the First Anonymous's third essay, which argues that Petrarch's scholarly group who planned to live and work together might have instituted the bash' system eight centuries early if the Black Death had not claimed all but him. It also claimed Laura, the beauty whom Petrarch's poems apotheosized into one of those immortal goddesses of Love, like Juliet, Helen, Cleopatra, Lesbia, Dante's Beatrice, Abelard's Heloïse, and perhaps now Seine Mardi, for the paintings, poems, plays, and films keep flowing, the world's imagination hungry for portraits of this young Humanist who shone so brightly that the Prince of Utopians would give up bash' and Hive and life for her. Will her cult endure the centuries, I wonder, as Laura's has? It is Petrarch's poem 205 that I remember best, where he sorrows for the men centuries later who will read his verses and curse Fortune that they were born too late to see Laura's beauty while she lived. Laura had children, though, living shadows of her beauty, including one famous descendant, whose path you may curse or praise Fortune for not permitting you to cross: De Sade.

"Casimir, you must let me pour you a drink." Felix Faust lifted a decanter from the sideboard, cut crystal of an expense to match the aged nectar within. "I never expected you to get this far. What a wonderful world we live in where even I can be surprised."

"Thanks, Headmaster, that's kind of you." European Prime Minister Casimir Perry had stood timidly at the threshold of the *Salon de Sade*, as if afraid the ivory carpet would blacken under an outsider's feet. "Where is everyone?" He scanned the oval ring of seats, all empty.

"Fair question. You're the guest of honor tonight and should have arrived last so we could cheer you across the threshold." Faust poured himself a glass as well. "In fact, the rest of us were asked to get here twenty minutes ago. It seems there's crisis enough afoot to have all the other Hive heads running late."

"But not you?" Perry fidgeted with his embroidered cuffs, fresh from Madame's tailors.

"Unlike our colleagues, I delegate Gordian's entire administrative burden, so, while I may be surprised by this delicious crisis, I'm not expected to do much about it. Shall we sit?"

Faust gestured to the window bench, so freshly brushed that not a speck of lint had had a chance to colonize the velvet. Madame and her servants had outdone themselves for this occasion, transforming the oval sanctum from an earthly to a celestial paradise. Fawn-thin tables stood against the walls, lush with sweetmeats and covered platters alluring as unopened presents. If roast beasts and flame-grilled hunks on spits are a man's feast, this was a woman's: intricate patisserie, ribbon candy delicate as jewelry, chocolate truffles, bite-sized cakes, and bouquets of fruit sliced so thin that the light shone through their juicy petals like stained glass. The benches had been restuffed, virgin sheepskins piled on the floor, while the tools of love in their glass cases, both the museum pieces and those ready for use, gleamed clean. Even the curtains over the grand window were new, night blue glittering with constellations, which made the masses in the Flesh Pit below seem as distant as mortals glimpsed by Zeus and Hera as they lie locked in love's afterglow on steep and snowy Ida.

Perry stared into his glass. "I'd rather stand."

"My dear Casimir, this bench has the most interesting view in the world. There's a more telling cross-section of humanity down there than in the Censor's database, plus porn. How can you possibly prefer to stand?" His eyes softened. "You're nervous?"

"Of course."

Faust smiled. "The entire European Parliament doesn't make you nervous."

The Prime Minister rubbed his temples, which had amassed more care lines in his five decades than Faust's had in eight. "The European Parliament can't deny me sexual satisfaction for the rest of my life. Aren't you nervous around Madame?"

Faust laughed. "Only when I'm sober."

"How did they do this to us, Felix? I was too young to understand when

I got sucked in, but you're a psychologist, you must have watched it closely. Here we are, the most influential people in the world, prancing around in frills because it's the only way we can get turned on anymore." Perry ran his thumb around his glass, coaxing a soft note from the crystal. "Madame lured us all into this long before we were important, but how did they know we'd become what we are now? Are they really able to spot the ones who're ripe for this perversion when we're young, and then make sure only we can get into office? Or is everybody this kind of pervert deep inside, and it's just Madame that brings it out in us?"

Faust crossed his arms. "Don't give Madame all the credit. Some of us cultivated excellent perversions on our own."

Perry smiled. "I know you did, Felix, but Bryar Kosala? The Emperor? The King of Spain is the most morally upright person I've ever met, but even Spain—"

"That didn't stop you hiring Ziven Racer to knock Spain out of the election," Faust tested.

Perry went white. "I . . ."

"Don't worry, I haven't discussed it with the others, and I won't without good cause."

"How . . . how did you know?"

"I'm Brillist Headmaster, Casimir, how do I know anything? Don't worry, I won't blackmail you. I couldn't really—body language isn't proof enough for court."

"I . . . thank you."

"My point was, you took advantage of Spain's honorability, knowing they'd resign if someone tried to fix the vote on their behalf. You know in Spain's case conscience is a weakness."

Again Perry's eyes escaped into the amber ocean of his drink. "I never said I wasn't the worst of us, Felix. I shudder to list the things I've done to get to this room today. I think I was a good person when I was young, I really do."

Faust stretched back. "Think of our perversions as topiary. We all had the seeds in us, but it's Madame who made them art. Now, shall I have Mycroft fetch you something to fuck while we wait? The others are so set in their configurations, the two threesomes and the pair, that usually our debauches aren't very debauched, I'm afraid. I've been looking forward to you changing that."

"Is that Mycroft Canner?" Perry spotted me now in Jehovah's empty corner, my dull Franciscan habit anticamouflage against the sparkle of the house.

Faust's eyes rarely grow wide. "You haven't met?"

"I heard about Canner turning up as a Servicer a couple days ago, and stalking Tully Mardi. I guessed Madame must be connected to it somehow. That's Mycroft Canner, isn't it? I recognize the notch out of their ear."

Faust summoned me with a flick of his fingers. "Poor Outsider, the only one who's had to make do without Mycroft's services all these years. To be strict, though, it isn't through Madame's good offices that we have Mycroft, it's thanks to our excellent and unique Prince, Jehovah Epicurus Donatien D'Arouet Mason." His eyes glittered. "Which name will you use for our dear scion now, Perry? As one of Madame's elite, you're entitled to use something more personal than 'the Prince D'Arouet,' but you must pick carefully—everyone is judged by which they use. Dibs on Donatien."

"Dibs?" Perry frowned. "Why do you get dibs on one?"

"As one of the candidates in the initial debate over who the child's father was, I got to contribute a name. But you weren't around twenty-one years ago. Tough luck."

Perry did not answer, for I had drawn close enough to be inspected. His face grew slack before me, a distanced awe, like a child gaping at a cobra in a zoo. "Incredible. Madame really does collect the worst of us." More words were on his lips, but others snuffed them.

"Twenty-nine years!" It was a woman's scream, shrill through the closed and paneled doors.

A man's voice followed. "Bryar! It's not as if I conspired against you personally."

"Twenty-nine years you've been controlling the CFB and you never said a word to me! Not one!"

"Her Excellency Cousin Chairwoman Bryar Kosala," the crier announced, finishing just as she burst in, a tidal wave of satin and accusations.

"You knew!" she shrieked. "And now you're too coward to show your face!"

"My Lord," the crier called behind her, "the Compte Déguisé."

This title heralded, not a man, but two servants wheeling a chaise. A manikin lounged in it, sporting a coat of green velvet, a burgundy-violet waistcoat, a strip of black mask, and, through loudspeakers, the voice of the Anonymous. "Bryar, be sensible!" he pleaded, desperation clear despite the computer's modulation. "You know I'm not hiding from you, I'm hiding from the Outsider. You expect me to reveal myself now, of all times?"

Faust laughed even as Perry scowled.

"It's not as if I actively conspired to take control of the CFB," the Anon-ymous continued. "It's Danaë and Julia Doria-Pamphili you should be angry at, they're the ones who actually tried to take it away from me and use it for their own ends. I didn't take it to abuse it, and really I didn't even take it, I . . . inherited it."

"Inherited?"

"Exactly. This isn't about us, Bryar. The Anonymous has directed the CFB for over a century, and I've been the Anonymous a lot longer than we've been together."

"And that's supposed to make me feel better?" Her voice cracked. "Not only has the person I loved been secretly dictating my political actions for thirty years, but other people I didn't even know were doing it before them!"

The manikin's bearers fled before Bryar's wrath like hounds from a whip, leaving the chaise and toy Anonymous to plead alone. "What was I sup-posed to do? It's not a system either of us could fix."

"How about, 'By the way, darling, your life is a lie'?" Faust cut in, smiling.

The bouquets of lace and satin which dripped from the half-sleeves of Kosala's gown were not cut to accommodate the brandishing of fists. "Felix, I swear, if the words 'I knew the whole time' come out of your mouth, I'll show you something your numbers say I shouldn't be capable of! Probably involving my foot and bits of you that don't want to meet it!"

Faust swished his dregs. "I can see why Madame wanted Mycroft here as chaperone tonight. Mycroft, pour the Chairwoman a glass of sherry, would you? There's a good monster. Perry, care for seconds?"

"Perry?" Bryar realized only now that the quiet figure half screened by tiers of canapés was neither Spain nor MASON. "Why didn't you tell us Perry was already here?"

The Outsider tiptoed forward. "Sorry this is coming on an awkward night."

I had never seen Bryar's eyes so cold.

Perry managed not to wince. "Good to see you, Chair Kosala. I know you know this already, but you look wonderful in a dress." He paused, hoping for a smile. None came. "And that's the Anonymous over the intercom?"

"We say Déguisé here," Faust corrected, "the Comte Déguisé. Déguisé, may I present Prime Minister Perry."

Silence is harshest when the speaker has no real face.

"It's an honor to meet you, Monsieur le Compte." Prime Minister Perry gave ample pause, but the voice behind the puppet did not stir. "I realize," he almost stammered, "it will take you longer than the others to trust me, but I can't tell you how thrilling it is to actually be able to talk to you, negotiate with you, get input. I've admired you my whole life. You're the voice of sense in all this." Again the Prime Minister paused, tense hands fidgeting with the buttons on his pocket flaps, but, again, silence. "And you control the CFB?" he continued. "That's strange news. It's not a problem if you're a Cousin, but you're not a Cousin, are you?"

"That matter is not for you to worry about," the Anonymous warned. "It is between Chair Kosala and myself. Understood?"

"Yes."

"Yes, My Lord Count," Faust corrected. "The forms don't all drop just because you're inside, Mister Prime Minister."

"Of course, Headmaster. My apolog—"

"His Grace," the crier interrupted, "Ganymede Jean-Louis de la Trémoïlle, Duc de Thouars, Prince de Talmond, President of the Humanists, with His Excellency Chief Executive Director Hotaka Andō Mitsubishi, and Her Highness Danaë Marie-Anne de la Trémoïlle Mitsubishi, Princesse de la Trémoïlle et de Talmond."

If divine Aurora, called Eos by we from whom the Romans stole her, limped to Olympus freshly wounded by a dart from vengeful Aphrodite, and crossed Zeus's threshold leaning one arm on Helios her golden brother, and the other on her dark companion Night, so her rosy dawn veil was framed by soft darkness on one side and sun-fire on the other, I doubt if even virgin Artemis could resist a blush. Perry staggered at the sight, and his gaping face glowed in the light reflected by Danaë's kimono, which shimmered with the subtle, mingling colors of the dawn, each thread awakened to brightness by reflections from Ganymede's gold as he pressed against her, careful as a guide dog. Andō, on her other side, had one arm locked around her waist, the loose black of his formal hakama and kimono darkening his limbs like storm clouds. Even I staggered.

"You're sure you want do this?" Ganymede settled his sister onto a sofa with meticulous care, like a gardener transplanting roses. "You don't have to stay tonight if you don't want to."

"I should be here." She pulled the pair of them down around her like shells around a tender scallop. "I must greet our guest."

No starving man has ever stalked a loaf of bread so fixedly as Perry's eyes locked on Danaë. "I hope I'm more than just a one-night guest, Pr-incesse," he corrected, tripping over the syllables. "But are you all right? You seem unwell."

"My wife is tired." Her husband sat forward, blocking as much of Danaë as possible from the Outsider's view. "That is all. Mycroft, brandy."

I delivered the glass to the Duke, who held it as his sister alternated between timid sips and resting her head against his golden coat. No, tonight's coat was something more than gold. Have you seen yellow diamonds, reader? The sunburst brightness that mocks gold, "You dull, opaque old metal, you're barely fine enough to coat the outside of my treasure box, while I, I capture the light itself, slice it into shards and turn it into me!"

I have spoken with several doctors hoping one could identify this prescient illness which affected Danaë *before* the day's dooms showed their faces. One proposed anemia, another that she sensed the anxieties of her adopted children, but I suspect it is simply a sensitivity, like orchids, or old men's knees which tremble at the scent of danger in Fate's breath. The skill is natural enough in this creature, who maintains herself ever on exhaustion's threshold, so her favorite weapons, hysteria and fainting, remain keen.

"His Majesty," the crier began anew, "Isabel Carlos II, King of Castile, of Aragon, of Navarre, of León, of Galicia, of Granada, of the Canary Islands, of Jaén, of Córdoba, of Mallorca and Menorca, of Murcia, of Algeciras, of Seville, of Toledo, of Valencia, of Gibraltar, of the Algarve, of the Two Sicilies, of Jerusalem, of Sardinia, of Corsica, of the Indies and Mainland of the Ocean Sea, of the Islands and Mainlands of the Ocean Sea, Archduke of Austria, Duke of Burgundy, of Athens and Neopatria, Count of Barcelona, Count of Flanders, Lord of Biscay and of Molina, and former Prime Minister of the European Union."

We will forgive the King of Spain if tonight of all nights he did not have the patience to wait through his full list of titles before entering. He nodded in geritocratic order to the others, first to Faust, then Bryar, then the Anonymous, and last the trio, pausing to frown his sympathies at Danaë, but all these he passed, stopping only at Perry. "Welcome inside, Prime Minister." He offered his hand. "You have worked very hard to get here. I hope to see that energy do the world much good."

Perry trembled as he took the king's hand. "Thank you, Your Majesty. I doubt you can believe me, but I'm sorry I had to come here at your expense. I have far more respect for you than for anyone else who's ever set foot in this room . . ."

"Careful," Faust objected.

". . . and I hope I'm right that you will see brighter days when this is over."

Spain accepted the glass of manzanilla I had waiting for him. "Thank you, Prime Minister. Membership in this circle represents a common hope that we with power may do more good for the world as colleagues than as adversaries. I hope you will embrace that."

Duke President Ganymede is never so cross as when he is forced to sit through the titles of a true king. "If Your Majesty wants Perry to dig their claws out of your heir," he jabbed, "you should just beg and have done."

"Ganymede!" It was Andō who scolded the Duke this time, though Danaë too dug reproachful fingers into her brother's lace. "Spain is not our enemy."

"No, but dynastic troubles are. If Perry really meant well by His Majesty, he'd get his claws out of the Crown Prince. Do you know how many nights this month Leonor Valentín has—"

The crier's voice rose once again. "His Imperial Majesty Cornel MASON, *Princeps Senatus, Pater Patriae, Praeses Maximus, Dictator Perpetuus Imperatorque Masonicus,* and Madame D'Arouet."

The hostess entered on the Emperor's arm, the breadth of her skirts keeping him at a civil distance. MASON always seems grim at Madame's, his suit of imperial gray transformed from grave to ominous as military flaps and cording replace the plain Masonic cut. Today the darkness spread to Madame as well, the salmon damask of her gown trimmed with festoons of black lace, as when a state funeral fills a mourning city with its trappings.

"Dearest friends," Madame began, her chilling portrait face offering its perfect portrait smile. "You are, you know, my dearest friends in the world. I cannot say how much it means to me to have you all gathered around me like this. I like to think this little world I have created enables communication which would otherwise be segregated by the walls that protocol erects between us. Here you are friends, not governments. You can speak honestly, care, cooperate, help each other as friends should, with patience and compassion instead of laws and faceless treaties. I hope to see you all remain friends tonight, setting aside personal allegiance and vendetta to help each other weather these grave days."

"Madame!" Kosala cried, red-faced. "You shouldn't share other people's secrets with the company without asking them. I don't want—"

Madame shushed the Cousin Chair with an open palm. "I was not speaking of your situation, Bryar. We are all of us, I think, aware that something is threatening the Cousins. We love you, Bryar. Not just Déguisé, we all love you, and owe you and your Cousins an incalculable debt for your help and charity and most humane activities around the world. You know you have but to ask for help for it to be yours, and the time for that will come soon. But, for the moment, I was not speaking of your trouble, but of something graver." Her eyes turned on the Outsider with a glistening and fragile sympathy. "I am sorry, Prime Minister, to load crisis upon you on your first visit. This should have been a time for you to enjoy the warmth of friendship, not to see it tested right away."

Perry nodded stiffly, his nub of ponytail hissing against his velvet collar like a drummer's brush. "It is all right, Madame. I did not join this company for the company. Go on."

Gratitude in tear form sparkled in the corners of her eyes. "There is no one in this room, our newcomer aside, who has not at some point employed my Son, not in the individual offices He serves for each of you, but as a polylaw. He investigates what no other can be trusted to investigate, and we rely on Him to settle in secret what is best kept secret. He has found an exception."

"An exception in whose opinion, Madame?" Andō challenged. "Yours?"

She shook her head. "Yours. We all drafted the rules together of what crimes were too great to remain concealed even if exposure might harm the commonweal." Madame's throat quivered like a puppy's as she swallowed hard. "Remember, friends, we are friends."

"His Imperial Highness," the crier called at last, "the Prince D'Arouet."

Are you surprised the crier stops short, reader? That no encyclopedia of titles trails after Jehovah's name? A list of His offices in every Hive would fill a paragraph, and with His full name and the styles bestowed by His pedigree the list would outstrip Mason's and approach Spain's. I think in early days it was Madame who chose not to remind each Power how many others laid claim to the Child, but it is now Jehovah's preference; He is offended enough by the time it takes to move from one location to another, and cannot stand to lengthen the delay.

Jehovah entered smoothly, His suit pure black as always, black buttons, black lace, black striped minor's sash, even the embroidered vine-work black on black and restful to the eye like shadow. "The illusion that the human race is capable of peace is over."

Doubt and fear shot from eye to eye around the room like electricity; hyperbole does not come from His lips.

"What do you mean, Epicuro?" It was Spain who spoke first, Spain least shaken, perhaps because all the others had secrets enough to fear that He referred to theirs.

"For two hundred and forty-four years peace between the Hives has been maintained by the Humanists and Mitsubishi, by employing the Saneer-Weeksbooth transportation network as an assassination system." He did not look at anyone, nor raise His voice as He spoke the revelation flatly. "Europe joined the conspiracy one hundred and twenty years ago. The victims total two thousand, two hundred and four. Your long supposed peace is made of murder. The Seven-Ten list theft was engineered to lead us to this truth."

How fiercely all in the room wished they could imagine that Jehovah would joke.

"What is this, Jed?" Kosala asked first, mumbling like one not fully wakened from a dream. "An assassination system? You mean criminals inside the Hives are—"

"The Hives themselves. Their leaders." Still He looked at no one, but His gaze seemed to accuse the air itself, and the defective race that breathed it.

"Whom have they been killing?" Caesar asked.

Jehovah turned slow eyes upon his Imperial father. "Human beings."

"Why?"

"World stability."

"You have proof?"

"Yes."

Behind Jehovah the crier announced, "The Honorable Mycroft Guildbreaker, *Prases Minor, Nepos Imperatoris, Familiaris Regni, Ministerque Porphyrogenis,* and the Reverend Father Dominic Seneschal."

The two wore the formal livery Madame had designed for this room, Dominic his black suit, Martin a light gray uniform, corded and military to match his Emperor's, with white cording on his right shoulder to represent the white sleeve of his *Ordo Vitae Dialogorum.* The pair brought printed lists on paper, and handed one to each Power within the room, ready to be kept forever as evidence, or destroyed at once, as the holder willed.

"Who knew about this?" Kosala asked. "It's some low-level conspiracy, right? It can't have been the leaders, they . . ." She winced as she found her eyes already straying to Andō and Ganymede. "You didn't know, right? Andō?"

Would he have tried to lie, I wonder, had he not raised his eyes to find Jehovah's staring at him? Men tell me that Jehovah's eyes look dead, a blackness which focuses on nothing and reflects nothing, lightless as the emptiness of Space. They must, I think, be atheists who say this, for, to me, the black of heaven that we see behind the stars is more alive than anything.

"This system is older than its current leadership," Andō began, "remember that. We inherited this, one of the powers of our offices. We could no more abandon it than you could throw away that black sleeve, MASON."

Caesar's eyes fell to his left hand. "Have you killed Masons?"

"One thousand and twenty-one Masons," Jehovah supplied, "seven hundred and eighty-two Cousins, two hundred and fifty-six Brillists, twenty-eight Hiveless, and one hundred and seventeen Europeans in the years before Europe joined the conspiracy."

"I want Andō to answer, *Fili.*"

Never let it be said that the Mitsubishi Chief Director cannot meet Caesar's iron gaze. "I have a duty to my Hive as you do, MASON. This is part of it."

"That's right," Perry chimed in. "It's like the Emperor's duty to torture their successor, or how the Déguisé inherited all the duties of the Anonymous, even the shady ones." He avoided Bryar's hot glance. "We didn't create this system. You think we want the world to be dependent on murder?"

I spotted tears in Spain's eyes. "You knew, Prime Minister?"

Perry forced himself to face the King. "Yes, Your Majesty, I've known for years, ever since I was appointed to the Special Means Committee. That's what they . . . we . . . do. The committee was created a hundred and twenty years ago by the subministers that made the deal to join this three-way alliance. It's been so good for Europe, you can't possibly imagine. The committee existed to let Europe participate in the system without the knowledge of the Prime Minister, to protect you and your predecessors from involvement with the assassinations because . . . because . . ."

"Because His Catholic Majesty goes to confession," Madame supplied.

Kosala could hardly keep herself from ripping the paper in her shaking hands. "You mean because Spain has a conscience, unlike some."

"Conscience?" Andō repeated, hoarse with scorn as if Kosala had just recommended some useful artifact to its inventor. "My conscience could not be clearer. Thousands, perhaps millions of lives are saved by every war we stop. All your charities have never given so much as a band-aid to so many."

"War?"

Just as, at sunset, the battlemented fortresses scattered across the Greek coast by the old Venetians stand in black blocks against the sea's rose gold, so Andō stood stark against the sparkling twins. "War, Bryar," he confirmed. "Riots. Slaughter. Death. Déguisé can tell you, they watch the numbers more closely than any of us. How many close calls have we had, Déguisé? How many ripples in the Hive balance that would have exploded if something invisible hadn't tipped us back from the brink?"

"I . . . the self-correction. It's tr-ue." The words cracked as they rose from the Anonymous's manikin. "That's what the self-correcting push is. I'd noticed it. I didn't understand it until now, but the worst of the trends always reset, settle down just before the point of no return. I always worried about recessions in the past, economic contraction, but since Sniper shared Tully Mardi's speech at Ingolstadt this morning I've realized the ripples have been threatening something a lot worse than a recession. The Hives are not as friendly to each other as we like to think. It's true. It has been stopping war."

"What are you saying?" Bryar cried. "That it's okay? That they should get away with murdering thousands of people?"

"Of course not," the Anonymous replied, "and certainly not in secret to further their Hives' interests against the others. They've been doing that, too, I can see it now. The inexplicable resets always favor those three Hives."

Kosala rushed a pace toward the doll, as if to seize or slap it. "That's what matters to you most? Hive bias? Then I suppose it would've been okay if they did it for everyone equally?"

"We did." Andō's declaration brought not only Bryar's glare, but everyone's. "A ship that boards too much cargo will sink, however strong. The Masons have benefited from this as much as we have. So have your Cousins. We can even save your CFB now if you like, we have a plan all ready. We were going to do it for you in the spirit of goodwill, but if you'd rather we can let you fall apart."

Would you expect the lady to threaten tears here, reader? That Kosala did, but threatened fists as well.

Headmaster Faust glanced up from reading. "I have students on this list."

Director Andō nodded acknowledgment. "Not as many as you would have lost in wars."

Faust glared. "I was talking to the system's creator, Andō, not to you."

"The system is three hundred years old, Felix. Its creators are long dead."

The old Headmaster shook his head. "Not their ideas. The Humanists created this. No one else sees history as composed of individuals. On their own the Mitsubishi would target corporations, Masons governments, Europe nation-strats, me bash'es, the Anonymous ideas. Only the Humanists still think the world is made of individuals." He leaned forward. "Ganymede? You can't pretend you aren't the heart of this."

The Duke President had sat detached, giving the papers a half skim as he continued to sooth his trembling sister. "This list is just names." He looked to Jehovah. "Does Your Highness have more exact proof?" Even in such crisis His Grace does not forget the title due an Emperor's Son.

"Not yet, Your Grace," Jehovah answered, "but the Commissioner General is close to proof."

Ganymede's lips pursed for a moment—a stifled wince perhaps? "The Commissioner General. How many of their staff know?"

Kosala's face grew dark. "Ganymede, you still haven't answered if you knew."

The Duke crossed his arms, the yellow diamond fabric flashing like the Sun without its warmth. "A leader is responsible for the actions of his Hive, regardless of personal involvement. Even if I didn't know, if my Hive is guilty then I am, so are Andō, Perry, His Majesty, and all others who have led our Hives in the last three centuries." He waited for Spain to nod. "But blame can wait. What matters now is that we stop the police from exposing this without warning and throwing the world into—"

"Donatien," Faust interrupted, "is Ganymede a murderer?"

It had to be asked, but all eyes, even Faust's, flinched slightly in the silence before Jehovah's slow and lifeless answer. "You are all murderers," He pronounced, "you and your whole world. We had thought that, if humanity left the trees far enough behind, you could leave the war of all against all with them. We were wrong."

I sobbed here. So did Caesar, once, the sob stifled stillborn in his throat like a too-hard swallow. He saw it too, I think, the specter of Apollo stirring in Jehovah's words like a harmonic, played by no one but rising unbidden from the perfection of a chord. We will never be free of you, will we, Apollo? We had not heard these words since Death and I extinguished what we thought was the vital part of you, yet here we hear your voice again, the stronger since it rises from His lips. I choked.

MASON was stronger. "Mycroft, is Ganymede a murderer?"

Stares tortured me for three long seconds. "Yes, Caesar. Yes, he is." Should I not have answered him? I have thought long about it. By law I must answer the Emperor, but it is by choice that we obey or break the law. It is not as if I think the Duke's guilt would not have come out had I stayed silent. But the choice won me another enemy. Until that moment, Ganymede had thought all the Powers were equally my master, Caesar no more than he, all second to Jehovah. Now he knew otherwise. The Duke does not forgive in general, and certainly not me.

"Would you like a copy of the list, Princesse?"

Martin and Dominic had not brought a copy for the lady, but an aide had followed them in, sliding quietly around the back in a monk's habit much like mine, dull as dust against the gold. Smiling her silent thanks, Danaë reached for the list, then screamed like a rabbit ripped in twain by hounds hot in the hunt, and slipped into that kind of lifeless faint which made Homer call Sleep and Death twin brothers.

"Danaë!" Husband and brother cried her name together, but Ganymede's scream tasted of a special panic, as a conjoined twin might scream seeing his other half die first, knowing that he will follow.

"It's true, isn't it?" The aide's hood fell back to reveal a red and seething face. "Danaë is my mother."

"Carlyle Foster!"

I barely had time to throw myself between the Duke and sensayer before Ganymede seized a dagger-long pin from Danaë's golden hair and lunged. "I'll kill you!" he screamed. "Parasite! You stay away from my sister! Away!" The steely needle inched close to my throat, while the Duke's other hand raked me with fingers fierce as talons—better me than Carlyle. "You planned all of this, didn't you!"

I seized the Duke's wrists, sleek as ivory, and forced him back until Andō could grasp him from behind.

"Ganymede, control yourself!" Andō ordered. "The child didn't plot this, they know nothing."

The Duke strained against our grips, his gold mane bright as fire against Andō's black. "Get that creature out of here!" he ordered. "And I want whoever let it in here flogged! No, bring the one responsible to me, I'll do it with my own hands!"

Lounging against the shelves of toys and Plato in Jehovah's corner, Dominic could not entirely suppress a smile.

"Carlyle, come with me." Kosala reached for the sensayer's shoulder. "You shouldn't be here."

"Don't tell me I shouldn't be here, Chair Kosala!" Carlyle slapped Kosala's hand away like an intruding insect. "I'm the one who gave Papadelias the evidence to expose this whole conspiracy. I'm the one who was almost killed last night by Thisbe Saneer trying to cover it up. I'm the one all of you have been trying so hard to keep in the dark, even you! When we met here before you told me you were just here as an outside inspector." Carlyle's hot eyes ranged her tight-corseted bodice, custom made. "You lied."

Bryar had a few inches on Carlyle and used them, glaring down with the stern authority of Teacher, Queen, and Mom combined. "It's my job to protect you, and yours to listen to me. I wish you had."

Carlyle's throat convulsed. "I was happy as a Gag-gene. I didn't want to know. But I was trying to save you and the CFB. This is the price I paid." Carlyle winced, feeling tears leak. "You can't leave me with half the truth. I was born here, wasn't I? I'm part of this . . . I won't call it a bash'."

Kosala swallowed hard. "Please wait outside for me. I'll come as soon as I can, but we have more important things to—"

"No," MASON judged, "we don't."

Bryar's frown looked hurt. "Cornel . . ."

A true modern like you, rational reader, would not perhaps allow such melodrama to distract you from Earth's crisis, but decades at Madame's have taught even Caesar to think in terms of sentiment and honor. "Foster may be a Cousin, Bryar, but that doesn't make this your decision. I am the *Praeses Maximus*. I guard the list of Gag-genes in the *Sanctum Sanctorum*, and if anyone had told me Carlyle Foster had set foot in this house, I would have summoned them at once to warn them of the danger. It's too late now." He stepped a short pace toward Kosala, his limp as bad as I had ever seen. "Foster is in pain, Bryar, the greatest pain they've ever experienced." He glanced at his Good Son, the Source of this strict kindness. "Nothing else is urgent enough to justify extending that."

Kosala hesitated. "I know, Cornel, I just . . . not here in front of everyone."

"Why not?" Carlyle's eyes shot from Power to Power, these distant faces, seen so many times on screens. "Why not in front of everyone? I get the feeling I'm the only person in this room who doesn't know."

I did not know, but did not contradict.

"What do you know already?" Caesar asked. I knew this voice of his, a special tone reserved for courtrooms, where office makes MASON play the cruel judge, while in another chair he might be merciful.

Carlyle looked to the princess curled on the couch, tresses leaking from her fallen hair like molten sun. "Danaë is my mother. Is anyone going to deny that?"

All saw the sheen of gold too strong for the brown tints of Carlyle's hair to overwhelm, and stayed silent.

"And my father was some rival of Director Andō's for Danaë's hand, yes?" Carlyle continued, each word aimed at Ganymede like a dagger. "Some other young politician Madame was trying to corrupt? But there was some deal made between Director Andō and President Ganymede." Even in rage, the good-hearted Cousin would not drop their titles of respect. "The two of you used the Saneer-Weeksbooth assassination system to eliminate my father, didn't you?"

Ganymede laughed, as if to remind the company that a Duke is above spitting. "Don't be absurd. Andō was not yet a Director then, and I had never set foot outside this house. How could we use a system we had not even heard of? Merion Kraye was a villain and a coward and I needed no assassin to deal with a worm who would not even face me in an honorable duel!"

Director Andō half released the Duke, as if testing to see if his haughty calm was real or feigned. "Merion Kraye was, as you say, Foster, a politician," Andō confirmed, "a young European, and a client of Madame's, on the middle level. They sought Danaë's hand but, realizing I was the stronger suitor, they . . . disgraced her."

"You mean they raped her?" Carlyle translated.

"No." MASON's bronze face set statue-hard, but other faces in the chamber seemed unsure.

Carlyle scowled. "Isn't that what 'disgraced' means in your crazy ancient prejudice?"

Andō's stern face turned sterner. "Kraye broke Danaë's heart. Kraye wooed her, lured her, made promises to her, pressured her into an illicit meeting—with a solemn vow that it would be an innocent one—and there, when the lady would not satisfy Kraye's mad jealous demands of eternal and monogamous fidelity," here he glanced at golden Ganymede, "Kraye attacked her. He was caught in the act, her blood on his fists, and would not accept the consequences like a gentleman, kept abusing her with slanders no gentleman should utter. Ganymede and I were only two of the many who offered to duel to avenge the lady's honor, but Kraye refused. When DNA proved the child was Kraye's they went mad with rage, attacked the lady, and Madame, and others. Madame dismissed them forever from this house, and Kraye killed themself soon after."

Carlyle scowled. "That's not an answer, it's a penny dreadful."

"Tut," Dominic warned, his voice deferent here among the princes, but still with its growling undertow. "There, little Cousin, thou malignest our *philosophe*; Diderot never sold for a mere penny."

Carlyle turned to Dominic, hot. "You knew, didn't you? All of this?"

Dominic needs to work on hiding his smiles. "Come, this is good news. Thou art a prince, and, with Ganymede childless, next in line to be the Duke. If thou'rt acknowledged thou mayest use one of thine uncle's lesser titles. I looked it up for thee: Count of Laval is the obvious choice, but thou couldst make a case for Marquis de Royan."

Carlyle glared, the true blue diamond sharpness of a scion de la Tré-moïlle finally awakening in his eyes. Yes, reader 'his'; this is the moment for which I was commanded to use 'he' for Carlyle. Such are the deplorable laws of aristocracy that a bastard niece might matter little to the Duke, but a nephew, with a nephew comes inheritance, and barbarian blood upon the ducal throne.

If Dominic had another taunt, MASON silenced it with the raising of his merciful right hand. "Cousin Foster," he began again, "I understand you have been to this house before. You know what is practiced here. Madame and those employed here know how to lure people into their moral palette, as well as their sexual palette. The Merion Kraye affair was a stock, archaic tragedy dredged back from darker ages, but stock, archaic dramas are why people come here, and they choose it knowingly."

"And you just let Madame do this to people?" the sensayer half shouted.

"I am the law in Alexandria," MASON pronounced, "not here. Madame and those within this house are Blacklaws. Members who patronize Madame's establishment do indeed break laws sometimes, as Kraye did by committing assault, against the laws of Europe, but for the residents of the house itself, only the Eight Black Laws stand here. If here Madame wields sex as a weapon, Romanova has no Universal Law to contradict. If here affairs of honor are resolved by dueling, and those who refuse the combat, as Kraye did, are expelled from the establishment, Romanova has no Universal Law to contradict. To ask me to intervene is to ask my Empire to raise its hand against Romanova; this you do not want, for a thousand reasons."

That fear—a thousand times the scale of petty Seven-Ten lists—made the Cousin pause.

"Exactly!" Ganymede confirmed. "This is a civilized house. My sister did nothing wrong. It was that monster Kraye—that criminal—who brought the poison, Kraye who broke the law, assaulted my sister, and tried to destroy her, and my family honor!"

"That isn't true!" Casimir Perry could hold back no more.

Ganymede's eyes flashed murder. "What would you know, Outsider?"

"What do I know?" Perry seethed. "I know the two of you conspired to ruin an innocent man. I know Hotaka Andō paid a king's ransom for your services, bought you from Madame, set you up in the outside, built your mansion at La Trimouille, arranged your art contacts, your political career, all in return for what you did. I know that whore lying on the sofa over there is not the pure, virginal victim you all pretend. I know Madame knew it all, let it all happen, may even have planned it all themself. And I know that child is not my son!"

No one breathed.

Faust moved first, smiling as he checked his gilded pocket watch. "Seventeen minutes, twenty-one seconds, Madame. I win the bet."

Madame gathered her skirts, the lacy sea tangling as she attempted to navigate around a tower of cheeses. "Oh, were we counting from when you and Perry arrived, or from when we were all assembled? By the latter count it's under ten minutes, so I win."

Perry bristled like a cornered boar. "What bet?"

Madame's fan hid what must have been a smile. "You were doing so well, Merion. All you had to do was sit quietly through this and no one would have known. You'd finally made it back inside."

"You knew?" He paled. "You knew it was me?"

"You think I don't check all comers to my house? All comers to this room?" The Lady blinked. "A suicide is easy to fake, a face, a voice easy to change, but there are always traces. I never lose track of anyone." Delicately as a hummingbird teasing the nectar from a flower's heart, she lifted the silver cover from a tray to reveal a layer cake frosted with the chocolate greeting: "Welcome Back Merion Kraye." Faust alone contributed applause.

I heard a hiccupped gasp across the line from the Anonymous, to my relief, and saw raw and innocent astonishment on Caesar's face, Kosala's too, Earth's Mom and stony Father stepping close to one another, as if ready to battle back-to-back for their Hives and poor Earth's sanity.

"Merion Kraye?" Ganymede clutched the knife-straight hairpin tighter.

"Calm, Your Grace, calm . . ." Madame warned.

"Casimir Perry is Merion Kraye?"

"Your Grace, I thank you to keep your temper in my house." Madame did not raise her voice, but its firm timbre made the Duke—her ba'child as much as Heloïse—tremble.

Of all present, Carlyle had the most right to shudder. "You're my father? Casimir Perry?"

I wonder if Perry, or rather Perry-Kraye, realized he was backing steadily toward the exit, or that I moved in to block him. I doubt it, for he stared at Madame like a lunatic at his hallucination. "You knew it was me this whole time? And you let me back in? Let me become Prime Minister? The last time you saw me I swore I'd never rest until I destroyed you and all that you've created. Why would—"

"Because I asked her to, Merion." The King of Spain stepped forward, gently, as if trying to keep a cornered animal from panicking.

The Outsider paled. "Your Majesty? Why?"

Spain smiled. "You were young and foolish and in love, and you were one of the most promising political minds of our generation. You did not deserve to lose it all over one sour love affair. Europe needed you. I needed you. Madame recognized you easily after you took on your new persona as Casimir Perry. Madame told me who you really were, but I asked her not to tell the others. They might not have tolerated giving you a second chance."

Perry-Kraye scrunched his cuffs with tense hands. "A second chance . . . And then I cheated you out of your office . . ." The new Prime Minister was too ashamed to meet the King's eyes. "I rigged the election, I had Ziven Racer cheat so you'd have to drop out, all against my benefactor . . ."

"I know." Spain nodded, as a much-tried father nods. "And I forgive you. The important thing is that Europe be ruled well, not that I rule it. I trusted you to value your second chance, and not to squander it on some petty revenge. Was I wrong?"

Kraye held his breath like a man about to dive, and I edged closer, ready to grapple if his dive turned violent. It was a strange way to meet him, really. I had not known this man, you must realize, not as Merion Kraye, nor really as Casimir Perry, the Prime Minister whom I had glimpsed here or there upon a balcony when I ran Jehovah's errands at Parliament, no more. I had identified Carlyle's mother by hacking the Gag-gene records, but had not known the deeper scandal.

"I wish you were right, Your Majesty," Perry-Kraye replied, slowly as if trying to prove he meant every syllable. "I wish I could say I had climbed the steps of power with the people's welfare first in my heart, as you have. But at least you were half right. I haven't squandered my second chance. My revenge is nothing petty, but a true apocalypse which will destroy, not only my destroyers, but the world that made them!"

His eyes opened, sharp as stars, to lock upon Madame, but Caesar stepped in front of her, a wall of iron gray shielding the salmon petals of her gown. "Be careful whom you include, Kraye. A large part of the world is mine. And you, Madame, and Spain, you should not have hidden such a dangerous situation from the rest of us, not even," he caught the King's eyes coldly, "in the name of mercy."

Kraye laughed—I had not imagined any man could laugh in Caesar's face. "Count yourself lucky, MASON, you're hardly going to suffer, a little global turmoil, that's all. You were party to it too; it's less than you deserve."

Wise men do not intentionally make MASON frown. "I was not party," Caesar answered, "I was witness. Your violence was intolerable."

"I was innocent."

"That you were not."

"I never raped her!" Kraye's hand tightened around his sherry glass, as heavy as a sling stone, but Martin planted himself as a silent wall before his Emperor, as Dominic did before Jehovah. He was still with us, our disappointed God, silent in His Gravity, like a tombstone in the corner of a playing field. The rest ignored Him, or tried to. A glance at Him reminded us that we were fools to care about old scandal when we had just discovered humanity was beyond redemption. But He would not stop us. Rather, like a cliff in storm, He suffered silently as yet more proof of His conclusion played out before Him. This world is not good, reader, not as good as He deserves.

"I know you didn't rape her," MASON answered flatly.

Kraye staggered. "Wha—what?"

"You didn't rape her. You beat her violently, and slandered her."

"She slandered me! She accused—"

"She never said you raped her!" My heart skipped hearing Caesar raise his voice. "You assumed she would. You were so obsessed with expecting that accusation that you never heard the words any of us actually said to you. We said you assaulted her, and you did, with your fists. You fractured her cheekbone, gave her a severe concussion, and could have done much worse, and when we dragged you off of her by force, you said the worst things of her that can be said of a lady in this house. Blacklaws may do what they like here, but as a European you were bound by law, as well as decency, and you went far beyond the bounds of both. Your expulsion was just and reasonable, as prosecution would have been too, under the laws of your own Hive!"

Is that a flinch, Kraye? Is that seething brain of yours revisiting old memories, and finding certain keywords lacking?

"She did accuse me! She faked the test!" Kraye shrieked. "She told you all the child was mine. I never touched that whore, not once! It was Ganymede! Ganymede arranged everything to conceal the produce of their incest, and I fell into the trap!"

"Filth!" the Duke cried. "Villain!"

Andō's grip on writhing Ganymede began to loosen, the Director running short, not of strength, but of reasons to keep the Duke's weapon from tasting Kraye's throat.

Kraye's eyes hopped from Chair to King to Emperor. "How can you not see it? I was framed! Ganymede got Danaë pregnant and lured me in to take the blame!"

"Then my real father is Ganymede?" Stunned Carlyle barely had the strength to voice the words.

"Yes!" Kraye snapped. "Yes, you're the poison that started all this."

"No, Merion. This is our son." Danaë stirred from her swoon at last, tresses spilling down about her shoulders, exquisite as when Helios pours gold across dawn waves from harbor to horizon.

Kraye's eyes glowed with that maniacal, inhuman light which made past generations believe in possessing demons. "The queen of whores joins us at last."

"Danaë . . ." Ganymede wrapped himself around his sister. "You don't have to—"

She shook her head, blue diamond eyes almost black as she peered out through the jungle of gold let loose without her hairpin. "That is you, isn't it, Merion? I should have known you at once, that gait, those hands. Monster."

"Monster? Me? You're the one who betrayed an innocent man."

"Innocent?" Tears came to her, bright as dew. "Day after day you swore you would love only me forever, but the instant you thought another man had touched me, you tried to kill me! How is that innocent?"

"I did love you. You're the one who cheated."

"No!" Danaë wrapped her rose-gold sleeves about herself. "You never loved me. A feeling which dies that easily isn't love, Merion, it's lust. You wanted my body. If we had been united, how long would it have taken you to pass me over for something younger? Fresher? To tire of me as my good husband never has? You never loved me or you never would have stopped!"

He laughed. "And you think Andō loves you for real? You're just a tool to them."

"No, I am not." She held her head high. "After the scandal I thought I was ruined, never to wed. Hotaka came to me. He said he did not care whether I was a virgin on our wedding night. He did not want a bride, he wanted a wife. My company, my counsel, my trust, my powers to draw in friends and lay waste to his enemies, that was what he wanted, a partner for his long journey to break the Chinese hold on the Chief Director's seat and rule the Mitsubishi as they should be ruled. Madame and her tutors gave me this power over people, but Andō taught me to realize that I had it, and to use it, and trusts me to choose my own tools, and my own victims."

Dark Kosala dug angry fingers deep into her skirts. "You mean me, don't you? My CFB?"

Danaë smiled softly. "Later, dear Bryar, you, and the Count, and I can retire to settle that issue ourselves, but kindly grant me some moments more to deal with my betrayer."

"Betrayer?" Kraye mocked.

The Princesse faced him boldly. "Lifelong trust, that is what a husband and wife give one another, Merion, not the heat of passion."

"You expected me to trust you when you were suddenly pregnant with someone else's child?"

"That shouldn't have mattered if you truly loved me. You failed the test."

"Test?" His words grew chill. "You had your brother impregnate you to test my sincerity?"

She squeezed her brother's hand. "If you had loved me, you would have stayed by me, embraced any child of my flesh, whatever its sire. And then I would have loved you forever, just as you had promised me. What joy we would have shared! Instead you . . ." Her fingers strayed to her cheek, drawn by the tactile memory of old blows. "You never loved me. I should have realized it sooner. Ganymede warned me. Every day you smuggled in letters swearing to love only me forever, while every night you vented your impatient lust on my twin! You didn't want me for myself, you just wanted my body, and you didn't care what mind and personality were inside, mine or Ganymede's!"

The Prime Minister seethed, hands twitching with the urge to seize and tear. "You're angry because I slept with your brother? Your husband sleeps with your brother. Everyone sleeps with your brother. That's what your brother's for!"

Ganymede ran out of syllables, but, sparkling like sun gold on angry water, writhed and screamed.

"I should have listened to my brother," Danaë continued, strong. "But I wanted to think better of you, Merion, to think that you only turned to Ganymede in desperation in your wait for me. But I had to be sure. The pregnancy was my test, to make you think that I had been with another man, to see how you'd react. And it was my escape too, so we could be together. I knew you could never pay Madame as much for my hand as other suitors could, but if I was spoiled, scandalously with child, then petty lovers would turn away, and only you, my true, true love, would stay. It was the only way that we could have each other. It was my brother who brought me your seed."

"My . . . seed?"

Her blink glittered with tears. "I said he was our son."

"It's the truth, Merion," Headmaster Faust interrupted, signaling me to refill his sherry. "I ran the DNA myself, twice. Has it not occurred to you that, thanks to modern science, there are ways a sperm and egg can meet other than the customary dick up vagina?"

Kraye froze a moment. "No. No, it was Ganymede, their incest . . ."

Faust rolled his eyes. "Look at the child, you idiot. The twins are genetic duplicates. Except for one Y-chromosome swapped in, Danaë and Ganymede are the same lifeform. Their child would be practically a clone of Ganymede. Does Carlyle Foster look like a clone of Ganymede to you?"

Kraye's flinch was painful to see, doubt flaring torture-sharp where doubt had seemed impossible. I knew that feeling. "Artificial insemination?"

"True love would have stayed true, Merion." Danaë held his eyes with hers, as deep and deadly as the sea. "I said I was with child, and a true love would have sworn to keep on loving me regardless, to the world's end. Then I would have revealed that the child was yours after all, and we would have had our happily forever. That's what I'd planned. But I mistook the false lover," she practically spat the words in Kraye's face, "for the true," a warm squeeze of her steady husband's hand. "I never claimed you tried to force yourself upon me, Merion. I said you tried to kill me, which you did. And our child. And when they stopped you, you went mad with rage, and swore to burn the whole world down." Danaë rose to her feet, and faced her former lover with so calm and strong and fixed a gaze that all within the circle held our breaths. "You stole the Seven-Ten list, didn't you? You climbed the ranks enough to learn about O.S., and now you've exposed it because you want to see my husband and my brother burn, and you don't care if you burn with them."

Threat to her own woke Chair Kosala from her shocked silence. "Is this true?"

The Prime Minister slouched within his stiff suit, like a man relieved of an old weight. "The Japanese Mitsubishi made the Canner Device, by the way. It's not just a stealth device, it's designed to remote access the Tracker System's main computers."

"You did it?" Kosala stepped forward. "You stole the Seven-Ten list? You admit it?"

Perry-Kraye laughed as he relaxed at last. "Why shouldn't I admit it? I've done the world a favor! While you hypocrites are here debating how best to cover this up for the public good, I've scattered enough proof that the lot of you together can't even slow it down. The world will know. The Humanists are guilty, the Mitsubishi, the rotten heart of Europe, guilty! The four of us, Andō, the twins, and I, and all our filthy allies, we'll all go down together as we deserve, the rest of you will suffer through the aftermath, and no one can stop it, no one!" He raised his eyes to MASON, past MASON to the subtle, silent matriarch hiding behind her fan. "Not even you, Madame."

Carlyle's breath sped to the edge of panting. "That's your revenge? You're trying to expose the truth about the Saneer-Weeksbooth bash'?"

"And the Canner Device. Don't imagine for a moment that Andō isn't the worst of all! The three-way assassination alliance wasn't enough for Japan, they had to develop something they could use against their allies too. That's what the device really is! Using the tracker system like the transit system. I had the device for years and I could barely tap its simplest functions. You can't blame it on your predecessors, Andō, not when the set-sets trained to use the device all call you father!"

Wrath-blush rose in Andō's cheeks as he felt the others' stares.

"The tracker system . . ." Carlyle broke the hush. "They were tapping it, today, the Mitsubishi kids, I saw them! They were tracking me through it. And they were asking about the Canner Device too. Julia said they had a name for themselves . . . Oniwaban set-sets?"

Shock held them all, but I saw a different kind of shock and hurt on golden Ganymede. "O.S. . . . ."

"My children are not set-sets." Andō was too dignified to bellow, but his words had the same shock-force. "They were deprived of that, ripped out of training by rabid Cousins, Lorelei Cook and their Nurturist zealots. The children were torn from their computers, their senses half remapped, scattered to the corners of the Earth." He had a black look for Kosala. "A child has a right to grow up with its ba'sibs. I gave them that, gathered them back together when I learned how my predecessor, who ordered their training, had abandoned them to the false mercy of your Cousins. As strat-leader, I owed those children nothing less than the home you stripped them from."

Carlyle was breathing even faster now. "They asked Julia to help them find the Canner Device. No, Canner's prototype, that's what they called it, like there was another. You've been using your own Canner Device!"

"No one can use the Canner Device!" Andō shot back. "No one ever has, and no one ever will, the training process was lost when Lorelei Cook's Nurturists destroyed the training bash'. Kraye is just trying to spit every kind of poison they can here, lie or truth. They're trying to splinter us. They know we can still turn the tide back if we work together." Andō faced Perry-Kraye head on, his gaze as black as ash. "Trying to tear down three Hives because you were too cowardly to face an honorable duel."

"Not three Hives! The world!" the Outsider shrieked back. "This whole world is rotten to its heart! Look at yourselves! Madame has sucked us all into playing these idiotic roles humanity should have outgrown centuries ago!" Kraye was in his element now, strutting like an actor who had rehearsed his lines too long. "I haven't been plotting revenge for twenty-eight years for nothing. The first five years I was in a blind rage, working my way back from nothing, through crime, through politics, all so I could earn entrance back here, kill Andō and Ganymede in front of Danaë, then hack out the bitch's heart. But then I realized they aren't the cause. It was Madame who made us into this. Look at you, prancing around in skirts and holding the door for ladies! Even you!" He faced Carlyle at last. "The most powerful administrations in the world did everything in their power to keep you out of all this, yet here you are in a monk's robe running errands in a salon. You were born here and you should have died here, and that's not the worst! The worst is us." He waved to Andō and seething Ganymede. "The leaders of three of the seven Hives caught up in a stupid love revenge cycle. It's absurd! Madame's turned me into the fucking Count of Monte Cristo, and there's nothing I can do about it except to make sure my revenge doesn't just destroy my betrayers, but also the system that did this to the world!"

"Leaving what behind?" Carlyle stepped forward, bold, though not without glancing to silent Dominic—for what, reassurance? "What's supposed to happen to the world after you destroy it? You haven't thought about that, have you, Father?"

"Don't call me that!" Kraye snapped. "I have no interest in talking to the poison that started all this." He knocked Carlyle aside. "This is about us, Andō. Me, and you, and your mad, psychotic whore, and their whore brother!"

"Kraye!" The Duke broke free of Andō's grip at last. He seized the Prime Minister by his embroidered lapels, and pressed the hairpin's point against his throat. "You can't have thought this would end any other way."

Kraye smiled. "It ends with everyone going down together. Us first."

Kraye's hands locked like a bear trap around Ganymede's shoulders. They toppled, Kraye's maniacal strength crashing them both against the great window, which shattered like spring ice. They fell. Razor rain followed them, and Danaë's scream despairing as a siren, out into the void of laughter and chandelier light over the Flesh Pit four stories below. Screams multiplied like thunder, the shattering too, couches and banquet tables toppling as the guests below scattered like pigeons from the tumbling shards.

For all my speed, I had not even time to think if there was something I could do. MASON and Kosala gaped. Spain hid in the comfort of Madame's arms. Andō seized Danaë, dragging her back as she threatened to follow her brother, who tumbled, bright as if the sun had fallen in Icarus's place, with Kraye still locked around him like chains around a prisoner cast into the yawning sea.

Sniper caught them. With a swimmer's form and fencer's aim, Sniper dove under the pair and padded the Duke's head and fragile shoulders with its chest.

"¿Are you all right, Member President?" Sniper wheezed, winded as the three lay supine together on the Flesh Pit floor.

"¿Sniper?" The Duke kicked Kraye's stunned weight off of them both. "¿What are you doing here?"

"You told me to come." Sniper's right arm had strength enough to help the Duke off it, though its left arm hung at an unnatural angle. "I wish your message had been more specific. 'Rescue me upstairs' or 'rescue me from falling' might have helped."

The Duke inched back, wincing, trying not to touch a blade of glass which jutted from his arm. "¿Rescue me? ¿What are you talking about? ¿What message?"

"'Madame's, 18:00 UT, Sniper rescue me.' The order came through with your executive code." Sniper's winded whisper dropped to an even lower whisper. "Same message that told us to go through with you-know-what."

Ganymede gasped. "¿You did the hit?"

"We failed. The police and the Utopians were waiting. They knew we were going to strike. Cato says they must have hired a set-set."

"I sent no such message."

"Then it must have been Director Andō, or . . ."

Sniper's eyes awoke with fear as the second figure who had fallen with its President brushed blood from his familiar face, and smiled. "It's over."

"Prime Minister Perry?" It was not Sniper who said it first, but one, then a dozen of the crowd whose shock gave way to curiosity.

"That's the Prime Minister!"

"And President Ganymede!"

"What's going on?"

"Sniper!"

"Is Sniper hurt?"

"Why . . ."

"MASON?"

The crowd's eyes migrated up now to the shattered window wall above, where MASON, Chair Kosala, Director Andō, Princesse Danaë, Headmaster Faust, the King of Spain still in Madame's arms, Carlyle Foster–Kraye de la Trémoïlle, Martin, Dominic, Jehovah, and myself stood in our ruffled suits, and skirts, and habits, bare before the crowd, and before Sniper's floating cameras, which transmitted the image instantly around the world.

CHAPTER THE FOURTEENTH

The Suicide of Cato Weeksbooth

THAT NIGHT WE ALL FELT, I THINK, RATHER LIKE MACHIA-velli. Not the advisor to wicked princes that history imagines but the frightened politician, ever burning midnight's oil scouring letters and dispatches in his desperate effort to predict which of Europe's terrible giants—the pope, the kings of France or Aragon, the Holy Roman Emperor, the Swiss—would next send an army to sack and slaughter fragile Florence; the question was never if the end would come, just which. After Sniper's withdrawal, the Powers retreated to their cliques: Andō and Danaë to Ganymede's infirmary bedside, Chair Kosala to hear the hard truth about the CFB from the Anonymous, Spain with Madame, all milking what they could from the few hours before the excuse of Ganymede and Perry's injuries could no longer placate the press. Attempts were made to draft a statement, but none could agree which lie was best, or, if telling the truth was better, what the real true explanation was for why the world's elite had degenerated into violence while meeting at a costume brothel with Mycroft Canner.

My place that night was with Jehovah, not as His companion this time, nor guard, nor secretary, but as His translator as He answered the thousand questions and requests of every Power. The cold face shown by Providence that night had incited a dark passion in Him, for which the labels 'sorrow,' 'anger,' and 'despair' were equally inadequate. In its grip, He lost again that art always so hard for Him: selecting words humans can understand. On peaceful days His handicap, as one might call it, manifests only as hesitation, a pause before each sentence as He checks His words, but in crisis thoughts must flow freely. As the only creature who has managed to attain any fluency in Jehovah's 'language,' it fell to me to sit with Him and paraphrase the answers and orders that poured forth raw from His tongue, like sunlight which must be weakened by atmosphere before its thin remnants can succor fragile life. Here I fail, reader, not only you but Him. I could leave nothing more useful to posterity than a transcript of His actions that night, the plans He set in motion in every Hive, missions given to Martin, to Heloïse, to Aldrin and Voltaire, to Dominic (after the flogging ordered by the Duke), advice to Kosala, philosophy to Caesar, yet I hardly remember what He did or said. They are right, I think, who say the human mind cannot comprehend infinity. For all the billions about to be uprooted, I could think only of Bridger. Where was he? What was he doing? Was he, as I had instructed, watching silently? As disaster broke, would he still sit back and observe? Or would kindly folly drive him to try again to come and save me? Or everyone? I saw in my mind his small arms grabbed by some dark watchman, Papa perhaps, or Dominic, as he tried to approach me. Bridger in tears, in chains, seemed to float before me, a second specter joining Apollo's at my side. I drifted thus half dreaming until dawn, but so did you, reader, or, if you are more distant, so did your ancestors. It had been centuries since the whole world spent a sleepless night. We do not have time to follow every friend and foe through their dazed wanderings—you must turn to other chroniclers for that. Here I shall choose just one among Earth's countless frightened houses in which to have you pass this night, the one in which the impact of the news was harshest: the Saneer-Weeksbooth bash'.

Ockham and Lesley watched the broadcast together from the sofa, silent before the screen's cold glimmer, like refugees watching their last candle burn down. I work here from very incomplete testimony, but my mind's eye knows those two well enough to see them, sharing a blanket which Lesley's doodles had turned into a labyrinth to baffle Daedalus. Even in the dark their skin tones never blur, the tints of India and Africa, distinct like different hearty trees.

"You know what really gets me? Hearing people call these three brave." It is the Proxy for the Anonymous they watch, Humanist Vice President Brody DeLupa, fastest to rouse the rabble on this hottest of nights. "You're thinking it takes some guts to plead guilty to mass murder, but if they had any guts they wouldn't have gone along with it in the first place. The real shock here isn't that three members of Perry's coalition came forward, but that dozens of others have not." The screen showed DeLupa at the Rostra in Romanova, sweat dribbling down his cheeks whose stubble clumped like mildew. "Even outside Perry's coalition, they've all suspected what this 'Special Means Committee' really was. As far as I'm concerned, every last person who's sat on Europe's Parliament in a generation is as complicit in these murders as President Ganymede!"

Where are the others, you ask? As O.S. and the bride whose favor made him O.S. watch the doom alone? The set-sets are sprawled as ever on the floor, watching the same explosions in their digital world. The thumps and screams of the twins float from upstairs, comforting like a dog's familiar bark, while the stairs down to Thisbe's room are blocked by the old rope Ockham strings across to warn the others when his deadly sister is in too dangerous a mood. One can hear poor Cato pacing in his lab alone. As for Sniper, it was waylaid an hour by the doctor, another by the President, another by its fans, but arrives home now, limping half broken down the empty trophy hall.

"¡Cardie!" Lesley was the first to spot the living doll. "¿Are you okay? ¡We saw the fall!"

"I'm okay. The doctors patched me up fine, don't get up." Sniper can always force a smile. "¿What's happened since?"

Ockham's eyes stayed on the broadcast. "A couple self-serving European MPs have gone public about O.S."

"¿What?"

"Three snitches: Goodall, Kovács, and Korhonen." Lesley helped Sniper onto the sofa at her side, frowning at the splint plastered around its left shoulder, aglow with subtle heat. "They must have got wind that Papadelias had proof, and are trying to get ahead of the tidal wave."

Lesley's worry-red eyes held a thousand questions for Sniper, but they sat stunned before DeLupa's press conference as the Vice President drew floating cameras as carrion draws flies.

"People are saying we have to move slowly on this," DeLupa continued, "that we don't have enough proof yet, but we can't afford to move slowly when those accused are precisely those with the political and financial power necessary to make an investigation drag on for eternity. Korhonen's description of the system is clear: back when the King of Spain was still Prime Minister this so-called Special Means Committee worked in secret, or semi-secret since it seems most of Parliament knew about it, but ever since Perry's coalition drove the King out of office, this committee of murderers has reported, not just to them, but directly to the European Parliament, and Parliament approved the assassinations, every single member! They're all responsible! Some knew the truth from Perry's mouth, some only from rumor, but they all knew, or were willfully blind! Yes, maybe some PMs didn't like it, maybe some voted against it every time, but they all concealed it, or pretended it wasn't true, them and all their aides and secretaries, they're all accessories if not murderers themselves. When someone is an accessory to murder we arrest them, no matter who they are. It sounds absurd arresting more than a hundred people, but this is two thousand murders! Two thousand human lives! And if due process says we don't have enough evidence to bring them in yet, surely due process breaks down when it's the very powers that designed due process who need to be taken down. We have to act now, or Parliament will hide behind due process forever. As for the other Hives, with the Mitsubishi, the only question is whether Chief Director Andō is solely responsible or whether all nine Directors knew. President Ganymede's involvement is, of course, a great personal blow to me, both as Vice President and as a Humanist. I've long considered Ganymede a friend, but as the voice of the Anonymous I cannot defend their complicity in this. Korhonen made it clear, the Humanist President had veto to stop any hit at any time. Ganymede's name should be right at the top of the list of guilty, above even Ockham Saneer!"

"Crap," was Sniper's only answer. "They really did spill everything."

Lesley shook her head. "Everything but your name. No one's outed you as part of this bash' yet. You're still the innocent hero who risked life and limb to rescue the President from falling out that window. You'll need to make a statement."

"Yeah." Sniper started to slump against her, but pain made it choose the sofa over her warm but lumpy shoulder. "I don't have long, ¿do I? Perry's fleeing cronies don't know I'm with this bash', but the police do."

"None of us has long." Ockham lifted Lesley's hand in his, exploring again the feel of her ink-stained fingers. "Lesley and I have been talking," he began softly.

"¿Yes?"

"We think it's time to pass things to you, Ojiro."

"¡Ockham!" Sniper's throat cracked.

"I do not intend to be the last O.S.," Ockham continued. "The Humanists need us more than ever now. The millions who put names on the Wish List do not think we are wrong to solve some problems with death."

Eureka was rereading it even then, the Wish List, that old web 'joke' where Humanists could vote for names of people they 'wished' would meet with some unhappy end. I think it reassured her, the thought that others might have killed as she did in her place. I think it reassured them all.

"When they learn how O.S. really worked, a lot of Humanists are going to feel it was right, want to support us, but they'll be scared to say so. The Hive needs someone they respect to speak out and make others feel free to speak out too if they think we were right. They need Ojiro Sniper as the next O.S., and you need Lesley to help you keep the bash' alive."

"I agree." Lesley squeezed both their hands. "You need me to go with you, Ojiro." Sniper's first name, not spoken in that house since Ockham's accession, came stiffly to her lips. "The two of us together, we'll run. You know I have the best instinct for this. I realized first when we had to kill our ba'pas. I'm also the figurehead of O.S., the one the public is used to listening to when they're angry about crashes. You need me with you where I can make plans and speeches, and recruit allies."

It was a sound plan. Murder or no, the world still loved that little Lesley Juniper who had stood before the cameras, all curls and chubby cheeks, and pledged to dedicate her life to improving the transit network which had left her orphaned. Before you ask, yes, they were murdered, Lesley's parents, their deaths tipping the Cousins away from some pro-Masonic policy or other. She knew. She always knew. The eleventh O.S., Osten Saneer, realized, I think, what Lesley would become the moment young Ockham and Ojiro returned from informing the child of her ba'pas' deaths. There were no tears back then, just the petition "Can we keep her?" as if she were some rain-soaked kitten, baring ready fangs.

Sniper swallowed. "¿What happens to Ockham?"

"Prospero now," Ockham corrected, using his own middle name, half forgotten since his accession. "I will stand trial." He did not look at Sniper but the screen, as if the mob around DeLupa were already camped around his courtroom. "All we have done is follow the orders of our Hive President. The world needs to decide whether that was criminal or not. For that I need to stand trial. You two don't. Take Cato, take one of the set-sets, take a twin or both if they'll go, and keep protecting the Humanists. They need us."

Sniper says it was the figs that made it cry, a bowl sitting on the carpet, remnants of the poor programming of their overfruitful kitchen tree. Their home. "¿You're sure about this?" it asked.

Lesley sighed. "It's not as if staying here would let us be together." She squeezed both their hands again. "We need to do this, Ojiro. They're going to take the cars away from us. We'll need your resources, to carry on without. I know you've thought about the possibility of something like this, living on the run. You have your fans, your followers, your underground, the makings of a private army. There's not a town on Earth without a devotee ready to open their door to you. We need that now."

Sniper avoided her eyes. "I was never planning to strike out on my own."

She frowned. "I saw your encounter with Felix Faust this morning, in Ingolstadt. All your questions about J.E.D.D. Mason. You haven't said anything these past days, but I can tell you're working on something. ¿You have a plan?"

"Jehovah Mason, that's what Thisbe says. The *J* stands for Jehovah."

"¿Sniper?" Lesley pressed.

"I don't know. There's something much more rotten than O.S. going on. Listen." Sniper nodded to the screen, where the Proxy's tirade was giving way at last to questions.

"Vice President DeLupa, is this what the Hive Leaders were meeting about at this Blacklaw house in Paris? Does the Anonymous know anything about what happened between Prime Minister Perry and President Ganymede?"

The Proxy nodded with too-forced gravity. "The Anonymous and I can confirm the President's official statement. J.E.D.D. Mason has been investigating these assassinations for some time, and asked the King of Spain to arrange a meeting in a neutral space, to ensure that all the Hives were presented with the same evidence at the same time, and so the Hive Leaders could plan together how to announce the news so as to minimize global disruption. The King's choice of venue may seem strange, but it had to be done in top security and absolute privacy, and somewhere Hive neutral, and not in Romanova or the press would notice all the Hive Leaders gathering. Few places fit the bill. Remember, the King's hope in arranging the meeting was to protect global stability by forming a plan before the crisis broke. It's not inappropriate for the Hive Leaders to meet in private like that, any more than it was inappropriate in 2131 for Thomas Carlyle to meet in private with the leaders of the Cousins, Olympians, and Europe to work out the Hive system quickly before chaos could set in. I'd say Spain and J.E.D.D. Mason are the only ones acting with any sense in all this."

Hearing the Proxy speak is like watching children perform declawed and bumbling Shakespeare. Knowing the Anonymous as I do, I could hear—yes, I too watched this speech—how the true author would have read these words, and I winced each time the Proxy improvised. Take this last simile. Comparing today's meeting at Madame's to Thomas Carlyle's instantly made the world see the Powers, not as conspirators, but as architects of some grand transformation, the birth of an even more golden golden age; this rhetorical brilliance was the Anonymous. Spoiling it by suggesting in the next sentence that all but two of these great architects were idiots, that addition was DeLupa.

"J.E.D.D. Mason," Sniper repeated in a slow whisper. "Jehovah."

Lesley voiced the questions which loomed in Ockham's face as well. "¿What did you see at Madame's? ¿Ojiro? ¿What did the President say after they fell? ¿What was that secret meeting really? ¿Did we make the wrong call sending you there with your cameras? I figured the President's message would've said Cardigan not Sniper if they'd wanted you without the cameras."

A secondary screen below DeLupa replayed the footage from Sniper's visit: Madame's regulars giddy with delight as they dressed their living doll, now as a captain, now as a duchess, now as a groom. An eye accustomed to the view could see that the Flesh Pit was different with Sniper in it, all dancing and banquet tables, a masked ball, racy, with its fair share of bare breasts and crude gestures, but nothing like an orgy. It hardly seemed like a brothel at all, just a Blacklaw-run themed nightclub, scandalous only for using 'he' and 'she,' while every client who might have been ashamed to be caught there had retreated to the inner rooms. In the hour before the great crash, millions across the globe had seen Madame's great banquet hall through Sniper's cameras' eyes and decided it was a place they might try visiting, even booked a dinner there; they could not thereafter censure Spain's choice of venues without feeling the tickle of hypocrisy.

"The message we got wasn't from the President," Sniper answered, "it was faked by Casimir Perry. It was a setup. Perry wanted that meeting exposed, and O.S. too. They ordered me to go to Madame's, and they ordered us to make the Harper Morrero hit knowing Papadelias was watching."

Lesley frowned. "But Perry's guilty too."

"I know, but Perry doesn't seem to care."

"And what about the presence of Mycroft Canner at the meeting?" It was the reporter on the screen who asked first, but Ockham and Lesley wondered too: if even the Prime Minister would betray them, so might I.

DeLupa huffed. "The Emperor still insists that the *Lex Familiaris* forbids any public discussion of Mycroft Canner's sentence, but I agree, an explanation is in order. Don't forget, the victims of the Canner Spree were all influential people themselves: two *Familiares*, a leading Senator, Faust's successor-designate . . ."

Even the reporter paled. "Are you suggesting the Canner murders were part of this same conspiracy?"

"I can't comment on that, but if Canner was summoned there then someone at that meeting, probably Caesar, was wondering the same thing."

Lesley's hands clenched hard around her ba'sibs'. "If they blame us for Mycroft Canner there won't just be a trial, there'll be mobs and torches."

Sniper scowled. "Smells like *Vice* President DeLupa can't wait to drop the 'Vice.'"

Lesley flexed her toes. "¿Should that be our next hit then?"

"¿What?"

"We still have the cars for a few hours, I'm sure Sidney and Eureka can work up a list of targets that would calm things down."

"¡You can't be serious!" The words came through the lab door, which Cato Weeksbooth had cracked open just enough to let the others see a sliver of white coat, wild hair, tears. "¿You're going to keep going? ¿Now? ¡It's over! ¿Can't you see? ¡It's over! ¡The world knows! ¡And they hate us! ¡And they're finally going to tear us down like we deserve!" Cato's throat was too sob-sore to scream. "¡People don't want this! They don't want us to keep going. They don't want the world to be dirty like this. ¡They want it to stop! It's not just Ockham who should stand trial, it's everyone: Sniper, Lesley, Eureka, Sydney, me, the President, Andō, every Humanist who's ever put a name down on the Wish List, everyone. It's over. ¡Let it end!"

Sniper's black eyes met Ockham's. "¿May I handle this?"

"¡Don't come near me!" The lab door vibrated as trembling Cato held it across him, like the shield of a novice hoplite, fearing he will make the phalanx fall. Such an unkind mistress Science is, her branches so infinite, each subspecialty demanding a lifetime and a lab to even scratch the surface. Cato has been Science's True Disciple all his life, yet does she bless him now with knowledge enough to cobble a gun from the trash in his dustbin and defend himself? "Please, Lesley, they'll listen to you, please, I'm sure you understand. We're the last remnant of something dirty that's been keeping the world on this track instead of something better. It's time we died out."

Sniper again to Ockham: "¿May I?"

"It's your decision now, Ojiro Cardigan Sniper, Thirteenth O.S."

With a nod of respect to its predecessor, Sniper sprang with full Olympic speed, ripped Cato from the doorway's haven, and pinned him to the ground.

"¿You think you're different from the rest of us?" it pressed, seizing Cato's black hair in its right fist. "¿You think you're less guilty than the rest of us because you didn't want to do it? ¿Because you felt bad all these years? ¿Because we forced you? ¿You think you're innocent just because you would finish the program and then hide under your desk and cry and wait for me to come and push the button? That makes you the worst of us. Prospero, Lesley, me, we did this because we think it's right. We chose it. We believe in it, saving lives, helping the world. ¡You thought it was wrong and you did it anyway! Two hundred people you've killed, Cato, you, not the rest of us, you with your poisons, and your accidents, and the science you love so much. You could've ended it any time. You didn't."

Salt crusts would not let Cato fully close his eyes. "I still can."

Even injured, Sniper's left arm was not too numb to feel Cato reach for something in the depths of his lab coat pocket. Sniper seized Cato's wrist and twisted. "You know the penalty for pulling a weapon on—" It stopped short as Cato's fingers slipped, and a jar with one coarse white pill rolled out across the floor.

"¡Coward!" Sniper cried, its voice black. "Oh, no you don't. You're going to live through this, Cato. You're going to live to see what the consequences are when it all ends like you pretend you always wanted."

"¡Cardie! ¡Please! ¡I just want it to be over!"

"It's Ojiro now," Sniper corrected sternly, "and it won't be over." Twisting Cato's arm, Sniper dragged the sobbing Mad Science Teacher to his feet and steered him back into the lab, where festive flashing screens stood ready to weave more murder. "This is beginning, Cato, not ending, and you don't get to run away."

A bin of scraps and string and other bric-a-brac standing by for quick inventions supplied tape strong enough to strap Cato's hands behind him.

"¡No!" Cato wriggled like a scooped-up puppy, protest without real hope of escape. "Cardie—Ojiro—Don't make me, I can't face—"

"¿The Utopians?" Sniper supplied, cold. "¿Afraid they'll treat you as a traitor? ¿Letting them think of you as almost one of them all these years? ¿Or is it your students you can't face? ¡When they find out what your science was really for!"

The words, more than Sniper's grip, forced Cato to the floor. "This isn't what it's for," he whimpered. "It shouldn't be. It should be for the future, for Space, and Mars, and medicine, and talking to dolphins, and finding what the universe is made of. That's what I should have been, but I can't look at a spool of tape without thinking how to hide poison in the glue, or plant a pathogen in the fibers. ¡You made me into this!"

Sniper grunted, its injured shoulder straining as it strapped Cato methodically to a table leg. "We're all living weapons, Cato. That's why humans are born with fangs and claws. You can have a few hours to think about your choice."

"¿Choice?" Cato flexed to test his bonds. "You're not leaving me any choice. You never have."

Sniper straightened. "I am this time, Cato. That's your punishment: you get to choose. You can stay here, and stand trial, and see how sympathetic your precious public is when they hear your sob story about how you never wanted to commit mass murder, or you can come with me, and keep doing what you're so good at doing, to protect the world now that it needs us more than ever."

"It never needed us."

"It did. You know it did. And it does now. You may not care about the Humanists, but you can't honestly believe this mess won't touch Utopia. Once Ockham's arrested, Utopia will take over our cars. ¿Do you think the world won't see that as a coup? They helped the police unmask us, that's three billion very angry Humanists, Mitsubishi, and Europeans against half a billion Utopians. ¿You really want to sit back and trust it'll end well?"

Cato shivered like a fly in a web. "They're not involved. They're clean. This is our sin, everyone's but theirs. The world can't turn around and attack the only innocents. ¿Can they?"

Sniper fished a rag from the invention bin and wound it into a gag. "I don't expect you've got the guts to bite out your own tongue, but I don't have time to babysit you, and I'm not taking the risk."

"¡I'm not what the world needs!" Cato cried. "The world needs a real mad scientist, someone who could concoct something to save everyone, some world-saving wonder, not just death. If I were that—"

"You're not." Sniper forced the gag between Cato's teeth. "I'll be back by dawn. Have an answer ready: stay with me in O.S. and save the world, or rot."

I CANNOT SAY THE SIXTH DAY EVER REALLY ENDED,
BUT HERE, WITH DISASTER'S BREATH UPON THE WIND,
THE SLEEPLESS EARTH SPUN ON TO THE SEVENTH
AND LAST DAY OF MY HISTORY.

The Most Important Person
in the World

WE REACH AT LAST MARCH THE TWENTY-NINTH OF THE YEAR 2454. The birds of Cielo de Pájaros still teemed that morning, numberless as spirits over the rings of glass roofs which studded the mountainside's descent toward an Ocean black and barely crusted with the gold of infant dawn. Seven days had passed since Martin Guildbreaker and Carlyle Foster had made their first approaches to the Saneer-Weeksbooth bash'. Today it was Papadelias who came with Martin, with others behind them, police uniformed in Romanovan blue, who marched with reluctant awe across the bridge which gave Bridger his name. You did not know that, did you, reader? In childhood all names were '-er' for him, Stander, Looker, Aimer, Croucher, Canner, even Saneer, so, dwelling as he did beneath a bridge, Bridger. It is a name which, like all good names, means nothing. I hope you will keep calling Jehovah 'Jed Mason,' reader. An empty name is healthier.

Martin and Papadelias separated on arrival, each taking a squad to cover the two bash'house entrances, the Commissioner General taking Thisbe's door in the trench below, while the Mason took the front. His hand shook as he activated the intercom.

"This is Mycroft Guildbreaker, acting for Romanova. I am here for Ockham Saneer."

"Is the world about to end?" the master of the house called back. "If not, leave. I have eight hundred million lives to oversee."

Martin breathed deep within his square-breasted Mason's suit. "I'm afraid the sky is falling this time. Ockham Prospero Saneer, by order of the Universal Free Alliance I am here to place you and all members of your bash' under arrest for murder and conspiracy."

The twelfth O.S. did not yet open his fortress door. "I am a critical officer appointed by the Humanist government, and charged by the Alliance with the maintenance of the cars. I may not leave my post unless relieved, nor may I permit anyone to interfere with my bash'mates' work without an order from my President."

"I know." At Martin's gesture the Utopians stepped into line of sight, nine of them, somber in muted shades of ancient temples and nanolabyrinths, with a reluctant set-set riding their triceratops. "These replacements have trained on the Utopian Transit Network. My orders are to have the two most vital of your bash'mates remain here under house arrest to help them with the transition, while you and the others are conducted to Romanova."

One did not have to see Ockham's face to sense his frown. "Utopians are a strange choice."

The Mason swallowed hard. "The Humanist backup facility by Salekhard was destroyed in an explosion late last night. There are two survivors of the backup crew, both in hospital."

Even Ockham required some moments to digest that. "You realize this cannot be coincidence."

"It was revenge," Martin confirmed. "The perpetrators already confessed. They were the bash' of a Brillist killed in a car crash, and attacked the Salekhard backup facility with a homemade incendiary device. If your bash'house weren't in a major population center, they would have targeted you, too."

A pause. "Which Brillist?"

"Giller Edison." Martin smiled slightly. "Do you remember all their names?"

The door opened at last. This is the moment you should remember, reader, not, as the news replayed so many times, Ockham marching with hands bound behind him, the police escort fighting back the sea of hysteria that crowded around his jail. You must have seen that video, rioters pelting the silent prisoner with screams and tomatoes, like a so-called witch dragged as scapegoat to the gallows by the thirsty mob. That was not Ockham Saneer, but what we made of him, to our collective shame. Here, this is Ockham, standing in his trophy hall like the guardian statue outside an abandoned temple, facing vandal and storm with dignity. His clothes were his favorites, comfortable and alive with doodles, and the steel and deerskin of his boots were polished brighter than even I could make them. His belt he now removed, the holster with it, holding the weapon out for Martin to accept.

"I recognize that your preparations for my relief are sufficient, and your authority legitimate. As of 22:21 UT today I have been relieved. From this point I may do nothing without orders from my Hive."

Martin took the surrendered gun with reverence, then signaled his men to storm the house and capture all within. Ockham waited silent, stretching his wrists and shoulders to prepare for hours in cuffs.

"*Praeses!*" called one of the police, a Cousin herself but habituated to the Latin title Masons use for a polylaw of Martin's pedigree. "Cato Weeksbooth is in here, gagged and tied to a table leg."

"Injured?"

"Doesn't seem to be. We've also secured Eureka Weeksbooth and either Kat or Robin Typer, we can't tell which. No sign of anyone else on this level or the upper floor. No resistance entering the computer areas below."

Martin looked to his prisoner. "Why was Cato Weeksbooth tied up?"

Ockham met the Mason's eyes but answered nothing.

"Where are the others?" Martin pressed. "The other Typer? Sidney Koons? Lesley Saneer? Thisbe Saneer? Sniper? Do you know?"

"Cato, Eureka, and a Typer should be enough to break in our replacements." Ockham's voice had an unfamiliar lightness, relaxation from a man whose work had never until now been done.

An old blood Mason can only sigh surrender before such dignity. "All's secure up here, Papa," he called over his tracker, "but five bash'members are still missing. How are you doing downstairs?"

"Give me time, Martin," the Commissioner General wheezed back. "Some things have to be done subtly."

It is a unique definition of subtlety that includes a squad of eleven well-armed guards in gas masks and a percussive charge to blast down Thisbe's door, but perhaps Papa meant the subtlety of thought behind the execution. The instant the door shattered his force struck, like dancers pouring out into formation on a stage. They covered every corner of Thisbe's room: the closet, the underbed, the inner door, and trained a bank of the finest, fastest stun guns on their target.

She was there, Thisbe, soft in her house clothes, black hair sparkling shower-wet as she leaned her elbows on the table, sipping her fresh-brewed oolong. "Gas masks?" Subtly, within her throat, she laughed. "You look like giant fleas with those stupid rubber noses."

"No fast movements, Thisbe." Papa's voice sounded nasal through the filter of his mask, old technology which has needed little honing during our long peace. "Take your boots off slowly and set them on the table. You're under arrest. The charge is murder."

Her eyebrows twitched. "My boots?" Beneath the table, her toes played with each other, the landscapes traced on the metallic surfaces of her boots eclipsing each other like colliding layers of mirage.

"That's where you keep it, isn't it?" Papa accused. "It has to be."

"Keep what?"

"Your 'witchcraft.' We found smelltrack chemical residue on Carlyle Foster's clothes last night, and in the crashed car that killed Aki Sugiyama's fiancé, and on the late Esmerald Revere. You've won two Oscars for driving crowds to tears, I can't imagine suicide's much harder. You made Cato Weeksbooth design the delivery system, I assume. Buttons in the toes?"

The witch smiled. "That doesn't matter."

"Take the boots off, Thisbe. Now."

Gloves and guns creaked as the police tensed.

Thisbe swished her tea. "You realize this is a Masonic coup, right? Guildbreaker's manipulated you so they can wrest the transit system out of Humanist hands."

Papa nodded for his men to approach Thisbe, weapons primed. "I didn't say anything about the transit system. You're under arrest for the murders of Luca Cormor, Quinn Prichard, and Alex Limner."

Now the witch flinched. "What?"

"Your ex-lovers. Three of them. You made them kill themselves, just like you did to Revere and almost did to Carlyle Foster. And you didn't do it for O.S., either. I think you made them kill themsleves for fun. You like playing around with death, just like you like to play around with Mycroft Canner."

Thisbe's smile refreshed its darkness. "Jealous? Mycroft loves you too, you know. More than they love me, I think. Except when I make them love me more."

The Commissioner General, who marks my every heartbeat through his tracker, stood his calm ground.

Thisbe stroked her teacup's hot rim, smiling, as calm as if the weapons and guards were mere illusion. "None of this matters. Only one thing in the entire history of the world matters." She locked her eyes on Papa's. "You think I'd wait around here for you to arrest me if the world weren't at stake? In the name of your oath of office as Commissioner General to protect and serve the peace and happiness of all humankind, I demand that you drop everything else and help me find the child named Bridger."

"Bridger?" Papadelias repeated the strange name dryly. "Who's that and why should I care?"

"Because they have the powers of a god, and right now they're being fought over by Dominic Seneschal and Mycroft Canner."

The old Greek stiffened. "The powers of a god?"

"Bridger can transform matter and create life and death at will. Look, I have proof."

As the witch smiled on, the next grim conjuration in her spellbook crept out from behind her teacup, slowly. At first one's eye might mistake him for a beetle or a pet mouse, shy of predators, but not when the whole figure stood tall. "Good to meet you at last, Commissioner Papadelias. I'm called Croucher. I'm a plastic toy soldier that Bridger brought to life."

Papa cursed within his throat. "Stay calm, everyone. The masks aren't working, but you trained for this."

Thisbe scowled, stung. "You think I'd stoop to hallucinogens? Croucher's real, Commissioner. You don't believe me, have your tracker do a blood chem scan. You're clean."

Private Croucher shuffled forward, the low rim of his helmet forcing him to crane his neck to see the humans' faces. "I'm real, Commissioner. Your men can vouch, they're all seeing the same thing, a five-centimeter soldier with dark hair and green fatigues. A hallucination wouldn't affect everyone the same."

Papa looked to the others, who, after nervous moments, nodded.

"What are you?" Papa asked. "A U-beast? They banned humanoid U-beasts."

Croucher sneered. "I'm no windup robot. I told you, I'm a toy brought to life." He offered his mouse-thin arm. "Flesh and blood. Pick me up and feel me, show me to a doctor if you have to, but listen to me. We don't have long. The child who created me can create anything: an army of angels, a supervirus, a black hole, whatever they imagine, and they're freaking out right now. The world should not be left at the mercy of the imagination of a frightened thirteen-year-old."

The guards around leaned tighter on their triggers as Papa drew close enough to test the tiny figure with his fingertip. "How is Mycroft involved in this?"

The witch liked the tremor that had entered Papa's voice. "Send your goons away."

"Not a chance, and if you don't take those boots off within the next ten seconds I'll have you force-stripped." Though his voice stayed stern, Papa could not hide the light of wonder in his eyes as he felt the tiny soldier grip his fingernail, and stroke his knuckle as a rider strokes a horse. "How is Mycroft involved in this?"

Thisbe dismissed Papa's threat with a smiling sigh. "Mycroft is Bridger's father, or as close as. We've been raising the kid in secret for almost ten years, Mycroft, me, and Bridger's creations, like Private Croucher here."

Gingerly, as if afraid the marvel would pop like a bubble, Papa lifted

Croucher in his hand and studied close-up the rough face, too fine for anyone to sculpt. "Ten years?"

"Well, eight," Thisbe corrected. "That's why Mycroft kept coming back here, Bridger lived in the flower trench out back."

"The caves."

"That's right." She smiled. "But with the investigation and all, Dominic Seneschal stumbled on Bridger, and now they and Mycroft are chasing each other, and the kid, around the world. I'm not going to sit back and watch omnipotence be fought over by two homicidal maniacs."

"Four," Croucher barked.

Thisbe and Papa frowned together. "Four?"

"Dominic, Mycroft, Thisbe, and the Major." Croucher made the names so dark he could have been listing the Apocalypse's horsemen. "The Major's the leader of my army squad. There are eleven of us in all, and the Major rules us like a dictator. The Major's not like me. I'm eager to be a civilian again, and still able to think like one. The Major's soldier to the core, a child's abstract, insane, imagined model of a perfect soldier, only happy on the battlefield, and he and Mycroft raised Bridger on Apollo's *Iliad*."

Papa squinted. "You mean the copy of the *Iliad* Apollo Mojave left behind?"

An archaeologist poking in the remnants of Khartoum, or the Caspian coast, or Washington, who finds a bioweapon capsule slumbering from the last war, deadly again now that we no longer vaccinate, could not have nodded more gravely than Croucher. "The *Iliad* with Apollo's margin notes, bound together with the unfinished draft of Apollo's new version, the one the Utopians are always bugging Mycroft to finish. It's not just some storybook rewrite like they told you, Commissioner, it's also a handbook, based on the Mardis' research, step by step, of how to return this world to war. That's the mandate Apollo left to Mycroft in their will, to finish their guidebook for how to start a war, and Mycroft used it as bedtime reading for a child god! When Bridger was little they had nightmares about drowning, and in their sleep the bed would actually turn to water. They don't need to wish it consciously to transform things. Now that they're big, they've started having nightmares about bombs and armies. It's happening. This chaos, all around the world, the governments and leaders all unraveling at once impossibly fast, can't you see? The world is falling apart just as Apollo scripted it. Bridger caused this, making this world follow Apollo's script without realizing it, and Bridger is the only way to stop it turning into World War!"

I wonder if Papa would have shown more passion, shuddered, sunk into a chair, had he not been aware of his men depending on his calm to keep their own. "Then the Seven-Ten list scandal," he began, "O.S.'s exposure, Casimir Perry, the CFB, you think it's all because of this child Bridger?"

Croucher has long practice bracing himself against the folds of a trembling palm. "Bridger's power works by touch, but if you put a bowl of toy fruit in front of the kid he doesn't have to touch every piece to make it real, he just has to touch one, and it flows from that one through the others like contagion. The Earth is a very large bowl of fruit. Bridger probably doesn't even realize he's doing it, but between them Mycroft, the Major, and the book have Bridger convinced that the world is going to explode into war. Now it is."

Seventy years on the job were not enough to keep Papa from shivering. "Central, this is Papadelias," he called over his tracker. "Detain Mycroft Canner, now."

Smiles do not come naturally to Croucher's face, its natural ugliness hardened by scars, and blows, and jealousy. "Thank you for believing. It's important we move quickly, while you still have me here to advise you."

Few men pick up on fear so fast as Papa. "What's going to happen to you?"

"Once the Major realizes I've betrayed him he'll kill me, and let's have no illusions that anything you can do will stop him. Even if he doesn't, the miracle will wear off in time."

"Wear off?"

Even Croucher could not suppress a brief half sob. "Bridger has to keep giving us life from time to time, by touch, or the miracle wears off. He can't create life from nothing. Turning an inanimate thing into another inanimate thing is permanent, turning a living thing into another living thing is permanent, but something like me, life from a toy, it'll wear off, and I'll turn back into a lump of plastic unless Bridger keeps me alive. After this, the Major won't let him."

Papa frowned, soft. "I'm sorry."

Croucher is a master of the black chuckle. "Thanks for caring. Few would."

Papa snorted. "Still, if Bridger's powers wear off, I wouldn't quite call that omnipotence. If Bridger's forcing a war, won't it wear off once they're not thinking about war anymore? Or is that what you propose we do? Make them think about peace."

"I said it's permanent for everything but toys brought to life. You're not a toy, Papadelias. Neither are your ten billion fellow humans."

"Bridger's still a child," Thisbe cut in. "They're too timid to create things consciously without a toy as prop, but they're really far more powerful than that. I don't even think they actually need to recharge the toys they've animated, like Croucher says, I think they just don't have the attention span to make creations permanent unless they see and play with them again from time to time. One never stops playing with the world." The witch stretched as she smiled. "Bridger trusts me. I'm the only one who can talk them down and end this. Find them for me, bring them to me, and I can save the world." Thisbe signaled her tracker to flash an image up on Papa's lenses. "Here's a photo of Bridger. Mycroft probably knows where they are, and if they won't tell you, you can at least track the kid through the Pets Register. Bridger can't, or can't yet, interfere with computer databases."

Papa perked. "Pets Register?"

Thisbe smirked at her own cunning. "Bridger doesn't have a tracker ID, but I wanted them to be able to come in and out of my door freely, so we told the computer they're my dog. Pet registration is automated, and the computer doesn't have enough common sense to realize that a dog shouldn't be bipedal and say 'woof' instead of barking. All it requires is a silhouette and voice print."

"A dog?" Hush fell over Papadelias, not a soft hush or a calm hush, but an ocean of trapped activity, like snow's motionless groan the moment before the avalanche. I swear in the recording I can hear the ticking and clicking of his clockwork thoughts advancing step by step toward their determined end. "A dog . . . was that Mycroft's idea?"

The witch gives credit where credit is due. "Originally, yes. I modified—"

"Bring me Mycroft Canner!" Papa screamed, his tracker humming as he routed his call to minion after minion. "Get my whole team! Anybody who had today off doesn't anymore! I need the creators of the Pet Registry on the line, our best explosives team, burn experts, trauma experts, and every record we have of Mycroft Canner's dog! But above all bring me Mycroft Canner!"

Thisbe frowned. "Mycroft's dog? No, Bridger's registered as my dog."

"Have you slept with Mycroft?"

Even the witch blushes at times. "What?"

Papa had the good sense to return Croucher to the tabletop as passion tempted his fists. "Mycroft's been spending nights here for eight years, we all assumed you were lovers, but you said it was just an excuse to visit Bridger. Have you ever actually had sex with Mycroft Canner?"

"Of course, we—"

"The truth!" Papa seized her wrist.

"They haven't," Croucher answered for her.

"Never? Not once?"

"Not once," the Private confirmed.

Papa glowed, his hand still locked around Thisbe's wrist, hungry to lock around mine. "Can't you see it? Saladin Canner is alive!"

"Who?"

"Saladin!" Papa cried, a decade's climax in his fortissimo. "Mycroft had a dog, a dog we never found. For years after the murders the computers kept picking it up as a stray in random places all around the world, but whenever pet control went after it, it was gone, like a ghost. But it wasn't a ghost, it was Mycroft's accomplice, the ba'sib everyone assumed was dead: Saladin Canner! They were childhood lovers. The majority of Saladin's body was never found after the explosion that wiped out the Canner bash'. We assumed they died with the others, but they must have just lost their tracker in the blast, and Mycroft hid them. That's how Mycroft seemed to be in two places at once during the murders! Oh, very good, Mycroft! Very good!" His face glowed. "Hiding an entire second person for over twenty years! Hundreds of interrogations and not a hint, not one!"

The witch blinked, more insulted, I think, than surprised. "Mycroft has a lover?"

"It explains everything!" Papa cried, almost dancing. "How they could guard one victim while simultaneously going after the next, how they could beat a Utopian in combat, even why they were so uncharacteristically brutal to Ibis Mardi. That wasn't Mycroft getting sloppy, it was Saladin punishing a rival! Ibis who wanted to elope with Mycroft!"

Say it, reader. Call me traitor, failure, fool. I deserve it. During our two weeks my Saladin and I claimed victim after victim, untraceable thanks to our iron-fast law: never use the same trick twice. If you use a knife, throw it away; a disguise, burn it; a way to trick the trackers, use it once then never think of it again. Anything the cops have seen once they can recognize; reuse it and you may as well turn yourself in. Perhaps thirteen years of peace

made me complacent, but that is no excuse. I failed, recycled our most critical deception, the Pet Registry, and now my folly had given Saladin's scent
to the one hunter who would never stop.

"Saladin Canner," Croucher repeated. "So Mycroft's 'scary friend' does
have a name."

Papa spun. "You've seen them?"

"I think so," the soldier confirmed, "only very recently. Dominic found
Bridger's cave, so Mycroft sent this 'friend' to take Bridger off to a safe
house. A savage with no tracker, wearing Apollo Mojave's stolen coat and
clothes, with a killer's instincts and no hair or eyebrows. He said they burned
off in an accident in childhood."

"Eureka! That confirms it! Hahaha! Saladin!"

How, reader, can I describe the tone, the face, the fervor of Papa here?
If Fate had set all the treasures of this world before him, the Golden Fleece,
the Holy Grail, the Armor of Achilles, Asclepios's wand that raises loved
ones from Hades's hall, Papa would have chosen this. In fact, Fate had
offered him those treasures, and more, anything he could imagine Bridger
might create, but, within the room, only Thisbe seemed to remember that.

"This is all very fascinating," she began anew, "but significantly less
important than a child with the powers of a god."

"That's your opinion," Papa snapped.

She picked at a tangle in her ink-black hair. "I didn't expect you to actually be as insane as Mycroft makes you out to be. What idiot made you
Commissioner General anyway? You're not good at being a cop, you're just
good at stalking Mycroft."

"Commissioner?" The others could not hear the timid voice which called
Papa back over his tracker, but they could see the Commissioner's eyes go
wide. "Mycroft Canner's gone."

"Gone?"

"We moved in on Canner's tracker signal, but their tracker's on someone else, another Servicer who's wearing both Mycroft's tracker and their
own at once."

"Why didn't you tell me there was an interruption in Canner's signal?"
Papa snapped.

"What?"

"There must have been an alarm at the change in heartbeat when they
slipped their tracker onto another person. You're supposed to investigate a
blip like that coming from any Servicer, especially Canner!"

"Easy, Papa, deep breaths," one of his fellow cops urged—drugs and doctors may let Papa forget his hundred years, but his men do not. "There was no interruption. I've gone over Canner's recorded heartbeats and there's not a single blip since yesterday, when you personally verified they put their tracker back on."

"Then where is Mycroft Canner?"

"I don't know, Papa. Should I arrest this other Servicer?"

Rage rose in Papa now, deadly as a volcano, worse, for a volcano razes only its neighbors, while no corner of the Earth is out of reach of the Commissioner General. "Yes, arrest them. All. Round up all the Servicers that have been with Mycroft in the last day. Arrest Thisbe Saneer, and take their boots, and, while you're at it, get some polylaws started working out what legal hoops we have to jump through to arrest President Ganymede, and Director Andō, and Danaë Mitsubishi, and Casimir Perry, for that matter all the Mitsubishi Directors, and every single associate of Perry's coalition in the European Parliament."

"Me?" O.S. trained Thisbe to hand out death, but she shivered at the bite of cuffs around her wrists, like any amateur. "You need me," the witch warned.

"No, I don't."

Her glare leaked murder. "I'm the only human besides Mycroft that Bridger will listen to. You need me to stay here so you can bring them back and I can—"

"No, I don't," Papa shot back. "If I need to calm the kid I'll call a shrink."

"Too dangerous," she countered. "Bridger wo—"

"Less dangerous than using you." Papa gazed at her, closely. Do you know that zeal, reader, which true connoisseurs fix on their favorites: a gourmand on some rare spice, an archaeologist on some ship-shard from the sea's green depths, Papa on me? This was the opposite, sleeplike, a disappointed boredom, as when the spice turns out to be mere cinnamon, the shard some modern log, the murderer a self-important amateur who cannot even understand the leagues of subtlety which separate her from a Mycroft Canner. "If I want you, Thisbe, I'll have you dragged up out of your little box. Take Thisbe Saneer away."

He turned his back, our Papadelias, as his men marched the witch away. She struggled slightly, trying to bring the Commissioner's eye back to her, one last chance for him to see the folly of underestimating she who held even O.S. in fear. It baffled her, I think, how Papa could ignore her. They are both right. Thisbe is an unimaginative murderess, clever but with petty motive and repetitive, not in Saladin's league. But she is, I remind you one last time, reader, also a witch, and witches fester, and even if Papa's men did confiscate the boots—her chemical spellbook—I fear she has more hexes yet, and bitterer, as jail and boredom nurture her black heart. It may not matter; we may not last so long.

Papa laid his open palm flat on the table. "All right, Private Croucher. Let's go catch ourselves a Bridger, a Mycroft, and a Saladin, and stop a war."

Croucher leapt on, like a knight mounting his steed. "Yes, sir!"

Deo Erexit Deus

CHAGATAI WAS CARLYLE'S EXCUSE FOR TREADING AGAIN THE garden path to the little chapel in Avignon. The valet, Carlyle reasoned, seemed to know Jehovah better than any other sane person, and sanity was never more precious than in catastrophe. Over her feed the Anonymous's Proxy and Kosala continued to lash the airwaves with their rage, and news of the arrest of Ockham Saneer fed paranoia that the millions of cars would crash like meteors. Carlyle confessed to me, when I interviewed her to write this chapter, that she did not actually expect to find Chagatai alone in the kitch-ens. Rather, as the cross-less spire of the church loomed close, Carlyle felt not just hope but, as she described it, almost a premonition that the Master of the house, however rarely He might be at home in peaceful days, was near.

"Don't move!" Guards too quick for Carlyle to count burst from the door and seized her before she had a chance to knock. They frisked her, practiced hands folding and squeezing every loose inch of her Cousin's wrap, so not even a razor could have passed unnoticed.

"Consorbin inermis est, Caesar." (The Cousin is unarmed, Caesar.—9A)

"Let them come in."

Inside, a lone carved chair, severe enough for a monastery, broke the rows of icons and relic shelves that crammed Jehovah's hall. There sat MASON, fidgeting with the black cuff of his left sleeve as scenes of the world's degen-eration sparkled across his lenses. "Have you been taking care of yourself since last night, Cousin Foster?"

Carlyle, like any sane woman, trembled. "MASON? Why are you . . ."

"I am waiting to see my son. You were seen with us at Madame's. The press will be after you soon, if they are not already. I can chase them off, if you like. I am firmer with them than Kosala is. Or if you prefer shelter, my *Sanctum Sanctorum* in Alexandria is open to you."

The sensayer floundered. In the madness at Madame's, MASON had been one more of a bank of cardboard witnesses, while only Carlyle and her parents were true players. Only now, seeing the suit of imperial gray, the famous face without press light to hide the care lines, did it sink in that she had met the Emperor.

"I haven't had any trouble so far, but I haven't been home yet. Do you think . . . is . . ." Carlyle choked.

MASON is so accustomed to his presence striking others dumb that I think sometimes he is surprised to hear a stranger manage a complete sentence. "You are here to see Jehovah?" he asked gently.

"Yes. Are they . . ."

"Upstairs." Between his spoken words, Caesar's fingers fed others to the computer, which routed them across his Empire. "What do you think of the Prince of Asturias?"

Carlyle frowned. "You mean the Crown Prince of Spain?"

At such proximity Carlyle says she could see the gray in Caesar's hair, not sophisticated frosting as photographs suggest, but streaks of real age, subtly heavier on the right side, spreading. "Their Majesty once told me that Crown Prince Leonor had done more good by being born than they have in their whole life since. The existence of a living heir stabilized Spain and Europe, promising a safe succession, and giving the Spanish strat the hope it needed to endure the queen's suicide. Since then the Prince has run wild in bad company, aided their father's political enemies, has probably literally slept with Casimir Perry, and has done far more to shame the royal house than even the public knows, but still the King is glad they have a son, however rotten. Would you call such a prince good because their existence aids the world, despite their deeds?"

"No."

"Then you are not bad because of the evil which your birth has caused."

Kind words. Carlyle had not had kind words since Julia's, before she felt truth's poison arrow fly. "I don't . . . I don't . . ." I doubt there was a real full sentence in her mind.

Chagatai poked her head around the corner now, friendly in her livery, like a mastiff trained as perfectly to charm children as to rip throats. "Carlyle Foster! Good of you to come again. Are you here for me or for TM?"

It took Carlyle a moment to recognize Jehovah's Hiveless nickname. "I was hoping for the Tribune, yes," she confessed.

The valet's smile tried to ease the tremor in Carlyle's voice. "No worries, you're not intruding. TM said they hoped you'd come. I'll show you upstairs now, if you're ready."

"Now?" Carlyle frowned confusion. "But . . . I'll wait until the Emperor's finished, obviously."

Caesar shook his head. "I am the Emperor, Jehovah's father, and ruler of one fifth of the world; I wait. You are a priest; you don't."

"This way," Chagatai coaxed. "Unless you'd like a bite to eat first, or the bathroom."

Carlyle's feat dragged, leaden. "May . . . may I ask a question, MASON?"

"You may ask anything," Caesar invited. "Asking does not guarantee an answer."

"Why did you adopt Jehovah? Why let Madame's son be so close to you?"

"Because Madame is that close to me." Caesar's eyelids sagged, as if he longed to close his eyes in brief retreat. "I need a companion in this world who is neither my subject nor my enemy. My bash', what friends survive from childhood, are all Masons, my servants now, and all my colleagues are my rivals. Madame is not."

"But Madame is horrible. Everything they do is totally manipulative and self-serving, surely somebody else——"

"All motives are self-serving," Caesar interrupted, "and all people are manipulators around an Emperor. Selfish or no, Madame D'Arouet has done more for me and for the world's stability over the years than anyone, even Kosala or O.S., but Madame wields sex and gender instead of socially acceptable tools of politics. I cannot free them from that stigma, nor give them the office or recognition they deserve. Their child I can."

"Then you did it for Madame?"

"I cannot say power was not a factor. We all fought over Jehovah, hoping Madame's resources would go to whoever was named father, or had most influence with the child. Until the influenced reversed." MASON's brows narrowed, subtly, a mild anger but chilling, like thunder whose softest rumble still threatens a storm. "Stop dawdling, Cousin. Your answers are upstairs, not here. You must finish with my son before I can begin with them, and today of all days my patience is finite."

Fear more than Chagatai led Carlyle up the thin steps to the nave of the old church above. Its stone vault rose high, light and dim at once, like an overcast sky. Jehovah Epicurus Donatien D'Arouet Mason sat upon the front pew, facing the altarpiece where saints and angels crowded to watch as Christ in glory received His virgin Mother into Heaven with a crown of stars. Carlyle says that at first her eyes assumed Jehovah wore the same dark suit as always, but as she tiptoed along the center aisle she realized it was a bathrobe, black, barely enough to shield Jehovah's body from the stone chill. Jehovah's flesh was young, remember, just twenty-one, ten years younger even than young Carlyle, the structure of His face still smooth with childhood beneath His black hair—almost black, I should say, since it seemed as dull as graphite beside the true black of His eyes. Carlyle told me later of the thousand questions that schooled in her mind as she studied the impenetrable Figure who seemed more and more the center of this unraveling world, but somehow she could not fold her questions into words.

Jehovah broke the silence. "Have you come to help Me?"

The sensayer waited, uncertain whether the words were meant for her. "Help you how?" she asked.

The stone-still Speaker did not turn. "To understand the God Who made this portrait of Himself."

Carlyle looked to the altarpiece, the choirs of Heaven shimmering in their concentric circles of cracking paint and gold. "People made that, human beings searching for their own understanding."

"If God made Man and Man made this, it is still a Self-portrait. And if, as some say, God made Man in His Image, and His Image then made this, it is a portrait's portrait. And if Nature is the face of God, another Portrait, and Man is the spawn of Nature, it becomes a portrait's portrait's portrait. The Nature we see on Earth too is a microcosm, one might say a portrait of the Cosmos, and the Cosmos a portrait of the Laws of Nature, portraits spawning portraits like the spiral chambers of a nautilus repeating the face of God. Such a Creator seems desperate to show Himself to someone. And yet He hides Himself." As sometimes in city parks clever sculptors create false merrymakers, a bronze person sitting on a bench or strolling by a lake, life-sized and eerie, just so Jehovah's flesh sat frozen on the pew, the abstracted shape of a person without motion to make the person live. "Did you show proof of God's existence to My Dominic, or did he show it to you?" He asked.

Carlyle's breath caught. "Dominic told you about Bridger?"

"Bridger." Jehovah repeated the name meticulously, sound by sound, not two syllables but a series of phonemes, segregated like steps in an equation. "I have not heard that as a name before. When you and I met four days ago you were a Deist. Nothing but your Clockmaker showing His Face could change you so fast, and Dominic would not stray from My side unless he has found That Which I most want in this universe, and seeks to hide from Me that he has found It."

"Dominic, Mycroft, and Heloïse, they speak of you as if you were a god." The words just came out, Carlyle tells me, unplanned, as when you rub your eyes and only afterwards discover you were crying.

"I Am."

They are words Carlyle thought she was prepared for. She had heard them before, not just in textbooks, but in the wild like this, from another parishioner. Her training should have sorted the statement like any other, identified its proper label: Calvinist, Hindu, megalomaniac, and selected appropriate next questions to help a parishioner explore himself. But this was different, Jehovah's 'I Am,' subtly yet absolutely different, for such was the conviction with which He said it that Carlyle believed Him. Yet at the same time, Carlyle says, she could not believe that she believed, as if she were split somehow, watching from some dream bubble another version of herself who had gone mad. "I don't understand," was all she could answer.

"Neither do I." Jehovah moved at last, lowering His black eyes to look upon His hand, which He raised before Him with uneasy wonder. "I remember infancy," He began. "My nurse often put My hand against hers, and I realized Mine was growing larger, deducing thus that these large beings that fed and lifted Me must be what I was going to become. I had known I was becoming more powerful, mastering how to grasp a thing, to turn it in My hand, to make it near and far. With no experience of the finite I had assumed My growth would be infinite. In her I saw its limit. Was that all? To see? To grasp what is within reach? To plunge forward in time, freefall, knowing only what lies behind, while what lies ahead remains invisible? Tu ... Ya ..." He stumbled now, one word then another falling stillborn as He realized it would not serve with monoglot Carlyle. "All things being right," He tried at last, "I should have but to Will a thing for it to be, yet here I was reduced to these weak tools: hands, eyes, memory. Beyond these limits I would be forever powerless."

Carlyle felt pain imagining such thoughts. "They say no one can remember infancy."

"I make the most of what few tools I have." Jehovah lowered His hand, and let His eyes lock on the sensayer trembling in the aisle beside Him. "Your flesh will drain your strength less if you sit."

"Thanks." Carlyle sank onto the pew opposite.

"As I grew I met words," Jehovah continued. "These made sense. These one Willed into being, as is proper, and of them one could create anything, near or far or infinite or past or perfect. I thought I had discovered the real matter of this universe, but even words were too limited. Each person,

I learned, could only perceive words made in their presence, and no new words could be made, only the same repeated that I heard from them, like atoms, diverse only when they recombine. Even these might have been building blocks enough, but, as I added more variety to my words, they affected the so-called adults less. Tutors told me each adult could only understand certain groups of words called 'languages,' that what had power over my nurse did not over *Pater*, or *Papá*, or *Chichi-ue*, or *Monseigneur le Duc*. Even now for you, Cousin, I must use only words in the set named 'English,' for the rest would pass intangible through the coarse net of your understanding, as they do through Aunt Kosala's. The tutors promised that, with time, it would come naturally to Me, speaking only one language at a time, but how can it be natural to paint only with shades of red, or to build with atoms from only one column of His Periodic Table?"

Carlyle's breath caught. "You mean God's?"

"This Universe's God," Jehovah clarified. "I am not one small god among many, as you imagined Zeus, Anubis, and Apollo. I am the only God, the infinite, omnipotent creative Will, the source of all My universe, which is not this one."

"A different universe?" Carlyle supplied, understanding breaking in her eyes like dawn. "A different universe, with a different monotheistic God?"

Jehovah does not nod. "In My own universe I Am all, complete, sufficient, the First and Final Cause, perfect in Myself. Yet, for some reason, I find Myself born here. In this universe I can perceive what is within the limit of My human body's senses, remember what I have experienced, and wield the prostheses of human technology, but that is all. I have learned, I think, to eke out more from what this flesh can do than any human, but no finite thing can substitute for lost infinity."

The dream bubble burst here. Sensayer training awoke in Carlyle, ingrained doubt piercing the thin film of belief, so she fell back on routine questions. "How long have you known you were a God?"

"My universe does not have time," the foreign God replied. "I find it cruel, like death and distance and misunderstanding, barriers separating that which would rather be whole. I do not yet understand why This Universe's God would make such things. Space. Time. I met Time at the moment of My birth, but since meeting it, and in My native infinity outside it, I have always known What I Am."

"What happened to your universe when you left and came to this one?"

"I have not left," He answered. "I cannot leave My universe any more than Being can leave this wood"—he looked to the pew, solid beneath them both—"or Space this place. I Am My universe, always, Creator, touching, making, enabling, and understanding every part of it, though I also sit here in this flesh."

"So you can still sense your universe even though you're here?"

Jehovah closed His eyes, the only sense we have the power, at our will, to shut off. "If Unity, which grants absolute understanding of all things, falls under the label 'sense,' then yes. It is all right that you struggle to believe."

"What?" Carlyle's voice cracked, startled.

"That I am What I say."

Carlyle looked at her hands. "I believe that you believe it."

"Most of My fathers tell themselves it does not matter whether I Am a God or not, so long as I do My duty by their Hives. But you know better."

The sensayer nodded. "If it were true, the existence of another God and another universe, it would be the most important fact in the history of science, as well as the history of religion and everything else." She buried her fingers in her blond-tinged hair. "I'm trying to understand what you're describing, but it's a lot, and, for me personally, at least, belief can't come before understanding."

"I likewise find Anselm difficult," Jehovah answered.

Carlyle smiled; they have read the same theologians, this priest and This God, equal in that at least. "It will take me time," Carlyle continued, "to work through what it would mean for there to be two universes, and two monotheistic Gods. Until I explore all the implications, I'm not at the level where I can believe or disbelieve, since I can't yet compare it to my current beliefs. In my experience I have to examine a belief system for at least a few weeks, sometimes a few years, before I know it well enough to believe or disbelieve."

"Yes," Jehovah agreed, "here time does seem a constituent component of belief."

"Do you see time like matter, then?" Carlyle tested, growing eager. "Moments like atoms, so old things have more time matter? Or is it connected, like a string?"

Jehovah spent several silent breaths in thought. "I am nowhere near understanding Time. It seems to be a direction in which sentience can only move one way and perceive the other, but it also destroys, and twists, and swallows, making legacies differ from, or even oppose, intent. It annihilates, repeats, erases. It is too alien to me."

Carlyle remembers a chill as she tried to read emotion in Jehovah's eyes, and caught the full force of their starless, living black. "Sorry to ask so many questions."

"I welcome questions," This Kind God replied. "Now that this universe has taught Me what ignorance is, I will never willfully inflict it on a sentient thing, as My Peer does."

"Your Peer, you mean This Universe's God?"

"Yes. I would wish you a kinder Maker, but it is *impius* to feel anything less than absolute gratitude for the absolute gift of having been created."

Carlyle smiled at Jehovah's latinate pronunciation of the word, meant in its Roman sense, when piety was owed to states and parents as well as to religion. "It sounds like you don't like Them. God, This Universe's God I mean, you don't like the way They run things."

Slowly, with difficulty, always with difficulty come His answers. "I do not dislike, rather I do not understand. I need to find Him. I need Him to answer why He made His Universe so full of barriers, and ignorance, and limited perspectives, which make His sentient creations suffer and see evil in His plan. I need to know why He invented Pain, and Time, and Distance. I need to know why He creates portrait after portrait of Himself, but stays so hidden. I need to know how He found Me, how He created this flesh men call Jehovah Epicurus Donatien D'Arouet Mason, how He bound Me into it, and why He brings Me here as His Unwilling Guest, and then, strange Host, He hides."

Carlyle smiled. "You're not alone there. Everyone asks questions. Why am I here? Why is there Evil in the world? Why won't the Creator show Themself? I know you must study as much philosophy as Dominic. That's what it's always been about. Everyone throughout history needed those answers."

"Not as I do," Jehovah answered slowly. "My Mycroft put it best. No matter how many beast companions Adam encounters in the garden, he needs Eve. Before I met this universe I was complete, neither wanting nor imagining anything beyond Myself. Here, watching humans, I have learned what it means for a being to have equals, to speak with another, debate, learn, grow. Now that I learn of that, I need it. I have never before lacked anything in My existence, but knowing that I have a Counterpart, a Peer, I need Him." His eyes turned to the painted portrait of that Counterpart on the altarpiece before Him. "You called Him 'Bridger'?"

Carlyle froze, taking some moments to remember that it was she who had spoken the name in Jehovah's hearing. "Bridger isn't God," she replied. "I think they're more an avatar of God, a manifestation, a tool. Something through which God channels Miracles."

"But He is here. Your Clockmaker has shown Himself."

"Yes." Carlyle felt doubt's end here, the fear that these last days might be illusion, dream, over. She never doubted again. "Bridger is a child, thirteen years old. They have the power to make toys real, any toy, no matter how fantastic, even living things."

"Idea to actuality," Jehovah supplied. "By Will."

"Mycroft raised Bridger. Mycroft Canner." Carlyle swallowed hard, a part of her rebelling as she found herself trying to defend, of all men, me. "I know it may seem cruel that they never told you, but they wanted Bridger to grow up and become a full, strong person before meeting you. Maybe they figured it was inevitable that you would meet eventually. Fated."

"My fideist has nothing left to believe in but Providence."

For Carlyle, who knew both the theology and me, this sentence stripped me naked as a soul at Judgment. A fideist is a religious skeptic, one who believes that human reason, however lofty its ambition, cannot achieve real, indubitable Truth, and that the senses, however fertile science makes them, are likewise fallible and incomplete. Not to be trusted. Have all your calculations answered what the soul is made of, Science? Have all your electron microscopes found or disproved an afterlife? I, born to the think tank bash'es of Alba Longa, I, trained by the genius Mardi bash', I, with the finest education in the world, I, Mycroft Canner, had been so wrong that I murdered the living light Apollo to stop a war which never would have come. My logic was not wrong, the data gathered by the engines of human science not wrong. Rather the human animal I was could do no better than to err so absolutely. Reason failed. Evidence failed. I failed. Conviction had died in me in that room at Madame's where my strange trial took place. Absolute doubt permitted only one escape: to surrender to and trust the Providence, which had not only planned my sin, but guided me after, not to the death I expected, but to Ἄναξ Jehovah.

"If you have a criticism, speak it," Jehovah invited, sensing a hotter tension in Carlyle's silence than mere pensiveness. "You are human, far more adept at living in this universe than I. I err often."

Carlyle tried her best to face Jehovah sternly, but no human can. "You shouldn't expose people's beliefs to others like that. You did it before, at the Saneer-Weeksbooth bash'house. I didn't want to know that Mycroft is a fideist, and Mycroft wouldn't want me to know. That's private, intimate. That's how our culture works."

The God thought for a silent moment. "Thank you. I forget that humans often cannot see what is to me as transparent as the air between us. I will try harder."

"You can sense it, can't you? You can read people's minds, their thoughts. That's how you know people's religions. That's your power, isn't it? A special power, like Bridger's. People call it telepathy."

"My Peer, That Host Who brings Me here as Guest, does not grant that."

"What?"

Tired, that's how Carlyle described Jehovah here, exhaustion like Felix Faust's, whose brain saps its host flesh harder than brains were meant to. "I know the word 'telepathy.' It would be a precious sense, making the mind's world visible, a world of words will-shaped, more giving than matter. With telepathy I would be a sense less blind. No, I have no such sense."

"But you know things, see things about people, things no one could see from just a glance."

"I work hard to understand this world, its thinking creatures most," answered This tender Visitor to our rough world. "I make the most of the senses this flesh possesses. I see people with these eyes, hear with these ears, feel the temperature when a pulse races. I think of what that means. My Uncle Felix does no less. Is that a miracle?"

Carlyle opened her mouth, but thought caught her. "No. No, I guess, it doesn't have to be. You could just be very strangely good at reading people." She chuckled at herself. "After Bridger I was too . . . credulous." Shame made her blush. "Aren't you going to ask me where Bridger is?"

Jehovah spared the sensayer His gaze. "You do not know. If you did you would be agitated, debating inside whether or not to tell Me. Dominic too, right now, does not know. When I find Mycroft, I shall know if he knows. If he knows, then I shall discover whether I ask. If I ask I shall discover whether he answers. Blindly we move. That is how time works."

Carlyle felt dizzy, a metaphysical vertigo, as if she were in freefall, plunging into the pit of an unseen future, but somehow she had not realized she was falling until Jehovah made her see. She hugged herself.

"We must stop this conversation now," Jehovah judged, rising with a robot's slow efficiency, a minimum of muscles.

"Why?"

"We are increasing the cumulative total of human pain. You need rest. I have duties. *Patris* patience is at its limit. Strangely, I have been born into this universe as the Child of the leaders of your world, and the eight living leviathans which comprise humanity today compete to place Me at their head. Perhaps This Universe's God thinks it a kindness, power, to make Me as close to My customary omnipotence as possible, a soft bed laid for Me, His Guest. But, vast as Man's prosthetic powers are, a finite thing, however grand, is nothing against a lost infinity."

MASON arrived now, and it is possible that his footsteps, audible on the stairs, were what told Jehovah their conference was about to end. "Terminus est, *Fili*," MASON pronounced. "Foster, are you satisfied?"

Carlyle swallowed hard. "Yes. Yes, I . . . Yes."

Carlyle describes the Emperor's stare as graphite dark, not pure black like his Son's, but a darkness which threatens to spread its dark across the room. "Remember, Foster, the mad Roman Emperors had themselves proclaimed gods, and inflicted unspeakable horrors on their subjects, but the sane ones were proclaimed gods too, and they did fine."

"Then . . . Caesar, you know what Jehovah thinks they are?"

MASON would acknowledge no more. "You are needed too, Foster. Had you forgotten?"

Carlyle had forgotten so completely that she had no idea what the Emperor might mean, so she flushed red with guilt as she saw, at MASON's heels, the frantic and loving mob of her own bash'mates. They had dropped everything, the rest of the Foster bash', to come at Caesar's summons, routed through Kosala, the two guardians of Gag-genes quick to answer the pleas of these loved ones who had been listening madly to their trackers for any word from their stray sheep.

"Carlyle!"

"You idiot! Are you okay?"

"We've been going mad looking for you!"

"We saw you on the news."

"What were you thinking?"

"Vanishing for three days when the world's falling apart!"

"You're coming home. No arguments!"

"We've made your favorite, salmon and ravioli."

"You're coming home!"

I do not know them, reader. I imagine a swirl of Cousin's wraps cocooning Carlyle as they drag her door-wards under the gentlest arrest, but Carlyle rightly will not let me bring their names or details into this. The bash' is our oasis, the one innovation of our golden age which even O.S. does not make sour. In the coming dark do not, like Carlyle, forget to turn to yours.

Only one thing made Carlyle drag his feet. "J—" She caught herself. "Tribune Mason! Let me know if you find Bridger!" She strained against the net of loving arms. "I need to know! There's so much no one's been able to understand about Bridger, the source, the limit of their powers, why they exist at all, but with what you can tell just looking at people I'm sure you'll be the one to solve it. Please, I need to know!"

What is the lag before Jehovah speaks? Is it just language? Complexity of thought? Or, as I suspect, is it some disconnect between His eternal timeless Psyche and His sentences, which are designed to convey human thoughts, forged in the cage of time? "I will tell everyone."

Home would wait no more. Carlyle's bash'mates hauled her bodily to the car, and the comforts beyond.

"*Quid* need, *Pater?*" Jehovah asked, mixing English and Latin freely in the company of a father long accustomed to Him.

"I need Mycroft Canner," MASON answered. "We both do. The police are asking me fresh questions about Apollo's *Iliad*, and—"

"You listened," Jehovah interrupted.

Caesar will never feel at ease relying on Jehovah, as no ruler can rest whose cities thrive upon a riverbank, which could, at any moment, flood. "Yes," he confessed. "Mycroft is mad. A child that can bring toys to life is mad, but . . ."

"*Vero* many *Mycroftis operes* make sudden sense *si sit veritas*." (But many of Mycroft's actions make sudden sense if it is true.—9A)

The Emperor sighed. "Mycroft is missing. They slipped their tracker, even Papadelias has no clues. Do you know where—"

"Romanova."

"They contacted you?"

"No."

"Then how?"

Jehovah's gaze strayed to the filtered sky beyond the stained-glass windows, dimmed by the onset of subtle overcast. "Downpour *est* in Romanova. *Posset Mycroftem* (Mycroft can) visit Apollo's grave unseen."

The Rape of Apollo

HAS IT OCCURRED TO YOU, READER, THAT THESE ARE THE words of a dead man? All books will be someday, for authors die, and if by chance you read this while I live, then the second time you take up my history, the third, when your grandchildren read it, I shall surely have paid the ferryman what we all owe. I think all human beings, even I who have no right to ask more of the world, wish to see the future. I don't mean the whole future; after a millennium history must progress beyond one's ability to understand. What we want is to see the trajectories of those things we care about: our legacy, our Hive, our children. If we cannot watch the ship on its whole voyage, we can at least feel satisfaction seeing the white sails shrink toward the horizon. The Stoics said no man can be called happy until the end of time, for, if all his successes were undone after his death, he would be wretched in retrospect. I think, though, they were too demanding. No one can hope to follow the Utopians to the infinity they aim at, but if I dared ask anything more of Providence, it would be that I might live to know one thing. Will this cold Plan let them take that first step to the stars? Or will it make them, like the dandelion seed, catch in the nearby grasses, forced to take root beside their parents, though they aimed so high? If I lived long enough to see the seeds fly, reader, count me a happy man.

"Mycroft."

Caesar found me as Ἄναξ Jehovah prophesied, hiding in the downpour before Apollo's tomb. Even Romanova empties before walls of rain, the remnant citizens too hurried to peer past porches and umbrellas, let alone to spot a Servicer's dull uniform as I knelt on the cobbles. Wind tossed the rain in waves, slapping the walls, the flanking awnings, and Apollo's statue, whose stone coat seemed to soar with the gusting wind. There is a spot before the grave where nothing grows, no trace of those brave sprouts which elsewhere eke out their strangling existence in the pavement cracks. I cannot help but think that my tears made it barren, salt shed over decades of visits stolen whenever dark or downpour offered me concealment. If it was not my tears alone, it was half mine, half MASON's.

"You broke your parole." I could hardly see the Emperor behind me, a black pillar haloed by the runoff of the umbrella held by an imperial guard.

"I know I have no right to mourn Apollo, Caesar," I answered, struggling to breathe between my sobs, "but that doesn't keep me from needing to."

In another place his black-sleeved fist would have threatened violence. Not here. "You lied, Mycroft."

"I only slip my tracker when I have to, Caesar. Sometimes——"

"I don't care about your tracker." He spoke English, unwilling to exchange Latin with one who has no right to know it. "Apollo's *Iliad*. You pretended all these years it was a storybook, a modern retelling of the Trojan War. I never asked to see it because you said Apollo wouldn't want me to read it before you finished it, the more fool me."

I shuddered. "It is a storybook, Caesar. Apollo's unfinished novel."

"The police know better. It's a handbook for the Mardis' war."

"It's not."

His impatient hands grasped at the rain. "Give it to me. I should never have let you keep it."

"I haven't been trying to start the war, Caesar, I swear!" I answered. "I tried to stop it. Everything I did, I did to stop it. Do you think I could have done this to Apollo if there was any other way?"

I heard the Emperor's knuckles crack despite the rain. "What you did to Apollo and the others was sick beyond imagining. If you had just been trying to stop the war, you could have made the murders quick and painless."

"And what justice would there be in that?" I snapped, startled at my own heat. "The Mardis committed themselves to war and all its consequences: rape, torture, oppression, famine, flame, children half crushed by bombs crying to the dark as they wait for their broken limbs to bleed enough to let them die. What I gave them was a fraction of what they planned to give the world. Aeneas, Geneva, Kohaku, Chiasa, all of them would rather have killed themselves than live to see the future they were trying to create. Painless deaths would not have been just punishment for what they planned, and they knew it."

"You call it justice?"

MASON stepped toward me, hands hungry for some justice of his own, but he stopped before the somber, staring vizor of Apollo's statue. It had been a challenge for the sculptor, how to render recognizable in stone a figure so completely shrouded, the too-long sleeves leaving only fingertips peeking out, the mouth and nose barely visible between collar and vizor, hair showing only in moments when the hood fell back. The artist settled on two tricks. Reflections first, polishing the coat so the marble reflects the faces and colors of passersby, much like the Griffincloth reality. Motion was the second trick, a forward momentum in sculpted Apollo's gait, so winds lift the coat and drive the hood back, as if he were about to leap down from a ship's prow to make first footfall on a newfound shore, or into battle, to counter Caesar's violence with his own.

"You're right, Caesar," I answered, "it wasn't justice. A single body can only endure so much before it dies, and each of them deserved the suffering of hundreds of millions. The Mardis wanted to know what the war would be like. I gave them as much of a taste as one body can endure. Some of them—Mercer, Luther—they agreed it would have been more cruel to send them to death without a sample of the world they had dedicated their lives to studying, or at least they agreed before the pain began." I could see Mercer's face before me as I spoke, her eyes' light growing more alien during the vivisection, as she dictated notes about her own psychological degeneration to the recorder I let her set up to preserve for Felix Faust the final discoveries of his lost heir. "Trauma and cruelty we still have today but war, the most extreme realm of human psychology, we know nothing about, now that there are no veterans left to teach us what it meant. The Mardis deserved to taste that." My voice quaked. "Release me from this, Caesar, please. I cannot defend the actions of a self long dead. The Mycroft Canner who carried out those murders—"

"Was you, Mycroft," MASON interrupted, hard. "Don't dare claim to me that Mycroft died when I'm the one who had to let you live."

"I'm sorry, Caesar. I'm sorry."

MASON strode closer yet, a dark splash within the storm. "Show me Apollo's *Iliad*," he ordered.

"You don't want to see it, Caesar."

"There are many things I don't want to see. I had my guards search Aldrin and Voltaire. I didn't want to find their coats like Apollo's, filled with hidden weapons, weapon systems, targeting programs in their vizors. I keep telling myself it's for defense, that Apollo didn't want war, that they just wanted Utopia to be ready to defend itself. Utopia wouldn't have developed secret weapons, and sheltered Tully Mardi all this time, in order to finish making the war the Mardi bash' tried to begin. Utopia is hope for the future. They should have faith that human beings can improve with time, grow past war, achieve anything, even eternal peace."

"They do, Caesar," I answered through my tears.

"Then show me the book." Earth's sole Capital Power loomed close enough for the runoff from his umbrella to thunder at my heels. "Prove to me that all of this, the Seven-Ten lists and the CFB and Perry, are not the recipe Apollo left behind for making war."

"I don't have it, Caesar."

"What?"

"The book. I gave it to . . . someone more worthy than myself."

"To Bridger?" MASON leaned over me, sheltering me from the rain's blows while threatening worse. "You gave it to this orphan who can supposedly bring toys to life?"

Terror gripped me. "How?"

"Thisbe Saneer told Papadelias, and Carlyle Foster told Jehovah. Even hearing it twice from separate sources on the same day, I'm still not sure that I believe."

Papadelias knowing, Thisbe's betrayal, Carlyle breaking his word, these should have frightened me, but I could not feel fear. Jehovah knew at last. He had heard, not from me, but from a priest, an agent of This Universe's God. The world seemed repaired, as if I had looked under a tattered bandage to find an old wound finally healed.

"It's true, Caesar," I affirmed. "I have no way to prove it to you here and now, but it's all true."

He seized the back of my collar, hauling me up until I had to face him. "I don't care if they can bring toys to life or not, you had no right to give that book to anyone."

"It was for them!" I cried. "Nothing in history has ever been so clearly meant for someone. Providence had me find Bridger, me of all human beings, this impossible child, no origin, no bash', no parents, no explanation except . . . If you saw them, Caesar, you would think Apollo had come back to you: their eyes, their hair, precisely the right age to have been born at the moment of Apollo's death." I could not meet his gaze. "It is not strange for the deaths of saints to be accompanied by miracles."

Caesar shook me, anger commixed with disbelief, as if he had not imagined this madman was quite so mad. "You think Apollo came back from the dead as this Bridger?"

In the downpour I could no longer tell if I was crying. "Bridger isn't Apollo, Caesar. I hoped at first they would become Apollo, but they're a different person, timid, kind. They want to use their miracles to create a perfect world, to save everyone, the living and the dead. But they're also terrified. So many times leaders and governments have tried to use reason or science to remake the world, and so many of them, the first French revolution, Stalin's Russia, they were disasters, killed thousands, millions. The risks here are infinitely greater, even one mistake!"

He shook me hard. "And with that excuse, you kept the power for yourself."

"For myself?" I grasped Caesar's wrists to steady myself. "How can you say that when you know what selfish miracle I would choose in an instant if I were to let myself abuse the power? I haven't."

"What?"

I did not look behind me, but even the hiss of rain against the statue made the old pain worse. "You built this statue, Caesar. Look at Apollo, ready to leap down off the pedestal and tell us about some great new future they've imagined. Every day, every hour of every day, I could have brought Bridger here to bring Apollo back, just one touch. Providence didn't just make me kill Apollo once, I killed them over, and over, and over, and over. I kept them dead, every day, still, every day I choose to keep them dead." I let myself look up into the Emperor's eyes. "Do I deserve to endure this? Even me? Living knowing every day that I could give my life to bring Apollo back?"

"What?"

I shook. "Bridger can't make permanent life from nothing. If they didn't keep recharging it, the statue would only live a few days before turning back to stone, but we tried it on a cat once: with a costume Bridger can turn one living thing into another living thing, forever. We have Apollo's coat, Apollo's clothes. I could die as I deserve, and give this lump of meat over to the person in the world we both most want to live. These hands!" I raised my hands before me, seeing blood upon them even without Apollo's coat to stain them so. "I can't look at these hands without wanting to hack them off and give them to Apollo, but I can't! We can't bring Apollo back, Caesar! They would just do it again."

"Do what? Make war?"

I bit my tongue, hard enough to taste blood, measuring in my mind how hard I would have to bite to cut it off and choke and end my life, if I had had the right to.

Caesar seized my hand and pressed it against the statue's stone base. "Swear."

"What?"

"Here, with your hand upon Apollo's tomb, swear to me there are no war plans hidden in that *Iliad*. It's just a storybook, the Utopian weapons are just defensive, this chaos a coincidence. Swear!"

Strength left me, drained by that stone where his slim bones make their slow return to dust. It is half your fault he lies here, reader, and half mine. You denied him the Pantheon. I destroyed his chance to join his kin among the stars. The autopsy and chemical tests left what remained of Apollo's body too contaminated to be processed into that organic essence which, after the rocket journey, will become the soil of Mars. Year after year, those Utopians who could not live to see the terraforming done at least become a part of it, each ounce of powdered flesh another fertile plot of their new world. All his brief lifetime Apollo watched the launches, yet in death he could not even send his dust where dust is precious. That is my guilt. As for yours, only a handful of Apollo's kind have been buried on this Earth in the two and a half centuries since the Mars Project began, yet, for all Utopia has given you, you would not give this orphan shelter in your Pantheon.

"It's not the Mardis' war plans, Caesar. It's Apollo's. Apollo was trying to start their own war." The truth leaked from me slowly, like an infected wound milked of its pus. "Apollo came to Luther and Aeneas, before the Mardi bash' made up their minds, back when they were first convinced that the length of time that passes between wars was what determines how devastating the next one will be. The others were undecided, not sure whether they should try to start a war now to keep the next one from being so big it would wipe us out entirely, or whether they should believe that the peace was real, that humans could outgrow the violence as we outgrew the trees. They were uncertain, but Apollo was honest, and loved them, and told them point-blank that whatever the bash' decided, Apollo would make their own war."

"Why?" Caesar cried, his arm convulsing as he held me. "Apollo moved me to tears dozens of times, their future, their vision of the infinity of human potential. Now you're telling me that was a lie? That even Apollo believed we're doomed to eternal war? That the instinct to violence is so ingrained it can't be overcome?"

We both shook, I and Caesar, weak as leaves. We heard Apollo's words again, his certainty, his vision of our bold posterity which will stamp footprints onto worlds too distant for us to yet imagine how to find them, but find we will, he knew we will, as the boundary of human knowledge, art, and hope expands like a parabola sweeping ever closer to infinity. Have you wondered, reader, what made Apollo special? Why his classmate Aeneas Mardi introduced him so eagerly to Cornel then-not-yet-MASON? Why MASON brought him to Andō, Kosala, Spain, to the Anonymous? Rewrote the definition of *Familiaris* for him? Why they all relied on him as sole ambassador from this strange Hive whose crisscrossed constellations reveal no leader? His gift was this: he could explain Utopian thought in words the rest of us could understand. The wall that makes them alien, the vizors, U-speak, their cold and separate plans, was lifted somehow with Apollo, so the light that guides the rest of them, for once, could touch us, too. Perhaps it was because he burned brightest, enough to pierce the veil, or perhaps he alone among them tried to pierce it, not believing with the others that long peace and the desire to maintain this happy present had bred all ambition out of the rest of us. Some men are built to love many times, some once, and MASON used his once, not on Madame, not even on his Empire, but on Apollo.

"Apollo never lied to you, Caesar," I replied, gasping as my lungs lurched with the power of my tears. "How can you even think that? Apollo believed there was no limit to humanity, no world, no transformation, no dream beyond our power to make real, that with reason and ambition in our blood we can achieve anything, become anything! Just not in time."

He gripped me harder. "In time for what?"

"Mardi," I answered. "War day. Mars day. In two hundred and fifty years the next stage of the Great Project will be complete. Do you think a greedy, selfish Earth will sit back and watch the minority they most distrust take sole possession of a whole new world? How many wars were fought over the Americas? Over Africa? Over expansion? In ten thousand years, maybe in one thousand years, humanity will have progressed enough to no longer feel envy or greed or hate the 'other,' but in two hundred and fifty? Utopia is optimistic but not blind. When the terraforming is complete there will be war, all the Hives of this complacent Earth united against Utopia. The conflict will consume one or both, unless by then we have had another war to change the character of the Hives, or, at the very least, to leave some veterans to teach us again how to wage wars, and how to survive them."

"War now to prevent war later?"

"Not to prevent, Caesar. To soften. We no longer even vaccinate against the plagues which claimed the billions of the last war, but samples survive. Imagine if they were loosed on Mars, the new world uninhabitable for a century. Or imagine if they were let loose on Earth by those on Mars, fearing their own destruction. What if some new technology we've never tapped for war, Mitsubishi cloth or smelltracks, turns out to be able to wipe out a planet in a day? We need to find that out now, in a gentler war, one where no one is willing yet to go all the way. That was Apollo's project. They designed their special coat, the weapons inside, trained, wrote up plans for how the war would probably begin, how to proceed. Later the Mardis chose to join them, but Apollo would have done it on their own."

As a storm's first tremors in the still-sleeping deep shake a slim ship, not yet in danger but helpless against the tempest that must come, so Caesar's trembling shook me. "Apollo's coat showed ruins, soldiers, even myself uniformed for war."

I glanced back briefly at the Emperor's guards, his childhood ba'sibs for the most part, or Guildbreakers, reliable as caryatids in the face of secrets, dumb as stone.

"Yes, Caesar," I answered. "Apollo's coat is a simulation, this world one year into Apollo's predicted war. The people who don't appear in it, the ones it makes invisible, those are people Apollo thought would not survive the first twelve months."

"Including themself," he supplied.

I nodded. "Apollo would have died on the front lines. It's not a fate they wanted, but it's what they expected, and when we faced one another in battle—"

"What you did wasn't a battle, Mycroft," he interrupted, grim. "It was a murder."

"It was to save Earth and Mars together, Caesar! My attempt to let us vent our war rage without killing millions. I had to stop the Mardis, but if I could make people as outraged as a war would have, get Earth to vent its killing rage on me, instead of billions on billions, maybe it could've been a tiny war, we two, Saladin and I, against the Mardi nineteen, ending with all humanity, ten billion together, killing me. Apollo understood. Our battle might have been enough!"

"Not battle. Murder."

Something in me dared glare back at him. "What is a battle if not a confrontation between two enemies, armed and prepared to kill or perish in a struggle whose outcome will determine the fates of many? It was a battle, Caesar! Saladin and I against Seine and Apollo. We were soldiers. The first soldiers in three hundred years! The other Mardis' deaths, those I admit were murders, but Apollo was a battle, the first and only battle of Apollo's aborted war."

He choked. "Second."

"Caesar?"

"It was the second battle." He released me, turning to peer up through the alley toward the Capitoline Hill behind us, its columns bright as a lighthouse through the rain. "You think you shed first blood in this, monster? You were years too late."

"Caesar, who—"

"Apollo. Five years before my succession, they called me to meet them behind the Rostra. They had already realized I was *Imperator Destinatus,* that was easy, but it had never come between us, not before. I found them in tears, leaning against the *Milliarium,* and, in their coat, the column was defaced, singed, the inscriptions gouged or burned away. It was horrible."

I could well imagine it. I passed it almost daily on my way through the Forum to the Censor's office or Julia's, the *Milliarium Aureum,* the column by the Rostra on which are inscribed in gold the distances to the great metropolises of the world empire: to Brussels, Tōgenkyō, Alexandria, to Ingolstadt, to Casablanca, to Buenos Aires, soon to be the Humanist capital again after the fall of Ganymede and La Trimouille, and the mechanical device implanted in the stone which tracks the ever-changing distance to Luna City.

"Apollo said," Caesar continued, "that Mushi Mojave had been selected to go to study the ant colony they found on Mars. I didn't understand, I congratulated them on their ba'pa's good fortune, said it was wonderful, but that just made them cry more. I asked why. They said Mushi was the number-two ant expert in the Hive."

I nodded. "After Mirai Feynman."

"They said Feynman was offered the position first, but turned it down because they had a bash', a family, and going to Mars is dangerous. A Utopian said going to Mars was too dangerous."

I too remembered well Apollo's tears, hysterical, hearing that news.

"Then Apollo asked me which the world thought was more important," MASON continued, "the present or the future. I didn't understand. I kept trying to be a friend, but Apollo didn't want a friend, they wanted the *Imperator Destinatus.*"

Is this not, reader, the strangest of titles? *Imperator Destinatus,* the future Emperor. The successor's name is sealed in the *Sanctum Sanctorum,* never to be revealed until Succession Day on pain of the harshest penalties that justice can inflict, and even speculation is forbidden under Romanova's First Law. The title, then, exists only so it may not be used, like a god's forbidden name, which cannot be pronounced without invoking his wrath.

"Remember"—Caesar limped back a pace, gazing up at the statue's mirrored vizor—"I was not yet Emperor, did not yet understand the real relationship between Utopia, the other Hives, and mine. You know how passionate Apollo was. All it took was some new discovery about fish or enzymes to move them to tears, but I'd never seen them hysterical like this. Eventually they made me understand. Humanity has everything now, everything: power, prosperity, stability, longevity, leisure, charity, peace. Vocateurs earn society's respect doing the work they love, and those who aren't vokers put in their twenty hours and spend the greater part of life at play. Happiness has taken the place of wealth as our prime measure of success, and envy no longer hungers for rare riches hoarded by the great, but for smiles and happy hours which all Earth has in infinite supply. This is what past civilizations wished for, worked for, what emperors and presidents and prime ministers and kings are supposed to try to give their people. We have. We're done." He gave a little hiccup, my first proof that the water on Caesar's cheeks was more than rain. "Every life has the potential to be a good one, for the first time in history. And everyone's secretly afraid that it's fragile, that if we try to make it better, change something, if the Hive proportions shift too much, if science raises the life expectancy too fast, or Brill's Institute finally figures out how to upload our brains into computers, or make us all into impossible geniuses, it will fall apart. Golden Ages always end with Dark ones. The Exponential Age, from the Black Death to the World Wars, was all about growth, acceleration, future-building, change, recovery first, then progress, advancement, exploration, interconnection, every generation experiencing a new world, different, more advanced than the generation before, a state of constant change, mixed but usually more for good than bad. When our modern age began after the Chuch War, as the Hives rose and happiness with them, humanity slowed down. We started taking baby steps, not exponential ones, a few more cured diseases, new Olympic records, some new toys, but calling that enough. Too much change is dangerous. A happy world wanted progress to stop. Apollo understood in a way I couldn't what it meant to be the *Imperator Destinatus*: I was going to take on the duty to maintain history's greatest empire and protect my three billion citizens by not letting anything change. That conversation was the first time in my life I regretted being a Mason. The Humanists, Europe, the Mitsubishi, the Cousins, it's the same for them. They vie with each other, get better at what they're already best at, but change nothing. Even Gordian's experiments rarely leave their Institute. Now we've discovered O.S., the dark side of our paradise, and it's horrible, unforgivable, but what is two thousand murders to what we've already given up? The future. Only

Utopia thinks the future is more important than the present, that there are worlds that we could make which are worth destroying the one we have here. Or, at least, they used to think that, but if Mirai Feynman would rather stay home with their bash' and kids than study the first ants on Mars, maybe even Utopia is vulnerable to too much peace. Our happy world has made complacency contagious. Apollo asked me then if, in two hundred and fifty years when Mars is ready, there would be anyone left, even among Utopians, willing to give up all the pleasures of Earth's greatest Golden Age for the harsh life of a colonist. Then they stabbed me with a pocketknife."

I choked. "Apollo attacked you, Caesar?"

He squeezed his own left shoulder, his thumb tracing the contour of a scar beneath. "They said, if they were going to wound me, they wanted to do it honestly with their own hand, that, if everything was to be their fault, they should shed first blood. I didn't understand. I thought they were just being hysterical, but that wasn't it, was it?"

My chest contracted, as if the statue's gaze, though blind and stone, was strangling me. "Apollo asked me once if I would destroy a better world to save this one. That wasn't the real question, the real question was if I would destroy this world to save a better one. Apollo didn't just think the war was necessary to keep the next one from wiping us all out. They thought we had to make the world less perfect or no one would be willing to face the hardships of moving on. There are few people left anywhere who are willing to die for something, for their children maybe, but not for a cause, and certainly not for a patch of raw and barren Mars ground. Apollo thought that we need suffering to create people capable of enduring suffering. World Peace does not breed heroes." My lips trembled. "The day you're talking about, August twenty-second, 2426, the day Mushi was asked to go to Mars, that was the same day Apollo told the Mardis they had decided to make the war come, even if the others wouldn't help."

The Emperor nodded, no surprise left now. "Apollo drew first blood, my blood. You drew second, theirs. After Apollo's death, I tried to stay close to Utopia, invited other Utopian *Familiares*, protected them, even against Madame. I did everything I could to help them pursue their future in parallel to mine. I thought the Empire could sit unchanging and nurture them while they progress, separate but not enemies. That book, Apollo's plan, it's making us enemies. As MASON I can't sit back and let Utopia destroy this world, not even to protect a dream I share."

"They aren't doing it, Caesar." It felt strange smiling here, but the thought of adding some salve to good Caesar's wounds made me feel warm inside. "Utopia is innocent. This isn't Apollo's war."

"What?"

"O.S., the Humanist-Mitsubishi-Europe alliance, the CFB threatening the Cousins, none of it matches what Apollo planned. Their war was to be the Masons against the Mitsubishi over land, with Europe taking your side and the Humanists taking theirs, while the Cousins and Gordian would have stayed neutral. The situation happening now isn't remotely like Apollo's war plans. Some of the tensions are the same, the economic balance Kohaku Mardi predicted, 33–67; 67–33; 29–71, but the events, the sides, are totally different. Utopia wouldn't do it this way. They wouldn't tear down the Cousins, the group we need to keep the others from getting too vicious. They wouldn't expose O.S. and make the public call for blood, they wanted the smallest war possible, not a huge, angry one like this will be. This isn't Apollo's war. The weapons, Voltaire's and Aldrin's, they really are for self-defense. Utopia didn't do this. The war they're ready for is coming on its own."

"You're sure?"

"I've memorized Apollo's war plans, every step, how to make the war midsized and brief, contingency after contingency for keeping it from getting vicious, and to keep it from dragging in every Hive. This O.S. mess is precisely the kind of war Apollo didn't want."

His eyes grew narrow. "So there are war plans in Apollo's *Iliad*?"

I winced. "I can't show them to you, Caesar. The plans include strategies Utopia can still use to help keep the war contained, and minimize the damage. If you know the plans you'll react differently to events, then they won't work. Trust—"

"You lied about that book! You and Apollo, too many times for me to trust you now!"

"Lied, Caesar?"

"War plans are not a storybook."

Again the presence of truth where only more betrayal was expected let me smile. "I wasn't lying, Caesar. There is a story in the book too, one I was supposed to finish. Apollo was rewriting the *Iliad* with giant robots."

He half laughed. "Giant robots?"

"You know the old science fiction stories where the pilot rides inside a giant human-shaped robot. Apollo's *Iliad* was set in the future, a space war where Troy is on the Moon, with Hector and Achilles facing off in giant robot suits and smashing asteroids. It was badly written, too. If you saw a chapter, Caesar, you would laugh."

MASON frowned, uncertain, as if believing me only because the claim was too stupid to be a lie. "Why would Apollo waste their time on such a thing?"

A touch of lightness let my tears pause. "It was the only way Apollo could imagine a future war where one soldier still matters. Apollo hated war, could not forgive a universe where such horrible suffering was necessary to get to Mars. They desperately wanted to find something else worthwhile in war, something to make it more than an unforgivable but necessary evil. The Church War consisted of statistics, a hundred thousand dead here, a million there, mostly civilians, but even the majority of soldiers were killed by faceless bombs, and those who did see the whites of the enemy's eyes did so only in waves of thousands. Apollo saw nothing worthwhile in such a war, no thought, no heroes, and whether one soldier thinks their side is right or wrong, changing sides would make no difference. In Homer's *Iliad*, when Achilles refuses to join battle, the Argive armies fail without him, and when other heroes, Hector or Sarpedon, charge or fall back, the whole face of the war is different. Individual decisions matter when the heroes make them. Realistically no one soldier's decision can matter like that in a war, but without that there is no human face to it, the war becomes a mere machine of death. Apollo wanted a war of meaning, two sides embodying two futures, who would fight with respect and honor, putting their lives on the line for their philosophies, as it was when Saladin and I faced Seine and Apollo. Homer's heroes could have that, be that important to the course of the war, because they were part god. Apollo's future version had cyborg pilots bonded to special giant robots that only they could use, which made them overwhelmingly powerful compared to common soldiers. In Apollo's version the gods were powerful A.I. robots, so a human pilot in a giant robot suit was literally wearing a prosthetic god. There were only a handful of pilots who could do it, so when one left or entered battle, or switched sides, that individual decision could change the face of the war."

Caesar breathed deep. "Just like Homer's heroes."

I nodded. "Freud said all technology is a prosthetic god, a set of tools we weak humans strap on to give ourselves the powers we crave: computers for omniscience; trackers for omnipresence; medicine for immortality; armor for invulnerability; guns for Heaven's wrathful thunderbolts. Apollo just made that literal. Of course, Apollo didn't really think the war over Mars in two hundred and fifty years would be fought with giant robots, it was just the only way they could describe a war that would be meaningful, conscionable, with space for human dignity. It was Apollo's hope, the kind of soldier Apollo wished they could be, so they could die a hero, instead of faceless, one among a million. That's why I had to face Apollo in battle head-on, not catch them by trickery as I did the others. It was foolish of me. Apollo could have won, killed me, and lived to make their war. I risked letting that happen, but I had to test myself, my future, against Apollo's. Apollo deserved to fall like a hero."

I will not solve the mystery, reader. I will not tell you of Apollo's death. You know the facts. The eighth day of my rampage Saladin and I convinced Seine Mardi that the police who had her in protective custody were complicit in the murders. She fled, and sent word to Apollo, who was about to embark for the safety of the Moon, but he gave up his seat to Tully, and returned. He knew it was a trap, but knew too that, if he did not come, his love would suffer all my tortures, alone. The police found Seine dead of cyanide, one bullet in her side, with residue across her brow proving that she had worn Apollo's vizor for a time, though whether before, during, or after death science cannot tell. Apollo's body they found dismembered, sexually violated, and dead from blood loss, since my imperfect tourniquets could not prevent all leakage from the stumps of thighs and shoulders. His coat, vizor, and U-beast were gone, but in his stomach they found a placebo capsule, shaped just like Seine's cyanide, and well-chewed bites of his own cooked flesh, which he had volunteered to taste as we feasted with him, one last experience. A second pellet of real poison waited out of reach in the gutter beneath. These are forensic facts. As for the truth? Who died first? Whether Apollo mistook the placebo for poison, or whether he chose the placebo and the pain that followed? Did Apollo lend Seine his vizor to aid her in combat? Or perhaps, before the battle, he shared with her a glimpse of his Utopian vision? Or placed the vizor on her dead eyes to make her rest more peaceful? These answers neither torture nor you can wring from me, reader. At first I kept them secret because I felt no outsider could understand, but there have been such exquisite versions of our story since, the plays, movies, paintings, poems, imagining different Seines, different Apollos, different Mycrofts, different great conflicts of our times played out as artists reenvision the tragedy of the Utopian who died for love. For me to set out a script of cold facts now would only block what has become the font of something greater. You will accuse me justly of hubris as I make this comparison, reader, but, if some base historian proved once and for all that there was no Achilles to drag Hector breaker of horses round and round the topless towers of Troy, the world would have lost something.

"I wish you could have seen them, Caesar." A whimper rose in me, and, judging by Caesar's face the rain had eased enough to let him see how thickly the tears washed down my cheeks. "I saw through my periscope, just before they leapt into battle, the last kiss Seine and Apollo shared, with the weapons in their hands, and wind driving the tears sideways across their cheeks. I can still see them when I close my eyes. And it was equal. We shared a last kiss too, Saladin and I, I can still feel it, just like theirs, what would have been our last kiss in a world where they won the battle. I feel it, see it, taste it. I can't feel anything else, just that moment forever." My pacemaker kicked in, my heart racing as if the memory were draining all my blood to feed itself. "I had believed violence was better in the hands of individuals, one murderer expressing himself absolutely, not ordered by the state like soldiers are. But there, the four of us ready to die to test the futures we believed in, that was better. If we could only have one future, if one of our rival futures had to die, we could at least give each of ours a chance. I understood then what Apollo was trying to do in their *Iliad*. There is something a little good in war." I laughed inside. "Trial by combat. Maybe I already believed a little bit in Providence even back then, but I had to think that whichever of us would win was somehow meant to. Whichever one of us would win had the right future. Apollo died for that."

"Apollo died for Seine Mardi." Hers is the only name the Emperor pronounces with more hatred than my own.

"We don't know that. Maybe Apollo would have come anyway, to test their future against mine."

"They died for Seine." One could taste the hate in MASON's tone, Cornel's tone rather, for it is the person, not the office, she offends: how dare she, this Humanist, this child, this person who, try as we might, we could not find anything special in, no wiser, keener, brighter, more creative, more ambitious than any other person, how dare she alone enjoy Apollo's love? "I talked to Apollo's bar friends," Cornel continued, fists stiff as stone, "the ones who were with Tully, and attacked you. Apollo visited them in the bar the day they died. Apollo showed up all of a sudden, standing in the doorway with tears running down their cheeks, and when the others asked what was wrong Apollo said, 'I don't want to die. I want to drink with you, and live with Seine, and stand on Mars, and breathe the air we made, but I'd go mad, I know it, I'd go mad living on, knowing I left

Seine to go through this alone. I don't want to die. I just wanted someone to hear me say it.'"

We collapsed here into tears together, Cornel MASON and myself. I like to think that, for that moment, the labels left. I was not Apollo's pupil, nor his killer; Cornel was not the avenger nor the unrequited lover; we were just two people who had lost the same friend.

"I can't tell . . . who's right . . . anymore . . ." I gasped out through my sobs. "I won, but, when I killed Apollo, God made Bridger, and now someone else is making the war, not Apollo, not Utopia, not me. I don't know who. I don't know how. I don't know why. And it'll be a worse war, much, much worse. But there is one mercy, Caesar. You and Utopia don't have to be enemies. You should still try to stop the war, you have to, but if you fail, if it starts, both you and Utopia will have the same goal: making it as short as possible. You can be allies. Once the war has started we can even have Bridger bring Apollo back, and you two can be allies at last, and work together to make this the best . . . the least bad . . . war that it could ever be." I swallowed hard. "This Universe's God is not kind. If They were, They wouldn't have made me kill Apollo in the first place. More than that, a kind God wouldn't have made human nature such that achieving a happy golden age like this meant risking the whole human race getting too comfortable and scared, like Mirai Feynman, and giving up on setting out among the stars. But here at least, for whatever inscrutable reason, They have been kind. We can bring back Apollo. If the war is real, Caesar, and we can't stop it, then at least we can finally use Bridger's powers to give my body over to Apollo. The largest part of my debt will be paid at last, my guilty life traded for Apollo's better one, and all will be as it should be."

Silence gripped MASON, far too dark to interrupt. He was not looking at me but at the statue, and I saw in his rain-streaked face an expression I had felt many times myself but never seen on another. Now the statue was a seed to him, a chrysalis waiting to become the man, and, as he faced it he faced not Apollo's dust, but an Apollo he might walk with again, and speak to, and hear answers. "You know Jehovah won't let you kill yourself, or anyone," he answered at last, "not until we can prove we aren't all Gods."

I nodded. It may be strange to you, but it is the most natural of fears to Good Ἄναξ Jehovah. If He was born a God, why not all of us? Perhaps every human being in this world was a visiting God like Him, trained by society not to realize what we are, to think that the universes to which only we have access are mere imagination, not Realities themselves. And if we are all Gods and mortal, do our universes die with Us? Does every human death take with it another cosmos, infinite, life-filled, and better than this one? I could not prove to Him it was not so—can you?

The Emperor stumbled, his weak left foot giving way, but he concealed it by bending to lift my hat from where it lay, and pulling from within it the dripping gray *Familiaris* armband, which I carried always but so rarely wore. "I'm going to have them sew this to your sleeve. The world knows about you now, you need the visible protection of my law or the next angry mob may do worse than knock you down."

"Yes, Caesar." I took it from him, wringing it out in my hands.

"It's too dangerous for you to walk the streets alone. Ever. Ever again. If I catch you out unguarded one more time, or even trying to get out, I'll lock you in a cell in Alexandria, and the only time you'll ever leave again is if I lend you out to someone who has their own cell ready for you. And I'll have you hobbled. Surgically. I mean it, no second chance."

"Yes, Caesar. I understand." A deep breath. "What now, Caesar? You have caught me, you must have more need for me than this."

"We need you at the Capitolium. The Censor has called an emergency session of the Senate to hear Jehovah present their findings on O.S., but we need you to help write their speech. Jehovah is still too distraught to make themself comprehensible to anyone but you."

I looked to the Capitolium on the hill behind us, the clouds now lightening over the temple which, in real Rome, would have held offerings to Jupiter, but here housed the constitutions which govern the many kingdoms of man—not much difference.

"You have an idea of how Jehovah fits in all this, don't you?" Caesar tested.

I sighed slowly. "Not a clear one, Caesar. History's largest war is coming. In the middle of it, Bridger was born human with the powers of a God, and Jehovah was born a God with no more powers than a human. When you first meet Bridger it's instinct to ask: Why me? Why did God show this miracle to me, of all people, when so many better people throughout history prayed their whole lives for this and got nothing? It takes some time for the selfishness to wear off. The real question isn't why me, it's why now? Why, out of all the moments in history, would God show Their face now? It is not coincidence. I don't know if Jehovah is here now because Bridger is necessary for the war, or if Bridger is here now because Jehovah is necessary for it, but I am sure they are here so they can meet, and meet at this moment of humanity's greatest testing, the first true universal war. God, the God Who made us, is the only other member of Jehovah's species. *Deus*

Monotheistus one might say. Jehovah needs to meet Them more desperately than any *Homo sapiens* ever has. This Universe's God is not so cruel as to deny Him that. That's why Bridger is here." I looked up into MASON's uncertain eyes. "I've never been sure, Caesar, if . . . do you believe Jehovah is a God?"

"Whether they are or not, my duties are the same." He handed me my tracker, kept safe and dry in the depths of his pocket. "If you slip that again without my permission I'll kill Saladin."

I had not thought I had the strength left to shudder so. "Understood, Caesar."

"Papadelias has arrested the Servicers who helped you. Papa's as eager to talk to you as I've seen anyone be eager for anything in my entire life. I can put them off for a few hours, until Jehovah is done with you, but no longer."

"Thank you, Caesar."

"Where is Bridger?" he asked.

A sob leaked. "I don't know."

I did not fully understand how true my words were until after I spoke them, when I set my tracker back into my ear and switched it on.

"Mycroft!" It was the Major's voice, harsh over the intercom the instant my signal went back on line. "Where in Hades have you been? Bridger's gone! We went to the Sniper museum to get more equipment from the toy stash, but the police were waiting, your Papadelias, with men everywhere, and some kind of electropulse, it fried the teleporter, all our radios, everything. They captured Boo and Stander-G. Bridger turned invisible and flew off to who knows where. We've lost touch completely."

"Bridger's alone?" I cried, unable to care whether Caesar or anyone could hear me.

"They've got their nonelectrical equipment, but that's it. It's been two hours and no contact."

I cannot call this feeling fear. It is not fear after the dam breaks, when you watch the floodwaters wreaking their unalterable destruction. It is not fear as you watch the armies already locked in battle. It is not fear as you are dragged in your coffin-cage to the execution chamber where you know your justice waits. If I still doubted there was a God, I would have felt doubt here, but all I felt was resignation, Providence's clockwork clicking on.

"There's nothing we can do, Major," I answered. "If Bridger wanted us, if Fate wanted us to be with Bridger, we would be. They don't. There's absolutely nothing we can do."

The Major paused. "I'll count to ten, shall I?"

"What for?"

"Till you admit you don't believe that either."

Aristotle and Alexander

AULUS GELLIUS PRESERVES FOR US A LETTER OF PHILIP OF Macedon to Aristotle reporting the birth of his son. I thank the gods, says Philip, not just that he is born, but that his lifespan overlaps with yours, that with your teaching he may prove worthy of us, and of the kingdom that will be his. The letter is a fake, of course, but mere fact has no power to erase so potent an idea. So many moments, from the first cave scribbles to the stars, Fate could have chosen to give us our Alexander, but it sent him when the Philosopher was there to teach him, so that the two, in meeting, might make this world.

"You're waiting to see who's safe, aren't you?" Tully was hoarse from preaching, weak from standing, our warmonger still unequal to Earth's IG embrace. "You're hoping your own Hive will be exonerated when J.E.D.D. Mason and Papadelias present their findings to the Senate, as if only the guilty Hives will suffer. You still think this is a trial, where the bad guy will be punished and the innocent will go home and sleep snug in their beds. It isn't. No one sleeps snug anymore. The Censor knows it. That's why they've frozen the stock market, and set a cop on every street corner in Romanova. The exposure of this assassination system isn't just a scandal coming to light, it's the end of the system which has kept the peace for two hundred and fifty years. The end of peace!"

Tully paused, expecting the crowd's voice to rise in agreement, criticism, shock, some noise, any noise, but the spectators crowding the Forum stood in sickly quiet, like children dragged from their predawn beds, not yet ready to register the waking world.

"The Censor's doing their best," Tully continued. "They've called this emergency Senate session, so at least we'll get it over with, and get the story from neutral investigators instead of all the Hives accusing each other at once, but that's not enough. Nothing's enough. When that door opens tonight," he pointed, "and the Senate session ends, the worst won't be over, it'll be beginning!"

The crowd's eyes followed Tully's gesture to the bronze doors of the Senate House, a stone's throw to his left, where the Senate Guard in Romanovan gold, white, and blue stood pale with awareness that they were no longer ceremonial. How did this day come, reader? This nightmare day, when the Enemy, the Mardis' spokesboy, stands, not on his soapbox in some mildewed alley, but on the Rostra! That high, wide, marble-covered podium in Romanova's Forum, where Tribunes and Senators announce the conquests of science, the triumphs of Olympians, the births of laws, and the deaths of heroes, and where now Tully harangues the thronging thousands, while floating cameras feed his words and gestures over the tracker network to another billion souls. The Forum had not been so packed in living memory. Downpour had ended, and drizzle had no power to deter the curious swarm, who filled the nooks and streets as plaster fills a mold. The marble porches of the law courts, the Hive embassies, the secular temples where Quaestors and secretaries trembled at their desks, even the Sensayer's Conclave, silent with panic after Julia's arrest, all were solid crowd. A pack of daring students had even climbed the triumphal arch which framed the steep steps of the Capitolium at Tully's back, hanging off the reliefs where our stone heroes—Thomas Carlyle, Jean-Pierre Utarutu, Sofia Kovács, and King Juan Valentín—turned forests of rifles into plowshares, and poured cornucopias of aid over what the world's mistakes had left of her poorer regions. Papadelias's Alliance Officers, more used to desks than mob scenes, joined the City Prefect's outnumbered force to carve out lifelines through the crowd, standing as living dikes around the landing patch for the arriving Senators. The elected representatives of Earth did not march into today's session, but dribbled from their cars, clumping in groups, Cousins clinging to Cousins, Japanese Mitsubishi to Japanese and Korean to Korean, most silently cursing the day they had been selected by the stockholders, suggested to the CFB, appointed by the Emperor, elected by the mob, whatever means each Hive preferred to fill those seats reserved for it in the illustrious body which oversees the Universal Free Alliance.

"I know!" the Enemy pressed on, fired with confidence that this day, this hour, was why Fate had spared him. "Many of you still don't believe in the assassination conspiracy, but I have proof. That's why Sniper arranged for me to speak here today. This is what the Mardi bash' studied, what I study, the tensions and forces that make society erupt into violence. I'm certain, and if you read the data I've released then you'll be certain too. Over the past two hundred and fifty years the world has come within a knife's edge of war a dozen times, and certain convenient deaths are the only thing that nudged us back from that edge. It was a system. We can trace it. It's real. And it's over."

I do not know Tully Mardi. I babysat him as a child, pulled his hair, but of that stage of his life when he became a person I know nothing. To my eye the Graylaw Hiveless sash around his waist was pure pretense, a way to seem a friend to everyone, while in his heart he encourages atrocities which would make the darkest Blacklaw sick, but that is my hatred talking. Perhaps he means it. Perhaps he has his own reasons for continuing his murdered parents' path. Entrenched as I am on the side which must forever call him Enemy, I cannot know.

"We're still on that knife's edge now." Even Tully sighed before continuing. "We have been for a few years. Peace isn't natural, not in a world where the Mitsubishi are squatting on all the land, where a half billion Utopians spend a giant chunk of the world's income on what everyone else sees as their crackpot Mars obsession, and where a growing third of the human race has pledged allegiance to a dictator who every day acts less like the Emperor of Alexandria and more like the Emperor of Romanova! Only the Saneer-Weeksbooth assassinations have kept us from degenerating into war already. Now we've lost that, and not quietly, we've lost it in a way that leaves us all pointing angry fingers. There have already been deaths: the Salekhard transit system backup crew, some Servicer lynchings; less than an hour ago a guard outside the Mitsubishi Executive Headquarters was killed by a mob throwing stones at the Chief Director's window. This is my last chance to convince you. You shouldn't spend the next few hours glued to the newscast from the Senate hearing, you should spend it barricading your doors, checking your fire extinguishers, teaching yourself basic first aid, and thinking about what side you and your family will be on, because there will be sides! Soon! There will be sides, and war!"

At the Rostra's edge, one could see its keepers exchanging hushed hisses with three Hiveless Senators. What a painful moment for those entrusted with the scheduling of this spotlight of spotlights. The public never stops complaining about how politicians monopolize the Rostra, dooming common citizens to an eternal waiting list. Now that Sniper's influence had handed the stage to a private citizen for once, the mob would not forgive these guardians if they silenced him, yet instinct urged them, and Senator after frightened Senator as well, to cut off Tully's stream of words, which seemed less a speech than a shaman's conjuration, drawing in some waiting doom.

"I'm the Canner survivor!" Tully declared at last; I had wondered how long it would take him to play that card. "I know better than anyone: humans are violent animals. In peacetime that violence gets vented in bar brawls, hate crimes, sports, and, yes, in murders, and the more and worse murderers there are the closer war is to surfacing. The last decades didn't just produce Mycroft Canner, they produced hundreds of thousands of people who idolize Mycroft Canner, who celebrate them, photos, music, movies, plays. Cannerism is a symptom of war waiting to erupt! The Censor may measure it in statistics, but you can measure it yourself in how many people you've seen smile or joke about Mycroft Canner, or Jack the Ripper, or any of these human monsters that some fraction of the world inevitably loves. Mycroft Canner was—is—a monster, the same monster that's forming mobs now in La Trimouille, and Brussels, and Tōgenkyō, that sacks, that pillages, that turned the world into Hell in 1914, and dropped the Bomb on Hiroshima, and Rome, and Washington, and laughed as it raped Ibis Mardi's corpse, and bombed New York after it was evacuated, just to watch the famous skyline burn. We can't delude ourselves into thinking the monster's gone. This world is ready—overready—for war, and it will come, because we are the monsters! Violence, Mycroft Canner, all of it is part of human nature, and it cannot change!"

"But I rehabilitated Mycroft Canner."

Death-soft Jehovah stepped up on the Rostra now at Tully's side. No one would stop Him, not the Senate, not the Rostra Keepers, not while His armband, dense with insignia, bore the sigil of a Graylaw Hiveless Tribune, *Tribunus Plebis,* that inviolate office trusted with the mandate to veto any Senate motion which threatened the freedom of the Hiveless and, through them, everyman. I would not call it hush, but the crowd's tone eased as He appeared, His black figure healing them as darkness heals the closed eye after day's long labor.

"See," He gestured, "here they stand."

Yes, reader, there I followed, at His command, behind Him. My wrists itched beneath the crowd's stare, my ankles too, my flesh insisting I should be bound still in my coffin-cage, as when the world first watched proud Papadelias parade his captive monster—long years ago in your experience, reader, but always yesterday in mine. I could not conceive of a billion people watching. In my mind the thousands blurred into one great eye which pierced through me, like the Great Judge's eye in those dreams I used to have, which others would call nightmares, recurrent the last year before my crime, when I previewed in my sleep the trial which would never come.

"Mycroft Canner . . ." Tully seems to lose the present as easily as I do.

On that platform, as close to sacred as a secular thing can be, my presence was as horrific in his eye as his in mine. "Tribune Mason, you saved Mycroft Canner?"

Jehovah's voice, soft always as if wary of waking some sleeping child, seemed weak and intimate over the sound system designed for rabble-rousers. "Thirteen years ago the public asked the law to take a life in anger. Those who witnessed Mycroft Canner's crimes could imagine no lesser punishment, but you also recognized the tragedy: there was genius in Canner, which could have achieved great things if set on a course to help, not harm. I asked MASON and Chair Kosala to make Mycroft Canner a Servicer. Thanks to their mercy, that genius has helped the world, served others, even saved lives. Death is infinite loss and I will not cheapen it by saying whether Mycroft Canner has yet saved as many lives as they took, but, even if they saved only one, that is a life we would have thrown away if we had fallen back into the old lie that death can undo death."

"But you lied. Tribune, all of you lied to everyone, making us think Canner was dead."

Jehovah seemed the dead one now, as still as stone between Tully and me as we both shook. "The public in its wisdom did not ask My Imperial father what happened to Mycroft Canner. All these years you trusted them to have dispatched justice. I hope you will not now feel that they, or I, betrayed you by substituting mercy. Is My hope wrong?"

My other guilty patrons, Caesar and Kosala, mounted the platform of the Rostra now, the Cousin Chair sharing the Emperor's security on this most tumultuous of days. Caesar's stone poise never changes. As for Kosala, her dark Indian hair worn loose hid most of her expression, but one could guess her feelings well enough from her husband, Censor Vivien Ancelet, who followed a cold and careful distance from his wife. He fidgeted with his dreadlocks, not daring to look at her, nor at the human sea summoned here by the Senate session he had been forced to call. The mob he had predicted, even minimized through careful calculation of the best moments to freeze the market and announce the session, but he had not predicted Tully.

"What Jed says is true," Chair Kosala confirmed. "The Servicer Program—"

"Get off the Rostra, puppet!"

"Charlatan!" Shouts rippled through the crowd.

"We all know what J.E.D.D. Mason's about to report!"

"The CFB is a lie!"

"The Anonymous controls the CFB, and you, Kosala!"

"Why don't you send Brody DeLupa up here, have them tell us what the Cousins think they think!"

The Emperor moved to intervene, but Kosala stopped him with a glance, harsh-seeming from a distance, in which only we beside her could see the glint of tears. "The Servicer Program," she continued, "exists to keep the potential good that convicts can do from being thrown away. There has never been a better use of it than sparing Mycroft Canner. Over the past thirteen years Mycroft has served as rescuer, laborer, translator, guard, continued what could be continued of their victims' works, helped with Brillist studies, the Censor's calculations, research, they even helped Papadelias and Guildbreaker uncover the Saneer-Weeksbooth conspiracy, saving who knows how many hundreds or thousands of people who would have been assassinated in the future. Surely everyone here can agree this is better, not just for Mycroft but for the world, than execution." She opened her arm toward me, the long trail of her Cousin's wrap sweeping out like a robe. "Mycroft, do you have anything to add?"

The gathered masses had surprising patience. I would have expected shouts and curses, but they waited, distant, like parents watching their infant take its first unaided steps, as the strength to speak gathered slowly in my shaking frame. I did shake, though I did not know it at the time. The video shows me, a sickly pale skeleton, digging my fingers into the tired brown hat that I clutched, as if by squeezing it enough I could shrink myself and disappear.

"H-hello. I'm M-Mycroft Canner." The microphones had trouble catching my first words, stifled in my throat as in a dream. "I know I don't deserve to live. I don't ask you to accept what's been done—I wouldn't. All I ask is this: please, blame only me. If the Emperor, Chair Kosala, and Tribune Mason deceived you, they only did it because they believe human beings are better than most of us do. Please don't punish them for having hope. And please don't punish my fellow Servicers either. Three days ago rumors started spreading that I was one of them, and since then six have been killed and hundreds injured by attacks which should have hurt only me, not them. In future if one of you finds me in the street, and asks if I am Mycroft Canner, I swear to you I will not lie, or run, I'll answer honestly, and take whatever punishment your anger wants to give, I deserve it all. But if you find a Servicer who says they aren't me, please believe them. Please don't attack the others. They have no more involvement in this than the bad luck of wearing the same uniform I do."

"Enough, Mycroft," the Emperor ordered. "Encouraging violence against one of my *Familiares* is a crime, even if it is against yourself. And you know you will not walk the streets again."

"Yes, Caesar." The command of silence was as welcome as a shield.

The Enemy stepped forward, or rather lurched forward on the crutches which helped him battle gravity. "Why are you protecting Mycroft Canner, MASON?"

Caesar did not grant Tully a glance. "The Emperor does not discuss the sentencing of *Familiares*."

"But in this case—"

"That is the *Lex Familiaris*, Hiveless," the Emperor snapped. "I will not break it. I will say only that, from now on, I shall never again let Mycroft Canner free to wander in public. Those of you who would use Canner as an excuse to vent on Servicers these violent instincts you're so expert on will find their target lacking, and yourselves prosecuted for your assaults with the full strictness of Cousin's law, and the harshness of my own. Now, leave here, Tully Mardi. The world's eyes, like mine, should be on the Senate and my son's report right now, not you and your vendetta. The Tribune would be within their rights to have you arrested for inciting riot. Go."

Tully smiled, as if he had not felt comfortable upon the Rostra until someone tried to kick him off. "I will not go, MASON, not while you're still hiding the real reason Mycroft Canner targeted my bash'. We predicted that this war was coming all those years ago, and Canner tried to silence us so we couldn't prepare the world for it, just like you're trying to silence me now!"

Mason's fists clenched, but in public he could not contradict the only living Mardi's claims of what the Mardis tried to do.

"You're still deceiving everyone!" Tully continued. "You think I don't have evidence? There's a recording circulating of you, MASON, and J.E.D.D. Mason meeting together with Mycroft Canner in Alexandria, only five days ago, both of you sharing secrets with Mycroft about the Seven-Ten list case, and proving both you and the Censor knew something about the Anonymous and Felix Faust lying about their own Seven-Ten lists, pretending they'd been tampered with, to try to cover up what really happened. You knew then what danger the public was in, and you did nothing!"

You must remember this scene, reader, when I took you into MASON's citadel in Alexandria, and let you hear for the first time the verbal knotwork that is Jehovah's Latin. The recording of that secret conversation had been leaked that morning, timed to do most damage, Perry's doing, or I should say Perry-Kraye, through the complicity of a traitor *Familiaris*,

Antonine Fusilier; MASON has not yet announced whether he will be executed when captured.

The Emperor was stone. "It is not your place, Hiveless, to interpret acts of which you have so little understanding."

"It's not your place to stop me, MASON." One must admire Tully for pressing on while tasting Caesar's anger face-to-face. "The world has a right to know what's going to happen when the Senate session ends today. If I were telling the people to attack the Senate, or to attack you, or Tribune Mason," he gestured at Jehovah, "you'd be right to stop me, but you have no right to keep me from warning the world there's going to be a war."

Martin and Dominic climbed up to flank Jehovah on the platform now, uncomfortable with how His stillness let Tully draw close.

"There does not have to be a war." Jehovah's voice seemed hollow next to Tully's, as a play's printed script reads hollowly without the actor's passion to ignite it. "You are right that history has been one long string of violence, and that this three-hundred-year peace was bought only through blood. That does not mean we cannot make real peace now. When I let Mycroft Canner walk the streets again, they could have tracked you down, Tully, and killed you. They chose not to. When I give my report today, every person in the world will have the choice to hurl hate and stones at whomever they blame, or to refrain. They may refrain."

I suspect Tully had not truly considered Jehovah his enemy until this moment. How dare He make the world think that my redemption proved mankind could be redeemed! How dare He make the world root for me! "Tribune," Tully replied, cold, "only you and the Commissioner General know the full content of what you're about to present to the Senate, so I'll ask plainly: do you honestly believe anyone in the world will be able to take it calmly? Let alone everyone in the world?"

Jehovah's gaze floated somewhere between Tully and the crowd, as if addressing an abstraction. "I would be a poor bailiff for the Humanists if I believed we have already seen the maximum of what a human being can achieve. What I will present today are proofs of what has already been said. Prime Minister Casimir Perry is actually the criminal Merion Kraye. The Anonymous has been secretly propping up the failing CFB for over a century. The Humanists have led Europe and the Mitsubishi in secret assassinations for two hundred and fifty years. These are facts we can endure—whether we will endure them we shall see. This is not the end of peace, it is the first chance we have ever had to make a real peace. In seeing how humanity comports itse—"

I saw red before I registered the sound, circus-bright red like finger paint against the marble, peppered with chunks of yellow-pink as Jehovah's brain spilled across the platform, Martin, Caesar, and myself. A gunshot. I had not heard a proper gunshot since Saladin had knocked the last weapon from Seine Mardi's hand, though the quick shocks of our handguns then were nothing to this blast, which thundered from all sides like God snapping his fingers. Jehovah fell, not dying but dead. His limbs, lifeless in life, convulsed as the nerves' last tangled signals filled his hands and legs with madness, then stillness. Martin and I caught Him between us, the warmth of His blood flowing across our knees. Everyone screamed. Thousands, the Emperor, myself. What mattered, where the microphones were strong enough to pick it up, was what we screamed.

"Jehovah!" That came from the Emperor.

"Jehovah!" from Censor Ancelet as well.

"Jed!" from Kosala.

"*Domine!*" and tears from loving Martin, faster than the rest of us to move past shock to grief.

Tully screamed, no words, just scream, and I likewise lost my many languages as adrenaline and blood-wind flooded my mind with fever.

The crowd too screamed, erupting into stampede as the Forum drained like a fractured water drum.

"Tai-kun!" This last scream rose from Chief Director Hotaka Andō Mitsubishi, who had not been with the others on the Rostra, but now gave away his hiding place watching from the doorway of the Mitsubishi embassy. "Let me go!" he shouted as his own guards dragged him back into the safety of the doors. "My son is dying! Let me go!"

Guards covered the Rostra, human shields pressing us down beneath a wall of uniforms, Masonic gray, Romanovan blue, Senatorial gold, Utopians too, Aldrin, Voltaire, Tully's nameless escorts suddenly visible as they leapt into motion. Only Dominic escaped the defensive prison, hurling his would-be protectors bodily aside as he leapt up onto the Rostra's railing to face the assassin. « Blasphémateuse! »

Sniper, rising, smiled at the compliment. It had lain in wait six hours, motionless beneath a camouflaged tarp on the roof of the law courts which stood to the other side of the Rostra, opposite the bustling Senate House. The proud assassin let its cameras rise around it now, broadcasting to all the world the clean pride on its face, and the twitch of its delicate nose as it scented gunpowder rising from the rifle, enormous in its arms. Sniper's Olympic medals are in pentathlon and pistol, not rifle, but I have watched it train in rifle too, freezing dead for the instant of the shot, even its heartbeat kept on hold for that immeasurable fraction when the weapon fires. With that skill in Sniper's arms, eighty meters' distance, and screaming innocents crowded on a balcony just below Sniper's rooftop perch, little wonder the guards hesitated before firing back. That vital half-second let Sniper slide from its exposed vantage on the roof's center peak down to the cover of the flat portico roof.

"The danger's over, friends, stay calm!" it called, lowering its weapon and relaxing in the cover of the portico's statue-studded gutter rail. "Sorry to startle everyone. I am— Hey!" Sniper jumped at the gray-purple flash of a phasing stun-rifle, fired by one of Caesar's guards, a modern marvel capable of passing clean through stone, but useless if it cannot find its mark. "I said stay calm!" the assassin snapped, its nose wrinkling like a child teaching a smaller child how the game is played. Too fast for us to see the means, it activated one of Cato's masterpieces, six devices hidden around the Rostra, each no larger than a grapefruit, whose activation filled the air with electric sting, and fried all the electronics around the Rostra: the cameras, microphones, trackers, and all the elegant, nonlethal weapons carried by the guards.

Sniper waited for its own cameras to take over the severed video circuits and route its voice and image to the watching world. The portico was a perfect stage, packed below with crowds and columns, but flat and open on roof level, enough like a sports track to make our athlete feel at home. "Much better. Hello, friends and foes. I am Ojiro Cardigan Sniper, thirteenth O.S." Its perfect doll's face smiled softly to the cameras and the world. "I'm sorry. I know this is going to break a lot of hearts, but I swore an oath to protect the seven Hives, and my Hive most of all. That duty comes before all others, even my fans. I am the current leader of the Saneer-Weeksbooth bash' assassins, a position called by the title of O.S. Many of you don't agree with what we've done in the past, killing unknowing individuals to protect unknowing masses, but that's over. Today is different. You may not like it, but Tully Mardi's right, even the best parts of history have had a little violence. All free peoples in every age and every continent have agreed that assassins are necessary for one purpose above all others: to kill tyrants. That's what I've done today. You've all been deceived. There was a conspiracy in this Seven-Ten list mess, a much darker one than my bash' and Hive committing homicides to protect the world. The real goal of the conspiracy was to expose us and the CFB in order to rip four of the seven Hives apart, and make J.E.D.D. Mason king of what remains!"

It is only thanks to the recordings that I can include these words, reader, for I heard none of them. Sniper had chosen its bullet well, explosive, scattering Jehovah's skull and its precious contents across the stone like storm's detritus abandoned on a beach. Ἄναξ Jehovah's warm blood drenched me, pouring like rain from the wreckage of His head as His heart kept up its duty, pointless now. My own body failed, wracked by pain and panic more physical than mental as I felt the vital core within me stop. As a long run makes even simple breathing a challenge, now an unimaginable pressure made everything impossibly hard: seeing, hearing, sorting touch from pain, supporting Jehovah's lifeless weight, supporting my own. I collapsed on the stone, my vision fading into neither bright nor dark, just fading. All I could think was that my fears were true. The Will Which Rules This Universe had sentenced me to death thirteen years ago, but Jehovah pitied me and made me His, and from that moment it was He, not This Universe's God, Who gave me life. Now He was dead, and all He made would die with Him, including me. His universe must be dying too, somewhere unreachable, those marvels He had half explained to me in shards of failing language: gradients of complexity, sentiences reveling in themselves without the impediments of Distance or of Time, a better universe, infinity of Good and Kindnness such as we will never know, lost. He had been so careful all His life, no sports, no unhealthy food, no rough play, riding only Utopian cars, not out of knowledge of the assassins, but fear that an accident, however improbable, in claiming Him might claim all His Creation. I wanted to pray that it not be so, that the true Jehovah might continue in His own world, He and His creations, separate and safe despite the death of flesh, but only This Universe's God remained to hear, and what could He do for us?

"Mycroft!" Martin did his best to catch me as I fell, and I remember wondering why the motion of his face was pale and slow.

"Their pacemaker!" The Censor was the first to realize. "The blast shorted Mycroft's pacemaker!" Strong hands caught me from all sides, good Vivien's strongest, like sun-warmed wood among reeds. "Lay them side by side." I saw him lean over me, angry, and I remember thinking he must want numbers from me, that I was late for my shift, or dozing in the Censor's office, drifting off halfway through an article. "Stay with me, Mycroft!" he cried. "I won't lose both of you, not in one day!"

"Then get out of the way!" Bryar Kosala shoved her husband aside, the arts of first aid ready in her hands. Flocking Utopians supplied all she needed, drawing medicine's clean tools from their coats, their many nowheres reduced to static, short-circuited by Cato's genius devices which Sniper had used to cripple MASON's guards, the Rostra's guards, and me.

"Utopian!" Dominic seized the nearest of them, Aldrin, by her coat of living static and pointed to Sniper's rooftop. "Give me a gun!"

Aldrin froze, the others too, feeling the world's eye on them. Gunpowder, of course, was unaffected by Cato's invention, as perhaps were new technologies: electron guns, magnetic pistols, inventions which a peaceful Hive should not have had concealed beneath their Griffincloth.

"Don't," MASON ordered, cold. His guards had dragged him to shelter behind the Rostra but could not shift him further, the sight of Jehovah's body filling his iron frame with a frenzy his six guards could barely match. "Not here."

Dominic turned a fraction of his red-hot hate on Caesar. "You choose them over Him?" He did not wait for a reply, but leapt from the Rostra, clawing his wild way across the backs and shoulders of those too fascinated by the blood to run. Does it surprise you that the bloodhound leaves Jehovah's side? That he does not stay, like Martin, clutching his Master's lifeless hand, or sobbing on his knees? You think perhaps that he has given up on his Master, turned to revenge now that fact has stripped hope. Not so. Dominic saw no damage or danger in Jehovah's assassination, only blasphemy. His mind had never recognized, even imagined, any Power other than Jehovah, so it could not register the concept that his God might die. His fingers, which did not care if they were scraped or broken, made a quick climb of the double porch of the basilica, using bystanders as footholds as he scrambled toward the infidel.

"J.E.D.D. Mason's real name is Jehovah Epicurus Donatien D'Arouet Mason." Sniper still faced the floating cameras and, as rumor spread across the Earth like an electric plague, he reached the largest audience a single person had commanded since Emperor Mycroft MASON during the Set-Set Filibuster two hundred years before. "The mother who gave their child a name like that," it continued, "is the leader of the conspiracy. They call themself Madame D'Arouet these days, but their birth name is Joyce Faust, one of Felix Faust's ba'sibs. Joyce Faust left Brill's Institute at nineteen and studied to be a sensayer, but instead of getting licensed they became a Blacklaw, moved to Paris, and founded the brothel where you saw all your leaders meeting in secret yesterday." At Sniper's cue the cameras split screened, showing again Ganymede and savage Perry-Kraye toppling through the shattered window at Madame's. "I'm glad now that I brought my cameras there, since now we can show you the truth. Madame has a network of clients—spies—in every Hive, in Romanova too, thousands of them, many in high positions in the government. Madame controls them using a horde of ba'kids, if you can call them that, children they engineered and trained at their brothel like set-sets, teaching them sensayer techniques and antiquated gendered sex tricks to make them experts at manipulating people using seduction and religion. Danaë Mitsubishi is one of them. Danaë helped make Hotaka Andō Chief Director. President Ganymede was also one of them, but broke away, and has been working secretly as much as they could to free the Humanists from Joyce Faust's conspirators without them noticing, but they did notice. That's why Joyce Faust decided to expose O.S. They'd rather destroy the Humanists than lose control of us. And here's another of their creations!"

Sniper pointed as Dominic hauled himself onto the roof, like a monster from the sea's depths hauling its black bulk on deck.

"See!" Sniper continued. "This is Dominic Seneschal, one of Joyce Faust's favorite creations. Look at them, look at *him*, wearing all the class and gender markers of the old days when people made slaves of each other. This Dominic was sent by Joyce Faust to corrupt the Conclave Head, Julia Doria-Pamphili, got them to do all the sick things you heard about in the arrest reports, and twisted them into manipulating their parishioners and the Conclave itself for Joyce Faust too. And now they've come to kill me rather than let me finish telling you the truth!"

Dominic did not answer the charge with words, but with his rapier, which has killed four Humanists and two Mitsubishi in legal duels, and I know not how many Blacklaw Hiveless in the war of all on all they so enjoy. There was no joy in Dominic's thrust today, though, none of the elegance which makes a master duelist an artist rather than a thug, just thirst to see the infidel destroyed. Sniper parried. The sportsman in it would not counter blade with bullets, but brought out its epée, that same hilt which had won it the silver in 2450, though this time with a razor combat blade. Sniper had dressed for the occasion, wearing the jacket portion of its fencing whites from the Olympics, with its riding pants below, and the light runner's shoes which had carried it the final three thousand meters to Olympic silver. Detractors claim that Sniper chose the Modern Pentathlon as its Olympic event out of weakness, that, lacking the natural talent or physique to excel at any one sport, the celebrity took advantage of its wealth to train in five; other critics, more vicious, say greed was its motive, since having multiple uniforms lets it sell more dolls and posters. Not so. I doubt if anyone since the baron who invented the event has viewed the pentathlon so sincerely as a test of military excellence: fencing, shooting, riding, swimming, running—the skills an old-fashioned soldier trapped behind enemy lines needed to fight for life, escape, and country. Others may whine that Sniper dishonored the sacred spirit of the games by staining its Olympic whites with blood that day, but that core of Humanists who still answer to 'Olympian' understood, and cheered.

"Joyce Faust's conspiracy had only one real goal," Sniper continued, jabbing with blade and words together, "to make Jehovah Mason ruler of the world by ripping down those Hives that can't be controlled, and tricking the remaining Hive leaders into choosing Jehovah as their successor before they realized the others intend to do the same!"

Dominic snarled, striking for Sniper's head, but the athlete had not sparred a decade and learned nothing. It ducked and, with a quick foot, flipped up the bulk of its discarded rifle, so the weapon tumbled against Dominic's shins. Dominic fell to his knees but kept his blade, a brief defeat, but enough for Sniper to flit out of range and loose another barrage of truth.

"It's an elegant way to conquer the world, I'll give Joyce Faust that." Sniper glared over at its enemy, half smiling. "Tell me, Dominic, I'm sure you of all people know: how did Joyce Faust convince Cornel MASON to adopt their child? Precedent says the Emperor can't pass power to a *Porphyrogene*, but one look down there's enough for anyone to tell whose name is really in the *Sanctum Sanctorum* in Alexandria." Sniper pointed with its blade at MASON behind the Rostra, his face slick with tears. "Is Joyce Faust still sleeping with the Emperor? Or did they only do it back around when Jehovah was born? Nothing like sex to make a man consider a child theirs, whatever DNA says."

"Blasphemy!" Dominic lunged like a mantis. "Thou, worm, hast put Tully Warmonger on the Rostra, risking World War, to lure *Maître* Jehovah to thy trap! He came today to bring peace to mankind, and thou interruptest that gift and assaultest His flesh, for what? To distract the masses from the exposure of thine own crimes! Villainy! Treason! A thousand times treason!"

Treason was a strange choice. Technically assault on a Romanovan Tribune was High Treason, but I suspect Dominic had in mind the more basic treason of a creation attacking the God Who had adopted it and its world, abandoned, as it seemed, by its own Maker.

"You're the one trying to distract the masses," Sniper shot back. "We all just heard Hotaka Andō say they think Jehovah—Tai-kun—is their child." Sniper retreated around the square track of the porch roof, teasing Dominic's blade with swift taps too irregular for its opponent to guess which might become a deadly thrust. "Madame even had Danaë make sure Andō wouldn't sire any other heir. Your Jehovah Mason would have inherited all Andō's shares and clients, and Andō even let them sit on the Directorate, the unofficial Tenth Director, poised to take control of the Mitsubishi when the other nine are arrested for their involvement in the assassinations."

Dominic slashed hard, taking advantage of his rapier's weight, which threatened to knock the light sport epée from Sniper's hand. "That has always burned thee, hasn't it, blasphemer? That there was an extra voice in the Directorate which would never accept murder as a means. How many more problems wouldst thou and thy base masters have tried to solve through blood if *Maître* Jehovah's Love for humankind had not restrained thee?"

Sniper paid back the taunt by scoring the first touch, its blade sipping blood from Dominic's elbow. "I cracked Gordian's files. Felix Faust has already assigned 'J. E. Donatien Mason and associates' as Gordian's new Brain-bash'. That includes you, doesn't it, Dominic? Is it fun being in Gordian's controlling think tank?"

The injury did not slow Dominic, or speed him, his rage already the maximum flesh can conjure. "Violating Romanova alone is not enough for thee, is it? Thou'rt set on wounding every Hive before thou goest down, just like thy beloved Mycroft Canner!"

No taunt could divert Sniper's momentum. "The Humanists and Cousins are too democratic to be controlled, so Madame's trying to destroy us outright. Utopia's too small to stand alone when all the other dominoes go down, and, as for Europe, I thought you were planning to tear Europe down too, until I snagged a hair sample."

Dominic's lunge grazed Sniper's arm. "Enough, worm!"

"With Casimir Perry and the whole of Parliament hauled off as criminals, Europe will be left traumatized, leaderless, hungry for a savior. Madame expects they'll come to heel as soon it comes out . . ."

"Enough!"

". . . that Jehovah's real father is the King of Spain!"

Dominic flailed, not caring if the epée pierced his shoulder so long as his rapier bit back at the blasphemer. It was not Sniper tipping Madame's hand which spurred this rage, I think, but seeing damage done to the honor of one of the few men Dominic had been conditioned to respect. No one imagined that His Majesty Isabel Carlos II had lived a widower these many years without some company, but to have his indiscretion exposed so basely, a mistress of ill repute, a bastard Son already come of age, the King's intimate secrets shouted across Romanova's rooftops like some schoolyard scandal, that made the courtier within Dominic burn. Doubtless you, progressive reader, see little crime in His Majesty's transgression. To the contrary, you admire the King's steadfastness in refusing to marry any other woman while Jehovah's mother lived, and admire too the care he took to see the Son he could not rear at least be raised as another monarch's Son. So thought the crowd, the world, looking, not at the shattered corpse, but at the photo archives, videos, the shape of Jehovah's lips, His hair not quite black, the royal resemblance, unthinkable before, now obvious. Chaos feeds that species of love we call nostalgia, nostalgia for trust in this case, for honor, for good leaders who were also good men: Thomas Carlyle, Mycroft MASON, and the many Spanish Kings and Queens who had served and protected the Hive system since its beginning. How proud would that proud ancestry have been to see a Prince of their blood, even a Bastard, deliver to the Senate the long-overdue truth about the assassinations, and so end centuries of murder. Now He would not. Across the Forum, fear's quick breathing, which had kept the cowering crowd mute, gave way to tears for the King He would have made.

"Where's the ambulance?" the Censor screamed, half to the guards, half to the heavens. "Where are the police?"

The ring of guards, clustered like cypress roots around the Rostra, wondered the same, trying trick after trick to awaken their dead trackers and contact the cars which should have come by now to spirit their charges to safety.

"Look at the sky!" someone cried. "The cars!"

Even in my state I saw them, hundreds, thousands, wild, round, pregnant like bombs, too chaotic in their courses for the eye to distinguish flight from falling. The lowest of the mad cars nearly grazed the Romanovan rooftops, stripping flags from flagpoles with their winds, while higher swarms sliced the clouds into grids. The sky was full, not a layer of steady traffic, not flocks of cars dispersing after a game, but full of cars, from the ground to the highest fringes where atmosphere gives way to dark.

"It's the Saneer-Weeksbooth computers!" Papadelias arrived at last, charging on foot down from his office at the best sprint his century-old bones could muster. "Sniper must have set the program before fleeing the house. They've launched the whole reserve, a billion cars flying wild, blocking everything, emergency zones, Utopian airspace, everything. We don't dare launch an ambulance, it would be hit in seconds. We tried calling a civilian car, but the network is rejecting new calls, not just here, everywhere. Cars already in flight won't land, and new ones aren't accepting passengers. The world's shut down."

Panic followed, cities not yet strangling but feeling the threat of strangulation, as when the heart has just failed and the body cramps by instinct knowing it will soon starve. That sky, streaked with heedless blurs, is now the most common nightmare image of our time. Everyone saw it, in the street, through windows, the last ignorant remnants startled from play or sleep by half reports: "The cars have stopped!" "They shot Tribune J.E.D.D. Mason on the Rostra!" "There's chaos in Romanova!" Experts tell us it was not those first minutes' freeze that did the real economic damage, but the panic as the whole world dropped its work, huddled in corners, jammed the network with calls to friends and bash'mates, as a population of ten billion all at once needed to find their loved ones safe. One billion had watched Tully on the Rostra—eight billion now found the channels that showed Sniper.

"I wish there had been another way to end this, but there wasn't." Sniper smiled as decades of training left it breath enough to preach, while its opponent panted. "As long as Jehovah Mason lived, the Hive leaders would have kept trying to make them their heir, and Joyce Faust's army of client-spies would have kept trying to destroy any Hive that didn't capitulate. Jehovah Mason would either inherit or destroy all seven, that was the plan. Tomorrow I'm sure leaders and experts will line up to question my evidence and motives, but don't let anyone persuade you that the global coup I stopped today would have been anything less than the total destruction of the Hive system. They'll say it's not a coup if everyone was willing to give Jehovah Mason power. They'll say Jehovah Mason was a good person, wise, competent, the best leader we could have had. They'll say most of the Hives would still have existed, even flourished, even if they all had one leader. They're wrong." An angelic calm dawned on Sniper's face. "The Hives are separate because they stand for separate things. I'm a Humanist. I'm not taking orders from any Mason, and I don't think a Mason should take orders from a Humanist. Different Hives think differently, and need to be led by people who think differently. It doesn't matter how wonderful or competent Jehovah Mason was, no one can think seven ways at once. The Hive system made monarchy popular again by eliminating the risk of tyranny, since if a bad Emperor came along, all the Masons would just switch Hives, but free choice requires options to choose from. Combining all Hives under a single ruler would leave this world no better than back when geographic nations gave people no choice. That's why my bash' has spent the last twelve generations killing people whose existence, whether they intended to or not, threatened to destroy the freest civilization—no, the *only* free civilization—that's ever existed. That's why Jehovah Mason had to die."

Dominic's blows grew fierce and faster, the rounded guard of Sniper's sword ringing like a bell in a child's abusing hand. Rage is an asset in the kind of rough, animal combat Saladin and I perfected, but fencing is an art, and Dominic's rage contaminated his stance as roughness muddies paint. Sniper lunged, a deep strike which skewered Dominic's wrist. The rapier fell from fingers no longer properly connected to the muscles which give grip its strength, but that would not stop Dominic. He hurled the weapon as it fell, and, as Sniper blocked the throw, Dominic flailed with his remaining hand and seized the blade of his opponent's sword. Sniper gave the hilt a twist, but pain could not dislodge the zealot. Sensing bloody fists dangerously close, Sniper released its sword and leapt off the rooftop onto nothing. The crowd screamed, then screamed more as the expected plummet turned instead to flight. Sniper ran across the empty air, as if that eternal inner flame which fires each new generation's athletes to break record after record had at last defeated gravity. Watch the footage in slow motion if you can, see how, like a dolphin chasing currents invisible within the sea, the practiced symmetry of Sniper's footfalls chased the wind. That wind turned out, in fact, to be a plank covered in Griffincloth, laid invisibly between the rooftops to enable Sniper's swift escape. I must point out, reader, the inhuman confidence it takes to sprint unflinching at Olympic speed along a walkway less than a meter wide and completely invisible, with only precipice below. I could not do it, nor could Dominic, who groped after his prey, marking the invisible path with his own blood as he lumbered forward over the heads of the crowd and stunned police. Even without cars, the cops had come, and they had almost finished surrounding the law courts, prepared to storm the roof. Now they could only watch their quarry soar over their heads to safety like some destructive angel, which does Providence's dirty work, then retreats to heaven beyond the reach of Earthly law.

Papadelias cursed fiercely, brightly, rich colloquial Greek burbling from him as this crisis-of-a-century fired his old bones with a vigor almost as fresh as youth. "Third squad stay on the ground," he ordered, "follow Sniper close as you can on foot. Ripper, Stark, and Bolenge, take Tully Mardi into custody. Everyone else, get the VIPs into the Censor's office, then lock it down. The Senate's already sealed."

Kosala seized Jehovah's limp arms and mine. "We can't move them without stretchers!"

Papa nodded to his men to drag her off by force. "Mycroft, can you hear me?"

I had heard all, and seen, but only now grew strong enough to speak. "Bridger."

I did not summon him. Rather, I named him when I saw him before me, the hood of the invisibility cloak falling back from eyes too tear-red any longer to look blue. He was above us, wracked with sobs, Hermes's winged sandals fluttering in protest as he made them descend toward the blood-smeared stone. "It's my fault!"

The guards drew their nightsticks at once.

"Let them through!" I cried, and mercifully Caesar cried it also, for my voice was too weak to reach even the nearest ear. "That's Bridger! Let them through!"

I wonder what the others must have thought, Martin, Bryar, Vivien, our Utopian guardians who found themselves hurled out of the way by Caesar's hands as this strange child descended with his play-stained child's wrap, and winged feet, and tears.

"It's my fault!" Bridger cried again. I doubt I could have understood words so twisted by sobs if I had not known his voice better than any other. "Mycroft, it's my . . . I shouldn't have . . . I didn't know . . ."

He had the vial already in his hand, potion bubbling like the part of flame that is more liquid than destruction. It had no scent as he uncorked it, but, as he poured it over the wreckage of Jehovah, the air's taste brightened, as when the Sun, emerging from cloud, makes spring grass tint the air with freshness. The Censor yelped feeling His dead hand awaken, fingers wriggling as the nerves which commanded them rethreaded themselves. The core of the brain regenerated first, blooming within the gore like an ugly orchid. All the nearby cameras were fried, but several spectators on balconies managed to record the restoration, and, with enhancement, one can see individual little arteries branching through the yellow-gray brain mass which swelled like rising dough. The miracle did not rewind the wound, did not draw the blood and shards of shattered skull back in, but grew replacements, the skull reknitting even as it rested blood-drenched on the pillow of its own discarded gore. It was not fast, Jehovah's resurrection. God can create a cosmos in an instant, but to let us understand, Caesar, Censor, Papa, Kosala, Tully, to etch His miracle into all our memories beyond the possibility of doubt, that took time.

"I'm sorry!" Bridger's words were shrill, like a cheap flute. "I shouldn't have let it happen! I just wanted everyone to be okay, but everything I do just wrecks things!" His nose was running, the parent in me noticed that.

I was not strong enough to reach his hand, but managed to brush his knee with feeble fingers. "Don't let Sniper see."

Papa understood my warning faster than the boy. He ordered the wall of bodies closed around us, the static curtains of Utopian Coats overlapping to shroud the scene from the assassin, still retreating from a foe it thought well slain.

The rooftops of the Forum were Sniper's playground now, path after invisible path tying building to building as it zigzagged an escape too tangled for the police to follow. Dominic plowed on, gaining ground as he grew used to the invisible paths, as if the blood he lost with every step just made him lighter. The world's eyes followed them, not us, missing the miracle as their darling-turned-villain raced for its life. Sniper ran out of roofs in the end, the Cousins' offices in the Temple of Venus & Rome marking the back limit of the Forum. Here Sniper vaulted down, not to the ground, but onto the back of Almirante, Sniper's favorite practice steed, a tall, gray Hanoverian gelding, and now the fastest vehicle in Romanova. Some have criticized the lapse in security that let Sniper set this up, but after decades of Sniper's state-sanctioned antics in the public and private sanctums of every VIP, what guard on Earth would find it strange if Sniper asked to park a horse even in the Emperor's bedroom?

Settled in Almirante's saddle, Sniper paused to flash its pursuer a salute, its own signature mock-pistol hand gesture, half courtesy, half taunt. "Go home, Dominic. We're both done. It's up to the Censor, the Senate, and the world now." It sighed, its doll's face sweet, even here. "It had to be done. Like Tully said, we were at the edge of war already. Even a well-meaning tyrant would have pushed us over. You knew that, but you didn't care."

"Aldrin!" Dominic screamed.

The Utopian needed no more instruction. She dispatched her unicorn, the slender black U-beast flowing dart-swift up the center of the Forum like the shadow of a crashing plane. Dominic mounted roughly, seeming too heavy for the doe-thin skeleton to bear, but whatever clever engineer had given the unicorn its processing power also made its frame stronger than Nature could. Sniper smiled at the sound of hoofs behind it, and led the chase, leaping rails and food carts and giving the young capital its first taste of the thunder of cavalry. The cameras and the crowd's eye joined the chase, or half the crowd's at least, for by now not a few of you had noticed something happening upon the Rostra.

"Domine?" Martin was the first to dare call to the reconstructed corpse.

It was hard to spot vitality returning to a body so lifeless even in life, but even Jehovah's Will could not keep His eyes from twitching to blink the blood away. *"Permanebam."* That was the word His lips formed first, even before breath had quite moistened them again. 'I continued,' there's a rough translation, 'I remained, endured, persisted—though this flesh died, I and My universe lived on, as you and I had so long hoped.' If English had a word for such an idea, Jehovah would have used that.

"Jehovah!"

For a few moments, the joy of His return drowned the shock of the miracle. Family crowded around Him, Censor and Kosala weeping freely as relief channeled their terror into happy tears. Caesar was quiet. He had understood what this miracle child was when he appeared, and, while joy for his Son's restoration crusted his eyes with salt, his mind turned already to what the world must do now that the Truth was known.

The world was not slow to start. "Did you see that?"

"J.E.D.D. Mason's okay!"

"Their brain, it was blown out! I saw!"

"It grew back."

"What did they do?"

"Was it the Utopians?"

The universal skepticism of our time would not let the word 'miracle' crop up so soon. Over the next weeks a credulous minority would begin to admit that they believe, and who knows how many others believe in secret now, afraid of seeming irrational before their peers. But still the majority prefers its other explanations, a hoax, an optical illusion, or some hidden healing technology Utopia will not yet share. You may believe or not as you will, reader. Had This Universe's God wished you to know Him without doubt, He would have worked His miracle before your eyes. Still, think, reader—whose side is Reason on? Her indispensable disciple John Locke, who freed a drowning Europe from the grip of Hobbes's dark sea, argued that no one would knowingly lie and claim they saw a miracle if saying so gained nothing while maintaining the lie cost dear; Reason and self-interest are against it. Were Locke with us today, he would no doubt turn Ockham's razor upon your disbelief too, and make you answer which is more plausible, that, as all of us who saw firsthand insist, God worked a miracle? Or that all Earth's leaders are willing to be called insane because they can find no less embarrassing lie to conceal the fact that the Utopians are hiding some amazing technological healing serum which, despite their vendetta against Death, they refuse to share with anyone besides J.E.D.D. Mason?

"You're Bridger, aren't you?" Papadelias laid a hand on the boy's shoulder, though he admits he half expected the child to vanish like a dream before his touch. "Come on, kid, let's get you inside somewhere safe."

"Get away!" Thor's strength in Bridger's arm hurled Papa back hard enough to sprain his shoulder. "Don't touch me! None of you! Stay back!" He brandished his magic wand, pregnant with spells more ominous than bullets.

Violence woke Kosala from her wonder. "What did you do?"

"I won't let anybody have it, no one!" Bridger clutched the resurrection vial in his other hand, the potion's residue glittering on the glass like a skin of sparks. "You're not ready for it yet! You're barely holding the world together with the people it has now. You think you can handle bringing everybody back?"

Jehovah's hand, shaking from the agony of circulation returning to fingers recently dead, locked around Bridger's thin wrist. ⌜"«¿Why tamdiu Me esperar nado to osshatta dixisti?»"⌟

Bridger reeled, hurling himself back as if Jehovah's black gaze burned.

"English, Ἄναξ," I urged. "Use English."

Jehovah flinched, as if the task stung like peroxide on a wound. "Why did You make Me wait so long?"

"I'm not God!" Bridger screamed. "I don't know what They're doing! I don't know what I'm supposed to do!"

If you had seen Jehovah's face as He tried to simplify his thoughts, reader, you would have felt as if you watched the captain of a crowded life raft, threatened with sinking by the mass of those who try to claw their way aboard, whose destructive desperation forces the shaking captain to shoot them, one by one. "As if it were not cruelty enough that change in time cannot create without destroying, once again He makes the agent He sends to bring about His better world love this one."

Bridger screamed. I never finished telling you the tale of Sadcat, did I? Years ago Bridger tried to heal a maimed cat by wrapping it in the plush fleece of an uninjured toy cat, but the healthy creature his miracle created had no sign of the personality of the original. 'Sadcat' we named it, a new creature inhabiting the stolen body of the old, while the original vanished, unmade, victim of a mistake Bridger seemed somehow unable to undo. The child screamed for hours when he realized he'd unmade a living thing, screams I can still hear, his small frame shaking in my arms. This scream surpassed that. Jehovah held fast to Bridger's wrist, the first full-body effort I had ever seen Him make, but, even with the fire of absolute Will within it, His human hand could not match Bridger's magic strength. The child pulled free.

"Bridger, wait!" I cried, but the weight of heart attack lead-dense across my chest twisted what should have been shout into dreamlike whisper.

"I don't want to destroy the world! You don't know I can really make a better one!"

"Wait!"

He vanished, pulling the invisibility hood over his head, so no eye, nor sensor, nor keen-nosed U-beast could find a trace of him. That did not mean he could not hear me.

"Come back, Bridger!" I shout-whispered. "Stay! There's no point hiding when the world's already seen you. You're here for each other, don't you see? Out of all the points in history This Universe's God could have chosen to show Himself, He did it when you could meet Jehovah and Jehovah you!"

Jehovah hushed me with a soft, black glance, then, in five perfect words selected from the six languages both He and I commanded, He ordered me to fulfill the purpose for which This Universe's God had forged me, by finding and protecting Asclepios son of Apollo, kindest of the gods, who, in his zeal to help mankind, would even break Zeus's law and raise the dead. It was a far better name than the one the child had chosen for himself.

Caesar, the Censor, Bryar, Papa, even Aldrin seized me as I tried to rise. "Where do you think you're going?"

"I must find Bridger."

"Not in your condition."

"I'm fine."

"You're not fine, you're having a heart attack."

I tried to pull free. "It was just a little spasm, not a full attack. I know the difference."

Their hands only grew tighter around me, and I could see the Censor's face and Caesar's darken with that concern mingled with rage which my constant self-neglect so often caused.

Papa frowned most gravely. "This happens every time you slip your tracker, doesn't it?"

"Their tracker?" Caesar repeated.

"This is how they slip it. I figured it out this morning when we caught one of their accomplices. Mycroft rewired their pacemaker to let them synchronize their pulse to someone else's, then they can slip their tracker off onto the other's ear without missing a beat." Papa reached down to the notch Saladin had bitten from my ear, the skin below sensitive where the tracker should have rested. "That's what this is for. We caught one of the other Servicers today wearing Mycroft's tracker in addition to their own, and they and half a dozen more of Mycroft's little friends have a nick cut out of the ear they don't wear their trackers on, so they can slip on Mycroft's. Problem is, messing with Mycroft's pulse like that damages their heart. Every time."

I forced them to let me sit up at least, eager to prove that I was ready for my task. "It doesn't spasm every time, Papa. Just sometimes. I'm okay, really. This is important. Let me go!"

Bryar Kosala's swift restraining hand was strongest. "We're taking you to a hospital, Mycroft," she announced with the unimpeachable authority of Mom. "You too, Jed, no objections. You were shot through the head. We won't believe you're okay until at least three doctors say so."

The Utopians closed possessively around the most promising medical miracle in history. "Our hospital is close."

She who oversaw forty-four of the hospitals in the city frowned at the mention of the forty-fifth, but knew when not to argue. Utopia's Nowhere Princes already crowded around Jehovah, scanning Him and the gore on the ground around with every instrument they carried, but snakes and sprites and Pterascanadons were nothing to the infinity of electric senses possessed by that block-long golem of distilled science we call a Utopian hospital. Kosala had to yield. "Fine. Papa, is it safe to move?"

The Commissioner General checked his tracker, still functional, since he had stood far from the discharge of the devices we have sinced named Weeksbooth Counterbombs. "Sniper's long gone, if that's what you mean," he answered. "They had a getaway car hidden in the river, flew off to who knows where, and with the cars still haywire we can't pursue."

I would smile later thinking on it: the athlete in Sniper, who had shot, fenced, run, and ridden its way to victory today, could not resist completing this last pentathlon with a swim. At that moment, though, I had no spare thoughts for Sniper, or anything besides the mandate which, for once, came equally from This Universe's God and from Mine. "I must return Bridger to Jehovah."

The Censor's soft hands caught me as I tried to rise once more. "Soon, Mycroft, as soon as the doctors say—"

I pinned him in a choke hold, my right elbow crushing his throat while the heel of my left hand stood ready to smash his nose up into his skull. "I'm sorry. I must go at all costs, and if Jehovah's universe continued safe even while His mortal flesh was dead, then, even if one of you also happens to be a God, I no longer need to fear that I'll destroy a universe by killing you."

I felt the bite, though not the snake. Voltaire must have planted it on me, one of his Swissnakes, its syringe-fangs loaded with something which made me limp at once, and summoned sleep's darkness soon after. I would not waken for five hours, but they were not wasted. Magnanimous Apollo sat with me, as he often does in fever dreams, rambling about his giant robots, and striding across Mars's soil, and his war, and when I woke I knew, as surely as I knew the task before me, in what hiding place I would find Bridger.

Chapter the NINETEENTH

Seven Surrenders

WHILE I SLEPT, THE WORLD SPENT THESE FIVE HOURS TRYING to make sense of how one woman could have twisted all seven Hives into passing power to a single Youth. Sniper's evidence flooded the net, even as its horse still thundered through Romanova, with Dominic hot on its heels. I will not give you what Sniper did: birth certificates, bank statements, DNA tests, wills—any truffle pig loosed in the archives can uproot such tedium. I was chosen as historian not least because my presumptive madness makes my testimony inadmissible in any court, so there are deeds that I alone may publicize without endangering those I describe. In evidence's place, then (and with the facts as purged of sentiment as I can make them), I offer you these seven scenes, scattered in space and time, which seem to me to be the moments at which each Hive fell.

* * *

Humanists first. It took the sweat-drenched Humanist Vice President and Proxy for the Anonymous Brody DeLupa only two hours to set himself up on the Senate steps, a stone's throw from the police barricade around the Rostra, still wet with Jehovah Mason's blood. "Murder on top of murder!" he raged, sputtering as he felt the mob hang on his words. "And when we finally expose the truth, they choose as their next victim Tribune Mason, the one good person responsible for trying to end their string of murders!"

The crowd around the Rostra had not so much thinned as changed, those who had endured the chaos firsthand wandering home to huddle with their bash'es, while, from the capital's depths, the morbid and the starstruck arrived in wide-eyed droves. The skies at least were clear. The Utopians had worked their magic, forty-seven minutes to cleanse the Saneer-Weeksbooth computers and restore that flying bloodstream which makes our modern world one living thing. At the Censor's urging, the Romanovan City Prefect had closed the capital to anyone without a diplomatic, legal, or bash' reason to enter, but that could not exclude the press, nor parasite DeLupa, thirsty for a stage.

"It's unthinkable!" the Vice President railed. "Sniper, who we thought was our brightest star, not just defending mass murder, not just committing mass murder, but crowning it with this attempt on the life of a Romanovan Tribune! Never in my life did I expect to feel ashamed to be a Humanist, but how can I not? We're the guilty ones! Europe and the Mitsubishi were complicit, but Humanists conceived this, Humanists controlled this, Humanists did this. Other politicians may be trying to sugarcoat it, but the Anonymous serves truth, and the truth is that our Hive's most prized conviction, our love of human excellence, has degenerated into a cult of celebrity which hands power to the most charming, regardless of how rotten they are inside. President Ganymede is a mass murderer. Whether they committed the crimes before or after taking office doesn't matter: we elected someone willing to commit mass murder."

DeLupa's hand rose by instinct to the tracker at his ear, reviewing the Anonymous's instructions, perhaps, or the newsfeeds hot with babble as every capital from Brussels to Tōgenkyō swelled with mobs.

"I know how self-serving this must seem," DeLupa continued, "the Vice President calling for the President's arrest, but it isn't what you think. The Anonymous doesn't want you to make me President. The Anonymous doesn't want you to make anyone President. In two hundred and fifty years, the Humanist Hive has not elected a single leader who refused to commit mass murder. Not one in two hundred and fifty years! Europe has had exceptions, the King of Spain, other good people who refused, that's why the so-called Special Means Committee had to run the murders secretly around them. The Mitsubishi hid it from their Greenpeace Directors, knowing Greenpeace has a conscience if the others don't, and the other Directors are chosen through patronage and family ties, so while it's sick that they've all been murderers for centuries, it makes sense, at least, since each murderer gets to groom a murderous successor, it doesn't mean everyone in the Hive is guilty. The Humanists don't have that excuse. We have open elections, the most open in history, and still we elect nothing but murderers! Worse, I . . ." He paused again, perhaps receiving fresh instructions from the Anonymous over the line. "Worse, I know why it's happened, and it's not corruption, or election fraud, or even ignorance. The Humanists elect nothing but murderers because the voters who elect them are all murderers themselves!"

DeLupa hurled a roll of paper down the steps with theatrical gusto, holding the end so the scroll billowed like a streamer in the post-storm wind.

"This has been circulating among the Humanists for decades now," he cried. "It's called the Wish List. If you want someone dead, you put their name on the list. If someone else wants them dead, they add a second vote. The rumor claimed that somewhere out there someone was watching the list and secretly granting these 'wishes.' The Anonymous and I, like many others, always thought this was a sick joke, but now we know it wasn't. The police just found the master Wish List, updated hourly, kept in the Saneer-Weeksbooth bash' computers. This . . . This is . . ." Again he touched his tracker, scowling as if the Anonymous's instructions came over the line too fast for him to follow. "This is not a government scheming to enrich itself, this is private individuals picking victims, and not a few. Each Hive Member can only vote for each name once, so if one name has a hundred votes that means a hundred different would-be murderers have added that victim to the list. The highest ranked name has nine hundred and eighty-nine million, four hundred and eight thousand and sixty-one votes. That's nine hundred and eighty-nine million individual Humanists who have willed to commit murder, at least ninety percent of the Humanist Membership, and we must assume . . . there must . . . be more since . . . since . . ." The red-faced Proxy ripped the tracker from his ear and hurled it on the steps. "Little wonder a nation of murderers would elect a willing murderer to lead them! Even now they're trying to stop me from saying what must be said"—he gestured at his tracker on the ground—"but I won't let them! I'm not directing this appeal to the Humanists, I'm talking to everyone else. Arrest Ganymede, yes, but don't make me President! You trust the Anonymous, I trust the Anonymous. If I became President, the Anonymous through me would lead the Humanists wisely until the next election, but the system wouldn't change! A system that reliably picks murderers, because the Hive members are murderers themselves! The Hive is the problem, this Hive which breeds competition, and glory-seeking, and backstabbing, and idol worship, and will keep producing murderers as long as it exists!"

The crowd on the steps below DeLupa began to churn, and murmur terms of fear.

"I'm not speaking as Vice President anymore!" The Proxy's cheeks puffed like an arriving wind. "I'm repeating the Anonymous's plea: Dissolve the Humanists! Dissolve the Hive! Make all current Humanists into Gray-law Hiveless, at least until they join a new Hive which will give them something better to believe in. They won't keep thinking like murderers without the poisonous Humanist atmosphere to twist them. They need to be split up, offered something better, new ideals, new guidelines. Let them—let us—become Cousins and Masons, and learn from their good models. Dissolve the Humanists! That's the only real way to make the murders stop!"

"Stop this, DeLupa." The bronze Senate doors behind him opened, revealing a wall of Senatorial guards, so polished, so ready, and so adrenalized by the day's danger that one might almost call them soldiers. Ektor Carlyle Papadelias stood at their head. "You don't have the authority to—"

"No one does!" the Proxy shrieked up at the Commissioner General. "Only the crawling, tiresome Senate has the authority to expel a Hive, but it has to be done fast! Now! And if the Anonymous is the only person in the world who dares to try, then—"

"You know the Anonymous has nothing to do with this." Papa scowled. "This isn't their idea, it's yours."

"What are you—"

Papa used his own tracker now to play aloud to the crowd a rough voice, garbled by computer modulation to sound more inhuman than not. "Friends, do not be deceived. I am the Anonymous. DeLupa has been my Proxy in the past, but I did not write the speech they just delivered, nor do I support their call to disband the Humanists. DeLupa is exploiting my name to trick you."

DeLupa sputtered like a rabid thing. "Don't listen! It's a trick!"

Papadelias sighed through his wrinkles like an old birch. "Don't try it, DeLupa. I'm Commissioner General. Everyone knows I know who the real Anonymous is; I have to for security reasons. Just give it up."

The Proxy stumbled as he turned toward his accuser. "Ridiculous! I'm the one who speaks the Anonymous's words! You're just abusing your office so you can prop up a fake Anonymous for your own ends!"

"I will stop you, DeLupa," the digital voice warned, "at all costs. If that requires me to reveal myself, so be it."

"You wouldn't." The Proxy's eyes sought the crowd's support. "Did you hear that? The real Anonymous would never—"

"You think I'm bluffing?" the computer warned. "I won't protect the office of Anonymous at the expense of shattering a Hive. You know there is a protocol if I need to reveal myself. I have already called MASON."

Papa's face reflected the black tone which the Anonymous's distorted words could not convey. "It's true," Papa confirmed, "MASON's in place in Alexandria, at the *Sanctum Sanctorum*, ready to open the vault, and furious that your antics have dragged them away from the hospital where their child may still be dying. I don't think the Anonymous is bluffing. If you push this they'll come out here, slap you across the face, and call you a liar in front of the entire world. Back off, or it's not the Humanists you're going to destroy, it's the office of Anonymous."

One of Papa's men held out a screen which showed the lighthouse tower of gray stone rising in the harbor of Alexandria. A gilded ziggurat crowned the tower, small but flashing angry in the overcast as sunset fired the bellies of the clouds. The guards, ba'sibs of MASON or past MASONs, had already unsealed the vault chamber, a round sanctum, no more than ten paces across, which formed the hollow heart of the gilded pyramid. In this heart's heart, a waist-high block of glass-smooth black technology held in its impenetrable womb the Masonic Oath of Office, and the name of the one who will be next to read it. Not a few of Earth's other Powers prefer sharing the Emperor's security to paying for their own. Earth's other great secrets slept in a ring of vaults nested in the round wall like a columbarium: the list of Gag-genes rested here, the Registry of Sensayers' Beliefs, logs of Censors' Office predictions, the wills and marriage contracts of Earth's remaining monarchs, and in Vault Four the true names of the Seventh Anonymous and their six predecessors. Here, with Jehovah's blood crusting his black left sleeve with brown, the Emperor waited.

"Last chance, DeLupa."

Brody DeLupa refuses absolutely to be interviewed. I do not know why he attempted what he did, whether he was a simple traitor, or whether deep down he believed that the Anonymous would want the Humanists dissolved. Beneath that grotesque shell he might be any kind of man, an innocent appalled to find himself surrounded by murderers, or a viper of Madame's positioned to backstab Ganymede should the Duke President turn rebel. It hurts not knowing, but you feel this all the time, do you not, reader? Frustration's itch as you boil with questions which I and my peers, distant or dead, cannot be made to answer. For your sake I did manage, at least, to ask the Anonymous why he picked DeLupa as his Proxy in the first place. He answered that, of the ambitious young Humanists he had found flocking Buenos Aires, DeLupa had seemed the emptiest.

The Proxy stepped aside, a few steps, just enough to let himself get both Papadelias and the crowd in line of sight. "I am the voice of the Anonymous. I am the one chosen to share their wisdom with the world, not you or anybody else. Dissolve the Humanists. That is the Anonymous's wish, not mine."

I have rarely seen Papa let himself look so tired in public. "MASON, if you would?"

I think the Emperor's silence was plain grief. Most would read rage or

Stoic dignity into the hush as he set chisel to stone, but a man with so few peers, and without ambition's poison in his veins to make him hate them, must mourn seeing one fall. Technology sealed the secrets, layers of ingenious keys and detectors, but the lowest layer was still the simplicity of mortar sealing stone, which crumbled ashlike across MASON's cuffs as he lifted the page within. "On this, the third day of May in the year twenty-four thirty," he read aloud, "I, the Sixth Anonymous, appoint as successor, and Seventh in my line, Vivien Ancelet."

"The Censor?"

No one moved at first, but murmur did not take long to turn its focus on the Censor's office, just out of shouting range along the street behind. Vivien Ancelet emerged, closing the doors behind him with a quick stroke of the old bronze. The crowd was too stunned to part around him, but let him slide between them, so the Censor's Guard struggled to keep pace with him, shoving back the crowds, many of whom reached out for a last touch of his dreadlocks or purple uniform, as this higher office lifted him away. He bent as he reached the steps, taking up the long scroll of the Wish List.

"A...Ab...Ad..." he skimmed aloud, "An...Ancelet: one thousand, two hundred votes for me. B...C...D...Da...De...Seventeen thousand for you, Brody. Ah, and here's your nine hundred eighty-nine million," he pinched the paper to underline the name he sought, "for Mycroft Canner." Vivien Ancelet mounted the stairs. "I don't think any Mason, Brillist, or even Cousin here can claim the Humanists are the only ones who've ever wished Mycroft Canner dead. Am I wrong?" He waited, but trembling DeLupa gave no answer. "I might be wrong. I don't know what this Wish List tells us about the character of Humanists. I'm Earth's greatest expert on big long lists of information, and I still don't know. Neither does the Vice President." He glanced at his Proxy, his face more fatigue than criticism. "Is there really something about the Humanist mind-set that encourages homicide? Or is this list something anyone would sign in jest if they didn't think it was real? I don't know. A couple months of study and maybe Felix Faust and I could figure it out, but raw data like this tells me almost nothing, certainly not enough to call for the dissolution of a Hive." He let the list fall from his hands, its white length stained gray by the rain-wet steps. "We can't handle a change like that right now. Change is the enemy here, too many changes, too big, too fast. Like Tully Mardi said, we've lost O.S., the system that's maintained peace for however long. We might lose the CFB, the heart of the Cousins. We've lost Sniper, that's irreparable now. We're going to lose Ganymede, Chief Director Andō, and Casimir Perry." Still-shy Vivien rocked in place as he spoke, fighting off the instinct to duck behind one of his own guards to escape the swarming cameras. "Now you've lost me, too, at least as your Anonymous. Madame D'Arouet— Joyce Faust—has been exposed. We might lose J.E.D.D. Mason, who, all else aside, kept things civil by making Andō and Caesar and Spain and Felix Faust all think of each other as family. If we don't lose J.E.D.D. Mason, those of you who saw the video of what happened after the shooting know something else very important happened there, something that's going to have huge consequences, perhaps bigger than all the others put together. The best thing we can all do over the next days is take it slow."

Vivien paused here, catching in the corner of his eye Bryar Kosala, who stepped out of the Senate doors behind to watch her husband and lover finally—in the public eye—reveal themselves as one. Those who warn of the dangers of mixing love with politics are right, about cases like this couple at least. Bryar Kosala's face as she stepped out here had the power to make or break her Vivien's speech, which would itself make or break the Humanists. All power here was hers. She might chill him to silence with the cold glare of the Cousin Chair for the Anonymous who undermined her CFB. She might comfort him with the tearful smile of a lover ready to soothe her lifemate's pain. She might stab him with the disinterested stare of a spouse betrayed by the awkward public partnership they had forced on themselves despite Madame's repeated warnings not to let marriage ruin their beautiful affair. Vivien felt the threat she posed to him, the Humanists, the world, his syllables stumbling even as he began to look at her. Whatever her inner thoughts, Bryar Kosala was merciful enough in that moment to wear on the outside the subtle, understated mask of a sympathetic friend. That let him carry on.

"We're all shocked by what's happened," the no-longer-anonymous Anonymous continued, stronger now that love's threat had been diffused, "and our instinct is to want shocking solutions, to destroy the system that's gone so wrong, to purge the guilty, and make something new. We mustn't be so rash. Before you listen to Sniper, or Tully Mardi, telling you a bloody revolution is the only way to make a new world, think about what you'll be giving up: utopia! Don't let one Hive using it as a name fool you, the Mars colony they're building, their space fantasies, those aren't utopia. This is utopia, right here! Right now! We have everything past generations worked for. Human history consisted of exploring, inventing, struggling, progressing inch by inch through toil and sacrifice to achieve what? Longevity, prosperity, safety, family, liberty, culture, art, the leisure to pursue happiness, the end of plague, the end of famine, peace: we have it all!" He gestured at the pseudoancient Senate house behind him. "If I had a time machine I could go back in time and find a king, any ancient king who ever lived, and bring them here and they would weep with envy for what the most modest of us has: a bash'house, warm in winter, cool in summer, comfortable clothes, appliances that do the work of a thousand servants, a bash' we choose, a spouse we choose, laws we choose, a job we choose, and enjoy, and only have to work at twenty hours a week, while the rest of the time we can listen to music at the touch of a button, read any book we want, travel the world in safety, dine as well as kings could, better!" He smiled to himself. "If I were Charlemagne or Julius Caesar I'd abdicate for that. This world is not perfect. It's scarred by mistakes, past and recent, but this is the utopia past generations worked to make for their descendants, not a perfect world, but the best one humanity has ever had, by far. This is the better world that history's future-builders dedicated their lives to making. We cannot throw away, because of two thousand deaths, the legacy which billions died building for us. This world is a utopia, not perfect, not finished, but still a utopia compared to every other era humanity has seen. Calm, slow change is what we need, to make this good thing better, not war, not revolution, not tearing it all down. If we all dedicate ourselves to saving this good world, and to improving this good world, we can preserve the good, and make the bad parts better."

The cheer woke slowly from the crowd, like dawn's incremental chorus. Such a speech deserved a cheer, acceptance, thanks for this benefactor who charged unwilling into the limelight when we needed him. I cheered when I heard it some hours later, though at the moment of its delivery the surgeon's anesthesia held me still. The live crowd around the Senate house was too shell-shocked to burst into anything warm or lively, but applause did come, hollow at first, but it swelled steadily until even Brody DeLupa found himself applauding.

"Anonymous," Papadelias invited, "would you like to come inside and address the Senate?"

Vivien swallowed hard. "I can't be the Anonymous anymore. I already have a successor prepared. The title will pass on to them now."

Papa nodded his sympathy. "Censor, then."

Vivien swallowed harder. "I'm also stepping down as Censor." He raised his eyes to face the crowd again. "I don't want everyone to think the Censor's always been the Anonymous. It was coincidence with me; the skills that let me track the previous Anonymous also caught the last Censor's eye, but that's the only connection between the two offices, and no previous Anonymous has been Censor or vice versa. Anyway, I filed my resignation as Censor as I left the office. My last act as Censor was to place a twelve-month freeze on the Senatorial proportioning. The number of Senators allotted to each Hive will remain locked as it is now. No matter how many people leave one Hive for another, even if one Hive dissolves, or two merge, or who knows what, the governing body that has safely maintained this utopia longer than any of us has been alive will stay in its present proportion, and stay in control. It's my hope this will make people wait, and think, and keep the changes slow. All day today my . . . the Censor's . . . office has been flooded with applications to switch Hives, more than we normally get in a year. If you have doubts about your Hive, there's no reason to switch today, you can switch tomorrow, next week, after six months, after we all know more about everything." He steeled himself, one last deep breath. "I know nobody trusts the Humanists right now. Nobody can trust Ganymede, and after this nobody can trust the Vice President, either." He dug his fingers hard into his Graylaw Hiveless sash. "Before I left my office, I filed an application to join the Humanists. It should be processed within a few days. In that time, the Humanist Senators should have no difficulty passing a vote of No Confidence in the current Humanist government. In the emergency election that follows, if I am nominated for office in the Hive, whether Preisdent or any other office, I will accept, and, since all the other Hives still trust me, hopefully I can help oversee the Humanists as we transition to a system without O.S."

A real cheer rose now, confident, unanimous, and, to not a few of us, frightening.

* * *

«Non, Altesse, les Utopistes et les Brillists sont différents.» (No, Highness, Utopians and Brillists are different.)

"Quomodo?" (How?)

The nurse sighed at her young Charge, eight years old then, too big for her to carry Him as she used to. «'Quomodo' n'est pas français, Altesse,» ('Quomodo' is not French, Highness,) she corrected gently as she set Him on His feet. «Dirons, 'Comment.'» (We say, 'Comment.')

«Comment?» the Child Jehovah parroted.

Felix Faust turned to watch the pair. Do not ask me how the thirteen years between this scene and now have changed Faust, reader; you may as well ask how they have changed the Sphinx. The master of Brill's Institute of Psychotaxonomic Science sat as ever by his window in the *Salon de Sade*, burying his grief over the loss of his prize pupil Mercer Mardi by studying the Flesh Pit where Madame's clients explored the depths of love. "Language trouble again?"

"It's been rough all day, Headmaster." The nurse brushed fluff off Jehovah's miniature jacket, black mourning silk fresh from the tailor's, since my murders were the first time He had needed mourning dress, and at the tender age of eight He had not yet started to demand that His clothes always be the color most different from the Light of This Universe's God. "We just had the most frustrating failure to converse with Papa Andō, didn't we, young Highness?" the nurse prompted.

"Hola, Uncle Felix." Jehovah tried to stop there, but His nurse's expectant frown commanded that He try again. "Vale... Ohayō... Bon... Guten Tag?"

"Guten Tag, Donatien." Faust patted his lap. "Come, sit on my Lap." The master Brillist used German with the boy, that modular, semielastic tongue that gives all nouns the capitalized dignity which its bastard cousin English reserves only for names, Gods, concepts, and the selfish I. "It's not your Fault, we've all had a hard two Weeks."

The Headmaster says he felt Jehovah shiver as He settled into his lap. Fatigue perhaps? Or something subtler? I cannot confirm, for at this moment I was still in my cage in Papa's prison van, dreaming of execution. "It makes no Sense that Things stop," the Child began.

Jehovah's uncle mussed His hair. "I miss Mercer and the Others too."

"How will you stop *Caesari* burying *Appollonem* in Pantheon?"

Faust tapped Jehovah gently on the shoulder, the barest pantomime of a slap. "You're Latinizing again. And why would I want to keep Apollo Mojave out of the Pantheon? It's a reasonable Suggestion, even if Cornel is still thinking with their Dick."

"You need them to be *conspicuousment* Outsiders," the Child answered, "to distract Everyone from noticing *ut* you're also Rivals for the Trunk."

Faust gave his Nephew a reassuring squeeze—back then Faust still thought Jehovah's physical detachment might someday develop toward some second stage. "Slow down, Donatien, one Idea at a time. What is this Trunk?"

"Of the Evolution Tree. A Tree has many Branches but one Trunk. When it's still young you can't tell which of the top Branches will become the Trunk, and which will branch off and lose Momentum. The Dinosaur Branch got as far as Birds, but only Mammals achieved Sentience. Humanity's Tree had many Branches too: Tribes, *archés que, nationesque, religionesque*. Some persist in Reservations, but *yappari* Hives turned out to be the Trunk."

Faust recorded all of this, and wants me to warn you that a mere transcript cannot capture the pauses as Jehovah hunted for elusive words, or the shifts in His tone and body language, almost absent, which Felix Faust, alone of all men, claims that he can read. In the original transcript, Faust also corrects Jehovah's German strictly after every line, but I shall omit this, since you, reader, are not attempting to raise a heptalingual Child.

"I'm not sure if Trees actually grow that way," Faust answered, "but I think I understand."

"*Itaque*, every *via* ... Branch ... worries it might not be the Trunk."

"You mean the Hives?"

"*Viae*," Jehovah corrected. "Branches. Ways. Going Ways. Only the leaving Hives say the Rest are wrong."

"Which Hives do you think are leaving?" Faust asked at once.

"You and Utopia."

Faust stroked the bristle of his chin. "You think we're dying out? I could see that, we are the smallest two."

"Not dying. You leave, explore, *exitis*, go." The Child flexed his still-growing fingers, not an idle fidget but deliberate practice, like an athlete impatient to rehabilitate after an injury.

"The Utopians are leaving, that's true," Faust confirmed. "I doubt if anyone expects many to stay once they have Mars."

"You go too. They go out, you go in." Jehovah illustrated this point, one small hand pointing to the infinity beyond the ceiling, the other to the equal infinity within His uncle's skull. "Either the Trunk is on Earth, or in Space, or Inside with Brain Words. If Either of you is right, the Majority is wrong."

"Majority," His uncle repeated slowly, playing with the word like caramel.

"Histories say scared Majorities hurt Minorities. That's why you hide. Utopia pretends *ut* because they're openly giving Implants to U-beasts they aren't secretly giving them to humans too, and you pretend *ut* because you don't make Set-Sets anymore you aren't making other, stranger Things. They make U-Beast Jokes to make Others forget Mars will be real; you make Number Puzzles to make Others forget your Machine-Brain-Copy will be real too." The Child reached up to touch His uncle's head above the ear, where thinning hair left visible the reddened pressure marks left from the Headmaster's last session with the mind-to-machine experiments that every Fellow at the Institute will claim are nothing. "Gordian isn't in Danger now," the Child continued, "because Utopia is so conspicuous that all the Afraid target them. You don't seem alien because they are more so. You need that. There has to be an Outsider or the next strangest will be named Outsider. If Caesar *Apollonem condit* in Pantheon, *si plus Utopianes* in Pantheon *qu*—" He caught Himself. "If there are more *Utopianes* in Pantheon than Brillists, you will be in Danger."

The Headmaster nodded, a slow commixture of agreement and praise. "Perfect. I'd never have phrased it as Branches and Trunk, but you're right, we do depend on the Utopians to focus Paranoia on themselves."

"How will you stop it?"

The Headmaster sighed. "I don't dare mess with the Pantheon Vote. Cornel MASON is a good Person in most ways, but if they found out I deliberately blocked Apollo from the Pantheon they'd destroy me."

The Child looked at His uncle. "People must not kill, we don't know the full Consequences."

"'Destroy' does not always mean 'kill,'" Faust corrected. "Do you want to help protect us, Donatien? To help protect me and my Hive?"

Jehovah took nine silent seconds to think. "You want me to keep my Fathers friendly *ad* you?"

"That would help, yes, but what I need most isn't that, it's this." Faust tapped the Child lightly on the temple, then eased Him forward on his lap, pointing through the window. "Look at that Pair there, in the Cleopatra Room, third on the left, the 3-5-10-9-3-10-3-10 and the 4-3-5-9-3-8-3-9. What do you think of them?"

Jehovah's black eyes took some seconds to digest the pair. "The recent Death of a Parent has made the one on top consider Reincarnation. The other I can't see well from here."

Faust held his Nephew close, and remembers wondering whether he did it because children build connections through touch, or to comfort himself. "Your Mother made a Bet with me when we built this Place, that they could combine de Sade's and Diderot's Techniques with Brill's to raise a Human-Creature more alien and 'Enlightened' than anything anyone had imagined Humans could become. I still say you're not too many Steps past Diderot's Rameau and Nietzsche's Zarathustra, but on the other hand you exist, which is a real Plus. I need you." He turned the Child to face him. "You're eight Years old and you can understand the secret Dynamics between the Hives, but not the Rules of Tag, or Grammar. You're what I need. Things are bad, Donatien. Something is brewing; your mother's smug Smiles are Proof enough. Gordian is vulnerable. Our old Brain-bash' is running dry, and, with the Mardis dead, there's no one else I know of with a Psyche novel enough to keep us fueled with Innovations through what's coming. You know what I mean, don't you? The Utopians fuel their Spaceships with whatever they can mine from the Space Rocks they've already reached, and the Resources on those Space Rocks limit how much further they can go. You're the only Outpost left on my Frontier with enough Resources to let me go further. I don't like to let your Mother's Fangs sink into Gordian, but we need a Brain-bash', and at this point, Donatien, it's you or no one."

* * *

"Thank you for inviting me to address you, Senators."

Bryar Kosala had refused to change her wrap, so faced the concentric tiers of Senators with her sleeves still speckled with Jehovah's blood and brains. The luminous egg-white marble of the hall around her crackled with the fabric hiss of Senators fidgeting in their seats, pretending not to be prisoners as the restoration of the transit network made the mob in the Forum outside swell and swell. The Senate ranks had never been so thin, patches of different Hives, who in peaceful days comingled happily, clumping with rows of No Man's Land between them. The Masons were in good attendance, the Cousins also, Brillists, the eight Utopian Senators clustered in the back row, and the four Hiveless Senators in the front near the Hiveless Tribunes, but the guilty Hives had deserted. The Europeans used the meeting of their own Parliament as an excuse, while the Humanists were simply AWOL, and the Mitsubishi sent only two Greenpeace Members and one lone Korean to make a savvy quorum call; without a two-thirds majority, even the Senate of the Universal Free Alliance could do nothing more dangerous than talk.

"Two weeks ago," Bryar continued, "O.S. used their assassination system to force *Black Sakura* reporter Tsuneo Sugiyama to retire and let Masami Mitsubishi write this year's Seven-Ten list. That's the same list that was later stolen and left in the Saneer-Weeksbooth bash'. This stunt was engineered to bring more attention to the list, and to one name on it: Cousins' Feedback Bureau Chief Darcy Sok. The resulting investigation of the CFB released a report last night, and conflicting versions have been circulating ever since. Jed Mason was to present a full report to you today, but Sniper's attack has made that impossible. I am grateful, therefore, that you have invited me to present the truth myself.

"The CFB sorts the suggestion letters by which the Cousins are run.

Since millions of letters arrive each week, sorting is done by a computer. Every letter is dealt with eventually, even unique ones, but the volume of letters in each folder after sorting is used as an indicator of how important the issue is, so, if the number of letters on a subject abruptly increases or decreases, that is when it receives the most immediate attention from the administration. We now know that the CFB staff has been altering this data by changing the computer's search terms. For example, the terms 'land grab' and 'turf slurp' are both slang for the Mitsubishi effort to buy up land, so letters using those phrases are usually sorted into the same folder. On January twelfth of this year, CFB staff intentionally altered the program to route these into separate folders, making it seem as if the number of letters concerning Mitsubishi land policy had suddenly dropped, whereas it had, in fact, increased. This prevented the Cousins' Board from taking action to place more blocks on Cousins selling land to Mitsubishi. That's just one example. The records I have uncovered reveal hundreds of such alterations made every year, which have controlled the flow of information, and effectively dictated much of the Hive's policy for decades. No records survive from the beginning of this system, but it seems to go back over a century. The common belief within the CFB is that they invented the trick in the twenty-three forties, but the Anonymous quickly realized what they were doing and blackmailed them into allowing the Anonymous to dictate the alterations they made."

Kosala flinched here, catching her eye straying to the ex-Censor, who sat in the non-voting seats with the Minor Senators, and a number of other officials who had taken shelter in the Senate from the mobs outside.

"Now," she continued, "this makes it sound as if the Anonymous has been corrupting the CFB to their own ends, but the facts do not support that. Upon deeper examination, the alterations I discovered are primarily reactive, engineered to conceal brief spikes or drops in the number of letters on a subject, and always relating either to some new Masonic law or policy, or to a subject that the Anonymous is about to publish an editorial about. For example, the surge in letters about the Mitsubishi land grab was caused by the Emperor passing a law restricting sale of land by Masons to Mitsubishi, and the spike of letters on that topic lasted only three weeks, after which the number of letters normalized and the CFB restored the search terms to their original arrangement. In other words, the Anonymous and the team at the CFB have been altering the letter sorting to prevent Cousin policy from being dictated by short-term, emotional reactions to Masonic policies or the Anonymous's own editorials."

Kosala let herself glance at Vivien again, her expression neither forgiving nor reproachful, but seeming to agree with him that, if the pair had had the power once in their lifetimes to stop time and take some private hours before the world churned on, they would have spent it here.

"I found it hard at first," she continued, "to believe that the corruption could be so innocent. I was sure we'd uncover some incidents of the Anonymous stifling suggestions which came from the Cousins themselves. I found none." She froze a moment. "Let me clarify that. I didn't just find no incidents of the CFB conspiracy squashing Cousin-initiated movements, I found remarkably few confirmable Cousin-initiated movements, at least relating to matters of political policy. The number of letters advocating particular political actions or policies seems to spike or fall primarily in reaction to sudden outside events, the Masons or the Anonymous, or in response to world-famous incidents like the Mycroft Canner murders. These spikes are short-lived, usually normalizing after a few weeks. The information I have seen suggests that, if not for the Anonymous controlling the CFB, the Hive's core political policies would have been dictated all these years by wild short-term oscillations of opinion, resulting in a chaotic and panic-driven system incapable of long-term stability. I wanted to ask the former Censor Vivien Ancelet to testify about this. Obviously, since the Censor was also the Anonymous and running this conspiracy, that is not appropriate, but I did put the question to their Deputy Censor, Jung Su-Hyeon A-ancelet Kosala." She tripped over her own ba'child's name here, her eyes ranging the benches as if afraid someone would rise to cry nepotism, but no one did. "It is Jung Su-Hyeon's belief that, if these reactive political swings had been allowed to dictate policy, the Cousins would have suffered crippling economic decay over the past century, or even fallen apart, rather than remaining the second-largest Hive. In brief…" Here she paused, with the face of one who looks out over the cliff's edge, and must jump. "In brief, this conspiracy's effect has been to conceal and protect the Cousins from the fact that the feedback system does not work as a form of government. For many things it works well—local issues, disaster response, social protections, health and human services—but it does not work for political decisions, the quick but considered responses to actions by other Hives, or to global crises, that all governments need to be able to make. The feedback system cannot do it, and has only ever seemed to do it thanks to corrupt intervention."

She paused again, a long pause this time, brushing back her black hair as if to fight off the temptation to hide behind it, and scanning the room once more, giving others the chance to interrupt with heat and fury which might have taken the spotlight from her. Fury was not so kind. "An hour ago," she continued, "the Anonymous spoke publicly for the first time in history. They urged us all to move slowly, to keep our reactions to this crisis in check in order to preserve what they have called utopia. I disagree. I don't believe this world where four out of seven Hives are ruled by corruption can be called a utopia. I don't believe that, having recognized our long-term dependence on these corrupted systems, we should try to keep ourselves dependent on them. I don't believe that any delay can prevent this crisis from being anything but what it is, the complete transformation of the Alliance. Better to act honestly and quickly than to succumb to corruption and base means to prop up what is already broken." Her eyes flicked across the ranks of Cousin Senators, some weeping openly, others still stunned. "The CFB has not been shut down," she continued. "Letters are coming in, in unprecedented numbers, and a new and uncorrupted staff has been there all day sorting them. One billion, two hundred million letters have been received so far today, representing more than two-thirds of the Hive. They have proposed a range of actions, but two demands above all are supported by the vast majority of letters. These ideas do not initiate from the Masons or the Anonymous. They could be called rash reactions to a short-term fear, but, since they represent the first uncorrupted voice the Cousin Hive has had in over a century, it would be the ultimate betrayal of my office to ignore them, or even delay acting on them. The first demand is that I resign as Chair." Could you, like Kosala, reader, deliver such words without even a wince? "This cannot be treated until the Administrative Board convenes tomorrow morning, but if at that time the board consents, I will step down. Meanwhile, so long as I remain in office, I shall pursue the second suggestion, supported by over one billion Cousins, who have requested that we enter negotiations with Emperor Cornel MASON, first to have the Masonic Hive take over administration of our most vital social services, schools, hospitals, and such, to buffer them through this transition, and second to begin the process of merging the Cousins with the Masons, not fully but as a sub-Hive, like Greenpe—"

"Aunt Bryar, stop!"

The Titan armies, risen from Tartarus for their revenge, with the Hundred-Handed Ones raging beside them, a club in every hand, could not have stirred the Senators to more surprise, more outcry, more astonished awe than the sudden entrance, panting, disheveled, and in tears, of a young nun.

"Heloïse!" Kosala cried. "What are you doing here?"

"Thank Heaven I'm not too late!" The habit thrashed around Heloïse's knees like rough surf as she rushed, the veils across her forehead slipping back to let her red-gold curls trail free. "I've just come from the hospital. The draft survived! *Seigneur* Jehovah wouldn't let the doctors start their tests until He knew it was safely on its way to you!"

Kosala met the little nun in the center of the house floor, standing close as if hoping her flowing wrap might shield the stranger from Senators who gawked like zoo-goers. "What draft?" she asked.

Heloïse pressed a packet into Kosala's hands, twelve crumpled pages, dense with ink and dyed red-black with gore. "An interim constitution. *Seigneur* Jehovah had it in His jacket. He and I spent all last night drafting it. You can use it to transition away from the CFB!"

"An interim constitution?" Kosala's eyes locked on the pages, though whether on the words or on the crust of blood I cannot say. "For the Cousins?"

"He thought you might need one. It's ready to implement. It uses strats and interest groups to divide the Cousin population into two hundred and twenty voting groups, which will each elect a representative to a temporary Assembly, which will then draft a new permanent constitution."

These words hardly reached any ears as the thunder of astonishment churned the House. Perhaps, reader, you would enjoy guessing which Senators are clients of Madame's and which free. Review the photographs: where confusion washes like Death's white mask over a Senator, there the nun's rough figure is as alien as a centaur's; on the other hand, where shock mingles with blush, or where faces hide behind hands, these perhaps have laid lustful eyes on Sister Heloïse before.

"Order!" The Presiding Speaker rose now, Jin Im-Jin, a tiny, white-haired Korean Brillist old enough to remember four Emperors, and to frown down from the hard-earned Speaker's seat at whippersnappers like Faust and Papadelias. "Order! Order! Chair Kosala, you will answer for this interruption. Who is this . . . person?"

"I can answer for myself!" Heloïse faced the Speaker, curtseying a quick apology. "Madam Speaker"—the Speaker grimaced at the title—"my name is Heloïse D'Arouet. I am Tribune Jehovah Mason's bash'mate and fiancée. Before the doctors put Him under, the Tribune appointed me his Proxy *In Extremis.*" Gasps rose anew as Heloïse produced from the folds of her scandalous habit the Tribunary sash of gold-edged gray which Tribune Mason wore when filling his Graylaw office here the Senate. "The Tribune is determined not to let this assassination interfere with duties which have been trusted to Him, either in His office as a Tribune, or as an Executive of the Cousins' Chief Council's Office."

The tiny Speaker took a long and thoughtful breath. "There is good precedent for selecting a bash'mate as Proxy *In Extremis,* but why did the Tribune involve you in drafting the constitution? You say that was last night, before the assassination attempt, yes?"

'Attempt' already, reader; how quickly mankind hastens to erase the miracle; the assassination *succeeded.*

"He had me help because I grew up with gender."

All other faces were pure shock, but on the Speaker's face shock mixed with a Brillist's delight at human bizarreness. "What do you mean by that?"

"The Tribune and I both grew up with gender, so we can see and talk about the Cousins clearly, where no one else can."

"What do you mean?"

"Being a Cousin is all about gender. Specifically about the feminine. I don't mean anything biological, I mean the old cultural construction. All the eclectic things we associate with Cousins—nurturing, helping, healing, child rearing, tenderness, charity, welcoming the lonely, comforting the sick, tempering the violent—they're all things that, in olden days, were associated with the feminine. That's what all the Cousinly activities have in common, but because we're scared to say the words no one knows how to articulate it anymore. None of you can articulate what the Cousins are about, can you? Not without gender." She turned to the benches, inviting answers, but remember, reader, how hard it is at the best of times to interrupt a nun. "The old concepts of masculine and feminine were huge," she continued, "complicated, centuries in the making, and deeply rooted in people, consciously and unconsciously. They facilitated bigotry and oppression, yes, but they had a lot of other social functions too. People who identified as feminine were caretakers, peacemakers, hostesses, consciences to balance the aggressive masculine. In the last centuries of the Exponential Age gender began to be liberated from biology, but that process wasn't nearly finished when the Church War came. The worst cults in the war were also associated with gender oppression, so after the war the nascent Hives tried to purge all gender differences so abruptly that there was no time to come up with substitutes for all the other social functions gender used to have. Imagine if an ancient surgeon, on seeing penicillin work for the first time, had renounced his scalpel, calling on all fellow surgeons to vow never again to cut into a patient when pills could cure without wounds, totally ignoring the fact that there were countless illnesses for which surgery, perfected over centuries, was still a more effective treatment than nascent pharmacy. That's what happened when we suddenly silenced gender. The broad, vague, cultural concepts of masculine and feminine had served a lot of social functions beyond oppression. Back when half the race identified as feminine it meant that half the race was devoted in some way to nurturing, peace, and charity, and we never developed a substitute for that. Since masculine was the empowered gender, the rushed transition encouraged everyone to act masculine, and all at once humanity went from a race of half peacemakers to a race where those with instincts toward the feminine felt ashamed of the label, or ended up sheltering in its only acceptable modern form."

"The Cousins?" Speaker Im-Jin guessed, Brillist eyes bright with delight at this unique new specimen, and at the equally unique shock on the faces of the many members of the gawking Senate.

"Exactly, Member Speaker," Heloïse continued. "The Cousins are our feminine. They're where the people who felt drawn to feminine concepts gathered in the wake of the Great Renunciation. That's the heart of the Hive, but the words are taboo so no one dares admit it, and it feels like the Hive is weak and teetering. Of course it's teetering! The Masons would teeter if we banned the word 'Empire' and Gordian if we banned the word 'psyche.' How could the CFB's computer sorting figure out what the Hive really wants when the words we need to express it are forbidden? Motherly affection, sisterly devotion, uxorial duty, filial piety. Those concepts are the real heart of the Cousins, and we need them now more than ever, with violence and talk of war looming before us. To let the Cousins be themselves we have to undo the silence of the Church War and accept the fact that gendered thoughts are still in us, not innately, but because our ancestors chopped down the tree without killing the roots, so new shoots have sprung up. Gender has changed since three hundred years ago, having less to do with sex and bodies, but it still affects our thoughts. We teach it unconsciously, just as our ancestors did, in stereotypes, associations, pre-modern stories, subtle differences in how we treat children we see as 'boy' or 'girl.' We can't stop passing it on, or even study how we pass it on, when we won't admit that it's happening. We stopped the conversation too quickly. After the shock of the Church War, the survivors declared that equality and feminism had won when we had only slapped a patch over the surface. We need to admit that gendered concepts are still affecting how we think, and let the Cousins voice them, now. Think of the Set-Set Riots. How many fewer people might have died if the Cousins had felt free to say overtly why they were really upset? That their motherly feelings judged it inhumane to do such things to children. Without that vocabulary, the real cause of the conflict couldn't even be discussed!

"Now violence is threatening again. If we lose the Cousins, Earth's last humane, feminine, temperate voice will die, and we will have nothing left to intercede when other forces quarrel. Tribune Jehovah Mason understands this. He and I were raised with masculine and feminine. We had it in our minds when we drafted this interim constitution, assigning extra representatives to humanitarian groups, teachers, doctors, daycare workers, office managers, grandbash'parents, new parents, veterinarians, therapists, all the voices of nurturing that have always been the core of the Cousins. Trust us! Call for the Cousins to elect an Interim Assembly that will finally actually reflect the values that have always defined the Hive. Then, when the Cousins are re-made, a revised form of the CFB can be a part of—"

Who would dare interrupt her righteous tirade? Only God, or rather His works, manifest in the mingled screams of men and women which burst in through the doors and windows in a universal shell of human grief. Order collapsed like sand castles before a flood. The agenda, Kosala's announcement, even the rebuttals that had built up like battle-hungry legions during Heloïse's speech, all were swept clean away as the reporters watching from the balcony, one eye on their newsfeed lenses, screamed:

"Brussels!"

"Parliament!"

"A bomb!"

"A missile! Three!"

"It's burning!"

"Someone just blew up the European Parliament!"

I, still a prisoner of the operating table, was one of perhaps a thousand people in the world who did not watch. The Senators, like you, reader, or like your ancestors, tuned in and watched the flames which boiled around the columns of the Parliamentary Hall, like the bloody juices of some demon's gut unleashed upon the stone. A mob had assembled in the streets of Brussels, with stones and Molotov cocktails hidden behind their signs and chants, but they scattered now like blasted sand before the inferno which, in their fervor, they might have created themselves, had someone not beaten them to it. Stone shards flew like hail. More missiles followed, sky-bolts trailing white smoke like celestial fingers pointing to the target of Providence's wrath. Even riding the Space Elevators, children invited by Utopia to enjoy their first taste of humanity's next destination froze to watch the trails bloom around Brussels like the starburst of a dandelion.

Commentary followed, the more resilient reporters struggling to narrate what they could understand of the barrage. Others, honest about their ignorance, resorted to film, replaying the impact of the first missile on the dome, or the last footage of the session within. Parliament had been full, every bench filled by the Prime Minister's summons, wings crammed with judges, aides, and Europe's Senators, who had accepted Perry's invitation to share the security of the Parliament House, and so escape the Romanova mob. Casimir Perry himself, bandaged and bloody from his fall at Madame's the night before, had been at the podium at the final moment, railing at the assembly like a man possessed. « I'm no more guilty than any of you! Everyone in this room consented to the O.S. murders, not once but a hundred times! It is impossible to deny! Every one of you voted for 'special means' more than thirty times since Spain was voted out! And you protected it with your silence for decades before! You are guilty, all of you! The world— » The first blast knocked him to the ground, and buried a third of Parliament in stone and flame. « You see! We all deserve judgment! The world knows it! The world will be our judge! » Flame followed.

In Romanova, Heloïse was most prepared to break shock's spell. "Aunt Bryar, come!" She tugged the Cousin Chair's limp hand. "The world needs you! There are victims! Fires! Orphans! Burns! Europe is wounded! It needs your ambulances, your nurses, your councilors! It needs your Cousins! Come!"

Bryar Kosala paused, eyes locked on her husband the ex-Censor and ex-Anonymous—Hiveless and soon to be a Humanist, but with the French nation-strat band still bright around his wrist—who sat doubled over in his seat, winded by sobs as the heart of Europe burned. She followed Heloïse.

* * *

"Madame must marry me!" King Isabel Carlos II paced like a tormented lion in the too-small chamber outside Madame's bedroom. "She must! There is no other solution!"

"Don't talk nonsense." Felix Faust never seems so exhausted as when he must repeat himself. "You're the King of Spain. You can't marry a prostitute. What would your friend the pope say?"

Spain jumped like a startled hare at every rustle from the bedroom, where a cloud of maids oversaw Madame's convalescence after the latest tests to track the health of her impending Son. The obstetrician had shooed out all visitors, too many suitors competing to hold Madame's hands and ask repetitious questions. When the images of the Fetus were ready for viewing, the gentlemen would be summoned to share the moment with the blushing mother-to-be, but until then they were banished to her little foyer, whose painted cherubs seemed to grin with glee at the discord sown among Earth's leaders by the doctor's confirmation of the father.

"I'll abdicate if I have to!" The King fidgeted as he paced, fingering the hem of his blue Prime Minister's sash, its row of gold stars perfect with his waistcoat of champagne silk. "I won't leave my child to be raised in secret like some object of shame."

"Your Majesty, why do we have to say it's your child?" Twenty-two years ago Censor Ancelet looked more haggard than he does now, sleep-starved, scrawny, all the symptoms of self-neglect which would not be cured until marriage merged his tiny all-vocateur French Graylaw bash' with Kosala's huge and loving Indian Cousin one. "Without the test," he pressed, "could anyone in this room say with certainty the child wasn't ours?" His eyes tested them all, the King first, then Faust, Director Andō, and the Emperor.

Ganymede raised an idle alabaster hand. The young Duke lounged on the central sofa, the perfection of his flesh, still sparkling with youth, nude except for a translucent faux-Greek drape of the sort that only sculptures, nymphs, and gods can get away with. This was seven years after Danaë's marriage, and the twins had succeeded in winning Andō the Chief Director's seat at last, but Ganymede himself had not yet made the transition from *objet d'art* to President.

"That's a fair point." Andō's voice brightened. "It could as easily be my son. Who's to say it's not?"

"It's not," His Majesty answered flatly. "Things would be simpler if it were."

"Then why not let it be? What the public doesn't know—"

"Is still fact."

Andō made fists within his sleeves, the timed dyes of the Mitsubishi cloth just starting to ripen from summer green to autumn gold. "Isn't who raises a child more important than—"

"You can't be serious, Andō." Ganymede did not lift his murder-blue eyes from a volume of la Fontaine, whose verses served as distraction from his irritation at the arrival of a Child who would irrevocably outrank him. "A royal prince given over to a common businessman to raise? Marrying my sister may give you the effective rank of Earl, but you're only a Mitsubishi by adoption, and even the Mitsubishi are barely nobility."

Andō spun, glaring less at the Duke than at the acquiescing silence of the King and Emperor.

"Eight minutes." Headmaster Faust sighed at the ivory watch face embedded in the knob of his antique cane. "Eight minutes without a female chaperone and we're already at each other's throats." He snickered at the problem. It was a marvel, really, that such a mixture rarely degenerated into duels: the Chief Director and King Prime Minister locked in a room with their foe the Emperor, an acerbic young Ganymede, and Faust's gadfly sense of humor. Kosala (not yet Chair) was not there to add her maternal restraint, and even the authoritative calm of the Comte Déguisé was absent, for that glorified bureaucrat we call the Censor was weak in those days, barely important enough to visit this inner circle, since He Who six years later would unmask him as the Anonymous was still in the laborious process of gestating.

"Anyway, there's no need for us to fight over this." Faust tried his best to smile the tension away. "The child will stay with its mother, that's the way kings usually dispose of their bastards, isn't it? Unless Spain wants to go the other traditional route and pretend the child is their nephew by some convoluted logic."

"You'd like that, wouldn't you?" Andō was fastest to accuse. "Giving the two of you equal claim as uncles?"

Faust snorted. "I don't think much can be done to keep me from being the child's uncle."

"I won't have it raised a Brillist, Felix." The Chief Director slammed the wall. "I won't!"

Faust's smile died. "You'd prefer a set-set?"

"Stop, both of you." Stress made His Majesty's voice kinder, like a nurse trying to soften a diagnosis. "It's not what we want that matters, it's what the child needs. They will be second in line to the throne of Spain. If the Crown Prince proves unpopular, there may be a faction that tries to make this child King, or Prime Minister. They need to grow up prepared for that, to have support, a bash', a family, ready to help the child refuse if others try to exploit them for their power games."

"That's what I'm offering," Andō answered, harsh. "Myself, a father, family, I can give the child that, you can't. Let me raise the baby as my own and, whatever its parentage, no Spaniard will want it on the throne, and no

European will want to make it Prime Minister. It's the right solution." He searched the others' faces for signs of softening. "You think I'm basing this on nothing? Madame came to me. They said——"

"They said they think of you as the child's true father," MASON interrupted, slouching on his bench like a storm-tired tree. "They said they don't care what the DNA test says. They even said they planned to name the child after your favorite philosopher as a tribute. Which one was yours, Andō? Epicurus?"

The Chief Director's fists trembled with the desire to contradict.

"The Emperor's right, Chief Director," the Censor ventured, tense and formal, knowing himself a mere clerk among kings. "This was no accident on Madame's part: twenty-nine years running a brothel without a single pregnancy, then suddenly, at a moment that all of us are poised to think ourselves the father, a bouncing baby boy. It's not coincidence, and it's also not coincidence that the actual father is the only one of us for whom the bloodline really matters." His tone stayed calm, but passion and his left fist spilled his whisky. "With the exception of Their Majesty, none of us has children of our own. None of us is likely to, not while the only women that can excite us are the ones Madame controls. This right here, this is Madame's goal, all of us squabbling for a chance to raise their child, when this whole stunt was obviously planned to give Madame a stronger hold over us."

His Majesty Isabel Carlos II faced the Censor with a soft sigh. "No one here will deny that this is a scheme on Madame's part, but in my case, scheme or not, it worked. A father has a duty to their child, and to the mother of that child, which no political circumstances can negate."

The Emperor fingered the crystal facets of his own glass. "You're seriously ready to destroy yourself over this, aren't you?"

His Majesty remained majestic. "I will not let my indiscretion harm my people, or my son."

"He's precocious!" Madame's cry burst out with a bugle's bright enthusiasm as her maids opened the door to admit her gentlemen. She lay on top of the sheets, her vast yellow gown embroidered with a blushing maiden's birds and daisies. A wig was impractical in bed, but her hair remained concealed by a modest ruffled bonnet. "Come in! You must see! The doctor says she's never seen so much brain activity at twenty weeks. He's wriggling around like a little athlete, opening his eyes already, and she says if she didn't know better she'd swear he was trying to propel himself around by grabbing the umbilical cord!"

"Is something wrong with the child?" Spain asked at once.

All looked to the doctor, a graying Utopian, who sat in the corner reviewing the 3D model of the womb projected by her otter, while her coat showed the voyage of a microsubmarine exploring the rose-warm labyrinth of someone's bronchia. She shrugged. "We don't think so." I omit her technical monologue, since none of the prospective fathers followed it well enough to summarize. "Its development is strangely accelerated, but probably fine."

"He's more than fine," Madame insisted, beaming. "He's perfect!" She loosed one of the ties of her gown and bared the warm bulge of her belly. "Come feel."

However many millions of generations may be born upon this Earth, I think life's miracle will still inspire awe enough to freeze us, as a schoolchild freezes, afraid the dream will end when he dares stamp his first footprint on the lunar dust.

The mother waited, blinking impatience. "No one?"

The first who did dare place a palm on her bare orb was a child who lurked among the servants, nine years old, already silent as a hunter, uniformed in the deep blood-crimson which was his favorite color before Jehovah grew old enough to choose black.

Madame smiled at her young creation. "Dominic at least is a brave boy." She touched his shoulder. "Canst thou feel thy master?"

The child did not answer, but stood, eyes shut, lost in the depths of touch. I asked Dominic once if he remembered what thoughts passed through him as his short fingers felt the taut warmth of the life which would so dominate his own; he struck me for my audacity.

"Madame," the King Prime Minister began in his delicate tenor, "we have been discussing the child's future."

"I will not marry Your Majesty." She blinked to prove her sigh was tearful. "I will not so damage Your Majesty's reputation, nor will I have my child caught up in a power struggle with your late Queen's surviving son."

"Madame——"

"It would hurt all of us." She took the royal father's hand, gazing up into the face that adorned so many coins and portraits. "I know you want to do right by our child, but the honorable thing in this case is not the kind thing, not to our child, or to me, or to yourself. Tell him, Caesar."

Madame looked to the Emperor, who drew close on her other side. Together, reader, we have seen Cornel MASON's black-sleeved left hand quake many times with rage, sometimes with prudent fear, his instincts scenting something rotten on the edges of his Empire, but his steady right hand, that I find hard to imagine trembling. They say it happened when he entered the *Sanctum Sanctorum* to take the MASONIC Oath of Office, which even the successor may not read until the moment he must take it. They say it happened when Apollo had Mushi let him touch a Mars ant. They say it happened as he set his palm against Madame's bare skin and felt the Baby kick.

Caesar's words were firm as a portcullis slamming down: "I will adopt our child as *Porphyrogene*."

All turned. All gasped.

"Caesar?" The mask of makeup on Madame's portrait face was too thick to show whether she blushed.

As the steel cage of a splint is gentle to the millimeter toward the limb it heals yet also hard as armor, so the Emperor's hand stayed stiff but gentle on her belly. "For a royal prince to be raised as an imperial prince instead is surely neither deprivation nor dishonor."

Spain's tears flowed freely now. "You would do this for me?"

"For themself," Director Andō cut in, flushing with passion. "For control."

"No, the opposite: for all of us." Not harshness but warmth rose in Caesar's eyes, in his face, a human warmth which caught Andō off guard. "This is our child." He looked to Andō first, then Spain, Faust, the Duke, the staring Censor, "I'm sure you feel it too, all of our child, the child of our . . . connections, to each other and Madame, as much as if this were a real bash'." Even brooding Andō could not resist the word, the smile it coaxed. "We can't be a real bash'," Caesar added quickly, "but this child should be raised among us, all of us, or as close to among us as we can make possible. As *Porphyrogene* the child will grow up at the center of world politics, and the public will think it perfectly natural if my peers and collagues come to know them, and spend time with them. That way you will all be able to help raise them, not only here, but out in the public world, as ba'pas should."

Warm feelings rose in all their faces, longing, friendship, many different things named love, even the primordial tenderness called parenthood, except in Ganymede de la Trémoïlle.

"Do you propose to raise the Prince away from here, Caesar? In Alexandria? Not at Madame's?" Here the Duke-Consul's impossibly blue eyes show his reflexive fear, Madame's creation remembering how hard he fought to break from her, to seize even the tiny hint of freedom he now enjoyed having his own houshold at La Tremouille. A childhood in Alexandria could spare this child that fight, but, on the other hand, to be raised outside this house in Paris is to be raised a sexless, cultureless barbarian; can the noble Duke wish that upon a babe who shares the blood of Charlemagne?

"Oh, he must stay here with me!" came the Lady's sweet but absolute reply. "He must have the proper tutors and attendants"—she smiled down at little Dominic—"and here he can spend time with His Majesty"—a nod to Spain—"and all of you, freely, outside the public eye. But I do think it would be a great thing for him to learn outside ways as well, and to see Alexandria, and Tōgenkyō." A smile for Andō. "And, yes, Felix, you may take Him to the Institute." A more teasing smile for her brother. "And I trust Your Grace too will be at His little Highness's service, to tutor him in what you have learned dallying among the Humanists?"

Before this Matriarch, who had crafted him day by day and gene by gene but never let him speak the word 'mother,' the Duke could only take his place beside young Dominic and bow. "Of course, Madame. It will be an honor to aid in the Prince's education."

See victory in her smile.

"Good, I'll need that," the Emperor confirmed, smiling with unaccustomed warmth upon the Duke-consul, and winning in return a glance of blue perplexity. "I'll need all of you. Precedent dictates that the *porphyrogene* should not be my successor. Nonetheless I hope our child will someday hold high office"—he squeezed Madame's hand—"the world will expect it, in Romanova perhaps, or among the Humanists, or in another of your Hives. I want all of you to act as bash'parents, to spend time with the child, bring them to your capitals, teach them the ways and mind-sets of your Hives. I want you all to give them Minor offices when they're old enough, so they can get to know all the Hive governments, and choose freely among them when they come of age." He met the eyes of each colleague in turn. "I don't want to make them *Porphyrogene* to take them away from the rest of you, I want to make them *Porphyrogene* so that all of us can spend as much time with our child as we like without the public finding anything strange in it, and so they can have a free choice of Hives, as all children should have. I know your objection, Andō," MASON pressed before the Chief Director could interrupt, "but think carefully. Being *Porphyrogene* will not make our child a Mason, it will give them the freest choice of all, since they will grow up assuming that my seat—the only seat so tempting that it trumps all other choices—is not an option. I'm the only one who can take away that option, and thus make all others equally appealing."

Doubt morphed to delight in faces around the room, then into doubt once more.

"What will you tell the public about the child's parentage? It'll be obvious it isn't yours." It was Censor Ancelet who had the thought first, his own dark African complexion making him acutely aware that he and deep bronze MASON were the two in the room who would least resemble this child of two pale parents. "The Celebrity Youth Act will seal the records, but if Spain spends a lot of time with the child people will talk."

"Unless there's a rival rumor!" Headmaster Felix Faust cut in, his eyes and fingers lively with delight. "You're lucky, Andō, thanks to Queen Yijun you're going to have your wish."

Spain turned at this invocation of his Chinese ancestress. "What?"

"You take after your grandmother quite strongly, Spain," Faust answered, pointing to His Majesty's perfectly straight black hair, "and it's visible in your little Leonor as well. If it's visible in this child too then a credulous public should be willing to believe it's Andō's."

"Andō's . . ." the King Prime Minister repeated.

Was the Chief Director's frown embarassement? Or frustration that the old Brillist had read his thoughts? "My offer stands to take responsibility for the child," he began, stepping forward to place a hand beside MASON's upon Madame's belly. "I know you will not lie to the public, Spain, but if a rumor spreads that I'm the father, it will divert gossip, and strong Mitsubishi ties on top of Masonic ones will firmly eliminate the chance of entanglements with the Spanish succession."

"I don't . . ." Spain hesitated, ". . . what about the Princesse?"

Duke Ganymede scowled on behalf of his married sister. "The rumor will wound her little compared to the fact that Andō needed to wait for today's test to be sure it's not his child."

If the rebuke stung Andō, he did not show it. "I will support this plan," he confirmed, "the adoption and the rumor. This will be best for your people, Spain, and for the bash' that the group of us can almost be for this child."

"And for Madame foremost." Now MASON set his grim left hand upon the warm bulge that held the child, so his right could grasp Madame's. "I have no doubt, Madame, that such a loving mother as yourself will not rest until you have made your son the most privileged child in the world. Safer for all of us, I think, to get it over with."

As when Medusa's stare makes stones of heroes, the room froze at Madame's smiling silence as she weighed MASON's words. "You are right, of course, Cornel," she pronounced at last. "I would like nothing better than to give my child every privilege, and I shall commit my full resources to that end. But I cannot accept your offer, generous as it is."

"May I know your reasons?"

"You're entitled to know, my dear." She squeezed his hand in hers, but sighed at the other, its black sleeve. "The *Porphyrogene* must be a *Familiaris*. I will not have my son in your power to execute at will, especially if, as you propose, he will be raised by all of us, and thus have sympathies for many rival fathers, tempting him to stray."

MASON frowned. "You think I am looking for a legal excuse to kill your son? My affection for you aside, Madame, I and all here know what the consequences are of breaking friendship with you. You could destroy me."

Her head slumped back against her pillow in a show of delicate fatigue. "You are the Masonic Emperor, Cornel. It is hard to believe you fear anything, besides your law."

The others waited for MASON's next move, all silent except for Spain, who hiccupped with soft sobs, neither joy nor sadness, but commingling passions too multiform to have a name.

"Let them be a *Familiaris Candidus,* then," Caesar offered, "the office I created for Apollo Mojave. With a *Familiaris Candidus* the Hive retains the authority to override my justice should it prove too harsh. While the child remains a Minor, Romanova's Third Law will guard them from my Capital Power," he nodded to the Censor, "and, once they pass the exam, veto will rest in the leader of whichever Hive they choose." He nodded to the others: Andō, Faust, the bright Duke-Consul, Prime Minister Spain. "You already control five Hives, Madame, and neither the Cousins nor Utopia will tolerate death."

"That is a good solution . . ." The blushing mother smiled slightly, her fingernails playing across the creases of the Emperor's palm. "I know the depths of your affection for me, Caesar, but I can't help wondering why you would give this gift so freely, if not to have my child in your power."

MASON's shoulders twitched, a gesture Faust claims was common in years closer to the harsh Masonic testing which robbed Cornel of his foot and younger self. "All that I have I will share with our child," he answered, hollow-voiced. "You have less reason to attack what you can freely exploit. I ask no more."

"But will you love him?"

MASON is hard to blindside. "Love?"

"You can't expect me to trust my child to a father who will not love him. It wouldn't be healthy, not to mention proper." Madame laughed brightly as she placed her right hand palm over Caesar's left against the hot skin of her belly. "Will you love him?"

A hush; as centuries are too rough a measure for the passing of an age, so seconds cannot track the tides of emotion which flowed across Caesar's face, eroding away his masks of stone and iron and baring something human. "We both know I will have little choice."

"In that case, Caesar, you have made me the happiest woman in the world."

* * *

« Hilliard Wolfe ? »

« Confirmed dead at Parliament. »

« Fisher Yilmaz? »

« Confirmed dead at Parliament. »

« Aster Zinc? »

« Dead in their bedroom. »

« This can't be happening. »

« Have we heard back about Peckory Ingrams yet? »

« Dead in their home, Papadelias just confirmed it. Clubbed with a shovel. »

« That's it for the current Commissioners. What about the Justices? »

« That's no good, Perry called them into the session too. »

« This can't be happening. »

« Did they all attend? »

« We may as well go through them. Cooper Aubrey? »

« Confirmed dead at Parliament. »

« Sol De Léon? »

« Confirmed dead at Parliament. »

« Lindy Gaylord? »

« This can't be happening. »

« Would you stop saying that! » The others could only take it so many times without snapping. « Get a grip, Czerwinski! You're not helping! »

Jay Czerwinski, personal assistant to the late Vice President of the European Economic and Social Committee, was, in fact, rocking forward and backward in her chair hugging her knees, an activity only minimally less helpful than those of many others in the office, who twitched and shuddered as they scanned videos of the still-flaming wreck of the European Parliament.

On screens around them, lists of the dead and missing were too long to do anything but blur into one horrific alphabet. Seven others remained with Czerwinski: two speechwriters, the personal assistant to the Prime Minister's Deputy Chief of Staff, a Deputy Counsel, two security guards, and the scheduling secretary for Tuesday through Thursday. The rest of the staff of Prime Minister Perry's offices were dead with their master in the flames, had fled from the mobs, or were simply gone, empty cabinets and blank hard drives testifying to cold premeditation. Feeds replayed footage from Romanova: DeLupa, Kosala, Heloïse, ex-Censor-Anonymous Ancelet, their desperate faces positively cheerful contrasted with the ashen cheeks of these few who remained in Brussels's inner sanctum. Wind batted a litter of papers across the office floor, and in and out through the shattered mouth of what had been (before the riot) a most charming window, ceiling-high with a magnificent view of the Parliamentary Hall, whose carcass still belched smoke into the sky.

« This is pointless. They're all dead! All of them! »

« Shut up! » Courtesy was dead too. « There are hundreds of people in the line of succession, we won't know until we check them all. Lindy Gaylord? »

« Confirmed dead at Parliament. »

« They're all dead! They were all at the session, and the ones who weren't were murdered in their homes. It's a conspiracy! It's O.S.! »

« It's not O.S., idiot, O.S. is on our side. There must be something else we can do, an emergency protocol, somebody we're supposed to call to summon special forces. »

« I don't know how. »

« The security database was just deleted an hour ago, can we restore it? »

« I don't know how. »

« Maybe there's a hard copy in Perry's desk. Can anyone unlock it? »

« I don't know how! »

« The Director of the Registry of Gifts has a copy of the desk key; their extension should be listed in the purple book on the bookstand in the corner under the Picasso. Next call the Brugmann and Saint-Pierre Hospitals, they both have emergency teams trained in case something happens here, and call Professor Erasme Torbert Bordet at the VUB history department, they've retired now but they were the officer in charge of emergency forces when I was in office, they should still be able to get us started. »

« Your Majesty! »

A sun-bright angel, flaming sword and all, could not have brought more joy to the tear-streaked cheeks of these survivors than the King of Spain, who alighted straight from his car through the shattered window. Half his old staff followed shortly, some of his cabinet too, former Secretaries of State, Treasury, an ex-Justice, an ex-Auditor, and a pack of seasoned clerks, who found their old desks as comfortable as familiar horses.

« We thought we might be of some assistance. » King Isabel Carlos II faced each volunteer in turn, not smiling but assessing them with solemn, grateful calm. « Who is in charge here? »

« Ge . . . eh . . . we . . . » After a quick scan of her panicked fellows, the Deputy Counsel Marden Navarro settled on, « We don't know, » but her silent eyes answered just as clearly, « You are now, Your Majesty, » perhaps adding, « praise God. »

Spain's nod thanked her. « Chair Kosala should arrive shortly with disaster relief. Meanwhile, we should forget the EU lines of succession and start to examine the lines of succession of the nation-strats to find substitutes to repopulate the Parliament and European Council, and arrange a broadcast to calm the press. Scaliger and De Vries »—even Perry's people he knew by name—« can you two help my former Press Secretary draft a statement? »

« Of course, Your Majesty! »

Further commands from Spain and Spain's staff rained like healing dew upon the room. Panic turned to action as experienced hands plucked out folders and backup discs, not much changed from their arrangement of five years before.

"¡Everyone's dead, Your Majesty!" Navarro lapsed into Spanish with her King, as if that small comfort might soften the news. "¡Even the ones who weren't at Parliament¡ Council Members, MPs, and others. ¡They've all been murdered!"

« I know. It was Merion Kraye. That is Casimir Perry. » The King did not chide his subject, but would not let his royal title hijack any facet of that office: not its powers, not its titles, not its French. « I received a message from Kraye just after the first missiles hit. It's a prerecorded confession. I have already sent it on to Papadelias. Kraye intentionally gathered as many officials as they could at Parliament before the attack, and published the whereabouts of others on the net so mobs could find them if Kraye's own agents failed. »

« Then Kraye—Perry—planned the missiles! »

« They expected an attack. We can't be certain yet if they arranged the missiles or trusted public wrath to do so, but the rest of the deaths, those who weren't lured to Parliament, those I'm sure they planned. »

« How? »

Perhaps His Majesty had already guessed what forces Kraye had gathered, Madame's castaways, hundreds, burning for vengeance, happy to be aimed like bullets at the clients and allies of she who had destroyed their loves and lives. But if he knew, the King knew too that there is a time for details, and a time for action. « Deloucé, call the stock exchange, make sure it's shut down. Czerwinski, call the Mayor's office and get a report on what emergency action they've taken. Southcot, go through the list of building staff and confirm who is physically here, who is missing, and who is dead. Tiburon, tune in to the three emergency broadcast channels, Brussels's, Papadelias's, and Romanova's, and keep us updated. » His Majesty paused, spotting tremors in many hands. « I am asking you to exceed your duties, not your capacities. This crisis is a horror beyond what anyone should have to face, but it is not beyond what the human race has faced in the past, and overcome. We are not weaker than our ancestors. We will do this. » Spain hesitated, but accepted as the Deputy Council offered him the Prime Minister's chair. « I know it is an unendurable task, Navarro, but I must ask you go through the Parliamentary and Consiliar Rosters name by name a second time. In crisis there is a tendency to declare the missing dead before it is known with certainty. There must be some who slipped through Kraye's net. »

« Yes, of course, I . . . » She winced. « I'm sorry, Your Majesty, but you ought to know, among the confirmed dead, Crown Prince Leonor Valentín . . . they were standing right by Perry in the video, you can see . . . they . . . It was quick. »

In ancient days the treasons of dynasties could so harden a monarch that he might watch his child put to the sword without so much as a moist eye; not anymore. « Yes. » Spain tried to hide his face. « Yes, I saw. »

Navarro said it hurt more even than the sight of flames, seeing the King's cheeks wet with tears. « Is . . . » she began, « how is . . . your other . . . »

« Epicuro Mason is recovering. »

The news heartened all, as shade salves the laborer's sun-seared shoulders.

« I can't tell you how glad we are to have you here, Your Majesty. I mean, to have you back. This never would have happened if you were still Prime Minister. »

« We don't know that, » His Majesty replied.

She was afraid to contradict the King, but the room's silence urged her on with its panorama of agreeing faces. « Maybe not, Your Majesty, but we do know your family was the biggest restraint on O.S. all these decades. You, Epicuro Mason, your predecessors, you're the only ones who tried to keep us off this path. If Europe had an Emperor like the Masons do— »

Spain stopped her there. «I failed to prevent this as much as anyone. It is no credit to me if I'm the one Kraye chose to pick up the pieces.»

* * *

"The Utopian is here, Madame."

"Ah, welcome. I had begun to wonder if your Hive was boycotting my little establishment."

Madame elected to receive this visitor in her nursery, vivid with painted animals and red damask. Madame's intimates testify that she became even more beautiful during the years of Jehovah's childhood than she was before His birth, rich-voiced, bright-eyed. If so, it was the idea of motherhood more than the act that changed her, for with three nurses, eight servants, ten bodyguards, five tutors selected by His fathers, and four more chosen for the Boy by her, she spent barely enough time with the Child to train Him to recognize her as the Matriarch to whom He owed French and obedience.

"Sit, friend," she invited. "Sit."

"I prefer to stand." The Utopian faced her squarely, hands clasped behind as a silent promise that no beasts or wonders would pounce forth from the sleeves. "I have a message for you. We surrender."

"What?"

"We know what you are doing here. Your conquest of the other Hives has progressed beyond their ability to counter. We have no desire to destroy ourselves fighting back alone. I am here to negotiate terms."

Madame tapped her chair arm with the day's fan, albino peacock feathers streaked with poppy red to match her gown. "That's a very cold way of describing the situation."

"You are a self-made siren. You'll understand why I ward myself."

She blinked at the compliment. "What is your name?"

"Mushi Mojave."

"A relation of the late lamented Apollo. My condolences."

The vizor, at least, showed no flinch. "Thank you."

"You're the one Cornel brought here to represent Utopia at Mycroft Canner's trial, aren't you? I didn't recognize you with your coat switched on." Her eye followed the simulated ants trailing their odysseys across her floor. "Apollo's only been dead a few months. Did you Utopians really have so much invested in one person that you surrender now without trying anything else?"

Mushi did not move. "Is one of your demands for our surrender that we reveal what other strategies we have tried against you? If so, I am instructed to demand equivalent information in return."

She stroked her cheek with a rosy nail. "You're determined to play soldier to the end, aren't you?"

"I am not playing," the Utopian replied. "Since you built your empire by exploiting play, I'm sure you realize that. What are your terms?"

The poise and softness fell from Madame's face all at once, like a storm's last sheet of rain. "Fine. No playing. First, no resistance to my current or future conquests, or my Son's."

Utopia: "Agreed." Mushi sealed the bargain with a nod. "For your part, you will not try to dissolve or weaken Utopia, or encourage attacks against us, be they physical, legal, economic, propagandistic, or intellectual."
Madame: "I hope you're not expecting me to actively protect you."
Utopia: "No, just that you agree not to attack us yourself, not to cause your conquests to attack us, and not to feed the general ill will against us; it is already strong enough."

That last touch made her smile. "True. Agreed, then. Second term, I want all your resources at my disposal."

Mushi's response was instant. "We will not divert resources from Mars."

Madame sniffed. "I meant your people, not your money, the teams you hire out for contract work. When I ask for something I want your best, and promptly."

Utopia: "You want to hire us without payment?"
Madame: "Without payment, without waiting, without questions, without objections, without receiving less than your best people, best artists, writers, designers, accountants, teachers, doctors, architects, the best of every field, whenever I ask, and with appropriate discretion. What you do for me is not to be shared or repeated."

Three breaths passed as silent debate flickered from Mushi's vizor across the constellations which cocoon Utopia's earthly empire. "We will complete specific quests. We will not proactively pursue your goals."

A slow laugh percolated in Madame's throat. "I don't trust anyone I did not raise myself to understand my goals. It's your arts I want, not your people. I may ask you to make a gun for me, but it will be my own creatures who pull the trigger."

"Utopia does not accept commissions to build lethal weapons," Mushi answered quickly.

Madame: "It was just a metaphor."
Utopia: "Utopia does not make anything that can be adapted into a Harbinger."
Madame: "A what?"
Utopia: "Nukes, CMWs, bioweapons, chainbombs, positron cannons, armed satellites . . ."

She laughed as at a child. "Why would I need those when I have sex?"

"You would be surprised how many innocent-seeming projects can be adapted into Harbingers. At times you may request something which, without your knowledge, borders on such arts. We reserve the right to refuse."

Madame fingered the lace-trimmed choker at her throat. "What God-fearing woman could say no to that? I hope everyone who hires you faces that same restriction."

Mushi would not step up to her taunt. "We should fix a cap on how many Utopians you may indenture to your quests at once. Shall we say—"

"The cap will be the necessity of discretion," she supplied, "that is to say, as many as I judge it safe to employ without the risk of others sniffing out the alliance between us."

Digital eyes narrowed. "You wish to shroud our surrender from the other Alphas? That is agreeable to us as well."

Her smile widened. "I thought it would be. Better for you if the other Six still think the freaks are operating in isolated ignorance, yes?" She waited, searching the bare quarters of Mushi's face for shadows of an answer. "It's better for me, too," she continued. "Not a few of my gentlemen might have heart attacks if they heard I'd snared you, too."

"MASON already knows."

Her painted brows arched. "Did Cornel tell you to come here?"

"No. MASON shared some information with us about the . . ." Mushi hesitates, uncertain how this grim and regal mother will react hearing her Son called by the honorable title of 'The Alien.' "About the *Porphyrogene*, and the various Alphas' relationships with them. Or rather MASON confirmed système

some information. It was just therefore that we tell them our decision before we came to you. As for your proposal that we trust you to keep the number of Utopians you indenture to a shroudable level, we accept. Have you other demands?"

She took a long breath. "I want hostages, two of your finest here at all times, and a further dozen I can summon at will."

A pause for consultation. "We will want to orbit them out in turns, shall we say five-year shifts?"

"Acceptable, but I mean it when I say I want your finest. I want them to be brilliant, competent, with full access to your technology, the ability to translate your U-speak, many other indispensable traits. Have them be authors, artists, or inventors, too, hostages you'll really value, I know how you hate losing authors and artists. And make them useful. They're to serve while they're here, servants and tutors for my Son. It isn't right that He be tutored in the secrets of only six of seven Hives."

The vizor could not conceal a smile of pride. "Many of us fit that description, but we will find some hostages with skills likely to prove useful to you, and whose loss will hurt us deeply."

"I shall have Caesar make them *Familiares Candidi.*" Her smile swelled. "Caesar can be our neutral arbiter, to verify for me that those you send me are indeed as excellent and valuable to you as you pretend."

Utopia: "Agreed. In return we request full research access to Micromegas."
Madame: "I never expected such a graceless people to call Him by so elegant a name. That will be easy; as servants and tutors, you'll have the fullest access."
Utopia: "Not just for the hostages, for our researchers. You had us in at the beginning."
Madame: "Your gynecologists you mean? Nothing but the best for my little Prince."
Utopia: "In recent years Headmaster Faust has been making efforts to block our access."
Madame: "Has he indeed? Well, I can't blame him; such a Specimen has never walked the Earth, nor may again. If I ran Brill's Institute, I'd never let Him leave, if I could help it, and I certainly wouldn't let you near Him."
Utopia: "We will do nothing invasive, but we want to document their development. As you say, Micromegas may be unique in the scientific record."
Madame: "My great experiment."

Utopia: "We want to keep records in terms the world can understand, not just the Brillists."

Madame: "A full chronicle of my Masterpiece. You'll share everything with me?"

Utopia: "Of course, and publish nothing short-term without your permission. These records are for the future, not the present."

Madame: "Agreed, then, full access for research, within the limits set by His tutors. You mustn't tire or trouble the Boy."

Utopia: "We will be careful. What is your next demand?"

Madame's swift fingertips tapped at the ebony chair arm, like the patter of a mouse. "That's all I can think of off the top of my head. You have rather put me on the spot. I'll want some time to think of more terms."

"A fortnight?" Mushi offered.

"That would work. Come again in fourteen days. Meanwhile the agreement can stand as it is."

Utopia: "We have three more terms now."

Madame: "A most demanding surrender. Go on."

Utopia: "We require that you forbid Utopians from becoming members of your club, and that you discourage all Utopians from coming here, apart from the researchers and hostages. You will have them, no others."

Madame: "If you insist. If this surrender proves sincere, I've no further need to bring you in, and you tend to make other clients uncomfortable."

Utopia: "Forbidding and discouraging are different—we expect you to do both."

Madame: "Well observed. Agreed. What is your second term?"

Utopia: "The Moon is off-limits to you and your creatures. Micromegas may visit if they wish, but not the others. You get the Earth, we get the Moon."

Madame: "You get the bare rock, I get the fertile one? That's fine. What about Mars?"

Utopia: "Since Mars won't be ready for two hundred and fifty years, we can leave that to another generation to negotiate. We will not let you endanger the terraforming—"

Madame: "I wouldn't want to. That's acceptable. What's your third term?"

Utopia: "We want the future."

She blinked. "That's not a small demand."

"True, but you don't care about it. You want to conquer the world to prove you can. You want your child to eclipse Augustus and Alexander. You want to show your enemies they were fools for throwing away the old weapons of sex and religion. You don't care about establishing a dynasty. Two generations are as good to you as twenty. We want what comes after."

Madame frowned. "What does that mean in practical terms?"

"We will not fight you or Micromegas for control of anything for the next hundred and fifty years. You will not interfere with our preparations for events thereafter."

"You mean Mars?"

"I mean everything. It's no more than the other Alphas have already granted. This world is content. The other Hives vie one with another for power and population, but a peaceful, happy Earth is utopia enough for them. The next step for humankind is left to us, and in return we share our practical inventions, let the others mass produce our cures and tools, and enjoy our art and stories, for Earth's benefit. That is the agreement between us and other Hives, implicit but universal. It's never been threatened before because power has been too diffuse for any few people to be in a position to change such an ingrained attitude. A global monarchy is different. We cannot sit back and let you take control until we are certain you will let our work continue."

"Your work for the future." Madame's shoulders tensed with the strength which makes the she-wolf fiercer when she has cubs to defend. "I have your word that your preparations won't threaten my empire, or my Son's?"

"None of them are intended to, but if any do by accident you will have our full resources ready to help you reestablish yourself. You get the present. One hundred and fifty years, a long lifetime. Leave us the future."

She made them wait, Mushi and the others watching from their distant cities, though whether the prolongation was deliberate or deliberation I cannot guess. "Agreed," she said at last. "Just two more petty things."

"What?"

"Hand me your vizor, and address me as Madame."

"What?"

"Address me as Madame. You haven't yet. Even Caesar uses the title now, but you're deliberately avoiding it, as if that keeps you clean. You're not clean, any of you, not anymore. As for the vizor, I'm tired of being curious, all the rumors about what you keep hidden in there." She extended an impatient hand. "A good servant would not make me wait."

She did wait, though, this calmly staring Matriarch, while debate sparkled across the constellations of Utopia as they felt the first tug of the yoke. "Just a moment, Madame. I need to evacuate it first."

"Evacuate? Oh!" Madame both winced and giggled as a platoon of Mushi's ants emerged from the vizor, making a forced march back into the safety of hair and coat. "Yes," she laughed, "and you shall tell the hostages when you send them that if any of your vermin so much as fright a lady beneath my roof, you'll bring them here no more." Her eye followed the last retreating ant into the depths of Mushi's collar. "Are those robots or real?"

"Both, Madame." Mushi blinked hard as the vizor slid free. "I am instructed to remain as your first hostage. I do meet your requirements."

"Coming from the Mojave bash' I trust you do." Madame blew on the inside of the vizor before trying it, as if imagining that ants left dust. "I'll have my maids prepare you a cell." She smiled, gloating at the ambiguity which left Mushi guessing whether her hospitality would prove a cloister or a jail. "It's normal!" She exclaimed as the vizor settled in place. I have Utopia's permission to expose this secret, reader; it is sad to let the mystery die, but better that than let you think that all Utopians have their vizors engineered for war and combat, as Apollo did. "The world's unchanged!" She gazed about at arm, walls, ceiling. "I expected everything would look like your coat."

Mushi squinted against the bare air's unfamiliar cold. "We would hardly work so hard for our utopias if we let ourselves live in the illusion that they are already real."

She smiled at that. "What are all these floating tags on things?"

"Select one to zoom in. They're things you can fix or improve: stains or damage, litter, blank walls waiting for art, subjects for research, mysteries, hazards to life or health, clumsy technology waiting for a better alternative."

She lifted a cup from the nursery table, examining whatever suggestions the vizor made for its improvement. "You see this all the time?"

"Unless I'm watching a movie or something."

"It would drive me insane. Do all Utopians see this?"

"Almost all. It's our Infinite To-Do List. It staves off complacency. It's not easy to maintain a race of vokers in such a comfortable world."

Madame's eyes fell on Mushi, dazzled by the calls for medical research and coat improvements which, as she describes it, glittered in the air like fireflies flashing their quick prayers for attention. "It would have been Apollo who was sent for these negotiations, wouldn't it?" she asked softly, "if they'd lived."

"No."

"No?"

"MASON would never have let Apollo set foot here." Mushi's bare eyes faltered as they tried to meet hers. "Besides, Apollo was too passionate. Their description of the future would have been too moving for you to be content to give it up."

* * *

「Yes, Chief Director.」

Now only Tōgenkyō remains, reader, Asia's compromise capital, the lotus blossom towers with their inner sides alight with commerce's neon fire. Tonight their outer mirrors had more to reflect than Indonesia's seas. Lights of a thousand colors filled the streets between the petals. The day's disasters, the exposure of O.S., Sniper's attack on precious 'Tai-kun,' the exposure of the Anonymous, the flames at Parliament, all had fueled these Mitsubishi mobs. As sunset crept on in Romanova and midnight's black in Indonesia, the raging thousands brought their own lights to Tōgenkyō's streets, a few torch-warm, most electronic, cold as moon-bright ghosts. The blood they screamed for hid above, seven of the nine Mitsubishi Executive Directors sheltering in their administrative headquarters in the greatest lotus's central stamen spire.

"Where are the other two?" It was Korea's Director Kim Yeong-Uk who brought English into the room. The five Chinese Directors had been conferring in their own tongue, even the representatives of Beijing and Shanghai united for once by fear as all watched the dance of the police lights trying to shift the crowds below. Greenpeace's Director Bandyopadhyay was nowhere to be seen. As for Japan, Chief Director Hotaka Andō Mitsubishi sat at his desk, eyes closed as he concentrated on editing the files which flicked across his lenses, alone.

"Bandyopadhyay went to Delhi." It was the younger of Shanghai's directors, Wang Baobao, who answered, good at hiding fear. "They're trying to rally the ex-Greenpeace bigwigs and convince people of their innocence. I hear it isn't working."

"And Kimura?" Kim Yeong-Uk glanced to the empty chair where the second Japanese Director should have sat.

"They took their own life."

Mortality's hush fell across the room, the Directors watching as chunks like bites disappeared from the churning star-sea of rioters below: police releasing gas.

"I hear there are hundreds dead down there."

"There's no way to tell yet."

"How many of the dead are Japanese?" Kim Yeong-Uk asked it, and stared at the Chinese directors, surveying the too-festive spring colors creeping across their Mitsubishi suits: maple leaves sprouting from black stripes, geometric patterns maturing into cranes or flying fish. China's great faction leaders, Wang Laojing of Beijing and Lu Yong of Shanghai, had words only for each other; the rest had words for none.

Chief Director Hotaka Andō Mitsubishi did not look up from his work. "I imagine almost all those dead are Japanese."

Kim Yeong-Uk nodded. "I'm sorry this happened while you were Chief Director, Andō. You worked hard and did well. This isn't Japan's fault."

"Thank you."

"Will you follow Kimura?"

Kim Yeong-Uk says Andō smiled, as if grateful for the confidence shown by this bluntness. "No."

"But it is your fault, Chief Director." It was Wang Baobao who said it, looking to Lu Yong for approval, but his elder was too wary. He was not. "Bad enough the Japanese made the Canner Device, but, if you hadn't gotten mixed up with Ganymede and that Merion Kraye, none of this would have happened. Now you're not even going to take responsibility for it?"

Still Andō did not glance up. "If you'd care to 'take responsibility,' ask maintenance to show you how to unlock that window. I have work to do."

Lu Yong silenced Wang Baobao with a frown, and stepped toward the Chief Director's desk. "We need to plan. Now. All of us together." He added the last loudly as the others started to whisper again.

"Together." Kim Yeong-Uk nodded. "Agreed. Papadelias is downstairs with a crew of polylaws preparing to arrest us. I doubt our people can slow them down much longer."

"Arrest us? All of us? Our blocs will fall apart."

Wang Laojing held his head high. "I have plans in place. Replacements. My bloc will stand. If some of you have neglected such preparation—"

"Useless," Shanghai interrupted.

Beijing: "Useless?"

Wenzhou: "I agree. The whole world heard DeLupa's speech about murderers training murderers. Everyone who's in a position to replace us is also on the list Perry published naming those who knew about O.S."

Young Shanghai: "It isn't true! I never told any of my subordinates."

Wenzhou: "That doesn't matter. I can't prove my staff and successors didn't know, nor can any of you. What Perry constructed is a very crafty list of everyone close enough to us to keep our blocs together. Everyone who knows enough to sit at this table is about to be arrested if not lynched."

"Not everyone." Old Huang Enlai had lingered at the window, watching the lights war on, but he turned now and nodded to the empty board table, testing the faces of his companions. Would they see it? "There's someone who knows everything, who isn't on that list. Someone who's sat at this table almost as often as we have ourselves."

"Xiao Hei Wang!" Jehovah's Chinese name spread quickly through the others, wide eyes with it. "Xiao Hei Wang is innocent."

"Xiao Hei Wang could do it."

"They sit in on every meeting, know who owes favors, family history, everything."

"They could hold my bloc together."

"They could hold all our blocs together until real plans are made."

Korea nodded. "It's not a bad idea."

"The other Hives trust Xiao Hei Wang too, they'd trust the Mitsubishi under their leadership."

"Would Xiao Hei Wang have to join the Hive?"

"No. Outside contractors can hold shares in trust."

"They'd do it for us, wouldn't they, Andō?" Old Huang Enlai approached the Chief Director's desk. "Xiao Hei Wang thinks of you as a father. They've supported us against the Masons, fed us secrets behind MASON's back. They'd stay loyal, support our families, honor our requests and instructions, even from prison, and they'll have Madame's resources to help, and the world's trust."

"Xiao Hei Wang would do it, I'm sure. We can make them custodian of all our shares until a new board is selected."

"They'll protect our families."

"Maybe get us acquitted."

"No!" Hotaka Andō rarely raises his voice, but there is thunder in it when he does. "We have been defeated. That does not mean we hand the enemy their prize."

All stared. "What enemy?"

"Madame D'Arouet. Can't you see it? They planned all this to force us to pass power to Tai-kun."

"Madame?" Glances flicked fast as sparks among the others. "Why would Madame attack us? We're all their clients."

This should be no surprise, reader. To head a Mitsubishi bloc is to raise a high tower on ground besieged by earthquakes; Madame's patronage is the iron hidden in the tower's heart which makes these ten still stand.

"Madame is not our friend." Andō's shoulders shook, as if something threatened to erupt from him, sobs or laughter. "It's just as Sniper said: Madame is trying to tear down all the Hives and put Tai-kun at the head of what remains. Tai-kun nearly lost their life exposing O.S. They're the world's hero now. The Cousins, the Humanists, Europe, we're all on the edge of ruin, and Madame is counting on us to realize we can save ourselves by handing power to Tai-kun. Europe has given itself to Spain, and Prince Leonor's death makes Tai-kun Heir Presumptive. As for the Cousins, they're already implementing Tai-kun's interim constitution, and you can't doubt Tai-kun and Heloïse will be the architects of the permanent one as well."

"Heloïse?"

Andō met Huang Enlai's eyes. "A tearful maiden charges onto the Senate floor with a bloodstained constitution? My Hiroaki still has access to the CFB, and the Cousins are all sympathy vote. After 'Aunt' Kosala's touching performance at the Senate this morning, and in the Brussels crisis, they've received more letters demanding that Kosala remain Chair than they had before for their dismissal. Even more are demanding that the Board waive the requirement for Board Members to be Cousins, so they can appoint Heloïse, as well as Tai-kun. Madame knows how to use a broken system."

"Then Madame is trying to have Xiao Hei Wang take over three Hives at once?"

Andō's voice was steel. "All hives. You know Faust and MASON have already surrendered."

"MASON? But Xiao Hei Wang is Shan Huang Zi, they can't be Shan Tai Zi." (China has its own words for *porphyrogene* and *Imperator Destinatus*.) "Can they?"

Scared faces.

"Why would Madame do this? Kosala and most of Parliament were as much their clients as we are!"

"Because Tai-kun is soft," Andō answered.

Old Huang Enlai studied the Chief Director's face, perhaps more scrutable to him after their long years of colleagueship. "What are you thinking?"

Andō kept working through all this, eyes more on the lens data before him than on his colleagues. "Madame has never concealed their ambition. The reason we didn't see this coming is that Tai-kun already had an office in every Hive. But Tai-kun wouldn't let Madame exploit those offices, they've fulfilled the duties to each in good faith, serving loyally instead of manipulating. If Madame wants to conquer the world through Tai-kun, they have to force them into higher offices." Andō looked up now, testing each Director's face as if eager to spar with any who dared object. None did. "The Cousins and Europe are conquered already, Faust and MASON won't fight back against their own next of kin, and the Utopians capitulated long ago. Vivien Ancelet may have saved the Humanists with this sudden call for an election, but Ancelet is very close to Tai-kun too, and now they have to pass on the title of Anonymous. I believe that Tai-kun has long been their designated successor." He gave his colleagues time to gasp. "If we hand our Hive to Tai-kun too, Madame wins."

Beijing and Shanghai exchanged glances. "We don't have a choice," Shanghai began. "The Hive needs a leader. Better to appoint Xiao Hei Wang than let the Hive dissolve."

For once the two agreed. "Xiao Hei Wang has long been one of us, and still thinks of you as a father, Andō. And they're loyal to duty, and to promises. We can hold them to their pledges. If we press Xiao Hei Wang to keep our Hive separate, to defend Mitsubishi values, to defend us, we can let the others fall to Madame, then have Xiao Hei Wang restore us. If you ask, Andō, they'll promise, and if they promise they'll keep it."

"Tai-kun will not defend homicide. Right now our own Hive hates us for our part in O.S., and loves Tai-kun for their part in exposing the same. What we did with O.S. we did lawfully as leaders of this government, for the good of our Members and the world. If our Members have a chance to calm down and listen to us they will see that, and rally behind us, defending our right to self-sovereignty and exercise of lethal force. But Tai-kun will never think that way." Hotaka Andō turned again to editing the documents before him, a sense of rest falling across his face. "Tai-kun hates death absolutely. Family ties cannot trump that. If they take office they will be unable to hide their horror at homicide, and that will push our Members to condemn us even more."

Wenzhou's careful Chen Zhongren nodded. "The Members have loved Xiao Hei Wang since birth. Now that they've almost become a martyr for the Alliance, they'll love them even more. If we put Xiao Hei Wang in charge, the Members will never let them pass power back to us when they see us as a group of murderers. We have to hold on to our shares, insist on our own family successors, keep Xiao Hei Wang out or we'll never get back in. And Xiao Hei Wang is a pious son—if they rule, their mother rules."

Beijing agreed. "We must resist, keep our own in power, even if it's a fight."

"No," the Chief Director countered, soft but clear. "Everyone under us is going down, Kraye saw to that. Fighting it will just rip the Hive apart. We've lost. We have no choice but to surrender."

"Andō—"

"But not to Tai-kun." The Chief Director did not glance up, too armored in conviction's calm to care whether the faces around him showed hope or anger. "There is another who knows just as much as Tai-kun about the inner workings of the Directorate, who has the knowledge necessary to be our proxy and to keep our blocs together, who had no part in O.S., but whom our Members will be happy to throw off, and who will never be able to hold on to power in the Hive without us and our families' constant support."

"Who?"

Andō saved his file. "Before Kimura killed themself, they signed their shares over to me. My voting bloc is now almost a quarter of the Hive. As of this moment I have left all my shares in trust to Dominic Seneschal, for a duration of three years, on condition that they train a board of new Directors selected by the dominant shareholding groups."

"Dominic Seneschal? From Xiao Hei Wang's harem?" Behind closed doors some give a darker name than bash' to His devoted servants.

Andō rose, giving the arms of the Director's chair a light parting caress. "Dominic spies through Tai-kun's tracker almost constantly. They've been spectator at every Directorate meeting Tai-kun has ever seen. And they have no qualms about lethal force. With our instruction and support, they can manage our blocs almost as well as Tai-kun."

"But Dominic is from Madame's!"

"They're the worst of Madame's! A monster!"

Does the fear flush in their faces speak of past encounters?

"True," Andō confirmed. "Seneschal terrifies and disgusts everyone, especially the public. They could never hold power without us to back them. The Members will hate and fear them, and welcome us back when we're ready to return."

"But they work for Xiao Hei Wang. They'll follow them as slavishly—more slavishly—than anyone."

"No. You forget, Madame is our enemy, not Xiao Hei Wang. You all know what Madame has done to Dominic. Dominic hates Madame with a bitter, vengeful hatred, and if we give Dominic power they'll fight to destroy Madame with more savagery, and more intimate knowledge, than any of us will ever have. A gun in Dominic's hand is a gun aimed at Madame by the true enemy of our true enemy. And thanks to Madame's training, Dominic believes a man may only love something weaker than themself. Dominic is an obedient servant, but beneath that wants nothing in this world more than to see Tai-kun fail. That contradiction will make them self-destruct in office. They will steer the Hive through the immediate chaos, preserve its independence for their own needs, but when they try to move forward, in a world where Tai-kun rules the other Hives, they will be paralyzed between wanting to help and hinder Tai-kun, and their policies will become a mass of contradictions. The Members will start to hate them, cry for their overthrow, and then they will remember us and ours as the better, stable way, and welcome us again."

Chen Zhongren studied Andō closely, frowning. "You believe we can reclaim our seats, against Madame? We all got these seats in the first place thanks largely to Madame."

Andō met his eyes. "I have three billion voting shares, my own connections, family, my ten bash'children and their . . . abilities, and Ganymede and Danaë, who are mine, firmly, not Madame's, mine. Whether I reach out my hand from here, or from a prison, makes little difference to me. You may strike out on your own if you wish, but I am confident."

Chen Zhongren nodded. "Was this Danaë's idea?"

The others say Andō flinched here, as if the question found his armor's chink. "This is my solution," he answered. "The only solution. I will not let Madame unite all the Hives, not even under Tai-kun. Those of you who are too tired to fight may do as you will. The rest I hope will join me and help to build a weak new board with Dominic at its helm. Dominic will destroy those who destroyed us, and then we will destroy Dominic and take all back again. The other six Hives have fallen, but not irrevocably, not while we endure. Who is with me?"

I Was Wrong.

I WAS WRONG. I HAD LOST CONVICTION'S ARMOR WHEN I FIRST faced Jehovah at my capture, and for thirteen years I embraced doubt, which lacks the oak's strength but sways reedlike before all storms, and so ensures one will at least never again be wrong. Fool that I am, I cast that doubt aside. I was so sure. When I awoke I would fly with zephyr speed to bring Bridger back to Jehovah, who would marshal His many fathers to commit all Hives to sharing Bridger's gift with a grateful world. That was the Plan, and I, Its agent, thought I understood. As if the trowel that slops mortar on the stones can understand the exalted aim of the cathedral. Unleash your vengeance on me, reader, Furies, God; I who forgot the lesson bought with Apollo's blood deserve no less.

«Welcome back, Mycroft. You're now the new Anonymous.»

I awoke in the hygienic prison of a Utopian hospital bed. My doctors knew I would not consent to convalescence without restraint, and, weakened as I was, they still showed due respect to Apollo's murderer by fashioning my straps of Cannergel.

«There were four coups while you were under.» Papadelias sat at my bedside, warming me with soft Greek and himself with coffee. «Ancelet exposed themself as the Anonymous and resigned so the Humanists can rush an election to make them President. The Mitsubishi Directors have all been arrested, the Cousins have scrapped their government and are holding elections under an interim constitution, and the entire European government was assassinated, so Spain's taken over as interim... they're saying Prime Minister but Dictator is more accurate. I can activate your tracker if you want to see the news.»

It took some tries to get my voice to work again. «Je-Jehovah?»

Papa smiled to find one part of the world at least unchanged. «Jehovah's fine, just having tests run.»

«How long was I out?»

«Five hours. I had them replace your pacemaker with one that's Mycroft-proof.» He had the old one on the table beside him, flat like a cookie, its surface clouded with an organic residue my body had used to integrate this alien into itself. «How old were you when you designed that thing?» he asked. «Fifteen? Fourteen?»

«Fourteen . . . » The syllables were not easy, reader, nor would you speak with ease if you saw the better part of your heart severed on a table before you. It was the better part, not the clumsy meat pump biology had fit me with, but love's creation, mine and Saladin's, which Saladin planted to mark his territory, so every clock tick that measured my life's hours was his as much as mine. I knew every wire of it, could smell in my mind the damp grass of our garden hideout where we planned its insides under the microscope, and practiced our laparoscopy on steaks and eggplants—happy years. «Did they replace the meat part of my heart too?» I asked.

«Just reinforced it. They said your heart's not in bad shape considering, and so long as you can't slip your tracker anymore, I'm content.»

The Cannergel was soft enough to let me test the motion of my shoulder, the muscles slow but responsive beneath the bandages. «Make sure there are no records of who performed the surgery.»

«Saladin still territorial?» he tested, smug. «I don't know whether to be more impressed with you because you managed to keep me in the dark for thirteen years, or less impressed because you had help all this time.»

I avoided his eyes, studying the ceiling's warren of clear tubes, through which U-beasts of all styles, from Bunnybots to flame-bright Fiberoptifoxes, bustled delivering snacks and pills and therapeutic cuteness. «I had a ba'sib once named Saladin,» I said.

Papa sipped his coffee. «No need to pretend. I'll find them on my own, after we deal with this Bridger kid. No hurry.»

I felt my face harden. «Should I wish you good luck, then, hunting for a ghost? Or are you after Bridger so you can have them resurrect my dead ba'sib just to accuse them of conspiracy?»

He kept his laugh low. «Thisbe told me about the dog trick you used with Bridger. The rest is obvious. It's unlike you using the same trick twice. Keep it up and you'll be unmasked as the Anonymous in no time.»

«Ἄναξ Jehovah is the next Anonymous, not me.»

Papa shook his head. «Jehovah's too busy. They say it should be you.»

Objections gathered within me, political and moral, but Papa was not the One to voice them to. «What happened to your face?» I asked.

Papa touched the bandaged scratches which striped his left cheek from eyebrow to chin. «Ganymede resisted arrest. I need you to look at something.»

He pulled back the curtains, baring the remainder of the room. The right wall was a great window overlooking Romanova's streets, eerie since an emergency curfew kept the shops and alleys dead. Martin and his Emperor sat in silence against the room's far wall, performing a thousand tasks over their trackers as they awaited the return of the Patient Whose gurney should have nested in the space between their chairs. Two other beds stood parallel to mine against the near wall. The farther held a patient barely recognizable as human, mummified in bandages and gel slabs, as one might imagine Frankenstein's creation in its unnatural gestation; the near bed held a body bag.

«Who's that in the far bed?» I asked, craning my neck as I tried to make out a sense of height or build through the bandage cocoon.

Papa sniffed. «If they recover, the Chief Director of the Mitsubishi.»

«Director Andō! What happened to them? The mob?»

«No, not Andō.» He half laughed. «That's Andō's successor-designate, Dominic Seneschal.»

«Dominic? Director Andō didn't choose Jehovah?» I did not see at first the significance of servant inheriting instead of Master; it seemed trivial, such was the power of confidence's golden illusion.

Papa nodded. «I didn't see that one coming. No telling yet if Dominic will live to take the post, though.»

I peered at the bandages, mounded thick like snow. «What did Sniper do to them?»

Papa almost smiled. «They did it to themself. Dominic grabbed on to the outside of the car when Sniper took off out of the river, and managed to stay on all the way to Antwerp. They should be dead.»

«They rode on the outside of the car?»

«Full speed, wedged themself on somehow. The engineers always said it was impossible, but now they have a dozen explanations, something about a wind pocket in the inner angle, or back drafts, or something.»

Oh, miraculous chameleon, Science, who can reverse your doctrine hourly and never shake our faith! What cult ever battered by this world of doubt can help but envy you? «Will they be okay?» I asked.

Papa frowned. «The doctors say there's all kinds of damage: skin stripped off, windburns, freezing, oxygen deprivation, and they're still assessing the internal consequences. Actually, I think they're just curious to find out how Dominic did it without blacking out.»

My eyes widened. «They stayed conscious?»

«They were conscious at the end, at least, yes. Sniper stopped the car above a jail outside Antwerp, where Julia Doria-Pamphili was being held, and shot them through the window.»

«Julia?» I cried, straps straining as my startled shoulders twitched.

«Easy, there. Julia's fine, the bullet went through their heart but there was a hospital right by the jail.» He frowned. «If you can shed any light on Sniper's motives I'd be obliged, Mycroft. Had those two ever even met?»

I searched sincerely for an answer, but knew nothing then of the kidnapping and day of passion that had been in payment for giving Carlyle Foster—Kraye de la Trémoïlle to Dominic. «If Sniper wanted Julia dead they'd aim for the head,» I answered, «not the heart. That's all I know.»

Papa shrugged. «Before Sniper could take off again, Dominic jumped them from the car roof and held on hard enough to strangle.»

«Sniper's dead?»

With decades, even the unzipping of a body bag grows routine. «This is what Dominic caught.» Papa eased the bag open, baring the familiar face with open eyes still lifelike. «Sniper's cameras never left it for a second, it can't be a substitution. This is what shot J.E.D.D. Mason.» He aimed a light, highlighting the crinkling of synthetic skin, and shards of plastic vertebrae which poked out through the crushed gel of the poseable neck. «There's no robotics or modifications inside. Serial number checks out and everything. For all science can tell me it's a normal Sniper Doll.» He held my eyes. «Thisbe introduced me to Private Croucher.»

A sob gave my chest and shoulder their first taste of the incision's pain breaking through the anesthesia. «Then it *was* Bridger's fault. Bridger said it was, I thought they just felt guilty that they couldn't stop it.»

«Bridger brought this to life?»

I almost laughed. «It's your fault too, Papa. You fried Bridger's electronics when you tried to corner them at the Sniper Doll museum. They lost contact with their little soldiers, and must have animated a Sniper Doll to help protect them. Bridger always said Sniper looked fun and friendly.»

Papa's voice darkened. «Then you agree the real Sniper was never at Romanova?»

I nodded. «They're out there somewhere, watching, and, knowing Sniper, they won't rest until they've killed Jehovah again. They'll try again, soon.»

Papa almost smiled. «Sniper's ahead of you.» He reached to my tracker and set it to mimic his as he flicked through pictures of Sniper standing beside images of burning Brussels and other fresh events to prove that it still lived. Papa's sigh was not an easy one. «They're transmitting manifestos in all directions, swearing they won't stop until they've liberated the world from Madame and Epicurus Mason, and calling on all free people who still love their Hives to join them.»

I expected to see Sniper smug in the photos, the showman's glint in its eye as it paraded costumes tailored for its new Rogue Assassin persona, but there was no play now. It wore its Humanist boots, a practical shirt, almost Hiveless gray, and its dark eyes were alight with a grave, steady fire, almost a grown-up's. Such a face even those who no longer play with dolls might follow.

«Go back,» I snapped, «two images ago, was that Tully Mardi with Sniper?»

«Yes.» Papa scrolled back to a still shot of Sniper and the Enemy, shaking hands before a wall-sized world map like two freshly allied heads of state. «We'd detained Tully for inciting riot, but Sniper's people busted them out, and Tully went, the fool. I would have dropped the charges if they'd cooperated, but now they've got resisting arrest and conspiracy and all sorts of crimes on their record. Sniper's no fool, though. Tully's stuck with Sniper now, on the run together, and Tully's making speeches at Sniper's side about how the war they've been predicting all this time is this one, Sniper against Epicurus Mason, independent Hives against unifying the Hives. By implication it's also Tully against you, with those who like you on Jehovah's side and those who don't on Sniper's. How many Humanists was it who put you on the Wish List again? Nine hundred million?»

I let my head fall back against the pillow, feeling the strange ease of one about to die, who sees the headsman's axe halted midair by royal pardon. «It doesn't matter anymore. We have Bridger.»

«So?»

I smiled. «So no one will care about Sniper's rebellion when Jehovah starts handing out immortality. That's why They've come to power now, don't you see? It's Providence. For the first time in history all the governments of the Earth will be united, not one common ruler right away but one Heir binding all rulers together. Ἄναξ Jehovah will make sure Bridger's gifts are distributed evenly to all, with no Hive privileged and none left out. They'll save everyone.»

The old man could not help but cock an eyebrow. «Bridger can really do that?»

«Bridger can do literally anything, they just need protection and support to do it. With Jehovah to oversee the transition they'll save everyone, even the dead. You think Tully Mardi will keep preaching when Bridger resurrects their parents? And Apollo?»

"Where is he? Where is my Son!" It was Madame's voice, shrill with love, which trumpeted down the hall outside in flagrant violation of a patient's right to hush.

Utopia: "We're running tests. They'll be back shortly. Please wait in here."
Madame: "What tests? Is there a problem?"
Utopia: "We're just gathering data. Please wait inside."
Madame: "No! Enough waiting! I must see my Son!"
Felix Faust: "Let it be, Joyce, you're scaring them enough already."

Caesar and Martin rose as the lady entered, Papa too. She wore a sleeved traveling cloak, black velvet and long enough to cover the full circumference of her skirts, like the outer leaf of a head of lettuce. She had shed nothing of her home costume, not the mask of makeup, not the quaint block-heeled shoes that made speed impossible; even the wig stayed, silvery beneath her hood, though far less monumental than her usual.

Caesar spoke first. "You came?"

"Of course I came!" she cried. "It's been a nightmare, Cornel! I haven't ridden in a car in fifty years! I had Utopia take me, but Romanova has all these ridiculous emergency restrictions. They kept asking questions, said I needed 'known Members' to vouch for me. Flagrant Blacklaw discrimination!"

The scowl on Felix Faust told the other half of her story: his sister, monstrous in her skirts and corset, clinging to his arm, while he, still in the Brillist sweater of his public office, drew stares like a magnet.

"But what's happening, Cornel?" Madame pressed, seizing Caesar's arm too without relinquishing her brother's. "Is there any news?"

"Jehovah's fine," MASON answered.

"Is it true what I saw on the news? They came back from the dead!"

"As next of kin, Madame, I'm sure you'll be the first to hear when anything is certain. For now, we wait."

Her eyes, wrath-hot and hungry for a culprit, locked on Martin. "You've some nerve, sitting here cozy when your master nearly died. Why didn't you throw yourself in front of the bullet? That's what you're for, isn't it?"

No words have power over Martin in Caesar's presence save Caesar's own. "No, Madame, it's not."

Her wrath would not fade easily. "Even Dominic was some use. I hear he pursued the assassin. Was he victorious?"

"Best leave that issue to me, Madame," Papa interceded. "The less you say about revenge, the less likely Dominic here is to wake up to charges of unauthorized use of lethal force." Papadelias had already closed the body bag again and drawn a curtain to hide it, but the bandage cocoon that held the wreck of Dominic lay bare.

"Oh! Dominic!" Madame cried, drawing Faust and Caesar close across her like doors, as if she feared the gore might leap out and contaminate her. « My poor pup! »

"The doctors have done all they can." MASON pried her off, and closed the door. "I have a question for you, Madame."

She frowned at his tone, a different kind of serious. "What is it, Cornel?"

"I know there is nothing to keep you from lying to me, but I must ask, and if our long friendship is not enough to entitle me to the truth, I hope you understand that I am much better able to tolerate wrongs honestly revealed than lies uncovered later."

She blinked prettily. "What lies? What has you so concerned?"

"Did you plan this?"

"Of course I didn't plan it!" she shrieked, seizing his arm again. "You think I'd try to kill our Son?"

MASON tried, but failed, to pull his hand away. "Not that, the rest. You knew Casimir Perry was Merion Kraye. Did you know the rest? The Seven-Ten list theft, DeLupa betraying the Anonymous, the exposure of O.S. Did you plan it? Did you know?"

With only a brief frown at MASON's coldness, Madame shifted onto her brother's arm. "No, but it is my doing nonetheless."

"Explain," Caesar demanded.

"I shall be honest," she announced, her voice light with surprise, as if she had expected herself to decide the contrary. "You're right, I do owe it to you, Cornel, for our long friendship, which I hope will not end here,"—her smile beamed frankness—"and I know you will deal more kindly with me if I am frank with you. Besides,"—she glanced at Papa—"I have done nothing prosecutable, or even malicious. But nonetheless, I take responsibility. I did not plan this." Her voice was lovely, giddy, as if elated by the catharsis of confession. "I simply resurrected the weapons with which it was done. I made Danaë the sort of woman a man would burn the world for. I made Merion Kraye and Andō and my Ganymede the sort of men who would betray each other, and nurse vengeance for decades, and not just them. Ancelet, and Spain, and even you had jealous days in your youth, remember, Cornel? And you in the inner circle are hardly my only clients. I have dozens of girls and boys, each with dozens of suitors who have been seducing, betraying, dueling, and stalking each other for fifty years. The losers are banished from my house and, finding they can no longer take satisfaction elsewhere, they channel their appetites into grudges against the victors who still enjoy my favor, and high offices. There are many hundreds of talented young things like Kraye out there who, thanks to my children, have no goal in this world beyond revenge on some rival I exalted over them."

"And on yourself too, of course," her brother interrupted.

"Of course, myself as well," she conceded, smiling at tired Felix as she squeezed his arm, "but that's a danger I'm prepared for. The world isn't so prepared. Kraye as Perry proved the most talented at marshaling this little army of avengers, but I'm sure Papadelias will discover many co-conspirators who helped Perry create this chaos, so they could wreak revenge on whichever Director or Senator or Member of Parliament or whatever stole their love. The Eighteenth-Century aristocracy seduced, betrayed, and corrupted itself until its world self-destructed into revolution. I didn't have to destroy you, Cornel. I just turned all of you into Eighteenth-Century aristocrats and let you do it yourselves."

Whatever Madame's tone, MASON had no more reason to believe this was the whole truth than you do, reader. "Why?" he asked. "Why do all that?"

"Because I realized I could." She laughed even as she said it, as if hearing the childishness in her own tone. "Honestly, it was too tempting, all these fantastic weapons shut up in old etiquette manuals and romances, where no one but me recognized what they could do if someone brought them back into use. When you were a kid, did you never have the urge to build an atom bomb, just to prove with your own hands that people could?"

MASON shifted his stance, his weak foot weakening. "And you didn't care what happened to the world? To my Empire?"

She gave the matter some quick moments' thought. "I did care. I did, but this world already had all the signs of being on the brink of some great change, you've known that for years. Cataclysm was coming. I just thought I could shape the great change, make it my sort, the Eighteenth-Century sort. That way, instead of chaos, it would be a familiar kind of great change, something someone would know how to shape, and take in hand."

"And conquer?" MASON supplied. "You saw the chance to seize power during the cataclysm, and rule through your son."

"Rule through Jehovah?" She sighed. "No. Perhaps, a long time ago, when I was planning my pregnancy, I was setting things up to have you all pass power to my child so I could rule through them, but when the child was actually born, I didn't want to raise a pawn, I couldn't. You know I'm sincere, Caesar, in my way. I love the Eighteenth Century. I fell in love reading about it at Senseminary, that great moment when humanity realized experiments didn't just have to be done with sciences, they could be done with morals and religion, too. I wanted to do that, run an experiment like the American Experiment, or greater. I couldn't resist the chance to finish what my heroes started, not just the humanitarians like the Patriarch and the romantics like Jean-Jacques, but the underbelly, La Mettrie, Diderot, de Sade. The Enlightenment tried to remake society in Reason's image: rational laws, rational religion; but the ones who really thought it through realized morality itself was just as artificial as the aristocracies and theocracies they were sweeping away. Diderot theorized that a new En-lightened Man could be raised with Reason in place of conscience, a cold calculator who would find nothing good or bad beyond what his own analysis decided. They had no way to achieve one back then, but I did it. I raised an Alien."

MASON took a deep breath. "You have raised many aliens: Dominic, Ganymede, one might add Perry."

Lacking a fan to veil her mouth, Madame could not help but laugh in Caesar's face. "I appreciate the compliment, Cornel, but the others are dif-ferent, based on the realities of the Enlightenment, not its darkest dream. No. Even I only had the resources to do it once. Jehovah is it. The rest are either tools or practice, but Jehovah was raised with everything, all philos-ophers, all our languages, equal access to all the contradictory thinking of our Hives and of the past, so the many beliefs annihilated one another, leav-ing the canvas blank and ready. Those people our world respects most, emperors and kings, Jehovah saw fucking like animals since before He knew the difference between beast and man. No child could absorb social values after that. I birthed a Being Who believes in nothing He did not conceive

Himself. I hadn't realized Enlightened Man would turn out to be a God. Our Jehovah wants omnipotence, Cornel. He needs it, feels its absence as a depravation, just as much as you would with a blindfold. I can't give Him omnipotence, but I can at least use this great change to help Him conquer more of the world than Xerxes or Alexander or any other God-King ever ruled. If being the head of the Leviathan is the closest to godhood a human being can achieve, then I will help Jehovah eat up all the Leviathans."

Had you smelled Hobbes at work in Madame before, reader? He from whose brute shadow not even sun-bright John Locke could wholly free us? The Hive, the nation, multitudes united into one Leviathan with the Sovereign as its head, is, as Freud might put it, another of mankind's prosthetic gods: deputies substitute for omnipresence, laws for Justice, welfare for Divine Love, the long reach of the military for the angel with the flaming sword. I had not until this moment imagined that Jehovah would consent to being Master of the world, but a lost God, stripped of His native omnipotence like an amputee of his rightful limbs, might take every prosthesis offered Him.

The Father of Men and Gods, to grant Caesar the most appropriate of Zeus's titles, listened with patience to Madame's words, as he always had, whether in the privacy of her boudoir, the philosophisexual climax of a debauch, or at their first meeting, when he was still a young *Familiaris* brought to Paris by Charlemagne Guildbreaker for some discreet recreation. "Did you know this would lead to war?" he asked at last.

Madame blinked. "War?"

"War," he repeated, cold. "This 'great change' you say you felt was coming, you can't be the only person who hasn't realized it means war."

She laughed. "Cornel, we're sensible modern people, we've outgrown war."

"Outgrown?" he snapped. "How can you still have no inkling of the warning signs? Kohaku Mardi's numbers, the Censor's predictions, O.S., Sniper, Tully Mardi; Apollo died for this, Aeneas—even the original Enlightenment ended in bloody revolution! What were you thinking, unleashing that?"

Madame concentrated for some moments, like a bloodhound sniffing for traces of something infinitely subtle. "Fine, yes, I suppose war did occur to me as a possible side effect, or bloody revolution at least, but that's not a problem. War is useful. The names of warriors and conquerors last a lot longer than those of peacetime heroes. What better way for our Son to eclipse Alexander than to fight and win a true World War?"

MASON seized her arm, hard. "And you don't care who gets hurt?"

"Steady on, Cornel," Felix interceded.

"Not one word, Felix!" MASON thundered. "You knew your sister was doing experiments a thousand times more dangerous than rearing set-sets. You didn't care who got hurt either!"

Madame tugged against Caesar's grip, drawing his attention back. "Of course I care who gets hurt! Jehovah is the Alien raised free from conscience, I'm not. I've tried every perversion in Sade's book, but I still feel bad when I hurt people." She sighed. "And imagine my disappointment when Jehovah came out more horrified by homicide than anyone. Our poor young God; the war will be so hard on Him. I trust you'll help us get it settled quickly."

"Get it settled quickly?" Caesar's grip tightened, threatening to snap her wrist like a doll's thin porcelain. "And just how do you imagine we'll fight this war? You're obsessed with the Eighteenth Century, have you never looked at what came later? Wars get worse when people know less about them. What is war going to be like now that we don't even have territory? A war of all against all fought in every single street!"

She winced at his grasp. "Technology changes between every war. People adapt."

"The problem isn't technology," he seethed, "it's ignorance! In the First World War the first commander of the Russian forces boasted that he hadn't read a strategy book written in the past century. Germany's attack plan was based on the Battle of Marathon—490 B.C.! Result: disaster. Well, everything's Marathon to us now. There haven't been strategy books written in three hundred years! How am I supposed to imagine sending people into battle? What will they do? How fast will they break? How long should they train? What's a big enough force to feel confident enough to take on a mission? What's a reasonable length of time to leave them in a combat zone before they go insane? War makes people into monsters. How do I keep them from shooting themselves? How do I keep them from raping and pillaging? Brussels is in flames—how long until that happens in the capital, and all over my Empire?"

She tried to pull away. "Caesar, please! The propaganda of the name aside, Romanova isn't your capital, it's Ancelet's, or was. Romanova's never really had an Emperor before, but if it's anyone's now it's Jehovah's, and if you can't control yourself I'll have Him tell you to pack off back to Alexandria where you belong."

I do not believe Caesar is a violent man by nature; none of them were until we made them so, Madame and Dominic and I, creatures too terrible for words without violence to truly touch us. It was Caesar's right hand which held Madame's wrist, but his left rose, with its stark black sleeve, poised to strike. Before his fist could fall, a fiercer hand wrenched his fingers off the Lady and slammed him backwards with a fast strike to the thorax. Speed made Madame's defender almost visible, as ripples betray a fish, the edges of sleeves and hood flagging like slices of displaced space as the Griffincloth's computer failed to keep up with combat's savage speed. "Apol . . ." Caesar's awed voice hardened to iron even as he toppled, ". . . Saladin!"

Safe behind her invisible guardian, Madame pulled his hood back and patted the hairless scalp above the hairless face which the vizor still made seem half Apollo's. "Good boy."

Wrath more than combat winded Caesar. "You let that monster out of its cage?"

"Stay where you are, Papadelias," Madame warned, her quick eye catching the Commissioner General as he leapt toward his quarry like a child toward a mound of birthday presents. "He's legally my guard dog now, and you're no dogcatcher."

Papa stopped at Caesar's side, the gel-cuffs hungry in his hands. "I think a judge can resolve the species issue easily enough."

Madame shook her head, today's modest wig shining in the hospital light. "If you push to have him declared a human being, before you can get a judge to issue an arrest warrant I'll have him certified mentally incompetent, not responsible for his actions past or present, and remanded to my custody as guardian, beyond your reach. Alternatively we can leave him legally my dog, and if he ever hurts anyone you can force me to have him put down. Which do you prefer?"

The Commissioner General did not answer, but his slack face declared *touché.*

"Both of them?" Wrath's quake hardened MASON's fists. "You want me to let Saladin run free like Mycroft?"

"Not free, Caesar. In my custody." Her voice grew syrup sweet. "Saladin's a good dog, he won't run off, will you?"

Saladin slid back behind Madame, the Utopian coat settling over him until only a trained eye could track him by the shadows between the hem and floor. "No, ma'am! Are you kidding? First time I've ever had a mentor I could actually learn from, I'm not quitting."

"A mentor?" MASON repeated.

Saladin laughed. "All these years I thought the only thing for a Cynic to do when we realize all the social rules are crap was to go live free like an animal, but Madame's learned better. They didn't have to cut themself off from society to keep from getting tangled in the puppet strings. All they had to do was genuinely not care." He prowled toward me around the circumference of Madame's skirts. "I don't get it, Mycroft. We thought Cornel MASON was a keen mind, but you and I can spot a predator at fifty yards—how come they can't after sleeping with one for twenty years?"

My chest did not have strength enough to laugh, but the attempt gave anesthesia's gradual withdrawal an opportunity to highlight my incision with lines of pain. Madame did it. One night, sitting by his cage with tender musings and philosophy, and she made a convert even of my Saladin. Diogenes the Cynic was our childhood mentor, Saladin's and mine, the first of our wretched race to realize that honor, glory, ambition, wealth, success, all are artificial things, and that pursuing them only makes us miserable. True happiness is to live as Diogenes and Saladin dared, like a dog by the side of the road, eating when the urge comes, pissing when the urge comes, saving all one's energy for the happy exercises of the mind, which no tyrant can deprive you of. Legend tells us that Alexander himself visited the wise old man, offering Diogenes anything in the world the Conqueror could grant; the Cynic asked only that the Great King stop blocking the sunlight so he could keep reading. Saladin never expected to find a living teacher closer to Diogenes's model than himself, but Madame too drew kings to her silk-lined barrel with rumor's allure. It is true that, unlike Diogenes, Madame took advantage of how much one can exploit a king's offer when one doesn't care if one actually gets anything, but she who could play the puppet web like harp strings was still undeniably closer to Diogenes's ideal than Saladin, who dared not touch the strings for fear of being snared. When we first committed ourselves to the Cynic path, we had lamented that there was no master of the School to guide us eager novices. This was not a wish Saladin had expected Providence to grant.

The Father of Men and Gods faced the shadow cast by Apollo's stolen armor. "I have long known what Madame is, monster. Do not presume to understand my thoughts."

Madame perked. "Then you don't mind if I keep him? I know you can't stop me if Papa can't, but I won't keep him if it distresses you, Cornel. I want you to be comfortable around me."

MASON faced her squarely. "I thank you for your honesty in answering my questions, Madame."

She frowned. "What will you do now, Cornel? You're the trickiest.

Unlike the others, you can change any day the name sealed in the Successor's Vault in Alexandria, and neither public opinion, nor law, nor I, can stop you."

MASON: "The law forbids speculation about the *Imperator Destinatus.*"
Madame: "He needs omnipotence, Caesar. Yours is the largest Leviathan; you can take the biggest blindfold off him."
MASON: "The law forbids speculation about the *Imperator Destinatus.*"
Madame: "He is your Son. He really is, more than anybody else's, your Son."
MASON: "You say that to a lot of men."
Madame: "I lie to a lot of men, but not to you."
MASON: "What about Spain?"
Madame: "Nurture matters more than nature. Jehovah could be Kraye's son but They'd still be yours."
MASON: "And their mother? When Jehovah was born you promised Spain you'd marry them if the public ever learned who the child's father was. Will you break that promise?"

Madame's gaze fell away from Caesar's. "I can't deny that His Majesty has asked again that I marry him. And I've consented. With Crown Prince Leonor dead, Jehovah must be legitimated or the Spanish strat will fall apart, possibly Europe as well."

MASON turned away. "We both know Spain's views on monogamy. Things can't continue as they have been between us if you are Spain's Queen, it would eat them away inside, not to mention what the public would say."

She took the Emperor's hand. "I didn't want it like this, Cornel, you know I didn't."

He pulled away again. "You've told the truth this far, don't spoil it. If you didn't want this, you would have arranged things differently."

Madame's hurt might have been genuine. "I told you I didn't plan this, I just planned the creatures who could achieve it. You think everything went in line with my ideal? I loved Brussels. I was very proud of my Merion Kraye, I didn't want him dead. I've lost my Ganymede to the law, poor Danaë is half dead from the shock, and Bryar and Ancelet will never forgive me. I loved them, Cornel. And I love you."

I omit the next few exchanges, reader. MASON deserves some privacy, and what matter is it to history, the sentimental terms and gestures with which old lovers say goodbye?

"Jehovah!"

They wheeled him back to us now, lying on a gurney, not because of weakness, but in deference to the hospital habit of circumscribing patients in the geometric borders of a bed.

"My darling Boy! Are You all right?" Even Madame does not hug Jehovah anymore, not that her Son objected, but His black gaze chills even her too much. "How are You feeling? Does it hurt?"

He answered with a string of all tongues, interwoven like pointillist brush strokes, meaningless to untrained ears.

"What?"

The doctor was a tiny Utopian, trailing a coat of molten stone which made the room into the layers of a volcanic mountainside, hardening at a century per second. She shared Madame's frown. "No one's been able to understand much of what they've said since they arrived. Short exchanges make sense, but nothing long. But I understand that's normal when Mike is stressed, yes?"

I smiled hearing the grandest yet humblest of His many names. "It is," I answered, straining against the straps as I leaned forward far enough to see Jehovah's eyes. "Usually I translate when He's excited or upset."

The doctor nodded. "What're they saying now?"

Men say Jehovah's tone never changes, that He stays equally cold before the Senate House and gentle Heloïse. It is almost true, but Felix Faust, whose expertise can read the temper of an earwig, tells me there is one exception, slight, an ease which tints the pitch of His voice in one circumstance only: when I arrive. The Brillist definition of a bash'mate adds to the legal one, not just that you live together, but that you speak the same language, ideally the same group of languages, though mixed-tongue bash'es birth their own pidgin, each member injecting favorite foreign phrases into English. Bash' by this definition is not just a group of people, but that special group of people with whom one can communicate completely. Madame has never answered whether she was pleased or angry when her Great Experiment found another who could comingle English, Latin, French, Spanish, a little German, Japanese, and Greek.

"He's happy," I translated. "He says . . . He says proof that a God's universe survives His death means . . . means . . ."—tears leaked from me even as I struggled to paraphrase—"it means He doesn't have to worry anymore that, if all human beings are Gods like Him, then each death might destroy an entire universe. It reduces the possible tragedy of human history by a factor of infinity per human being that has ever died."

Each in that room—MASON, Martin, Faust, Madame, the Utopian

doctors who have studied Him since their surrender—believes in Jehovah's divinity to some different degree, some not at all, some partly, some completely, but whatever their beliefs they all believe that He believes it. So all paused now to consider how this new revelation would affect Him, and through Him everyone. Martin wept a few tears, delight at seeing so dear a Master relieved of that cruel fear which had gnawed at Him as viciously as the eagle at Prometheus. I sobbed outright.

The Utopian nodded pensively. "How do they feel physically?"

Jehovah answered, metaphysics pouring around me like a waterfall which cleanses soul instead of flesh. "He says He finally understands why He had to be born in a physical body to communicate," I interpreted. "He . . . He accepts it now. He says it was hard making contact, but He's glad This Universe's God gave Him a life here. They were both lonely." Lonely . . . glad . . . I do not dare call it translation, this blasphemy, inadequate, unclean; I may as well be a sighted mole describing to my blind kin the wonders of Luna City. 'Lonely' was nothing to the phrase which captured all the longing and eternity of Dante's Hell, and 'glad' not a thousandth part of the joy felt by this Sentience which had endured so long with nothing but toys and worms for company, but now heard at last the longed-for whisper through the dark, "I'm here."

"He says," I continued, "that when He died He left, and existed only in His universe for a few moments, but He still remembered this one. He understands now that in His universe He's always had the memories of His life in this one as Jehovah Mason, but without being born and experiencing time He couldn't understand before how to sort those memories linearly, they were just thoughts and opinions to Him, not a continuity. Now that He's had a chance to pass in and out of this universe and time again, He recognizes the memories for what they are. He's always had them . . . well, there is no 'always' without time, but they're part of Him, His Personality, His Self. He says those memories helped form the judgments He used in making His Own Universe. He says living here is what taught Him how to make it different there, better, richer. He used to think it was cruel making Him live here, but He sees now it was the only way This Universe's God could find to reach out and share the example of His Creation, so Jehovah could respond and grow. The beginning of their Great Conversation. He says . . . He . . ." I groped for words to do His feelings justice, but how could I? Imagine yourself a child born blind and deaf, who has spent all your life in pain, but you realize now that that pain, that burn, that stab in the dark that has never let up, was the only means a desperate kinsman could find to prove that you are not alone. I don't understand why it must be so hard for Gods to reach Each Other. Perhaps because Each is omnipotent within the perimeter of Its Own Mind, and reaching Another requires conceiving something outside One's Self, not easy when there are no senses, no external world, no hands driven by instinct to grope and reach out, and no 'out.' Whatever it takes for Utopia to make First Contact across the sea of stars, a thousand years' research, a thousand years frozen in flight, a thousand thousand lives, it will still be an expansion of the infant's first grope toward what lies beyond its reach; this was harder. "He says He'll return the favor if He can."

The Emperor did not have time for metaphysics. "What will you do now, *Fili?*"

This was, for once, easy. "He doesn't know. While He was in His universe He remembered His whole life, before and after His first death, but here He remembers only the past."

His father frowned. "I meant, what do you intend to do?"

"He says He will accept the powers offered Him," I answered, "and face His enemy. He says Sniper must . . ." I choked. "Sniper must die."

You will not be surprised, reader, to find His mother beaming with delight to hear her Masterpiece's defect—His fear of killing—finally corrected. Are you surprised to learn that His Imperial father smiled too? You should not be. He who wears that black sleeve, he who limps still from the cruel testing enforced by his predecessor, knows that certain strengths are necessary in a ruler.

I continued my translation: "As leader of O.S., Sniper will never stop, or compromise. It must . . . it must die." I stumbled here because I lied, though a lie is hardly a greater sin than the mockery of translation; He did not say in the abstract Sniper must die, he commanded that I, Mycroft Canner, must track it down and kill it. "Tully Mardi must . . . publicly submit . . . but not be killed, they would make too powerful a symbol dead. The truth, about Casimir Perry, Jehovah's succession, Madame, Bridger, all of it must be revealed to the public, so people may make up their own minds which side to fight on in the . . ."

I froze, but the others knew what came next, for, of all Jehovah's mingled tongues, English has the clearest, most concise word for 'War.'

"No!" My voice cracked. "Ἄναξ, there doesn't have to be a war now. You'll stop it! We have Bridger. You'll stop it, You and Bridger together, and You'll make a new—"

He spoke again, and sobs wracked me until I was glad of the Cannergel that held me down.

"What is it, Mycroft? Mycroft?"

I would not translate, not even for Caesar, but for you I shall, my precious, distant reader. I was wrong. That's how He began it: Mycroft, you are wrong. He sensed at once conviction in me, as out of place as a gun in Heloïse's hand, or a healing salve in Dominic's. I had believed that Providence sent Bridger and Jehovah to this Earth at the same moment, so they might meet, and Jehovah receive at last His greeting from This Universe's God. This had proved true, but, fool that I was, I had assumed that one kindness dropped by Providence meant more would come. Yes, Bridger and Jehovah were placed on this Earth to meet each other, but meet they had. First Contact was done. For all we knew, Sniper would shoot Jehovah dead before Bridger could return, or it would spirit Bridger away to use his gifts for Sniper's side and wreck Jehovah's empire. Nothing was certain. Nothing under Providence is ever certain until an agent goes and tries and makes it so.

"Release me."

All turned, startled by the speed with which my grief gave way to the cold demand.

Papa smiled. "Not a chance."

"I must find Bridger."

He shook his head. "You need to recover from surgery first."

I made a grab for Papa's wrist, but the straps held me too tight. "Bridger is everything: immortality, resurrection, cure, the weapon to protect the world, the weapon to destroy it, anything we can conceive. No one knows what this war will be like except that it will be the worst in history. Nothing but Bridger can guarantee that the human race will even survive. I'm the only one here who knows how to find them. Sniper knows about Bridger too; Sniper will be after them. I must bring them here, now, safe. Nothing in history has ever been so important."

Saladin moved as I spoke. Only I could see him, accustomed as I was to tracing the ripple-shadow which betrayed the Griffincloth. The Cannergel that held me was firm as adamant—but the same genius that had crafted it had filled Apollo's coat with blades to slice through adamant like tissue. We didn't need them. The Commissioner General and MASON together, on their authority as human beings more than as my custodians under the law, released me.

"Come back safe."

Saladin helped me rise. "Should I c—"

I winded him with a blow before he could complete the offer. "Stay here," I urged, apologizing with a kiss. "The world needs Ἄναξ Jehovah right now, and Jehovah needs a translator."

CHAPTER THE TWENTY-FIRST

Hero

I LEFT YOU BEFORE WITH TOO LITTLE OF DIOGENES. MADAME'S heroes, the Patriarch, the Philosophe, de Sade, you now know well, but the one mind in history that young Saladin and I acknowledged as our role model, him you doubtless see as just another Greek among many, instead of what he was: the most successful man in history. The great breakthrough of our age is supposed to be that we measure success by happiness, admiring a man for how much he enjoyed his life, rather than how much wealth or fame he hoarded, that old race with no finish line. Diogenes with his barrel and his sunlight lived every hour of his life content, while Alexander fought and bled, mourned friends, faced enemies, and died unsatisfied. Diogenes is greater. Or does that past-tainted inner part of you—the part that still parses 'thee' and 'thou' and 'he' and 'she'—still think that happiness alone is not achievement without legacy? Diogenes has a legacy. Diogenes ruled nothing, wrote nothing, taught nothing except by the example of his life to passersby, but, so impressed were those bypassers, that, after the better part of three millennia, we still know this about him. How many kings have three millennia erased? How many authors? How many books? I lied to the Utopians, reader. It is fitting that I confess before the end. I never intended to finish Apollo's *Iliad*. There was a storybook in there among the war plans, Apollo's giant robots, and Utopia expected me to finish what my victim started. It is ingrained in us, in them above all, this conviction that writing is the best immortality. They feared you would forget Apollo, as Alexander feared that he would fade away with no Homer to immortalize him. But Diogenes needed no Homer, so I do not think Apollo needed his *Iliad*. If his name survives three thousand years, that storybook will not be why. So I lied. This is the book I finished for Apollo, not his own. Still, it no longer matters. What do a few paper chapters matter when Bridger has already made so much so real?

<Major? Are you getting this?> My fingers labored at my tracker, testing different frequencies, hoping that the text function at least might have

recovered from whatever blast Papadelias had used that scrambled Bridger's electronics.

Major: <I feared you'd take much longer. Where are you?>
I: <East side service entrance of the Sniper Doll Museum. Are you inside?>
Major: <I am. Croucher's deserted, and they still have Stander-G, but the rest are with me, including Mommadoll. We're in the main showroom, pinned down under one of the dolls. There's someone here with very keen eyes. Whenever we try to move they shoot.>
I: <Has Bridger come back yet?>
Major: <No sign.>
I: <You're sure?>
Major: <What do you know that I don't?>
I: <You came here before because Bridger said they needed something from the toys they left here. If they didn't get it, then I thought they might come back for it.>
Major: <If so, I wouldn't know it. No visibility.>
I: <I'm moving in now.>

I dove full speed from the door to the cover of the nearest doll. No shot. Then, when I thought I was in cover, a bullet proved me wrong, grazing the pad of fat behind my left kidney. Sniper. It knew I would know the spot, clean skin until now, framed by the scars left by the explosion and those from where Seine Mardi shot me. Time and again, when Sniper and I rested after sparring and the athlete listened bright-eyed to the stories I could tell of every scar, its fingers would tickle that spot, as if marking out a patch of brick to add its own stroke to the graffiti. Sniper asked me once who I thought was the most dangerous person in the world. It was an impossible question, since in those days of secrets I could not mention any of the true contenders: Madame, the Major, Saladin, Tully still mongering the Mardis' war, Dominic, Danaë, who with a broken heart could bring a curse down on her enemy to rival Hera's, and, of course, the two true rivals: Bridger and Jehovah. I tried to sidestep, answering that it depended on the circumstances, for there could be no worse political adversary than the Anonymous, but if the question is being murdered in my bed I would dread no one more than Cato Weeksbooth. Sniper insisted on the abstract, and, succumbing to a slave's instinct to please, I answered that the most dangerous person in the world must be either Sniper itself, or me. I thought I was lying.

"I won't let you take the kid, Mycroft!"

Sniper's voice rose unfindable from somewhere in the ranks of hundreds of Snipers posed on their chairs and stands and pedestals, modeling all the fashions, costumes, and expressions coveted by a lustful world. The darkness of the closed museum did not do them justice, but in light they are a panorama of obsessions: aristocratic Snipers, slobby Snipers, so shrewd-seeming in a Mitsubishi suit, so strict in a Mason's, mild in a Cousin's, eerie in a Utopian coat which, like some perverse Geppetto, turns all passers into jointed marionettes, complete with strings.

"Why don't we let Bridger decide which side to take?" I called out, sheltering behind the bulk of a space-suited Sniper.

"Not a chance!" Its voice was as clear as a nightmare when the psyche forgets to add the realism of competing sounds. "The kid brings toys to life. You think this is coincidence? You think I'd give that up?"

"Bridger's not here for you, Sniper!"

"They're not here 'for' you or your Jehovah Mason either!" it shot back, and fairly. "They're here for everyone, the whole world. Even your bizarre theology must admit that."

Sniper was moving, I could tell that much, but the vaulted ceiling scattered sound, and through the mist of paranoia every plastic finger seemed to twitch. "Are you the real Sniper?" I asked.

It laughed. "Since we're talking about someone who's spent their whole life trying to become a living doll, I'd say I'm more real than the original!" A lesser marksman would have punctuated the declaration with a hail of shots, but Sniper does not fire unless it might hit. "You raised a very trusting kid, Mycroft. I could've convinced them to animate ten of me if I'd made up ten excuses."

I crouched, threading my way along a row of dolls modeling Sniper's pentathlon uniforms. "Where is the original?"

"Doing their duty as O.S., I imagine. Don't think having the Anonymous on your side will turn the tide. It may take weeks or months, but when the public really thinks about what Jehovah Mason is, they'll call a rat a rat and join me, not all of them, but enough."

Major: <You're getting close. We're under the doll in the white ballet outfit, three rows left, four up.>

I: <Should I come get you, Major?>

Major: <No. Keep Sniper busy. We need to evacuate Mommadoll.>

"You should've told me about Jehovah, Mycroft!" Even as I drew close, Sniper's voice was hard to pinpoint as the reflective ceiling scattered sound and light in shards. "We could've stopped this years ago, before any of the Hives got ripped apart."

"You're the one who's ripping them apart now, Sniper! Jehovah just wants peace. You've seen Bridger. If we're going to spread Bridger's gifts to everyone, it's best to have one united Voice to lead the transformation, Someone Who's thought a lot about world-changing questions: death, immortality, resurrection."

"Someone who MASON raised to remake the world in MASON's image?" Sniper called back. "The world's already had too much of that!"

I took a ball from a cricket-playing Sniper and threw it far to my left, hoping the sound would draw its fire and attention. Nothing. "People will die if there's a war, Sniper!" I called. "Thousands, maybe millions of people. Is that really what O.S. is for? You've spent your life protecting the many at the cost of the few."

"I'm no slave of numbers, Mycroft." Its light voice darkened as much as it can. "O.S. protects the Hive system, this way of life, a way of life worth dying for. And killing for."

"Jehovah's will be even better!"

"Jehovah's would be world dictatorship!"

"You don't know Jehovah, He . . ." No. This wasn't the right tactic. I had to goad Sniper, make it angry, make it rash. "There are more ways to be famous than to have the highest body-count to your name!"

At that it did shoot, a single bullet, close enough to pierce my shadow as I rolled for cover. "Don't insult me!" it called. "I could've crashed the cars. I had millions of hostages, I could've slammed every Mason flying into a Mason's house, or drowned Madame's in flames like Perry did to Brussels. I didn't. My duty is to protect the Hive system, Masons included. If the system can't keep going without an old-fashioned revolution, it's my duty to lead it."

"You can't control it!" I cried. "It's been three hundred years. The Mardis worked for decades and they still had only the vaguest idea what a war would be like after all this time."

"We both know it's far simpler than that. The side with Bridger wins."

I reached a row of military Snipers now, crawling my way forward through history's bloody centuries: hoplite, centurion, knight, samurai.

"They're here, aren't they? Bridger? Can you hear me, Bridger? It's Mycroft! I just want to talk to you!"

"Go away!"

Those two words were enough; Bridger's sob-strained voice rose muffled from behind the closed door of a storage hall far to my left. I spotted Sniper now, perched as guardian on the roof of a concessions stand beside the door. I had wondered what costume Bridger would choose for the Sniper it awoke as guardian: something friendly, a Cousin's wrap perhaps, a frilled apron like Mommadoll's, or something from the heroes gallery, Sun Wukong, or Robin Hood, he did love Robin Hood. He had chosen a Servicer's uniform.

"Bridger, call Sniper off, please! Let me help! Let me tell you what's happened!"

Inching forward, I reached World War Sniper, took a toy grenade from its pack strap, pulled the replica pin, and hurled the weapon onto the platform where Sniper crouched. Knowing a real bomb was not beyond my resources, it fell for the gambit, dove, and rolled out of blast range like a dancer, perfect form, but in that instant I was on it. We grappled on the floor, a strange combat, moves that we had practiced often on Sniper's training mats, suddenly intended to actually harm. Zeal's blush lit Sniper's face, its chance at last to taste the violence sleeping in my limbs that it had often tried to coax to wakefulness. It punched my temple, smirking as if imagining the envy on real Sniper's face when it would see the bruises its proxy had inflicted. I did not have time for play.

"Bridger, help!" I cried. "It's going to kill me!"

Life left the doll, as instant as the snapping of a neck. Should I apologize? It was a lie, a dirty, cheating way to win, but combat is not sport. Even Seine Mardi fought dirty in the end.

"Go a-way, My-croft!" Panicked, shallow hiccups made Bridger's words staccato as a drum. "I'm not going to change my mind!"

I made my tone warm. "What happened in Romanova wasn't your fault."

"It is my fault! I got scared and careless, just once, and the Sniper I brought to life wrecked the whole world!"

I pried the doll's arms from around me. "That's why you need help. I'll protect you, you know I will, always!"

"You can't! Everybody knows, Mycroft! Everybody saw me, the Hive leaders, videos, the whole world. They'll all be after me now."

"That's why you need to come with me, where it's safe."

"It's not safe, even with you. I can't handle this. I can't handle the whole world hunting for me and the whole world counting on me."

I moved close to the door, calling softly through its crack, as through the pillow door of a play-fort where children run to pout. "Of course you can't handle it alone, but you're not alone. May I come in?" I tried the handle, but the lock stayed firm.

"Stay away!" He choked on the violence of his own syllables. "I don't want anybody to touch me! Nobody!"

"Okay. I'll be right here when you decide to come out. Do you want some tissues? I have some, I can stick them under the door."

Bridger sniffed to prove he didn't need them. "I did what you said, Mycroft. I watched, I spied on your Jehovah. Do you think they're actually a God like they say?"

I stole a trick from Carlyle. "What do you think?"

"I think they're scary. When I hear them talk, they're different, more different than anything else, like everything else I've ever seen is part of one familiar thing, but they're something else. Every word they say it feels like it's true, but at the same time like I shouldn't be hearing it."

I wondered whether the presence of This Universe's God in Bridger let the child sense somehow that Jehovah was separate, an Intruder in the fixed perfection of our Maker's Providence, a free and separate Will. "It's true that Jehovah's scary," I answered, "but they're also Good. We can rely on Them. They understand what you can do better than anyone. Jehovah's the right Person to help you." I could hear Bridger moving on the far side of the door, the rustle of fabric a few feet inside.

"That's not what you said before," he countered. "You said before I had to wait to meet Jehovah, that they'd twist me into something I'm not, if I met them too soon."

I smiled. He could not see, but sometimes a smile can be heard in one's tone even over distance. "You met Them when you were intended to, no earlier or later."

"They're right, aren't they?" His voice grew thin. "I'm going to destroy the world."

"Of course you aren't, you're going to save it."

"I don't like it when you lie to me. You know I'm not going to save this world, I'm going to destroy it to make a better one, just like Apollo wanted."

"Apollo never wanted that!" I snapped, glad now that he could not see my reddened face. "Apollo was willing to destroy this world to guard a better one, but only because there was no other choice. They tried to start a war now to keep Utopia from being wiped out in the war that will come when Mars is ready, but that's not what they wanted, it was never what they wanted."

I heard Bridger thumping, hunting through boxes, uncertain where my Servicer friends had packed whatever it was he came for. "I can't handle this, Mycroft. I know me, and I can't. I'm not like you and the Major and your scary friend. I'm frightened. I wanted to keep hiding until I got stronger inside. I can't face this now. I'm going to go crazy."

"No you're not. We're here to help you."

"I am! I'm going to go crazy watching a war I started. I'm going to go crazy running from a whole planet full of people who think I can grant their wishes. I'm going to go crazy having to choose between leaving dead people dead, and bringing them back and overwhelming the world with resurrected people. I'm going to go crazy trying things, and having them go wrong, over and over, with consequences nobody can predict. And I'm going to go crazy being around Jehovah."

I leaned against the door's cold panel, mirrored steel. Why? Did I hope my warmth would reach him somehow? Or, hearing his predictions, was I too weak to stand? "I know it seems impossibly hard, but we'll help you. We'll do everything we can."

Tears' hiccups made his voice shrill. "Why'd you raise me like this, Mycroft? You and the Major could've raised me stronger, like a soldier. Then maybe I could've handled this."

"Then you would've remade the world the way a soldier would. That isn't what you want, is it?"

"How do you know I haven't done that already? How do you know I didn't cause this war?"

I smiled again. "Because I trust you."

"I don't want to destroy this world. I like this world."

"Then we'll save it, together."

"No." There was a special, almost surprised firmness in this 'no,' as if Bridger's young mind was unsettled finding himself exercising this grown-up-like responsibility of choice. "I've made up my mind. I'm too dangerous. I can't handle being scared, or watching horrible things happen. I'll panic, and snap, and just wish for everything to go away, and then it will."

"You wouldn't do that, Bridger. I trust you."

"Of course you do! Because I want you to!" Sobs broke into a scream. "Can't you see it? Everybody says you were a completely different person before you met me. What if it's true? I was scared! I just wanted somebody nice to hug me, and keep me safe, and tell me stories. I turned you into this! You're not Mycroft Canner! You're a fantasy, like Boo, and Mommadoll, my fantasy of what I wanted from the first real grown-up I ever met!"

The suggestion struck like lightning. I had not thought of it. Perhaps you, wiser than I, had, reader, but it is far easier to doubt another's existence than to doubt one's own. My mind searched itself for proof, dredging up memories, actions, continuity, excuses. It couldn't be true. "I'm not your invention, Bridger," I answered, more for myself than him. "I have too many memories of things you don't understand."

"Stander-G remembers fighting at Lyrnessus. I don't know where Lyrnessus is!"

I shook my head. "I have too many other loyalties. You wouldn't have made a Mycroft that felt like I do about Ἄναξ Jehovah."

"Maybe I only changed the surface, maybe I made you nice and kind and loyal like this, where you should be fierce and free and scary, like your friend!" He paused for breath. "I almost turned them into Apollo, when they first showed up, your scary friend. They looked so much like Apollo. Apollo would know how to fix everything, I thought. I almost did it. Think about how sad you would've been. Just like Sadcat, and as long as I exist I might do the same thing, accidentally, anytime, to anyone, to everyone!"

Alarm far worse than fear of Sniper's bullets set on me like frost. "As long as you exist? What are you doing in there, Bridger? Bridger!"

"It's like Croucher said, I can't control my powers. I'm turning the whole world into a war story like Apollo's *Iliad*. Just by being so scared of it, I'm making it be real. I can't stop it! Can you imagine how much worse it'll be if I go crazy? I can't handle this power. No one can."

"Jehovah can. That's why you're here together. Providence planned this. Jehovah has the experiences, the thinking of a God. You're omnipotent, They know how to handle omnipotence. They'll guide you. You each have half of what you need."

Conviction's heat made Bridger's words strong, not fiery, but like a candle, just strong enough to hold its own. "If that was the plan then Providence would've given Jehovah my powers in the first place. They're not for Jehovah. They're not for anyone. No one should have them, especially not me!"

Major: <Mycroft, what's happening over there! We just lost Mommadoll, she reverted to toy form. Is Bridger hurt?>

"Bridger?" I called. "What are you doing?"

"Mommadoll wouldn't want to see this." His voice broke, the sorts of sobs that usually come only with pain. "I'm done, can't you see that? I brought Jehovah proof that God exists, that's what my powers were for, you said so yourself, so did Jehovah. You don't need me anymore. Everything else I do just makes things worse."

"You're not done, Bridger. We need you more than ever. You can stop the war, all of it, by working with Jehovah—"

"You know that's not true! I can't prevent the war, it's already started! All I can do is pick a side."

"You can do more than that. You can end it sooner, make it less bad. Win the war!"

"I don't know how!" His words began to slur, the half-formed syllables of a child speaking more to himself than anyone. "You should've raised me as a soldier. That's what you need now, a soldier, a replacement for Apollo, not someone like me. Then I can disappear."

"Disappear?" I tugged at the door, remembering now the boxes of old clothes we had hauled from Bridger's cave: coats, T-shirts, wigs. "Bridger, you're not putting on a costume, are you?"

"I want the world to be safe. I'm not the one who can make it safe."

"No! Bridger, we need you!" I slammed the door with my shoulder. "Not Apollo, you!"

"This power shouldn't exist."

Tears leaked from me, desperate, but how many more, reader, must have been streaming down his cheeks, a child with such thoughts.

"Apollo's statue!" I cried. "You don't have to transform yourself. You can animate Apollo's statue! Apollo will guide you through it! Come, we'll go to Romanova together!"

His words could barely break his sobs. "I don't want to see any more like what's happening at Brussels and Tōgenkyō. I don't want to live through this."

"You can't, Bridger!" I hurled myself against the flat steel, feeling my shoulder pop, but if we do not care what bones we break when fighting for our lives, what could I care fighting for everyone's? "You can't destroy yourself! Everyone on Earth, everyone in history, we've been waiting for your power! Waiting for you!"

Aimer: <Mycroft! Can you hear me, Mycroft! It's the Major! The Major's reverted! What's happening?>

My blood spattered the steel as I pounded the door. "Bridger!" I screamed. I learned then that I had never truly screamed before, not to the desperate maximum a body can. "Don't do it! We need you! I need you! I love you! Bridger!"

I am hardened to many kinds of pain, reader, of body and of mind, but I had no more armor against this new pain than if I had never held Apollo's body in my arms. Desperation turned to prayer: Don't take Bridger. Please. Don't take this child whom I love, not as others before me have loved a son, a brother, a savior, a master, but whom I—strange creature that I am—love in all these ways at once, all rolled together into a new kind of love, abject and irrevocable, that has as yet no name. Do not take that from me too, after taking Apollo. Reader, whatever curses you have for me— worm, monstrosity, unholy brute—I deserve them all, I who, in the moment of humanity's great loss, raised so selfish a prayer. To Whom? To Jehovah, Who has no powers here? Or to His Peer Who rules This Universe, my intractable Maker, Who had long since Judged that my evil requires more ingenious punishments than death? But my old crimes, weighed against this new one, were like the theft of an apple weighed against a patricide. It would be my fault. All the hopes of humankind lost—my fault. I saw it, even as my fists battered the door, as impassable as the barrier between today and thirteen years ago. I did this. I taught Bridger weakness. I taught him to tremble, flinch, hide, run. Providence made me our savior's caretaker, and now he proved too weak because I made him so. A new, more fitting prayer bled through me: Don't let my failure doom everyone. Don't take away the hope, the better world, the wonders Bridger could conjure for Utopia, for all of us, because of me. Don't make the living stay mortal and the dead stay dead because of me. Apollo, Seine Mardi, older heroes, Patriarch Voltaire, Diogenes, Odysseus, MASON who will die someday, Papa, good Spain, my Saladin, and every victim of the coming war, they all could walk the Earth another hundred years, five hundred, live to walk on Mars, on Titan, on the ship decks wrought of substances undreamt-of which will someday bear us to the Sea of Stars. If there are still colors in grief's palette that I—orphan, parricide, traitor, wanderer, fool—have not yet had wrung out of my flesh, then let me suffer them, not all the world. Don't take Bridger. Don't leave us here alone to fight Apollo's war because of me.

"We lost him." A man's voice came through the door, rough, where the child's should have been. But not Apollo's.

"Major?"

The door opened, easy from the other side. The veteran's cheeks were wet, though whether with Bridger's remnant tears or with his own I could not say. "We had him and we lost him, our one chance." The fatigues hung slack around him, man-sized on a body that was still a boy's in scale. Bridger had been thorough. He launched the Major into life with all his gear, his pack, his helmet, bedroll, ammunition, rifle on his shoulder, while Bridger's own kid-bright backpack rested in his hands, personal effects packed neatly for the tearful loved ones. "I'll kill it," the Major announced. "Sniper. I'll kill it."

I slumped useless before him, grief's convulsions too severe to let me stand. It was not despair. Despair is a numbing blackness, which offers at least the consolation that there is no next task to face; I had tasks still.

"Sniper did this!" the Major continued, his voice iron enough to make MASON's seem weak. "We could have saved everyone, living and dead, and Sniper destroyed it, Sniper, with its petty duty, and its Hive System. I'll kill it. I'll run it through, and feel its blood across my hands, and taste its last breath as it gasps away its life!"

I choked down breath enough to start my pleading, "Major, stop."

"And then I'll gather all its stupid dolls and burn them!" He kicked the one that lay beside me, his eyes taking pleasure as the neck flopped limp. "How far do you think the smoke would reach? A million toy corpses burning, but not the real one! Never the real one. No funeral rites for Sniper, no mourning fans and speeches. I'll haul it to a field somewhere and watch the dogs and birds feast on its heart!"

"Stop, it won't help."

"And then the others, Ockham, Tully Mardi—there's one you should've finished off long ago. They did this with their petty ambitions. I'll make their bodies carrion, all of them!"

"Stop, Achilles. It isn't Sniper's fault, it's ours."

He turned, just enough to glance sidelong at me, while the helmet's shadow veiled his expression. "So, you did know."

I choked. "I felt like saying something would make it more true."

He fidgeted with the rifle at his shoulder, where his shield should be. "How long have you known it was me?"

"I wasn't positive until Lieutenant Aimer turned so conspicuously into Patroclus."

"Have I always been . . . myself?"

"I don't think so," I answered, softly. "At first I think you were just an abstract soldier, but as Bridger matured, and their concepts of war and death matured, you matured with them. When they read the *Iliad*, it changed you. We both helped Bridger read it, over and over, Homer's version and Apollo's version too, so you became Achilles bit by bit." I felt my breath grow steady, loss's sorrow easing as a different sorrow took its place: pity. "I've always wondered which war you remember: the World Wars, or Apollo's future war flying in your giant robot hero-god across the dark of Space, or Troy."

I wasn't sure that he would answer. The Major—Achilles—he was never one to open his heart, not in any version. He was my commander, and a king. He owed me nothing. Even if we had been friends, co-parents, I had lied to him these long years, pretending I did not hear his Greekisms, his invocations of Hades and the other deathless gods, his fear whenever his Lieutenant Aimer volunteered for some mission. I had lied by feigning ignorance; even if I said nothing, I had lied.

Achilles flexed his veteran shoulders beneath the pack and straps. "You know, even when it isn't in my hand, I can always feel the rifle with me." He stroked its stock, then reached out, grasping at something invisible in the air before him. "And the controllers"—his hand fell to his side now—"and the spear. I remember all three, not jumbled, three full lives. I remember growing up on the mountains with Chiron the centaur who taught me to hunt, and with Chiron the flight instructor who made me best pilot in the forces. I remember losing Patroclus three times. And Hector, I remember the feel of Hector's blood, the stink of Hector's corpse growing fouler day by day, three times, a different smell each time. I remember dying, too, Apollo's arrow, Paris. Three times. More than three, so many versions." He turned to me. "You know what else I remember? I remember the Odyssey. I remember when Odysseus came to see us in the Underworld, do you remember that part?" He paused. "We were all there, Tiresias who knew too much, and my Patroclus, and that blowhard Agamemnon. I said then that I would rather be the lowest man alive, breaking my back to plow another's land for a starvation wage, rather than be what I was, the most honored of the dead. I meant it. Ten years I've been a tiny plastic toy baby-sitting a child in a gutter, and I've thanked the gods for every day. I think that's why they picked me as guardian. I understood Bridger's gift better than anyone. The dead want to live. Even those of us who never really existed in the first place, we want to live, not all of us, maybe, but most of us. We want it more than anything. Even if it means being a toy, or a slave, or suffering like you and I have, Mycroft, we want to live. That's more important than the Hives and what might happen to this world, wonderful as this world is. Bridger would have given life to everybody, everyone who ever died, or will die, more, even to people who were half fictitious like me, everyone that anyone ever believed would want to live. We could have. They tested us, the Fates, the gods, your Providence, it has so many names. They gave us one chance to let everybody live. We failed."

I had thought I'd mastered my tears, but Boo emerged now, sniffing for his absent master, his friendly, furry face confused but not yet sad. Halley came with him, Apollo's long, green Pillarcat, abandoned at Romanova after Tully's arrest. The U-beast had tracked us somehow, locked onto me perhaps or Bridger, seeking a familiar scent. I hardly had strength enough to speak as my tears flowed free. "You know Fate better than that, Achilles!" I had not intended the reproof to come out as a scream, but it did, sharp as the grief that spurred it. "Fate doesn't taunt. This was all planned. Paris takes Helen. We lose Bridger and Apollo. The war begins. It's all one Plan. You being here now in Bridger's place, that's the Plan too."

Achilles scowled. "I've never really understood Fate, not in fiction or reality."

"I understood it once." I shuddered, gazing at my own tear-blurred hands which seemed (not only then but always) red with blood. "I understood it, after I killed Apollo—no, after I learned I hadn't had to kill Apollo, when I met Jehovah and realized that, by letting me think I understood the way the Hives worked, Providence had tricked me into killing the best person in the world." I choked. "I understood then, but these past years, seeing Bridger's powers, I let myself fall into the delusion that Providence might be simple. It isn't simple. It isn't kind. It isn't working toward some happy end where we're all saved, and every bad thing that happens turns out to be for the best in ways we can't yet see. It isn't cruel either, though it often seems so." I tried to meet his eyes, but faltered. "It's not trying to destroy humanity, or torture us, or leave us in the dark alone. It's something else. There is a guiding Principle, not Good, not Evil, not Justice, not even Progress, something else that we can't understand or name yet, one of these God-sized concepts that even Jehovah can't describe in all His languages. Providence planned this war. It's going to let millions die, let cities burn, make us tear down the better part of the world we've built, but it's not going to let us wipe ourselves out. That's why it left you. A kind God would have left us Bridger. A cruel One would have left us nothing. This One left you.

You know how to fight this war, Achilles. We have no idea what's coming, but you do. You've fought this war before, a future war, with flying cars, and tracker computers, and new weapons made from *Mukta* fuel and U-beasts. You've already fought Apollo's war. You can teach us."

The veteran rubbed his hands, exploring their calluses, so many kinds, too thick to let the nerves beneath feel much anymore. "It won't start with new weapons. It'll start with bats, and kitchen knives, and scared people defending themselves against neighbors they can't trust. Then Sniper's hero delusions will spread, people imitating war movies with the guns and planes and missiles hobbyists have stashed in their basements. Innovation will take longer."

I felt my own tears changing, hope diluting grief. "But you know the old weapons too. You fought at Troy with bronze and horses. You fought the World Wars with guns and planes. You know how to lead men into battle, what will break a soldier, and what won't. You trained in the trenches, and with Chiron, and in Space. You know how to fight this war. You know how to fight every war ever, because you have."

Achilles did not look at me. Long years of breaking bread together, and wiping Bridger's tears, were not enough to make him ready to share sentiments more private than his rage, even with me. "Then we have work to do." He rummaged in Bridger's backpack, Hermes's winged sandals fluttering in protest as he jumbled them among folds of cloak, and futuretech, and wands. "I'm keeping Excalibur, and a couple of these." He pulled healing and resurrection potions from the depths. "Take the rest to your Utopians. They'll use it right, analyze it, learn from it, maybe reproduce it someday." He dropped the bag at my side, knowing my arms would be too weak to hold it. "You're right, the gods didn't leave us with nothing. We have these, and we have me. I'll teach you and Jehovah how to fight your war. I know how, any war, all wars. It's all I do know. The Mardis worried what would happen with no veterans left to teach the current generation what war was like. Their prayer at least was answered." He paused as if to laugh. "Take me to Romanova. Have Jehovah call your allies in, the Emperor, Anonymous, Spain if you can, Kosala, I'll brief them all at once. And call your Servicers. Thanks to you they're closer to a ready army than anything else on Earth." He frowned finding me immobile, weeping still. "Mycroft?" he tested.

"Yes?"

Achilles took a long breath, ready to move on. "Get up. I won't win this war without you. You know that."

The first lesson you will learn when war reaches you, reader, is that our limits in civilian life, the point at which we are too tired, too distraught, too weak to go on, are not really our limits. I rose and saluted.

CHAPTER THE TWENTY-SECOND

Last Prayer

Now I have fulfilled the strict command to give you truth. I bared myself, my secrets, and Jehovah's secrets, even those which will make you call Him mad. I exposed His mother, His fathers, and many sins and crimes which great and wary rulers would rather have silenced. I showed you Bridger. I showed you the resurrection that you witnessed, but cannot quite believe in. And I told you who this strange man is who now stands often at Jehovah's side, small as a boy but hero-strong, and calls himself Achilles Mojave. I do not ask you to believe, just play-believe, since often things we play-believe in—superstitions, bedtime stories, luck—still make us feel a little better when hard choices come.

It has been three months since I began this history. In that time the sides have taken shape, the trials begun. MASON's black hand is now outstretched, the Cousins are reborn as peacemakers, Dominic holds the Mitsubishi together by the skin of his fierce teeth, and more souls every day flock to the bull's-eye flag of the "Hiveguard" who follow Ojiro Cardigan Sniper, thirteenth O.S. Kind Ἄναξ Jehovah will not let the bull's-eye be banned, or even discouraged, since for This blinded God (five senses are as blindness to One Who was omnivoyant) each morsel of communication is as precious as desert rain. Earth, while He helps rule it, He decrees, will have honesty, if we cannot have peace. Achilles fears that someday soon a brawl, or street scuffle, or hatemongering word, will be the spark that triggers open war. I pray this book is not that spark.

If you are my contemporary, reader, brought to this history to understand the days of transformation you are still living through, be patient, pray. Do not act rashly, spurred by your revulsion at the dark underbellies I have exposed here. Do not hate Cornel MASON, Ancelet, Kosala, Ockham, even Ganymede. So many on all sides of this are bloodstained, perverted, mad, but also noble, wise, untiring servants of your interests, who will give their days, their years, their deaths, to guard this world for you, or make a better one. I do not ask you to forgive them all, just to have reasons beyond rash grudges or affections when you choose to fight and kill for one side, or the other. As for Ἄναξ Jehovah, if your theology cannot admit that He is more than a madman, at least believe that it is a madness which makes Him Good. By His command I may not ask you to fight for Him. His Wish is only that you look with love—as He does—upon this world, this human race, its many branches, and judge carefully which one you will fight to make the trunk.

If, on the other hand, you are a distant reader, and our coming war is, for you, just one more memorial, standing in some quiet park where you grew up, laughing and chasing beneath the strange skies of whatever world Utopia's toil has earned for you as birthright, pray for us. Our war may have been a thousand years ago, more, but God our Maker hears all prayers, past and future, even if He rarely makes His answers visible. If Providence sent Achilles to guide us in our day of greatest need, if we survive this war, rebuild, and if in future days some blessed generation is judged worthy to receive a second chance at what God tried to give us when He first sent Bridger, it may be that He grants humanity all this because you, child of a nobler future, asked Him to.

HERE ENDS
Seven Surrenders,
THE SECOND HALF OF
Mycroft Canner's History
of these Days of Transformation.

HERE BEGINS
THE CRISIS STILL UNFOLDING,
whose Chronicle,
freshly begun, he names
The Will to Battle.

AUTHOR'S *Note* AND *Acknowledgments*

ADA PALMER

Books by their nature require many people: editors, publishers, test readers, proofers, designers, publicists. But books also require interlocutors, the many voices, scattered in geography and time, to whom the author responds. I thanked many people in the first volume, but it felt strange acknowledging the contributions of the present when the true list of contributors reaches deep through time. Side by side I should thank Denis Diderot, Alan Charles Kors, Homer, James Hankins, Voltaire and Émilie du Châtelet, Patrick and Teresa Nielsen Hayden, Alfred Bester, Miriam Weinberg, the Marquis de Sade, Diana Griffin, Gene Wolfe, Patty Garcia, Arthur Conan Doyle, Liana Krissoff, Montaigne, Anita Okoye, Yevgeny Zamyatin, Heather Saunders, Aldous Huxley, Irene Gallo, Robert Graves, Tom Doherty, Samuel R. Delany, Victor Mosquera, Victor Hugo, Amy Boggs, Suetonius, Ed Misch, Peter Chung, Crystal Huff, Barbara Tuchman, Irina Greenman, Osamu Tezuka, Lauren Schiller, Thomas More, Lila Garrott, Robert Fagles, Jeremy Brett, Francis Bacon, Michael Mellas, Derek Jacobi, Jonathan Sneed, Jack Pulman, Carl Engle-Laird, Petrarch, Jo Walton, Pierre Bayle, Doug and Laura Palmer, Yoshiyuki Tomino and Hajime Yatate, and many, many more. And you. Because even this list is only two-thirds of the conversation, past and present. You are the third. As I write these words *Too Like the Lightning* has launched, and, around the globe, the diasporic conversation is beginning, responses, more of them and more enthusiastic than I had dared imagine. The intensity of it these past months has taught me how even happiness can be exhausting. But I am also holding my breath, much like Mycroft at the end here, not knowing how the wide world will react to this second half of his history, the hard half, where we lose the lightning before it lightens. Because the most important part of this, your part, the part that conquers time's diaspora, comes next. So thank you in advance for being part of it, coequal with Homer and Diderot, in our long conversation.